Kitty's Greatest Hits

THE KITTY NORVILLE BOOKS

Kitty and The Midnight Hour
Kitty Goes to Washington
Kitty Takes a Holiday
Kitty and the Silver Bullet
Kitty and the Dead Man's Hand
Kitty Raises Hell
Kitty's House of Horrors
*Kitty Goes to War**
*Kitty's Big Trouble**

OTHER NOVELS

*Discord's Apple**
*After the Golden Age**
Voices of Dragons
Steel

*A Tor Book

Kitty's Greatest Hits

Carrie Vaughn

A TOM DOHERTY ASSOCIATES BOOK
New York

This is a work of fiction. All of the characters, organizations, and events portrayed in these stories are either products of the author's imagination or are used fictitiously.

KITTY'S GREATEST HITS

Edited by David G. Hartwell

A Tor Book
Published by Tom Doherty Associates, LLC
175 Fifth Avenue
New York, NY 10010

www.tor-forge.com

Tor® is a registered trademark of Tom Doherty Associates, LLC.

Library of Congress Cataloging-in-Publication Data

Vaughn, Carrie.
Kitty's greatest hits / Carrie Vaughn.—1st ed.
p. cm.
"A Tom Doherty Associates book."
ISBN 978-0-7653-2696-6 (hardcover)
ISBN 978-0-7653-2957-8 (trade paperback)
1. Norville, Kitty (Fictitious character)—Fiction.
2. Werewolves—Fiction. 3. Vampires—Fiction. I. Title.
PS3622.A9475K57 2011
813'.6—dc22

2011013448

First Edition: August 2011

Printed in the United States of America

0 9 8 7 6 5 4 3 2 1

COPYRIGHT ACKNOWLEDGMENTS

To all the editors who opened doors,
especially George Scithers, Darrell Schweitzer,
Patrick Swenson, and Shawna McCarthy

CONTENTS

Il Est Né

Hugging himself, shivering, David curled up under the reaching bows of a pine tree. A moonlit drift of snow glowed silver just a few feet away, outside his shelter. More snow was falling, and he was naked. If he simply relaxed, he wouldn't be that cold. But he was afraid. More afraid every time this happened.

He didn't know where he was, but that didn't bother him so much anymore. And how strange it was, that something like that didn't bother him. *That* was what bothered him. Not knowing, not remembering, had become normal. He didn't know where he was, but he knew exactly how he got here. It was getting harder to claw his way out of this space, to keep this from happening. He was losing himself.

The fire had taken him again. Blood rose and changed him. In a helpless surge, another body of fur and teeth, claw and sinew overcame him. The hunter, the wolf. He couldn't stop the Change. He could flee, stumbling into a wild place where no one would see him, where he wouldn't hurt anyone. Better that he stay here, because the pull was getting harder to resist. Easy to say that this was where he belonged, now.

Sometime in the last year, since this curse had landed on him, his thinking had switched. He wasn't a human who turned into a wolf. Instead, he was a wolf trapped in human skin. The wolf wanted to run away forever. Might be easier, if he just never returned to human. But he did.

At some point, he drifted back to sleep and woke to bright sunlight gleaming off the snow. Blinding, almost. It would be a beautiful day, with a searing blue Colorado sky, crisp snow, chilled air. And he couldn't really sit here under a tree, bare-ass naked, confused and depressed, all day.

Ultimately, that was what drew him back to civilization. He was still human, and the human grew bored. He'd walk, find a road, a town, steal some clothes. Figure out the date and how long he'd been out of it this time. Wander in the company of people, until the fire took him again.

Just because Kitty couldn't go home for Christmas didn't mean she had to be alone.

At least, that was the reasoning behind forcing herself to spend part of the day at a Waffle House off the interstate. It was the holidays, you were supposed to spend them with family, with voices raised in celebration, toasting each other and eating too much food.

Not that any of that was happening here. It was her, a couple of truckers, the waitress, the cook, a glass of middling nonalcoholic eggnog, and Bing Crosby on the radio. All in all this was one of the most depressing scenes she'd ever witnessed.

She was reading Dickens while sipping her eggnog. Not the obvious one, which hadn't lasted long, but *Bleak House*. The title seemed appropriate, and at three inches thick would last her a good long while.

Just a couple more hours, she thought. Long enough to have supper in the company of other people—no matter that no one had said a word to each other in half an hour. Then she'd go to her rented room, call her family to wish them happy holidays, and go to bed.

The music cut off, and Kitty looked up, ready to complain. The Christmas carols had been the only thing making this place bearable. How pathetic was that, clinging to old-school carols piped through the speakers of a cut-rate stereo? Behind the counter, the waitress pulled over a footstool and used it to reach the TV, sitting on a shelf high on the wall. She popped a VHS tape into the built-in slot.

As if she felt Kitty watching her, she—Jane, according to her name tag—looked over her shoulder and smiled.

"*It's a Wonderful Life,*" Jane said. "I play it every year."

Oh, this was going to make Kitty *cry.*

The fact that Jane had spent enough years here to make it a tradition, not to mention she had the movie on videotape rather than DVD, somehow added to the depressing state of the situation. That could have been a lot of Christmases. Jane wasn't young: wrinkles had formed around her eyes and lips, and her curling hair was dyed a gray-masking brown. Waitressing at Waffle House didn't seem like much of a career. A stopgap maybe, a pay-the-bills kind of job on the way to somewhere else. It wasn't supposed to become your life. No one should have to work at Waffle House on Christmas every damn year.

Kitty set her book aside and leaned back in the booth to get a better view. There were worse ways to kill time. She'd watch the movie, then blow this Popsicle stand.

Amazing what people left on their clotheslines in the dead of winter. It was a small-town characteristic he'd come to depend on. Blue flannel shirt, worn white tee, wool socks. He wasn't desperate enough to steal underwear and went without. He found baling twine in a trash can and turned it into a belt to hold up a pair of oversized jeans. The work boots he found abandoned behind a gas station were a size too small. He didn't look great. He looked homeless, with shaggy brown hair and a five-o'clock shadow—five o'clock the next day. He *was* homeless. He only bothered because he felt he ought to. Walk through town and remind himself what it was like to be human. He *wanted* to be human. Wearing clothes reminded him. He'd loved his job—raft guide in the summer, ski instructor in the winter. Stereotypical Colorado outdoor jock. He and some of the guys wanted to start their own rafting company. He was going to go back to school, get a degree in business—

Not anymore.

David cleaned up as well as he could at the gas station restroom. The nice thing about stealing clothes off a clothesline—at least they were clean. He scrubbed his face, his hands, slicked back his hair, guessed that he didn't smell too awful. Squared his shoulders and tried to stand up straight. Tried to look human.

He regarded himself in a cracked mirror and sighed. He wasn't a bad-looking guy. He was young. He should have had his whole life ahead of him. But he looked at himself now and saw only shadows. His eyes gave off a shine of helplessness. Hopelessness. Their brown seemed more amber, and something else looked out of them. He was trapped in his own body. He washed his face again, trying to get rid of that expression.

He could usually find an evening's work somewhere, washing dishes or sweeping up, if someone felt sorry enough for him. Enough to pay for a meal—a cooked, human meal. He hadn't yet resorted to panhandling. He'd rather run wild in the woods and never come back.

Near the interstate, the minimalist main street of this small town seemed quiet for an early evening. No cars drove by, only a couple were parked on the street. The only place open, with its sign lit up, was the Waffle House at the edge of town.

The smell of the town seemed strange after his days in the forest. His nostrils flared with the scent of oil, metal, and people. An inner voice told him this wasn't his place anymore. He ought to flee. But no—he was here, he'd make a go of it. Trying to soften the tension in his shoulders, willing himself to stay calm, he headed to the restaurant.

The bell hanging on the door rang as a man walked in. *What do you know, another angel gets his wings.*

Kitty glanced over to see him, but his scent reached her first: wild, the musk of lupine fur hiding under human skin. In instinctive response, her shoulders tightened with the motion of hackles rising. She sat up, her hands clenching, the ghosts of claws reaching inside her fingers.

He was a werewolf. Just like her.

He froze in the still open doorway, his eyes wide. Clearly, he'd scented her as well, and was shocked. He looked like he might bolt. Their gazes locked, and Kitty's heartbeat sped up. A stare was a challenge, but this wasn't right, because the guy almost looked terrified. Like he didn't know what to do.

"You want to close that, honey? You're letting the warm air out." Jane smiled over the counter at the guy, and that broke the tension.

Kitty looked away—another bit of wolf body language, a move that said she wasn't a threat, and she didn't want to fight. She forced herself to settle back—and could sense him relax a notch as well, lowering his gaze, turning away. She desperately wanted to talk to him. What was he doing here? She didn't know of any werewolves within a hundred miles.

It was why she was here.

The man—young, disheveled, wearing ill-fitting clothing and a haunted expression—slouched inside his flannel shirt and moved to the counter.

He spoke softly to Jane, but Kitty held her breath and made out what he said. "Uh, yeah. I'm a little hard up, and I was wondering if there was anything I could do to earn a cup of coffee and a pancake or something."

Jane smiled kindly. "Sorry, there's nothing. This is our slowest night of the year." The man looked around, at faded tinsel garlands strung around the walls, at the movie playing on the TV, and blinked at Jane in confusion. "It's Christmas," she said.

He glanced at the TV again with a look of terrible sadness.

This scene pushed all Kitty's curiosity buttons. The urge could not be denied.

It was all she could do not to rush straight at him, but if he'd been startled and tense with her just looking at him, she could imagine what that would do. He was on edge—more wolf than human almost, even though the full moon was over a week away.

She walked toward him, her gaze down and her posture loose.

He backed up a step at her approach. She tried to put on a pleasant, nonthreatening face.

"I'm sorry, I don't mean to interrupt, but you look like you could use a cup of coffee. Can I buy you one?" She laced her hands behind her back. He started to shake his head, and she said, "No strings, nothing funny. Consider it a Christmas present from another one of the tribe who doesn't have anywhere else to go." She glanced at Jane, who smiled and reached under the counter for a cup and saucer.

"Hi. I'm Kitty." She offered her hand. Didn't really expect the guy to shake it, and he didn't. It wasn't a wolfish gesture. She'd never seen a lycanthrope look so out of place in human clothing.

He took a moment to register the name, then pursed his lips in a stifled laugh. He actually smiled. There was a handsome guy under the hard times. "I'm sorry, but that's the funniest thing I've heard in a while."

She wrinkled her nose. "It gets a little old, believe me."

"How did a were—" He cut himself off when Jane returned with the pot of coffee.

"Why don't we go talk about it?" Kitty said, nodding back toward her booth.

A moment later, they were sitting across from each other, each of them with fresh cups of coffee. Jane also brought over a plate of pancakes. David gazed up at her sheepishly, blushing. Embarrassed, Kitty decided. He didn't like the charity. But he drowned the pancakes with syrup and dug into them.

Around bites, he finished his thought. "How did a werewolf end up with a name like Kitty?"

"The better question is how did someone named Kitty end up as a werewolf. That's a long story."

"It's almost as bad as a werewolf named Harry."

Perish the thought. "Oh my God, your name isn't—"

"No," he said, ducking his gaze. "It's David."

"Well, David. It's nice to meet you. Though I have to say, I wasn't expecting to see another one of us walk through the door. Are you from around here?"

"No. I've been on the road awhile."

"That's what I thought."

He hadn't yet taken a sip of his coffee, but he wrapped a hand around the cup, clinging to it like he could draw out its warmth. He hunched over, gazing out at the world with uncertainty. He probably didn't realize how odd he seemed, coming out of the cold without a coat. Werewolves didn't feel the cold as much.

Staring at the tabletop, he said, "I've never met another one. Not ever. But I could tell, as soon as I walked in here I could smell you and I knew. I almost walked right back out again."

"What, let a little old thing like me scare you off?" She'd meant it as a joke, but he flinched. She willed him to relax. His hand around the mug squeezed a little tighter. He set his fork down and pressed his fist to the table.

His voice was taut. "You seem so calm. How do you do it?" His eyes flickered up, and the look in them was stark. Desperate.

She froze, nerveless for a moment. Is that how she looked? Calm? She was exiled from her pack, driven from Denver by the alpha werewolves, and so was spending Christmas at a Waffle House in a desolate corner of the state and not with her family. She felt like she was on the verge of losing it. Without an anchor. She'd lost her anchor—but David had never had one.

"What about the one who turned you?"

"I was camping by myself, something . . . something attacked me. It looked like . . . I remember thinking, this is impossible, there aren't any wolves here. I knew something was wrong when I woke up, and I didn't have any wounds, no scars, and I didn't—"

He stopped, swallowed visibly, clamped his eyes shut. His breathing and heart rate quickened, and his scent spiked with fur and wild, wolf trembling just under his skin.

He didn't know how to control it at all, she realized. He hadn't had anyone to teach him. He'd been running as a wolf recently. Probably woke up with no idea where he was—no idea that it was Christmas, even.

Suddenly, her own situation didn't seem so bad.

"Breathe slowly," she whispered. "Think about pulling it in. Keep it together."

He rested his elbows on the table and ran his fingers through his hair. His hands were shaking. "I turn all the time. Not just on full moons. I can't stop it. Then I run, and I don't remember what happens. I know I hunt, kill whatever's out there—but I don't remember. I try to stay away from people, far away. But I just don't remember. I don't want to be like this, I don't—" His fingers tightened in his hair, his jaw clenched, teeth gritting. His wolf was right on the edge. Always right on the edge.

"Shh." She wanted to touch him, steady him, but didn't dare. Anything might set him off. And wouldn't that be a Christmas to remember? Werewolf rampage in a Waffle House in southern Colorado. . . . He might have done okay by Jimmy Stewart, but she'd like to see Clarence the angel fix that mess.

He looked at her. Square on this time. "How do you do it? What's your story?"

"I had a pack," she said. "They found me right after it happened to me. Like you, in the woods, attacked. But they took care of me. Told me what had happened, taught me how to deal with it."

"Does that happen?"

"Yeah, it does. There are probably more of us out there than you think. We keep quiet, stay hidden. At least, most of us do." And that was more story than she should probably go into at the moment.

"Where are they? Your pack."

Her smile turned wry. "I left. Or got kicked out. Depends on who you ask."

He looked crestfallen. The concept of a pack—the idea that he might not be alone—seemed to have heartened him. But that opportunity had once again become remote. "I didn't know. How was I supposed to know something like that was possible? I've been so alone."

What were the odds that his wandering brought him here, to her, perhaps the one werewolf in all the world who'd listen to his problems and want to help?

She said, "It doesn't have to be like that. You can control it. You can lead a normal life. Mostly normal, at least."

"How?" he said, teeth clenched, voice grating. Like she'd told him he could fly to the moon, or dig a hole and find a million dollars.

"You have to really want to."

Donning a smile that was more grimace, he glanced through the fogged window, to a graying, snowy parking lot. He spoke with sarcasm. "You make it sound so easy."

"I didn't say that. It's not easy. I spend a lot of time arguing with my inner Wolf."

"So do I. I lose."

"Then you have to figure out how to start winning."

He chuckled. "You ever think about going into the self-help business?"

She almost asked him if he listened to the radio much, or watched TV recently. Obviously he hadn't, or he would have already said something about her talk radio show.

She smiled slyly at the tabletop. "The idea had occurred to me."

David seemed calmer. Once or twice, Kitty had been accused of talking too much. But she found that talking improved almost every situation. Talking could make a lone werewolf on the run feel a little less lonely.

Jane marched in from the kitchen, straight toward the TV. Frowning, she pressed a cell phone to her ear. "Okay," she said. "What channel?"

She pulled her stool under the TV again and stopped the tape. A cheerful Donna Reed cut off midsentence.

In place of the movie, Jane turned on a news station, turned up the volume, then moved away to watch.

A young news reporter was standing in a winter landscape, a windblown field in the foothills nearby, a few stray snowflakes drifting around her. She was lit with a harsh spotlight, striking in the evening darkness, and speaking somberly.

". . . series of gruesome murders. The violence of these deaths has authorities concerned that the perpetrator may be using an attack dog of some kind. Police would not give us any further details. Authorities are asking residents to stay inside and lock their doors until the killer is apprehended."

Behind the woman a crime scene was in full swing: three or four police cars, an ambulance, many people in uniforms moving purposefully, and what seemed like miles of yellow caution tape. The camera caught sight of a spatter of blood on the ground and a filled body bag before the scene cut away.

A male reporter in a studio repeated the warning—stay indoors—and a scroll at the bottom listed the information: five deaths within the space of an afternoon, violence indicating a highly disturbed, animalistic killer.

Jane folded her phone away, hurried to the door, and locked it. "That's just a few miles up the road from here. I hope nobody minds," she said, regarding her customers with a nervous smile. No one argued.

He said he Changed, and hunted, and didn't remember.

For a long moment, Kitty stared at the stranger across from her. Nervously, he glanced away, tapping his fingers, slumped in the plastic booth like he didn't fit in the confined space.

She shouldn't have automatically been suspicious, but David's situation raised questions. Where had he come from? What had he been doing before he woke up and found—stole—the clothes he was wearing? Was it possible? The only thing she knew: David was a werewolf, and werewolves were capable of violent, bloody murder.

"Get up," she said to him, growling almost. She didn't like the feeling rising up in her—anger, which stirred her Wolf. Quickened her blood. Had to keep that feeling in check. But she'd offered him friendship and didn't want that to have been a mistake.

"What?" he said, voice low.

"Come on. In back. We have to talk." She jerked her head toward the bathrooms, down a little hallway behind her. Glaring at him, she stood and waited until he did likewise. She stormed into the back hallway, drawing him behind her.

Kitty pulled him into the women's restroom. If anyone noticed, let them think what they would. Keeping hold of his collar, she pushed him against the wall. Working on sheer bravado, she tried to act big and strong. He could throw her across the room if he wanted to. Trick was not to let him try. Dominate him, play the alpha wolf, and hope his instincts to defer to that kicked in.

"Where were you before you showed up here?" she demanded.

Whatever attitude she'd been able to pull out worked. He was almost trembling, avoiding her gaze. Mentally sticking a tail between his legs.

She hadn't been sure she could really pull it off.

"I was walking," he said. "Just walking."

"And before that?"

"I was out of it." He grew more nervous, looking away, scuffing his shoes. "I turned. I don't really know where I was."

"What do you remember?"

"I never remember very much." His voice was soft, filled with pain.

She understood what that was like—remembering took practice, control. Even then the memories were fuzzy, inhuman, taken in through wolf senses. He didn't have any of that control to begin with.

"Did you hunt?" she asked, hoping to spark some recollection. "Did you kill?"

"Of course I did! That's what we do, what we are."

He tried to pull away, cringing from her touch. She curled her lip in a snarl to keep him still.

"Think, you have to think! What was it? What did you kill? Was it big? Small? Did it have fur?"

He growled, his teeth bared, and an animal scent rolled off him.

She'd pushed him too far. She almost quailed and backed down. His aggression was palpable, and it frightened her. But she fought not to let that show. Stood her ground. Being alpha was a new feeling for her.

"So you could have killed someone," she said.

He pulled away and covered his face with his hands. She barely heard him whisper, "No. No, it's impossible. It has to be impossible."

He didn't know. Honestly didn't know. Now, what was she supposed to do about that?

She tried again, calmer this time. Pulled out whatever counseling skills she'd picked up over the last year.

"Try to think. Can you remember images? Scents, emotions. Some clue. Anything."

He shook his head firmly. "I don't know what it's like for you, but I don't remember anything. I don't know anything!"

"Nothing?"

"It's a blank. But you—how can you remember? You don't actually remember—"

"Images," she said. "The smell of trees. Night air. Trails. Prey." A long pause, as the memory took her, just for a moment. A flood of emotion, a tang of iron, euphoria of victory. Yes, she remembered. "Blood. Now, what do you remember?"

He dug the heels of his hands into his temples and dropped to a crouch. Gritting his teeth, setting his jaw, he groaned, a sound of anguish. Every one of his muscles tensed, the tendons on his hands and neck standing out. He was shaking.

Alone, out of control, he was over the edge. She knelt by him and touched the back of his head—simple contact, chaste, comforting. "Keep it together," she said. "Pull it in. Hold it in. Breathe slower. In . . . out." She spoke softly, calmly, until he matched his breaths to the rate of her speech. Slowly, he calmed. The tension in his fists relaxed. He lowered his arms. His face eased from a grimace to a simple frown.

She stroked his hair and rested her hand on his shoulder. "It's possible to keep some control and remember."

"I used to have a life," he said. "I just want my life back."

She didn't know what to say. Of course he wanted his life back. So much easier if everything could go back to the way it was before. Nearly every day she thought of it. But if you wanted that life back, you had to fight for it. Fight for that control, every day.

"What am I going to do?" he said, voice shaking, almost a sob.

"Nothing," she said. "We wait."

If he hadn't done anything, nothing would come of this. Nothing would lead the police to him. But she didn't want to even suggest that much. In case he had done something, and the police did come for him.

David took a moment to recover after Kitty left the bathroom. Not that a moment alone would help. He felt fractured. The parts of his being had scattered, for months now.

He didn't understand her at all. She was like him—the same, another monster, a werewolf. And yet she was completely different. So . . . with it. And he didn't understand how she did it. How she looked so *calm.*

If he couldn't remember what had happened, maybe he could learn what happened some other way. He couldn't sit here waiting for the cops to find him and haul him away. Not that they could. The moment he felt danger, he knew what would happen—he would turn, and run.

He stepped to the end of the hall that tucked the bathrooms away from the restaurant. Kitty had returned to the booth. The waitress poured her more coffee, which she sipped. Hunched over the table, she looked out with a nervous gaze. He could see the wolf in her, intense brown eyes flickering to every movement, watchful, alert. Part of him was afraid of her, her strength and confidence. She'd had him cowed in a second.

She believed he was a murderer, and he couldn't deny it. Couldn't say that she was wrong. He couldn't be sure that she wouldn't call the police. He'd only known her for an hour. She might be a monster like him, but she also seemed like the kind of person who would tell the police. A law-abiding werewolf. He never would have believed it.

He had to prove that he didn't do it.

From the hallway, he ducked and slipped to the back of the kitchen, moving quickly so Kitty or the waitress wouldn't see him. She'd think the worst.

One guy in the kitchen, a Latino wearing a white apron, looked at him. "Hey—"

David didn't slow down but ran straight through the kitchen, unlocked the back door, and slipped out. Outside, he paused, taking deep breaths of chilly air through flaring nostrils. Night had fallen, gray and overcast. A light snow fell. A dusting of it would mask scents.

Thinking like a hunter, a wolf—he shook his head to clear his vision of the haze that covered it for a moment. Couldn't let the wolf take over. Had to stay human. What had Kitty said? *Keep it together.*

His breathing slowed. He straightened his back and felt a little more human.

The lot behind the restaurant was lit by a single, fuzzy orange lamp. Only one car was parked here. Snow coated it, so it had been here a while.

Beyond that lay an interstate wasteland: scrub-covered verges, cracked parking lots and frontage road, ancient gas stations. Cars hummed on the distant freeway, even on Christmas.

A set of flashing lights traveled along the frontage road. David took off at a run after the police car.

In less than half an hour, he reached one of the murder scenes.

He caught a scent—blood, thick on the ground. A hint of rot, meaning guts had been spilled. Not fresh, the slaughter had lain open to air for a while.

Human blood. Somehow, he recognized it.

But did he recognize this place, this situation? Or was it a false memory? Did he recognize the scene from the newscast?

Moving low, almost on all fours, touching the ground with his hands every now and then to keep his balance as he ran, he approached the site. He kept out of sight, hiding among the dried vegetation, banked with crusted snow. *This would be easier on four legs. As a wolf.* He fought to ignore the voice whispering at him, clawing at him. He wanted to keep his awareness.

Police cars blocked off a place where a pickup truck had pulled over along the road. Yellow tape fluttered, marking off almost an acre of land within it. A half dozen people moved around the space, bent over, examining the ground.

David stopped and lay close to the ground, hidden, and studied the area as well as he could. Three body bags on stretchers lay by an ambulance. The pickup truck's doors were open, lights shining around it. Its interior was covered in blood.

Did he even know what he was looking for here? What he hoped to find? He had to admit, he didn't know. He just wanted to see the bodies. See that it had been guns or knives that had done this, spattered all that blood over the truck. Not teeth and claws.

But he could imagine a scenario: driving along the road, this family, or maybe group of friends, saw a huge wolf loping alongside them. Curious, they stopped to watch, because wild wolves weren't found here. Maybe they stepped out to take a picture. And it wasn't a wolf, and he was drawn by the promise of easy prey, of slaughter—

He buried his face in his arm to stop the vision. He choked on a sob, because his mouth was watering. At the same time, he wanted to vomit.

That wasn't a memory. Just an overactive imagination. He couldn't remember. *Couldn't.*

He imagined Kitty's voice telling him to slow his breathing, to hold the panic at bay. To keep it together.

Crawling on his belly, infantry-like, he inched forward to get a better look.

Kitty expected David to follow her back to the booth after he had settled down. They'd wait for news, hope for the best.

Surely he'd remember *something* if he'd killed someone. Surely. But who could say? For all her bluster, she knew so little about it.

Minutes passed, and he didn't return. Not that she could blame him if he'd decided to avoid her. Maybe stay in the bathroom, hiding from everyone. This whole spending the holidays with people thing left something to be desired.

Finally, she went back to the bathrooms to check. He wasn't in the women's anymore. For the best, probably. She knocked on the door to the men's. "David?" she called, and got no answer. She opened the door a crack, peered in. Empty. So where had he gone?

From the back hallway, the kitchen was visible, all stainless-steel surfaces and stove tops. The single cook on duty leaned on a counter, looking out at the TV. And on the other side of the room was a door to the outside.

Her heart thudded, contemplating what he was doing. She'd been stupid, confronting him like that. Now she'd driven him off. Who knew what he would do, an out-of-control werewolf roaming the countryside?

Of course, now it was up to her to clean up the mess. Or at least keep it from getting worse.

Crouching to avoid drawing the cook's attention, she dashed across the kitchen and went through the door, which was already unlocked. As if someone had been this way already. Outside was freezing. But her blood was warm, Wolf running through her, firing her senses. Scent, sound, feel—she searched for his trail by the way the hairs on the back of her neck tingled. She felt the heat of his footsteps on the ground.

Breaking into a jog, she followed his trail, the faint touch of his scent, like a taste in the back of her throat. She let a bit of Wolf bleed into her consciousness. A bit of the hunter, tracking one of her own.

She shouldn't have been surprised to find the trail leading straight toward what was clearly a crime scene of epic proportions. Flashing blue and red flared out over the countryside, turning the darkness into a surreal disco parody. The snow fell heavier now, large flakes burning on her skin. They glittered in the lights. She'd forgotten her coat, but hardly noticed; she was sweating from the exertion.

Not wanting to get caught, and certainly not wanting to answer questions about why she was out here, she dropped to the ground. She assumed David had done the same, since she couldn't see him silhouetted against the lights. Instead, she saw what must have been dozens of cops milling inside a taped-off area.

And she smelled blood. Great quantities of reeking, rotten blood and bile. People hadn't just died; they'd been shredded. Her human sensibilities gagged. The Wolf merely cataloged the information: several bodies, human, gutted, and they'd been out awhile. Carrion, Wolf thought. Kitty shook the thought away.

Had they been dead long enough for David to be the culprit?

Almost, she turned around and went back, because she didn't want to know.

Just a little bit farther, though. If she could smell the bodies, she ought to be able to catch a scent of what had done this to them. Since she couldn't get close, she concentrated on the land around them. If something had killed them here, then that same something had to have fled. The trail might be covered with snow now, but she might find a trace of it.

She smelled David.

Pausing a moment, she tasted it, fearing what it meant. But no, this was fresh. Still warm. The touch of him on the air was more human than wolf. He was in human form. His trail didn't have the reek of a predator who'd just devoured prey.

Ahead, she saw him, a dark figure stretched out on the ground, collecting bits of snow in the wrinkles of his clothes. She was in the perfect position to sneak up on him and pounce. In fact, her hands itched, the claws wanting to come out, Wolf wanting to grab this opportunity.

And wouldn't that be a complete and utter disaster? She refrained, not wanting to give him a heart attack—or a good excuse to turn wolf at this particular moment.

"David," she called in the loudest whisper she could manage, creeping up until she was beside him.

Despite her caution, he flinched and twisted back to look at her. Then he sagged with relief.

"What are you doing here?" he hissed back.

"Following you. Have you found out anything?"

He took a deep breath. "I don't think a werewolf did it. There'd be some trace of it, wouldn't there?"

There would. She'd smelled the aftermath of a werewolf-killed body before, and he was right—if David had done it, they'd be smelling blood, bodies, and *wolf.*

"Yeah, there would," she said.

He slumped and made a sound that was almost a sob. He'd come out here for no other reason than to reassure himself.

Tentative, she touched his shoulder. Leaned close to him in a wolfish gesture of companionship. "It's okay. It's going to be okay.

Let's go back now." Back to the warmth, light, virgin eggnog, Jimmy Stewart, and a wonderful life.

"If I didn't do this," David said, "who did? *What* did?"

"That's for the police to find out."

Something seemed to have taken hold of him. Some newfound determination. Like the evidence had given him confidence—proof that he wasn't an out-of-control ravening monster.

"We ought to be able to find something out," he said. "We can smell the trail. The police can't do that. If we can, shouldn't we help—"

"'With great power comes great responsibility.' Is that what you're thinking?" she said with a smirk.

Looking away, he frowned. "It can't hurt to try."

She wanted to apologize. She shouldn't tease him.

"So," she said. "You feel like a hunt?"

He stared out at the murder scene. He might have had a human form, but crouched there, his gaze focused, body tense, ready to leap forward in an instant, his body language was all wolf. She felt the same stance in her own body.

"Yeah," he said. "I do."

Together, they took off at a jog, keeping clear of the cordoned-off area and the circle of lights that marked it.

Prowling out of sight of the police, they found a trail, the barest scent of blood on the air. Probably not so much as a drop was left on the ground for the police to find. But it was there, lingering, fading rapidly because of the falling snow. If they were going to do this, they needed to hurry.

They ranged back and forth along the same half-mile stretch of prairie leading away from the frontage road, looking for the sign they'd discovered: blood on the air, and oil, like the person they were looking for worked in a garage. There was something indefinable—something she as a human being couldn't describe. But the Wolf inside her knew the flavor of the smell. This was a predator they were looking for. A taste of aggression rather than fear, like there'd be with prey. The feeling put her on edge. She was sure, though: The murderer was human.

A few miles from the interstate, another set of police cars gathered around a house at what looked like a junkyard. Acres of wrecked and rusting cars lined up on the land around it, roped in by strings of barbed-wire fencing. The familiar ring of lights and yellow tape bound the house. And the tang of blood and slaughter drenched the air. This scene was more recent than the other.

"What is this?" Kitty whispered. "Is some guy roaming the countryside murdering people he just happens across?"

The thought of a crazed murderer running around out here didn't frighten her; she was a werewolf. Unless his weapons were silver, he couldn't hurt her without really working at it. Even so, this was turning into one of her more harebrained adventures.

"What are we going to do if we find the killer?" David said.

"Call 911?" Then she grumbled, "Ignoring for a moment the fact that I didn't bring my cell phone and I'm betting you don't have one . . . we tell the police what?"

"I don't know. I thought you were the one with all the answers."

Ha. Why did everyone think that again? Just because she ran her mouth more often than not was no reason to actually put any *faith* in her.

She had no desire to get closer to this murder scene, and the killer's trail was fading.

"Let's go," she said, and took off at a jog. After a moment's hesitation, David followed her.

It made her wonder, just for a moment, what it would be like to have a pack again. The thought made her lonely, so she shook it away. The thing now was to find this killer. Figure out a way to throw him at the cops. Or to stop him, if it came to that.

The guy was on foot. If he had left footprints, the falling snow covered them. They tracked by scent alone, but the smell of human blood was strong. Not exactly subtle. Nothing about these murders was subtle. Kitty could tell that much by the police response, without even seeing the bodies. She didn't have to be a trained profiler to tell these were unplanned. He was lashing out, haphazard.

David must have been thinking along the same lines. Briskly, they walked side by side, following the trail that the police hadn't found yet. "He's racking up a body count, isn't he? That's what this is about. Whoever he is, he's gone postal."

"Looks that way," Kitty said.

"We're going to have to kill him if we find him, aren't we?" David said.

"No." She shook her head. "I don't want to get in the habit of killing people. Even if they are bad guys. I don't think you want to get into that habit either."

He pursed his lips and nodded.

When they spotted another house up ahead, lit by the yellow circle of a lamp by the door, Kitty's stomach sank. They'd found his next target.

It wasn't really a house, but a weather-beaten single-wide mobile home, white aluminum siding rusting at the edges, sitting by itself at the end of a long dirt road. The minimum of what could be called a homestead. But it had a fenced-in yard with spinning plastic sunflowers sticking out of the snow, and a satellite dish attached to the roof, which was outlined in colored holiday lights. Somebody loved this place and called it home, and the killer had headed right for it.

She tugged on David's arm and broke into a run. Dodging the fence, they went to the front door. The place seemed peaceful. Soft, shaded light shone through the fogged windows. Faintly, the sound of Christmas carols played on a radio, muted. Maybe nothing was wrong. Maybe they'd made a mistake.

They hesitated at the base of a trio of steps leading to the front door. Their breaths, coming fast after the effort of running, steamed in the chill air. David glanced at her.

"What do we do?" he whispered.

"We knock on the front door," she said, shrugging. "If nothing's wrong, we can sing 'Jingle Bells.' "

He actually chuckled. The boy was coming around.

She mounted the steps first, raised a fist to knock on the door—and saw that it already stood open a crack. *Shit.*

Then she thought, *What the hell,* and pushed open the door all the way.

Her nose flared with the scent of blood at the same time she saw the spray across the linoleum floor of the entryway before her.

Wolf's senses sprang to the fore, the instinct to Change and defend herself ripping through her gut. She swallowed back bile and forced that feeling down, told herself to keep it together, stay human, keep that beast locked away. Her gut clenched, but she didn't shift.

Still, she looked over the scene with a hunter's gaze, and a growl burred in her throat.

Standing over his prey, the man glanced at Kitty with surprise. He was tall and thin—unnaturally thin, like he hadn't eaten well in some time. His clothes hung oddly on him. He wore a green canvas jacket, white T-shirt, threadbare jeans. All shone wet with blood. He was covered with red, presumably from his previous two stops. She could smell violence on him, illness, like an animal that had gone out of control, that no longer worked by instinct, but by madness, striking out at everything. His pale eyes gleamed with it. His ear-length hair was matted, uncombed, and an uneven beard grew around his slack mouth. His whole body was rigid.

He loomed over two people, a middle-aged man and woman, husband and wife probably, who lay in the middle of what passed for a living room—a plush sofa shoved up against one wall and a large TV in the opposite corner. They were both a little worn out and overweight, both wearing jeans and T-shirts—they matched the trailer, Kitty thought absently. They were trussed up like a holiday meal. That was the only way Kitty could think of it. Each had wrists and ankles bound fast in front of them with thin twine. Both were gagged with strips of cloth, so tightly their teeth were bared, their lips stretched back in grotesque smiles. Their eyes glared large and white with fear. Bloody marks shone on their heads, as if the killer had subdued them by hitting them with something. But they were alive, trembling, pressing themselves away from the killer even while bound.

He'd started with her, slashing her arms, spilling blood everywhere. He held an eight-inch-long serrated knife, dull-looking, something that might rip like the teeth of an animal. It dripped blood onto the floor.

The killer regarded Kitty and David.

Wolf, the voice of wild instinct, spoke to Kitty: *Can't show fear, can't show terror, then he'll know he's stronger and he'll attack, he'll kill. We must be stronger, we must dominate, we are alpha here.*

Wolf was right. Kitty wanted to scream, but she didn't. Instead, she looked him in the eye. Glared. Bared her teeth a little. He was in the wrong here. He must be made to relent—to show his belly. Cow him before they had to fight it out.

Beside her, David was doing the same. His fingers were curled, stiff, as if showing claws. For a moment, she worried. Much more of this, and he'd shift. Hell, they both might. And maybe that wouldn't be so bad—no way could this guy escape from a couple of werewolves with full-on claws and teeth.

The killer took a step back. He sensed something, obviously. The aggression, the challenge. The fact that these were a couple of monsters standing in front of him, no matter how harmless they might look. But he didn't know how to read the signs. He didn't know how to respond. A wolf would either return the challenge or back down—slumped shoulders, lowered gaze. Make himself small and helpless before them, to show that they were stronger.

This guy twitched, feet shifting in place. His grip tightened and retightened around the handle of the knife. His gaze shifted between them, the door, his captives, the knife in his hand, and back. He didn't know where to look, where to go, what to do. His eyes were wide, shocky, and his lips trembled.

Then he asked a strange question.

"What are you?"

I'm your worst nightmare, Kitty wanted to mutter in a bad accent. But she didn't. She wondered what he saw in them, though—two people with wolves staring out of their eyes, tense and glaring like they were ready to rip his throat out. The guy ought to be scared.

She had to swallow a couple of times before she could speak instead of growl.

"You're not going to do this anymore. You're not going to get away with what you've already done."

After staring at her for a moment, he bit his lip and made a noise that almost sounded like a giggle.

What had she thought he would do, put the knife down and his hands up and wait for the cops to get here?

He stepped toward her, and Kitty braced to defend herself—kicking and scratching his eyes out if she had to. She wasn't worried about the knife. It was stainless steel, not silver. He'd have to just about cut her head off before it would do real damage.

Not that it wouldn't hurt a whole lot in the meantime.

David moved to intercept him. His shoulders were bunched up, like hackles raised, and his glare seemed to bore through the killer. In response, the man stumbled back, clutching the knife with both hands and pointing it defensively. The knife was shaking, just a little.

Hell. Maybe she could just talk him out of it.

"You're going to put the knife down now," Kitty said, her voice low, rough. "You're not going to kill anyone else. We won't let you."

Then, unbelievably, he started crying. Didn't make a sound, but tears spilled from his eyes. Kitty thought, *Something drove him to this.* Something pushed him over the edge and he couldn't cope, and he was psychotic enough to begin with that he did this. This was something else that could happen when you didn't have a place to go home to at Christmas.

Wolf didn't have an ounce of sympathy for a predator who slaughtered for no reason, who didn't recognize territory, who didn't obey the rules. Wolf could spot the signs and see what was happening right before the killer tensed and raised his knife to attack. Shouting, he made a mad plunge for the door, ready to slash his way past her and David.

She'd have let him go. They could call in an anonymous tip, let the cops go after him. They'd saved these people—wasn't that enough?

But David stopped him.

She thought he was shifting, that he'd lost it and his predator had burst forth to meet this human predator in challenge. The killer lunged forward, ready to stab down and cut his way through to the door.

David ducked and tackled him. Planted his shoulder under the guy's ribs and shoved. Werewolves were stronger than people. David threw more power into the move than appeared possible. The killer swung sideways and banged into the flimsy plywood wall dividing the living room from the kitchen.

David didn't shape-shift. His wolf hadn't taken over. He had used the wolf's power and managed to stay in control, though he was breathing hard, and his teeth were bared.

He didn't let the killer recover. Pouncing, he pinned the guy to the floor, tossed the knife away, and leaned a rigid hand on his neck, pressing down with all his weight. The killer sputtered, gasping for air, thrashing, but he couldn't escape David's strength.

So maybe he wasn't entirely in control of himself.

"David," Kitty said. David flinched, startled, and glared at her, something amber and animal lurking in his eyes. He was *barely* under control. "Keep it together. You don't have to kill. Just keep it together."

"Then what do we do?" His voice was a growl.

"We'll leave him for the cops."

Kitty waited until he nodded, until his muscles relaxed, until he stopped looking like a wolf in human skin, before she knelt by the victims. But when she approached them, they screamed around their gags.

"No, no, I'm not going to hurt you," Kitty murmured. Once again, she wondered what she and David looked like from the outside. Were their eyes glowing or something? Maybe they were. Her senses were on a trip wire.

She moved slowly, and the husband let her work off the gag and the cords on his wrists. "Do you have rope or duct tape or something?" she asked.

He nodded quickly. "Kitchen. By the sink." Then, just like the killer had, he asked, "What are you?"

That question again. And those wide, fearful eyes.

"Doesn't matter," she said. She went to the kitchen and found a length of clothesline in the drawer by the sink.

Kitty helped David tie up the killer. They probably tied him much tighter than he needed to be. But she didn't want to take chances.

"I don't want to have to answer questions from the cops," David said.

"That's okay," Kitty said. "I don't think we should stick around." She turned to the couple, who were now free of their cords. "Call 911. Get help."

"Thank you," the man said breathlessly. "Thank you, thank you—"

"Thank us by not telling the cops about us. Okay? The guy got sloppy. You did this yourselves. Okay?"

Both of them nodded frantically. They kept looking at the bound killer like they expected him to attack. But he lay limp, staring unblinkingly at nothing. He whined with every breath. Like a hurt wolf.

In a moment, the man was talking on the phone, and Kitty and David stood by the door. She had a weird urge to say "Merry Christmas" or something before they left. The woman was looking back at her, cradling her torn and bloody arms in her lap, gasping for breath. But smiling. Just a little.

Kitty smiled back, then pulled David out the door with her.

They trudged back to town, led by the sounds of cars on the freeway and the faint glow of lights through the misty air. Snow was falling picturesquely. Her feet, and the rest of her, were soaking wet. David was using the snow to wash blood off his hands.

He looked at her. "Why the hell are you smiling?"

Kitty was grinning so hard she thought her face would break. "Why am I smiling? Because we totally saved those people. We're werewolf superheroes! We're Batman and Robin! That's so awesome!"

Then again, that might have been the adrenaline talking.

David wanted to howl at the night sky in joy and triumph. He'd almost shifted. He'd almost gone over the edge. Attacking that guy had come instinctively. It had been like hunting.

But he came back from the edge. With Kitty's help, he'd pulled himself back and stayed human. And that felt powerful.

The glaring yellow sign of the Waffle House shone like a beacon over the snow-covered prairie. Like the Star of Bethlehem over the manger. David felt a surge of relief when he and Kitty came back in sight of it. Civilization. A roof and hot coffee. Glorious.

No telling how much time had passed since they'd left. They crept in through the still unlocked kitchen door. The cook was gone. Both of them were soaking wet from running in the snow. At least it made the blood he'd gotten on him less noticeable. Almost, he could think about the blood without wanting to turn wolf.

Kitty rubbed her arms and shook out her shirt, squeezing water out of the hem. "Not the smartest thing I've done recently," she muttered. "The one time I didn't bring a change of clothes . . ."

David resisted an urge to reach out and hug her. From affection. From happiness. How long had it been since he'd been happy? Despite the adventure, the running, tracking the killer, and the violence of what he'd witnessed, the urge to turn wolf had faded, a whisper rather than overwhelming thunder. He'd taken a step toward asserting his dominance over that part of his being. The world looked brighter because of that.

Jane, the waitress, came in. "There you are. I thought maybe you'd ducked out on me, but your coat and bag are still here, but you weren't in the bathroom, and I was starting to worry . . ." She narrowed her gaze. "What are you two doing back here?"

David opened his mouth but couldn't think of what to say. It was Kitty who announced, cheerfully, "Oh, you know. Looking for mistletoe."

He blushed, which must have lent some truth to her excuse, because Jane quirked a smile and left again.

"Sorry," Kitty said. "But people tend not to ask more questions if you tell them you've been fooling around."

He wanted to burst out laughing. "Does this sort of thing happen to you a lot?"

"You'd be surprised."

He had a feeling he wouldn't.

Out front, they returned to their booth. Other customers glanced at them, but no one seemed unduly concerned. The TV was still tuned to local news. The same reporter stood by what looked like the same snowy roadside, speaking grimly at the camera. Similar text scrolled along the bottom listing details: five murders and two attempted murders at three different locations. But instead of "serial killer on the loose," the text now read, "serial killer caught."

Then David listened. "Police apprehended the suspected murderer just a little while ago. He appears to have been overpowered by his latest would-be victims, both of whom were injured in the encounter and have been taken to a local hospital. The police have made a statement that they cannot speculate on the exact series of events, and the lone survivors of these horrific events are not talking to reporters."

Maybe they were safe. The witnesses wouldn't remember them. No one would come looking for them. Just a couple more monsters in the night.

He and Kitty got refills on their coffee and made a little toast. "To Christmas," Kitty said. He just smiled. He'd faced down a killer. Captured a killer, and kept his own killer nature locked inside him. Now that he knew he could do it, he wondered if it would become easier. Wondered if maybe he could go home again. He thought he knew what Kitty would say if he mentioned it to her: He'd never know until he tried.

Maybe it wasn't too late to go home for the holidays.

"Thank you," he said to Kitty.

She glanced away from the TV. "For what?"

"For helping me. For teaching me. For making my day a little more interesting. For giving me hope."

She shrugged and gave a surprisingly shy smile. "I didn't do much but get in trouble. As usual."

"Well, thank you anyway. I think I'm going to go back home. See if I can't get my old job back. See if I can't cope with this a little better. I think I can do that now."

"Really?"

He shrugged. "I'd like to try. Not much future for me waking up naked in the woods every couple of days."

"Not unless you're in an industry with a lot of *X*'s in the job description." He had to laugh. "Just remember to breathe slowly," she said.

"Yeah." He started to get up.

"You're going right now?"

"I'm going to make some calls." He gestured to the front door and the pay phone outside.

"Do you need money or something? For the phone."

"I'll call collect. This is the one night a year I know my folks will be home. It's . . . it's been a while since I've called. They'll want to hear from me. I can get some money wired, then catch a bus for home."

He really was anxious to get going. Anxious to test himself. She seemed put out. She really wanted to help, and it heartened him that people like that were still out there.

"Here, take this." She dug in her bag and pulled out something, which she handed to him. A business card. "That has all my info on it. Let me know if you need anything."

"Thanks."

"Good luck." Smiling, she watched him leave.

He was at the pay phone before he took a good look at the card. It was for a radio station: KNOB. Her name: Kitty Norville. And a line: "Host of *The Midnight Hour*, The Wild Side of Talk Radio." She hosted a talk radio show. He should have guessed.

He hadn't talked to his parents in months. Not since he'd run away. He'd done it to protect them, but now, dialing the operator, he found himself tearing up. He couldn't wait to talk to them.

He heard the operator ask if they'd accept the charges. Gave him his name, and he heard his mother respond, "Yes, yes of course, Oh my God . . ."

He said, his voice cracking, "Hi, Mom?"

Thankfully, Jane turned the news off when the reporter started repeating herself.

The movie was long over. The carols were back, all the ones Kitty knew by heart. Jane must have had the same compilation album that her parents played when she was growing up. Funny, how it wouldn't be Christmas without them.

One of her favorite tunes came on, a solemn French carol. A choir sang the lyrics, which she had never paid much attention to because she didn't speak much French. But she knew the title: *"Il Est Né le Divin Enfant." Il Est Né.* He is born.

She dug in her bag and found her cell phone. Dialed a number, even though it was way too late. But when the answer came, Kitty heard party noises in the background—her parents, her sister, her niece and nephew, laughter, more carols—so it was all right.

She said, "Hi, Mom?"

A Princess of Spain

November 14, 1501, Baynard's Castle

Catherine of Aragon, sixteen years old, danced a pavane in the Spanish style before the royal court of England. Lutes, horns, and tabors played a slow, stately tempo, to which she stepped in time. The ladies of her court, who had traveled with her from Spain, danced with her, treading circles around one another—floating, graceful, without a wasted movement. Her body must have seemed like air, drifting with the heavy gown of velvet and gold. She did not even tip her head, framed within its gem-encrusted hood. She was a piece of artwork, a prize for the usurper of the English throne, so that his son's succession would not be questioned. King Henry had the backing of Spain now.

Henry VII watched with a quiet, smug smile on his creased face. Elizabeth of York, his wife, sat nearby, more demonstrative in her pride, smiling and laughing. At a nearby table sat their two sons and two daughters—an impressive household. All made legitimate by Catherine's presence here, for she had been sent by Spain to marry the eldest son: Arthur, Prince of Wales, heir to the throne, was thin and pale at fifteen years old.

All these English were pale, past the point of fairness and well toward ill, for their skies were always laden with clouds. Arthur slouched in his chair and occasionally coughed into his sleeve. He had declined to dance with her, claiming that he preferred to gaze upon her beauty while he may, before he claimed it later that evening.

Catherine's heart ached, torn between anticipation and foreboding. But she must dance her best, as befitted an infanta of Spain. "You must show the English what we Spanish are—superior," her mother, Reina Isabella, told her before Catherine departed. She would most likely never see her parents again.

Arthur did not look at her. Catherine saw his gaze turn to the side of the hall, where one of the foreign envoys sat at a table. There, a woman gazed back at the prince. She was fair skinned with dark eyes and a lock of dark, curling hair hanging outside her hood. Her high-necked gown was elegant without being ostentatious, both modest and fashionable, calculated to not upstage the prince and princess on their wedding day. But it was she who drew the prince's eye.

Catherine saw this; long practice kept her steps in time until the music finished at last.

The musicians struck up a livelier tune, and Prince Henry, the king's younger son, grabbed his sister Margaret's arm and pulled her to the middle of the hall, laughing. All of ten years old, he showed the promise of cutting a fine figure when he came of age—strong limbed, lanky, with a head of unruly ruddy hair. Already he was as tall as any of his siblings, including his elder brother Arthur. At this rate he would become a giant of a man. Word at court said he loved hunting, fighting, dancing, learning—all the pursuits worthy of any prince of Europe. But at this moment he was a boy.

He said something—Catherine only had a few words of English, and did not understand. A moment later he pulled off his fine court coat, leaving only his bare shirt. The room was hot with torches and bodies. He must have been stifled in the finely wrought garment. Because he was a boy the court thought the gesture amusing rather than immodest; everyone smiled indulgently.

Catherine took her seat again, the place of honor at the king's right hand. She gazed, though, at Arthur. She did not even know him. She did not know if she wanted to. Tonight would be better. Tonight, all would be well.

He continued staring at the foreign woman.

The evening drew on, and soon the momentous occasion would be upon them: Arthur and Catherine would be put to bed to consummate their marriage. To seal the alliance between England and Spain with their bodies. Her ladies fluttered, preparing to spirit her off to her chambers to prepare her.

In the confusion, the lanky figure of a very tall boy slipped beside her. The young prince, Henry.

He smiled at her, like a child would, earnestly wanting to be friends.

"You've seen it, too," he said in Latin. She could understand him. "My brother, staring at that woman."

"*Sí.* Yes. Do you know her?"

"She's from the Low Countries," he said. "Or so it's put out at court, though it's also well known that she speaks French with no accent. She's a lady-in-waiting to the daughter of the Dutch ambassador. But the daughter kept to her apartments tonight, and the lady isn't with her, which seems strange, doesn't it?"

"But she must have some reason to be here." And that reason might very well be the young groom who could not take his gaze from her.

"Certainly. Perhaps I'll order someone to spy on her." Henry's eyes gleamed.

Catherine pressed her lips together but didn't manage a smile. "It is no matter. A passing fancy. It will mean nothing tomorrow."

Arthur was *her* husband. Tonight would make that a fact and not simply a legality. With a sudden burning in her gut, she longed for that moment.

In nomine Patris, Filii, et Spiritus Sancti."

The bishop sprinkled holy water over the bed, where Catherine and Arthur were tucked, dressed in costly nightclothes, put to bed in a most formal manner for their wedding night, so that all might know that the marriage was made complete. At last, the witnesses left them, and for the first time, Catherine was alone with her husband.

All she could do was stare at him, his white face and lank ruddy hair, as her heart raced in her chest. He stared back, until she felt she should say something, but her voice failed. Words failed, when she couldn't decide whether to speak French, Latin, or attempt a phrase in her still halting English. *Why can he not understand Spanish?*

"You are quite pretty," he said in Latin, and leaned forward on shaking arms to kiss her on the lips.

She flushed with relief. Perhaps all would be well. He was her husband, she was his wife. She even *felt* married, lying here with him. Warm from her scalp to her toes—pleasant, illicit, yet sanctioned by God and Church. This was her wedding night, a most glorious night—

Before she could kiss him back, before she could hold him as her body told her to do, he pulled away. Unbidden, her arm rose to reach for him. Quickly, she drew it back and folded her hands on her lap. Must she maintain her princess's decorum, even here?

Arthur coughed. He bent double with coughing, putting his fist to his mouth. His thin body shook.

She left the bed and retrieved a goblet of wine from the table. Returning, she sat beside him and touched his hand, urging him to take a drink. His skin was cold, damp as the English winter she'd found herself in.

"*Por Dios,*" she whispered. What had God brought her to? She said in Latin, "I'll send for a physician."

Arthur shook his head. "It is nothing. It will pass. It always does." He took a drink of wine, swallowing loudly, as if his throat were closing.

But he had been this pale and sickly every time she'd seen him. This would not pass.

If they could have a child, if he would live long enough for them to have a child, a son, a new heir, her place in this country would be assured.

The wine would revive him. She touched his cheek. When he looked up, she hoped to see some fire in his eyes, some desire there to match her own. She hoped he would touch her back. But she only saw exhaustion from the day's activities. He was a child on the verge of sleep.

She was a princess of Spain, not made for seduction.

He gave the goblet back to her. With a sigh, he settled back against the pillows. By his next breath, he was asleep.

Catherine set the goblet on the table. The room was chilled. Every room in this country was chilled. Yet at this moment, while her skin burned, the cool tiles of the floor felt good against her bare feet.

She knelt by the bed, clasped her hands tightly together, and prayed.

December 15, 1501, Richmond

Another feast lay spread before her. King Henry displayed his wealth in calculated presentations of food, music, entertainment. However much the politics and finances of his realm were strained, he would give no other appearance than that of a successful, stable monarch.

Catherine did not dance, though the musicians played a pavane. She sat at the table, beside her husband, watching. Husband in name only. He had not once come to her chamber. He had not once summoned her to his. But appearances must be maintained.

He slouched in his chair, leaning on one carved wooden arm, clutching a goblet in both hands. He had grown even more wan, even more sickly, if possible. Did no one else see it?

She touched the arm of his chair. "My husband, have you eaten enough? Should I call for more food?"

He shook his head and waved her off. It was not natural, to treat one's wife so. He was in danger of failing his duty as a prince, and as a Christian husband.

But what could she do? A princess was meant to serve her husband, not command or judge him.

"Your husband will take mistresses," her mother told her, in her final instructions before Catherine set sail. She told her that it was the way of things and she could not fight it. But Isabella also said that her husband would do his duty toward her, so that she might do *her* duty and bear him many children.

Her duty was turning to dust in her hands, through no fault of her own.

In the tiled space in the center of the hall, the young Prince Henry danced with the strange foreign woman. Catherine had no evidence that this woman was her husband's mistress, except for the way Arthur watched her, desperately, with too bright eyes.

The woman danced gracefully. She must have been a dozen years older than her partner, but she tolerated him with an air of amusement, wearing the thin and placid smile, as though sitting for a portrait. Henry was a lively enough partner that he made every step a joy. His father was training him for the clergy, it was said. He might be the greatest bishop in England someday—the crown's voice in the Church.

Catherine begged leave to retire early, before the music and dancing had finished. She claimed fatigue and a sensitive stomach. People nodded knowingly at the information and offered each other winks. They thought she was with child, as any young bride ought to be.

But she wasn't. Never would be, if things kept on in this manner.

It was difficult to spy in the king's house unless one had command of the guards and could order them to stay, or leave, or watch. She did not have command of anything except her own household, which the English court treated as the foreigners they were. Really, though, her duenna and stewards commanded her household—Catherine was too young for it, they said. Her parents had sent able guardians to look after her.

Nevertheless, against all her instincts, after dark—well after the candles and lanterns had been snuffed—Catherine donned a black traveling cloak over her shift and set out, stepping quietly past her ladies-in-waiting who slept in the outer chamber. Very quietly she opened the heavy door, giving herself barely enough space to slip through. The iron hinges squeaked, but only once, softly, like a woman sighing in her sleep.

Two more chambers, sitting rooms, lay between her and Arthur. The spaces were dark, chill. Thick windows let in very little of the already faint moonlight. Her slippered feet made no sound on the wood floors. She kept to the paneled walls and felt her way around, step by careful step.

Guards walked their rounds. They passed from room to room, pikes resting on their shoulders. England had finished its wars of succession relatively recently; for the royal family, there was always danger.

If she were very quiet, and moved very carefully, they would not see her. She hoped. If they found her, most likely nothing would happen to her, but she didn't want to have to explain herself. This was very improper for a woman of her rank. She should go back to her own room and pray to God to make this right.

Her knees were worn out with praying.

She listened for booted footsteps and the rattle of armor. Heard nothing.

She reached the chamber outside Arthur's bedroom. A light shone under the door, faint, buttery—candlelight. A step away from the door she paused, listening. What did she think she might hear? Conversation? Laughter? Deep sighs? She had no idea.

She touched the door. Surely it would be locked. It would be a relief to have to walk away, still ignorant. She touched the latch—

It wasn't locked.

Softly, she pushed open the door and looked in.

Looking like an ill child far younger than his years, Arthur lay propped up in bed, limp, his eyes half-closed, senseless. Beside him crouched the foreign woman, fully clothed, her hands on his shoulders, clutching his linen nightclothes. Her mouth was open, and her teeth shone dark with blood. A gash on Arthur's neck bled.

"You're killing him!" Catherine cried. She stood, too shocked to scream—she ought to scream, to call for the guards. Even if they could not understand her Spanish, they would come at the sound of panic.

In a moment, a scant heartbeat, the foreign woman appeared before Catherine. She might as well have flown; the princess didn't see her move. This was some dream, some vision. Some devil had crept into her mind.

The woman pressed her to the wall, closing Catherine's mouth with one hand. Catherine kicked and writhed, trying to break away, but the woman was strong. Fantastically strong. Catherine swatted at her, pulled at a strand of her dark hair that had come loose from her hood. She might as well have been a fly in the woman's grasp. With her free hand she grabbed Catherine's wrists and held her arms still.

Then she caught Catherine's gaze.

Her eyes were blue, the dark, clear blue of the twilight sky over Spain.

"I am not killing him. Be silent, say nothing of what you have seen, and you will keep your husband." Her voice was subdued, but clear. Later, Catherine could not recall what language she had spoken.

Catherine nearly laughed. What husband? She might as well have chosen the convent. But she couldn't speak, couldn't move.

The woman's touch was cold. The fingers curled over Catherine's face felt like marble.

"You are so young to be in this position. Poor girl."

The woman smiled, kindly it seemed. For a moment, Catherine wanted to cling to her, to spill all her worries before this woman—she seemed to understand.

Then she said, "Sleep. You've had a dream. Go back to sleep."

Catherine's vision faded. She struggled again, tried to keep the woman's face in sight, but she felt herself falling. Then, nothing.

She awoke on the floor. She had fainted and lay curled at the foot of her own bed, wrapped in her cloak. Pale morning light shone through the window. It was a cold light, full of winter.

She tried to recall last night—she had left her bed, obviously. But for what reason? If she'd wanted wine she could have called for one of her ladies.

Her ladies would be mortified to find her like this. They would think her ill, keep her to bed, and send for physicians. Catherine quickly stood, collected herself, arranged her shift and untangled her hair. She was a princess. She ought to behave like one, despite her strange dreams of women with rich blue eyes.

An ache in her belly made her pause. It was not like her to be so indecorous as to leave her bed before morning. As she smoothed the wrinkles from her dressing gown, her fingers tickled. She raised her hand, looked at it.

A few silken black fibers—long, shining, so thin they were almost invisible—clung to her skin. Hair—but how had it come here? Her own hair was like honey, Arthur's was colored amber—

She had seen a dark-haired woman with Arthur. It was not a dream. The memory of what she had seen had not faded after all.

That day, Catherine and Arthur attended Mass together. She studied him so intently that he raised his brow at her, inquiring. She couldn't explain. He wore a high-necked doublet. She couldn't see his neck to tell if he had a wound there. Perhaps he did, perhaps not. He made no mention of what had happened last night, made no recognition that he had even seen her. Could he not remember?

Say nothing of what you have seen, and you will keep your husband. Catherine dared not speak at all. She would be called mad.

This country was cursed, overrun with rain and plague. This king was cursed, haunted by all those who had died so he might have his crown, and so was his heir. Catherine could tell her parents, but what would that accomplish? She was not here for herself, but for the alliance between their kingdoms.

She prayed, while the priest chanted. His words were Latin, which was familiar and comforting. The Church was constant. In that she could take comfort. Perhaps if she confessed, told her priest what she had seen, he would have counsel. Perhaps he could say what demon this was that was taking Arthur.

A slip of paper, very small, as if it had been torn from the margin of a letter, fell out of her prayer book. She glanced quickly around—no one had seen it. Her ladies either stared ahead at the altar or bowed over their clasped hands. She was kneeling; the paper had landed on the velvet folds of her skirt. She picked it up.

"*Convene me horto.* Henricus," written in a boy's careful hand. Meet me in the garden.

Catherine crumpled the paper and tucked it in her sleeve. She'd burn it later.

She told her ladies she wished to walk in the air, to stretch her legs after the long Mass. They accompanied her—she could not go anywhere without them, but she was able to find a place where she might sit a little ways off. Henry would have to find her then.

Here she was, in this country only two months and already playing at spying.

Gravel paths wound around the lawn outside Richmond, the King's favorite palace. Never had Catherine seen grass of such jewellike green. Even in winter, the lawn stayed green. The dampness made it thrive. Her mother-in-law Elizabeth assured her that in the summer, flowers grew in glorious tangles. Around back, boxes outside the kitchens held forests of herbs. England was fertile, the queen said knowingly.

Catherine and her ladies walked to where the path turned around a hedge. Some stone benches offered a place to rest.

"Doña Elvira, you and the ladies sit here. I wish to walk on a little. Do not worry, I will call if I need you." The concerned expression on her duenna's face was not appeased, but Catherine was resolute.

Doña Elvira sat and directed the others to do likewise.

Catherine strolled on, carefully, slowly, not rushing. Around the shrubs and out of sight from her ladies, Henry arrived, stepping out from behind the other end of the hedge.

"*Buenos días, hermana.*"

She smiled in spite of herself. "You learn my language."

Henry blushed and looked at his feet. "Only a little. Hello and thank you and the like."

"Still, *gracias*. For the little."

"I have learned something of the foreign woman. I told the guards to watch her and listen."

"We should tell your father. It is not for us to command the guards—"

"She is not from the Low Countries. Her name is Angeline. She is French, which means she is a spy," he said.

Catherine wasn't sure that one so naturally followed the other. It was too simple an explanation. The alliance between England and Spain presented far too strong an enemy for France. Of course they would send spies. But that was no spy she'd seen with Arthur.

She shook her head. "She is more than that."

"She hopes to break the alliance between England and Spain by distracting my brother. If you have no children, the succession will pass to another."

"To you and your children, yes? And perhaps a French queen for England, if they find one for you to marry?"

He pursed boyish lips. "I am Duke of York. Why would I want to be king?"

But there was a light in his eyes, intelligent, glittering. He would not shy away from being king, if, God forbid, events came to that.

He said, "There is more. I touched her hand when we danced. It was cold. Colder than stone. Colder than anything."

Catherine paced, just a little circle beside her brother-in-law. She ought to tell a priest. But he knew. So she told him.

"I have been spying as well," she said. "I went to Arthur's chamber last night. If she is his mistress—I had to see. I had to know."

"What did you see? *Is* she his mistress?"

Catherine wrung her hands. She did not have the words for this in any language. "I do not know. She was there, yes. But Arthur was senseless. It was as if she had put a spell on him."

Eagerly, Henry said, "Then she is a witch?"

Catherine's throat ached, but she would not cry. "I do not know. I do not know of such things. She said strange things to me; that I must not interfere if I wish to keep Arthur alive. She—she cast a spell on me, I think. I fainted, then I awoke in my chamber—"

Henry considered thoughtfully, a serious expression that looked almost amusing on the face of a boy. "So. A demon is trying to sink its claws into the throne of England through its heir. Perhaps it will possess him. Or devour him. We must kill it, of course."

"We must tell a priest!" Catherine said, pleading. "We must tell the archbishop!"

"If we did, would they believe us? I, a boy, and you, a foreigner? They'll say we are mad, or playing at games."

She couldn't argue because she'd thought the same. She said, "This woman made me sleep with a glance. How would we kill such a thing?" Even if they *wanted* to kill her. What if the woman was right, and if they acted against her she would find some way to kill Arthur? Perhaps they should bide their time.

"Highness? Are you there?" Doña Elvira called to her.

"I must away," Catherine said, and curtsied to her brother-in-law. "We must think on what to do. We must not be rash."

He returned the respect with a bow. "Surely. Farewell."

She hoped he would not be rash. She feared he looked upon all this as a game.

His Highness is not seeing visitors," the gentleman of Arthur's chamber told her. He spoke apologetically and bowed respectfully, but he would not let her through the doors to see Arthur. She wanted to scream.

"You will tell him that I was here?"

"Yes, Your Highness," the man said and bowed again.

Catherine could do nothing more than turn around and walk away, trailed by her own attending ladies.

What they must think of her. She caught the whispers among them, when they thought she couldn't hear. *Pobre Catalina.* Poor Catherine, whose husband would not see her, who spent every night alone.

That evening, she sent Doña Elvira and her ladies on an errand for wine. Once again, she crept from her chambers alone, furtive as a mouse.

I will see my husband, Catherine thought. *It is my right.* It should not have been so difficult for her to see him alone. But as it was the palace swarmed with courtiers.

She wanted to reach him before the woman arrived to work her spells on him.

Quietly, she slipped through Arthur's door and closed it behind her.

The bed curtains were open. Arthur, in his nightclothes, sat on the edge of the bed, hunched over. She could hear his wheezing breaths across the room.

"Your Highness," she said, curtsying.

"Catherine?" He looked up—and did he smile? Just a little? "Why are you here?"

She said, "Who is the woman who comes to you at night?"

"No one comes to me at night." He said this flatly, as if she were to blame for his loneliness.

She shook her head, fighting tears. She would keep her wits and not cry. "Three nights ago I came, and she was here. You were bleeding, Arthur. She hurt you. She's killing you!"

"That isn't true. No one has been here. And—what business is it of yours if a woman has been here?"

"I am your wife. You have a duty to me."

"Catherine, I am so tired."

She knelt at his side and dared to put her hand on his knee. "Then you must grow strong. So that we may have children. Your heirs."

He touched her hand. A thrill went through her flesh, like fire. So much feeling in a simple touch! But his skin was ice cold.

"I am telling the truth," said the boy who was her husband. "I remember nothing of any woman coming here. I come to bed every night and fall into such a deep sleep that nothing rouses me but my own coughing. I do not know of what you speak."

This woman had put a spell on them all.

"Your father is sending your household to Ludlow Castle, in Wales," she said.

He set his lips in a thin, pale line. "Then we shall go to Ludlow."

"You cannot travel so far," she said. "The journey will kill you."

"If I were really so weak my father would not send me."

"His pride blinds him!"

"You should not speak so of the king, my lady." He gave a tired sigh. What would have been an accusation of treason from fiery young Henry's lips was weary observation from Arthur's. "Now please, Catherine. Let me sleep. If I sleep well tonight, perhaps I'll be strong enough to see you tomorrow."

It was an empty promise and they both knew it. He was as pale and wasted as he had ever been. She kissed his hand with as much passion as she had ever been allowed to show. She pressed her cheek to it, let tears fall on it. She would pray every day for him. Every hour.

She stood, curtsied, and left him alone in the chamber.

Outside, however, she waited, sitting on a chair in the corner normally reserved for pages or stewards. Doña Elvira would be scandalized to see her there.

In an hour, the woman Angeline came. She moved like smoke. Catherine had been staring ahead so intently she thought her eyes played a trick on her. A shadow flickered where there was no flame. A draft blew where no window was open.

Angeline did not approach, but all the same she appeared. She stood before the doors of Arthur's bedchamber as regal as any queen.

Catherine was still gathering the courage to stand when Angeline looked at her. Her face was alabaster, a statue draped with a gown of black velvet. She might as well have been stone, her gaze was so hard.

Finally, Catherine stood.

"*Es la novia niña,*" Angeline said.

The princess would not be cowed by a commoner. "By the laws of Church and country I am not a child, I am a woman."

"By one very important consideration, you are not." She turned a pointed smile.

Catherine blushed; her gaze fell. She was still a maid. That was certainly not *her* fault.

"I demand that you leave here," Catherine said. "Leave here, and leave my husband alone."

"Oh, child, you don't want me to do that."

"I insist. You are some witch, some demon. That much I know. You have worked a spell on him that sickens him to death—"

"Oh no, I'll not let my puppet die. I could keep your Arthur alive forever, if I wished. I hold that secret."

"You . . . you are an abomination against the Church. Against God!"

She smiled thinly. "Perhaps."

"Why?" Catherine said. "Why him? Why this?"

"He'll be a weak king. At best, an indifferent king. He won't be leading any troops to war against France. He will keep England a quiet, unimportant country."

"You do not know that. You cannot see the future. He will be a great king—"

"One need not see the future to guess such things, dear Catherine."

"You will address me as Your Highness, as is proper."

"Of course, Your Highness. You must trust me—I will not kill Arthur. If his brother were to become king—you have seen the kind of boy he is: fierce, competitive, strong. You can imagine the kind of king he will be. No one in Europe wishes for a strong king of England."

"My father King Ferdinand—"

"Not even King Ferdinand. From the first, he wanted a son-in-law he could control."

Catherine knew it was true, all of it, the chess-like machinations of politics that had ruled her life. Her marriage to Arthur had given Spain another playing piece, that was all.

There was no room for love in any of this.

She was descended from two royal houses. Her ancestors were the oldest and most noble in all of Europe. Dignity was bred into the sinews of her flesh. She stood tall, did not collapse, did not cry, however much the little girl inside of her was trembling.

"And what of children?" she said. "What of the children I'm meant to bear?"

"It may be possible. Or it may not."

"I do not believe you. I do not believe anything that you say."

"Yes, you do," she said. "But more importantly, you cannot stop me. You'll go to sleep, now. You will not remember."

She wanted to fling herself at the woman, strangle her with her own hands. Tiny hands that couldn't strangle a kitten, alas.

"Catherine. Move away. I know what she is." The command came in the incongruous voice of a boy.

Prince Henry stood blocking the chamber's other doorway.

He had a spear, which seemed overlarge and unwieldy in his hands. Nevertheless, he held it at the ready, feet braced, pointed at the woman. It was a mockery of battle. A child playing at hunting boar.

"What am I, boy?" the woman said in a soft, mocking voice.

This only drove Henry to greater rage. "Succubus. A demon who feeds on the souls of men. You will not have my brother, devil!"

Her smile fell, darkening her expression. "You have just enough intelligence to do harm. And more than enough ignorance."

"I'll kill you. I can kill you where you stand."

"You will not kill me. Arthur is so much mine that without me he will die."

She'd made Arthur weak and subsumed him under her power. If that tie between them was severed—

Catherine's heart pounded. She could not stop them both. They would not listen. No one ever listened to her. "Henry, you must not, she is keeping Arthur alive."

"She lies."

The woman laughed, a bitter sound. "If Arthur dies, Henry becomes heir. That reason will not stay his hand."

But Henry didn't want to be king. He'd said so . . .

Catherine caught his gaze. She saw something dark in his eyes.

Then she tried to forget that she'd seen it. "My lord, wait—"

The woman lived in shadow—was made of shadow. She started to flow back into the hidden ways by which she came, moving within the stillness of night. Catherine saw nothing but a shudder, the light of a sputtering candle. But Henry saw more, and like a great hunter he anticipated what the flinch of movement meant.

With a shout he lunged forward, driving the spear before him.

The woman flew. Catherine would swear that she flew, up and over, toward the ceiling to avoid Henry. Henry followed with his spear, jumping, swinging the weapon upward. He missed. With a sigh the woman twisted away from him. Henry stumbled, thrown off balance by his wayward thrust, and Angeline stood behind him.

"You're a boy playing at being warrior," she said, carrying herself as calmly as if she had not moved.

Henry snarled an angry cry and tried again. The woman stepped aside and took hold of the back of Henry's neck. With no effort at all, she pushed him down, so that he was kneeling. He still held the spear, but she was behind him pressing down on him, and he couldn't use it.

"I could make you as much my puppet as your brother is."

"No! You won't! I'll never be anyone's puppet!" He struggled, his whole body straining against her grip, but he couldn't move.

Catherine knelt and began to pray, *Pater Noster* and *Ave Maria*, and her lips stumbled trying to get out all the words at once.

The prayers were for her own comfort. Catherine had little faith in her own power; she didn't expect the unholy creature to hear her words and pause. She didn't consider that her own words, her own prayer, would cause Angeline to loosen her grip on Henry.

But Angeline did loosen her grip. Her body seemed to freeze for a moment. She became more solid, as if the prayer had made her substantial.

Henry didn't hesitate. He threw himself forward, away from Angeline, then spun to put the spear between them. Then, while she was still seemingly entranced, he drove it home.

The point slipped into her breast. She cried out, fell, and as she did Henry drove the wooden shaft deep into her chest.

The next moment she lay on the floor, clutching the shaft of the spear. Henry still held the end of it. He stared down at her, iconic, like England's beloved Saint George and his vanquished dragon.

There was no blood.

A strangeness happened—as strange as anything else Catherine had seen since coming to England. With the scent of a crypt rising from her, the woman faded in color, then dried and crumbled like a corpse that had been rotting for a dozen years. The body became unrecognizable in a moment. In another, only ash and dust remained.

Henry kicked a little at the mound of debris.

Catherine spoke, her voice shaking. "She said she was keeping Arthur alive. What if it's true? What if he dies? I'll be a widow in a strange country. I'll be lost." Lost, when she was meant to be a queen. Her life was slipping away.

Henry touched her arm. She nearly screamed, but her innate dignity controlled her. She only flinched.

He gazed at her with utmost gravity. "I'll take care of you. If Arthur dies, then I'll take care of you, when I am king after my father."

Arthur died in the spring. And so it came to pass that Henry, who had been born to be Duke of York and nothing else, a younger brother, a mere afterthought in the chronicles of history, would succeed his father as King of England, become Henry VIII, and marry Catherine of Aragon. He would take care of her, as he had promised.

He was sixteen at their wedding, a year older than Arthur had been. But so different. Like day and night, summer and winter. Henry was tall, flushed, hearty, laughed all the time, danced, hunted, jousted, argued, commanded. Their wedding night would be nothing like Catherine's first, she knew. *He is the greatest prince in all Europe,* people at court said of him. *He will make England a nation to be reckoned with.*

Catherine considered her new husband—now taller than she by a head. Part of her would always remember the boy. She could still picture him the way he stood outside Arthur's chamber, spear in his hands, fury in his eyes, ready to do battle. Ready to sacrifice his own brother. Catherine would never forget that this was a man willing to do what he believed must be done, whatever the cost.

She wanted to be happy, but England's chill air remained locked in her bones.

Conquistador de la Noche

His life was becoming a trail of blood.

Ricardo de Avila fired his crossbow at the crowd of natives. The bolt struck the chest of a Zuni warrior, a man no older than his own nineteen years. The native fell back, the dark of his blood splashing, along with dozens of others. The army's few arquebuses fired, the sulfur stink clouding the air. The horses danced, tearing up the grass and raising walls of dust. Between keeping control of his horse and trying to breathe, Ricardo could not winch back his crossbow for another shot.

Not that he needed to fire again. The general was already calling for a cease-fire, and the few remaining Zuni, running hard and shouting in their own language, were fleeing back to their city.

City. Rather, a few baked buildings clustered on the hillside. The expedition had become a farce. Cibola did not exist—at least, not as it did in the stories the first hapless explorers had brought back. So many leagues of travel, wasted. Dead men and horses, wasted. The land itself was not even worth much. It had little water and was cut through with unforgiving mountains and canyons. The Spanish should turn around and leave it to the natives.

But the friars who traveled with Coronado were adamant. Even if they found no sign of treasure, it was their duty as Christians to save the souls of these poor heathens.

They had believed that Coronado would be a new Cortés,

opening new lands and treasures for the glory of Spain. The New World was more vast than any in Europe had comprehended. Naturally they assumed the entire continent held the same great riches Spain had found in Mexico. As quickly as Spain was eating through that treasure, it would need to find more.

Coronado tried to keep up a good face for his men. His armor remained brightly polished, gleaming in the harsh sun, and he sat a tall figure on his horse. But with the lack of good food, his face had become sunken, and when he looked across the *despoblado*, the bleak lands they would have to cross to reach the rumored Cities of Gold, the shine in his eyes revealed despair.

This expedition should have made the fortune of Ricardo, a third son of a minor nobleman. Now, though, he was thirsty, near to starving, and had just killed a boy who had come at him with nothing but a stone club. His dark beard had grown unkempt, his hair long and ratted. Sand had marred the finish of his helmet and cuirass. No amount of wealth seemed worth the price of this journey. Rather, the price he was paying had become so steep it would have taken streets paved with gold in truth to restore the balance. What was left, then? When you had already paid too much in return for nothing?

Ricardo had sold himself for a mouthful of dust.

Ten years passed.

It was dark when Ricardo rode into the main plaza at Zacatecas. Lamps hung outside the church and governor's buildings, and the last of the market vendors had departed. A small caravan of a dozen horses and mules from the mine was picketed, awaiting stabling. The place was hot and dusty, though a cool wind from the mountains brought some refreshment. Ricardo stopped to water his horse and stretch his legs before making his way to the fort.

At the corner of the garrison road, a man stepped from the shadows to block his path. His horse snorted and planted its feet. Ricardo's night vision was good, but he had trouble making out the figure.

"Don Ricardo? I was told you were due to return today," the man said.

Ricardo recognized the voice, though it had been a long time since he'd heard it. "Diego?"

"Ah, you do remember!"

He'd met Diego in Mexico City, where they'd both listened to the stories of Cibola and joined Coronado's expedition. Side by side they'd ridden those thousands of miles. They'd both grown skinny and shaggy, and, on their return, Diego had broken away from the party early to seek his own fortune. Ricardo hadn't seen him since.

"Where have you been? Come into the light, let me look at you!"

A lamp shone over the doorway on the brick building on the corner. Ricardo touched Diego's shoulder and urged him over. His old compatriot turned, but didn't move from the spot. Ricardo squinted to see him better. Diego had not changed much in the last decade. If anything, he seemed more robust. He had a brightness to him, a sly smile, as if he had come into some fortune, discovering what the rest of them had failed to attain. His clothing, a leather doublet, breeches, and sturdy boots, were worn but well made. His hair and beard were well kept. He wore a gold ring in one ear and must have seemed dashing.

"You look very well, Diego," Ricardo said finally.

"And you look tired, my friend."

"Only because I have ridden fifteen miles today over hard country."

Diego grimaced. "Yes, playing courier for the garrisons along the road to Mexico City. How do you come to do such hard labor? It's not fit for one of your station."

Typical hidalgo attitude. Ricardo was used to the reaction. Smiling, he ducked his gaze. "The work suits me, and it won't be forever."

"Hoping to earn your way to a land grant? A silver mine of your very own, with a fine estancia and a well-bred girl from Spain to marry and give you many sons? So you can return to Spain a made man?" Diego spoke with a mocking edge.

"Isn't that the dream of us all?" Ricardo said, spreading his arms and making a joke of it. He really was that transparent, he supposed. Not dignified enough to lead the life of dissolute nobility like so many others of his class. Too proud and restless to wait for his fortune to find him. But the secret that he told no one was that he didn't want to leave and take his fortune back to Spain. He had come to love this land, the wide desert spaces, green valleys ringed by brown mountains, hot sun and cold nights. He wanted to be at home here.

Diego stepped close and put a hand on Ricardo's arm. "I have a better idea. A great opportunity. I was hoping to find you, because I know no one as honest and deserving as you."

The schemes to easy wealth were as common in this country as cactus and mountains. Ricardo was skeptical. "You have found some secret silver lode, is that it? You need someone in the government to push through the claim, and you'll give me a percentage."

Diego's smile thinned. "There is a village a day's ride away, deep in the western hills. The land is rich, and the natives are agreeable. A Franciscan has started a church there, but he needs men to lead. To make their mark upon the land." He pressed a folded square of paper into Ricardo's hand. A map, directions. "You are a good, honest man, Ricardo. Come and help us make a respectable town out of this place. And reap the rewards for doing so."

Such a village should have fallen under the governor of Zacatecas's jurisdiction. Ricardo would have heard of a priest in that region. Something wasn't right.

"I still dream of gold, Ricardo," Diego said. "Do you?"

"The Cities of Gold never existed."

"Not as a place. But as a symbol—this whole continent is a Cibola, waiting for us to claim it."

"Just as we did the last time?" Ricardo said, scowling.

"But you'll come to this village. I'll wait for you."

Diego patted Ricardo on the shoulder, then slipped back into shadows. Ricardo didn't even hear him go. Thoughtful, worried, Ricardo made his way to the fort for the evening.

Ricardo followed Diego's map into the hills, not because he was lured by the promise of easy wealth, but because he wanted to discover what was wrong with the story.

The day was hot, and he traveled slowly, keeping to shade when he could and resting his horse by dismounting and climbing steep hills alongside it. He followed the ridge of mountains and hoped he had not lost the way.

Then he climbed a rise that opened into a valley, as Diego had described. A large pond, probably filled by a spring, provided water, and fruit trees grew thickly. A meadow covered the valley floor, and Ricardo could imagine sheep or goats grazing here or crops growing. Much could be done with land like this.

A small village sat a hundred yards or so from the pond. The Franciscan's church was little more than a square cottage made of adobe brick, with a narrow tower. Wood and grass-thatched huts gathered around a dusty square.

No people were visible, no hearth fires burned. Not so much as a chicken scratched in the dirt. Four horses grazed in the meadow beyond the village. They glanced at Ricardo, then continued grazing. Riding into the village, he shouted a hail, which fell flat, as if the empty settlement absorbed sound. Dismounting, he left his horse by a trough that was dry.

A smarter man might have traveled with a troop of guards, or at least servants to ease his way. He had thought it easier to travel alone, learn what he could, and return as quickly as possible to report this to the governor. Now, the skin of his neck crawled, and he wondered if he might need a squad of soldiers before the day was through. He kept his hand on the hilt of his sword slung on his belt.

He went into the chapel.

The place might have been new. A few benches lined up before a simple altar. The wood was freshly cut, but they seemed to have been poorly built: rickety legs slotted into flat boards. Those seated would have to be careful if they didn't want to tumble to the dirt floor.

In front, the wood altar was bare, without even a cloth to cover it. No cross hung on the wall. The place had the sickly beeswax candle smell that imbued churches everywhere. At least that much was familiar. Nothing else was. He almost hoped to find signs of violence, because then he'd have some idea of what had happened here. But this . . . nothing . . . was inexplicable.

"*¡Hola!*" he called, cringing at his own raised voice. He had the urge to speak in a whisper, if at all.

A door in the back of the chapel opened. A small body in a gray robe looked out. "Who is it?"

A shiver crawled up Ricardo's spine, as if a ghost had stepped through the wall. He peered at the door, squinting, but the man was hidden in shadow.

"I am Captain Ricardo de Avila. Diego Ruiz asked me to come."

"Ah, yes! He told me of you." He straightened, shedding the air of suspicion. "Come inside, let us speak," the friar said, opening the door a little wider. Ricardo went to the back room as the friar indicated.

Like the chapel, this room had no windows. There was a table with a lit candle on it, several chairs, and a small, dirty portrait of the Blessed Virgin. There was a trapdoor in the floor, with a big iron ring to lift it. Ricardo wondered what was in the cellar.

"Take a seat. I have some wine," the friar said, going to a cabinet in the corner. "Would you like some?"

"Yes, please." Ricardo sat in the chair closest to the door.

The friar put one pewter cup on the table, poured from an earthenware jug, and indicated that Ricardo should take it. He took a sip; it was weak, sour. But his mouth was dry, and the liquid helped.

The friar didn't pour a drink for himself. Sitting on the opposite side of the table, he regarded Ricardo as if they were two men in a plaza tavern, not two dusty, weary colonials in a dark room lit by a candle. The man was pale, as if he spent all his time indoors. His hands, resting on the table, were thin, bony. Under his robes, his entire body might have been a skeleton. He had dark hair trimmed in a tonsure and a thin beard. He was a stereotype of a friar who had been relegated to the outer edges of the colony for too long.

"I am Fray Juan," the man said, spreading his hands. "And this is my village."

Ricardo couldn't hide confusion. "Forgive me, Fray Juan, but Señor Ruiz told me this was a rich village. I expected to see farmers and shepherds at work. Women in the courtyard, weaving and grinding corn."

"Oh, but this is a prosperous village. You must take my word that appearances here aren't everything." His lips turned in a smile.

"Then what is going on here?" He had started to make guesses: Fray Juan was smuggling something through the village; he'd failed utterly at converting the natives and putting them to useful work and refused to admit it; or everyone had died of disease. But even then there ought to be some evidence. Bodies, graves, something.

Juan studied him with cold eyes, blue and hard as stones. Ricardo wanted to hold the stare, but something made him glance away. His heart was pounding. He wanted to flee.

The friar said, "You rode with Coronado, didn't you? The expedition to find Cibola?"

Surviving that trip at all gave one a certain reputation. "Yes, I did. Along with Ruiz."

"Even if he hadn't told me I would have guessed. You have that look. A weariness, like nothing will ever surprise you again."

Ricardo chuckled. "Is that what it is? Something different than the usual cynicism?"

"I see that you are not a youth, but you are also not an old man. Not old enough to have the usual cynicism. Therefore, you've lived through something difficult. You're the right age for it."

A restless caballero wandering the northern provinces? He supposed there were a few of that kind. "You've changed the subject. Where is Ruiz?"

"He will be here," Fray Juan said, soothing. "Captain, look at me for a moment." Ricardo did. Those eyes gleamed in the candlelight until they seemed to fill the room. The man was all eyes, shining organs in a face of shadows. "Stay here tonight. It's almost dusk, far too late to start back for Zacatecas. There are no other settlements within an hour's ride of here. Take the clean bed in the house next door, sleep tonight, and in the morning you'll see that all here is well."

They regarded one another, and Ricardo could never recall what passed through his mind during those moments. The Franciscan wouldn't lie to him, surely. So all must be well, despite his misgivings.

And Fray Juan was right; Ricardo must stay the night in any case. "When will Ruiz return?"

"Rest, Captain. He'll be at your side when you wake."

Ricardo found himself lulled by the friar's voice. The look in his eyes was very calming.

A moment later, he was sitting at the edge of a rope cot in a house so poorly made he could see through the cracks in the walls. He didn't remember coming here. Had he been sleepwalking? Was he so weary that a trance had taken him? For all his miles of travel, that had never happened before. He hadn't eaten supper. He wondered how much of the night had passed.

His horse—he didn't remember caring for his horse; he'd left the animal tacked up near the trough. That jolted him to awareness. It was the first lesson of this vast country: Take care of your horse before yourself, because you'd need the animal if you hoped to survive the great distances between settlements.

Rushing outside, he found his bay mare grazing peacefully, chewing grass around its bit while dragging the reins. He caught the reins, removed the saddle and bridle, rubbed the animal down, and picketed it to a sturdy tree that had access to good grazing, since no cut hay or grain seemed available. He had found water in a small pond in the meadow.

Fully awake now, studying the valley under the light of a three-quarters moon, Ricardo's suspicions renewed. This village was dead. He should have questioned the friar more forcefully about what had happened here. Nothing about this place felt right, and Fray Juan's calm assurances meant nothing.

Ricardo had reason to doubt the word of a man of God. It was a friar, another man of God, who brought back the story of Cibola, of a land covered in lush pastures and rich fields, of cities with wealth that made the Aztec Empire seem as dust. Coronado had believed those stories. They all had, until they reached the edge of that vast and rocky wasteland to the north. They had whispered to each other, *Is this it?*

Ricardo de Avila would find Diego Ruiz and learn what had happened here.

The wind spoke strangely here, crackling through cottonwoods, skittering sand across the mud-patched walls of the buildings. In the first hut, where he'd been directed to stay, he found a lantern and lit it using his own flint. With the light, he examined the abandoned village.

If disease had struck, he'd have expected to see graves. If there had been an attack, a raid by some of the untamed native tribes in the mountain, he would have seen signs of violence: shattered pottery, interrupted chores. He'd have found bodies and carrion animals. But there was not so much as a drop of shed blood.

The huts were tidy, dirt floors swept and spread with straw, clay pots empty, water skins dry. The hearths were cold, the coals scattered. He found old bread, wrapped and moldy, and signs that mice had gnawed at sacks of musty grain.

In one of the huts, the blankets of a bed—little more than a straw mat in the corner—had been shoved away, the bed torn apart. It was the first sign of violence rather than abandonment. He picked up the blanket, thinking perhaps to find blood, some sure sign that ill had happened.

A cross dropped away from the folds of the cloth. It had been wrapped and hidden away, unable to protect its owner. The thought saddened him.

Perhaps the villagers had fled. He went out a little ways to try to find tracks, to determine what direction the villagers might have gone. Behind the church, he found a narrow path in the grass, like a shepherd might use leading sheep or goats into the hills. Ricardo followed it. He shuttered the lantern and allowed his vision to adjust to moonlight, to better see into the distance.

He was part way across the valley, the village and its church a hundred paces behind him, when he saw a figure sitting at the foot of a juniper. A piece of clothing, the tail of a shirt perhaps, fluttered in the slight breeze that hushed through the valley.

"Hola," Ricardo called quietly. He got no answer and approached cautiously, hand on his sword.

The body of a child, a boy, lay against the tree. Telling his age was impossible because his body had desiccated. The skin was blackened and stretched over the bones. His face was gaunt, a leathery mask drawn over a skull, and chipped teeth grinned. Dark pits marked the eye sockets. It might have been part of the roots and branches. Ricardo might have walked right by it and not noticed, if not for the piece of rotted cloth that had moved.

The child had dried out, baked in the desert like pottery. It looked like something ancient. Moreover, he could not tell what had killed it. Perhaps only hunger.

But his instincts told him something terrible had happened here. Fray Juan had to know something of what had killed this boy, and the entire village. Ricardo must find out what, then report this to the governor, then get word to the bishop in Mexico City. This land and its people must be brought under proper jurisdiction, if for no other reason than to protect them from people like Fray Juan.

He rushed back to the village, went to the church and marched inside, shouting, "Fray Juan! Talk to me! Tell me what's happened here! Explain yourself!"

But no one answered. The chapel echoed, and no doors cracked open even a little to greet him. Softly now, he went through the strange decrepit chapel with no cross. The door to the friar's chamber was unlocked, but the room was empty. Not even a lamp was lit. The whole place seemed abandoned. He tried the trapdoor, lifting the iron ring—the door didn't move. Locked from the other side. He pounded on the door with his boot heel, a useless gesture. So, Fray Juan was hiding. No matter. He'd report to the governor, and Ricardo would return with a squad to burn the place to the ground to flush the man out. He wouldn't even wait until daylight to set out. He didn't want to sleep out the night in this haunted valley.

When he went to retrieve his horse, a man stood in his way.

In the moonlight, he was a shadow, but Ricardo could see the smile on his face: Diego Ruiz.

"*Amigo,*" the man called, his voice light, amused. "You came. I wasn't sure you would."

"Diego, what's happened here? What's this about?"

"I told you, Ricardo. This land is rich. We are looking for men to help us reap those riches."

"I see nothing here but a wasted village," Ricardo said.

A new voice spoke, "You need to see with different eyes."

Ricardo turned, for the voice had come from behind him. He had not heard the man approach—he must have been hiding in one of the huts. Two more came with him, so that together the four circled Ricardo. He could not flee without confronting them. He turned, looking back and forth, trying to keep them all in view, unwilling to turn his back on any of them.

The four were very much like Ricardo—young men with pure Spanish features, wearing the clothing of gentlemen. Others who had swarmed to New Spain seeking fortunes, failing, and turning dissolute.

Ricardo drew his sword. One of them he could fight. But not four. Not when they had every advantage. How had they taken him by surprise? He should have heard them coming. "You've turned bandit. You think to recruit more to run wild with you? No, Diego. I have no reason to join you."

"You do not have a choice, *amigo*. I brought you here because we can use a man like you. Someone with connections."

Ricardo smiled wryly. "No one will pay my ransom."

They laughed, four caballeros in high spirits. "He thinks we'll ask for ransom," another said.

Ricardo swallowed back panic and remained calm. Whatever they planned for him, he would not make it easy. He'd fight.

"Señor, be at ease," spoke a third. "We won't hold you for ransom. We have a gift for you."

Ricardo chuckled. "I don't think so."

"Oh, yes. We'll bring you to serve our Master. It's a great honor."

"I will not. You all are evil."

The men did not argue.

They began to circle him, jackals moving close for a kill. They watched him, and their eyes were fire. He had to run, grab his horse and fly from here, warn the governor of this madness.

It was madness, for Diego lunged at him, weaponless, with nothing but outstretched arms and a wild leer. Ricardo held out his sword, blade level and unwavering, and Diego skewered himself on the point, through the gut. Ricardo expected him to cry out and fall. He expected to have to fight off the others for killing one of their own. But the other three laughed, and Diego kept smiling.

Ricardo held fast to the grip out of habit. Diego stood, arms spread, displaying what he'd done. No blood ran from the wound.

Ricardo pulled the sword back just as Diego wrenched himself off the blade. Still, the man didn't make a sound of pain. Didn't fall. Wasn't bothered at all. Ricardo resisted an urge to make the sign of the cross. Holy God, what was this?

"This is why we follow Fray Juan," Diego breathed. "Now, will you join us?"

Ricardo cried out a denial and charged again. These were demons, and he must flee. He crouched, grabbed a handful of dirt with his left hand. If he could not cut them, perhaps he could blind them. He flung it at the man behind him, who must be moving to attack. In the same motion he whirled, slashing with his blade, keeping some distance around him, enough to clear a space so he might reach his horse. He did not wait to see what happened, did not even think. Only acted. Like those old days of battle, fighting the natives with Coronado's company. That had been a strange, alien world. Like this.

He'd have sworn that his sword met flesh several times, but the men stood firm, unflinching. Ricardo might as well have been a child throwing a tantrum. They closed on him without effort.

Two grabbed his arms, bracing them straight out, holding him still. A third wrenched his sword from him. His captors bent back his arms until his back strained, and presented him to Diego.

Ricardo struggled on principle, with no hope. His boots kicked at the dirt.

Diego regarded him with a look of amusement. He ran a gloved hand along Ricardo's chin, scraping his rough beard. Ricardo flinched back, but his captors held him steady. "You should know that you never had a chance against us. Perhaps you might take comfort in that fact."

"I take no comfort," Ricardo said, his words spitting.

"Good. You will have none." He opened his mouth. They all opened their mouths and came at him. They had the teeth of wild dogs. Of lions. Sharp teeth meant to rend flesh.

And they began to rend his.

He couldn't move. He'd been on a very long journey, and his limbs had turned to iron, chilled iron, that had been left out on a winter's night and was now rimed with frost. That image of himself—stiff flesh mounted on a skeleton of frosted iron, a red body fringed with white—struck him as oddly beautiful. It was an image of death, sunk into his bones. Memory recalled the ambush, arms clinging to him, breath leaving him, and the teeth. Demonic teeth, puncturing his flesh, draining his blood, his life. So he had died.

His next thought: What had he done to find himself relegated to hell? What else could this be? Like Dante's ninth circle, where the damned lay frozen solid in a lake, he was left to feel his body turning to frost, piece by piece. He tried to cry out, but he had no breath.

A hand rested on his forehead. If possible, it felt even colder, burning against Ricardo's skin like ice.

"Ricardo de Avila," the devil said. "You hear me, yes?"

Nothing would melt his body; he could not even nod. Struggling to speak, he felt his lips move, but nothing else.

"I will tell you what your life is now. You will never again see the daylight. To touch the sun is to burn. You are no longer a son of the Church. The holy cross and baptismal water are poison to you. From now on you are a creature of darkness. But these small sacrifices are nothing to the reward: from now on might be a very long time. You belong to me. You are my son. With your brothers you will rule the night."

Ricardo choked on a breath that tasted stale, as if he had not drawn breath in a very long time. His mouth tasted sour. He said, "Is this hell?"

The devil sounded wry. "Not necessarily. In this life, you make or escape your own hell."

"Who are you?"

"You know me, Ricardo. I am Fray Juan, and I am your Master."

He shook his head. It wasn't that the numbness was fading. Rather, he was getting used to the cold. This body made of iron could move. "The governor . . . the king . . . I am loyal . . ."

"You are beyond them now. Open your eyes."

His lids creaked and cracked, like the skin was breaking, but he opened them.

He lay on a bed in a dark room. A few lanterns hung from hooks on the walls, casting circles of light and flickering shadows. Fray Juan sat at the edge of the bed. Arrayed elsewhere stood four men, fierce looking. The demons.

He felt trapped by the shadows that had invaded his dreams. They would destroy him. In a panic, he waited for the jolt of blood, the racing heartbeat that would drive him from the bed, allow him some chance of fighting and escaping. But he felt nothing. He put his hand around his neck and felt . . . nothing. No pulse. He wanted to sigh—but he had not drawn breath. He had only taken in enough air to speak. Now, the panic rose. This could not be, this was impossible, dead and yet not—

This was hell, and the demon with Fray Juan's shape was lying to him.

"Diego, bring the chalice," Juan said, not with the voice of a sympathetic confessor, but with the edge of a commander.

A figure moved at the far end of the room. Even as Ricardo prayed, his ears strained to learn what was happening, his muscles tensed to defend himself.

"Hold him," Juan said, and hands took him, hauled him into a sitting position, and wrenched back his arms so he could not struggle. Another set of hands pinned his legs.

His eyes opened wide. Three of the caballeros braced him in a sitting position. The fourth—Diego, his old comrade Diego—brought forward a Eucharistic chalice made of pewter. He balanced it in a way that suggested it was full of liquid.

Ricardo drew back, pressing against his captors. "You wear Fray Juan's face, but you are not a priest. You can't do this, this is no time for communion."

Juan smiled, but that did not comfort. "This isn't what you think. What is wine, after the holy sacrament of communion?"

"The blood of Christ," Ricardo said.

"This is better," he said, taking the chalice from Diego.

Ricardo cried out. Tried to deny it. Turned his head, clamped shut his mouth. But Juan was ready for him, putting a hand over his face, digging his thumb between Ricardo's lips and prying open his jaw, as if trying to slide a bit in the mouth of a stubborn horse.

Juan was stronger than he looked. Ricardo screamed, a noise that came out breathless and wheezy. The chalice tipped against his lips.

The liquid smelled metallic. When it struck his tongue—a thick stream sliding down his throat, leaving a sticky trail—it tasted of wine and copper. With the taste of it came knowledge and instinct. Human blood, it could be no other. Even as his mind rebelled with the obscenity of it, his tongue reached for more, and his throat swallowed, greedy for the sustenance. Its thickness flowed like fire through his veins, and something in him rose up and sang in delight at its flavor.

The battle was no longer with the demons holding him fast; it was with the demon rising up inside of him. The creature that drank the blood and wanted more. A strange joy accompanied the feeling, a strength in his body he'd never felt before. Weariness, the aches of travel, fell away. He was reborn. He was invincible.

And it was false and wrong.

Roaring, he shoved at his captors, throwing himself out of their grasp. He batted away the chalice of blood. They lunged for him again, and Fray Juan cried, "No, let him go."

Ricardo pushed away from them. He pressed his back to the wall and couldn't go farther. He could smell the blood soaking into the blanket at his feet. He covered his face with his hands; he could smell the blood on his breath. He wiped his mouth, but could still taste blood on his lips, as if it had soaked into his skin.

He had an urge to lick the drops of blood that had spilled onto his hand. He pressed his face harder and moaned, an expression of despair welling from him.

"You see what you are now?" Juan said, without sympathy. "You are the blood, and it will feed you through the centuries. You are deathless."

Ricardo stared at him. The blood flowing through his veins now was not his own. He could feel it warming his body, like sunlight on skin. Sunlight, which he would never see again, if Juan spoke true.

He drew a breath and said, "You are a devil."

"We all are."

"No! I don't know what you've done to me, but I am not one of you. I would rather die!"

Juan, a pale face in lamp-lit shadows, nodded to his four henchmen, who backed toward the ladder, which lead to the trapdoor in the ceiling. One by one, they slipped out, watching Ricardo with glittering, knowing eyes. In a moment, Juan and Ricardo were alone.

"This is a new life," Juan said. "I know it is hard to accept. But remember: You have received a gift."

Then he, too, left the room. The door closed, and a bolt slid home.

Ricardo rushed to the door, and tried to open it, rattling the handle. They had locked him in this hole. A damp chill from the walls pressed against him.

Ricardo lay back on the bed, hands resting on his chest. Eventually, the lamp's wick burned down. The light grew dim, until it was coin-sized, burnished gold, then vanished. Even in the dark, he could see the ceiling. He should not have been able to see anything in the pitch dark of this underground cell. But it was like he could feel the walls closing in. He waited for panic to take him. He waited for his heart to start racing. But he touched his ribs and could not feel his heart at all.

Hours had passed, though the time moved strangely. Even in the darkness, he could see shadows move across the ceiling, like stars arcing overhead. It was nighttime outside; he knew this in his bones. The night passed, the moon rose—past full now, waning. The way the air moved over his face told him this. Eventually, near dawn, he fell asleep.

He started awake when the trapdoor opened. His senses lurched and rolled, like a galleon in deep swells. He knew—again, without looking, without seeing—that Juan and his four caballeros had returned. They had a warmth coursing through them, tinged with metal and rot, the scent of spilled blood. The thing inside him stirred, a hunger that cramped his heart instead of his belly. His mouth watered. He licked his lips, hoping for the taste of it.

Shutting his eyes, he turned his face away.

Another, a sixth being, entered the room with them. This one was different—warm, burning with heat, a flame in the dark, rich and beautiful. Alive. A heartbeat thudded, the footfalls of an army marching double-time. A living person who was afraid.

"Ricardo. Look." Juan stood at the foot of the bed and raised a lantern.

Ricardo sat up, pressed against the wall. Two of the caballeros dragged between them a child, a boy seven or eight years old, very thin. The boy met his gaze with dark eyes, shining with fear. He whimpered, pulling back from the caballeros' grasp, but they held fast, their fingers digging into his skin.

Juan said, "This is one of the things you must learn, to take your place among my knights."

"No." But the new sensations, the new way of looking at the world, wanted this child. Wanted the warm blood that gave this child life. The caballeros hauled the boy forward, and Ricardo shook his head even as he reached for the child. "No, no—"

"You cannot stop it," Juan said.

The child screamed before Ricardo even touched him.

It was not him. It did not feel like his body. Something else moved his limbs and filled his mind with lust. His mouth closed over the artery in the child's neck as if he kissed his flesh. His teeth—he had sharp teeth now—tore the skin, and the blood flowed. The sensation of wet blood on tongue burned through him, wind and fire. His vision was gone, his mind was gone.

This was not him.

The blood, life giving and terrible, filled him until he seemed likely to break out of his own skin. With enough blood, he could expand to fill the world. When they pulled the dead child away, he was drunk, insensible, his hands too weak to clutch at the body. He sat at the edge of the bed, his arms fallen to his sides, limp, his face turned up, ecstatic. He licked his lips with a blood-coated tongue. But it was not him. His eyes stung with tears. He could not open them to look at the horror he'd wrought.

He was not so cold anymore. Either he was used to it, or he could no longer feel at all. That was a possibility. That was most likely best. Even if this were not hell, what they had forced him to do would surely send him to hell when he did die.

If he did.

"It is incentive to live forever, is it not? Knowing what awaits you for these terrible crimes," Diego said with the smile of a wolf.

The friar had shown him what horrors this life held for him: he brought Ricardo a cross made of pressed gold. He kept it wrapped in silk, did not touch it himself. When Ricardo touched it, his skin burned. He could never touch a holy cross again. Holy water burned him the same. He could never go into a church. His baptism had been burned away from him. The Mother Church was poison to him now. God had rejected him.

But I do not reject God, Ricardo thought helplessly.

There were rewards. Juan kept calling them rewards. Mortal weapons could not kill him. Stabs and slashes with a sword, arquebus shot, falls, cracked bones, nothing would kill him. Only beheading, only a shaft of wood driven through the heart. Only the sun. He was immortal.

"You call this reward?" Ricardo had shouted. "To be forever shut out of God's heavenly kingdom?" Then he realized the truth: This was no tragedy for Juan, because the friar did not believe in God or heaven.

"Did you ever believe?" Ricardo whispered at him. "Before you became this thing, did you believe?"

Juan smiled. "Perhaps it is not that I don't believe, but that I chose to join the other side of this war between heaven and hell."

Which was somehow even more awful.

Ricardo stood at the church wall one night. The moon waxed again, past new. Half a month, he'd been here. He didn't know what to do next—what he could do. They held him captive. He belonged with them now, because where else could he go?

They told him that the blood should taste sweet on his tongue, and it did. He still hated it.

Perhaps he looked for rescue. When he did not report to the governor, wouldn't a party come for him? A troop of soldiers would come to learn what had happened, and Ricardo would intercept them, tell them the truth, and he would help them raze the church to the ground, destroy Juan and his caballeros.

And then they would destroy him, stake his heart, drag him into the sunlight, for being one of them. So perhaps Ricardo wouldn't help them, but would hide.

Did he love existence more than life, then? More than heaven?

A jingling of bridles sounded behind him. Ricardo did not have to look; he sensed the four men approaching with the horses.

"Brother Ricardo, it's good you've finally come into the air. It's not good to be cooped up all the time."

"I'm not your brother," he said. His voice scratched, weak and out of practice. He had taken breathing for granted, and had to relearn how to speak.

Diego laughed. "We're all you have, now. You'll understand soon enough."

"He has lots of time to learn," said Octavio, one of the four demons who had once been men, who followed Juan. Rafael and Esteban were the others.

Diego said, "Ride with us. We hunt tonight, and you'll learn at our side." It was a command, not a request.

He followed, because what else could he do? Except perhaps stand in the open when the sun rose and let it burn him. But suicide was a sin. Even now, he believed it. He would show that he did not forsake God. He would ask for forgiveness every moment of his existence.

Diego seemed to be Fray Juan's lieutenant; he had been the first of them turned to this demon life, years ago now. That was why he looked no older than he had when they returned from Coronado's expedition.

He explained what they did here. "Each of us is as strong as a dozen men. But there are still those who know how to kill us. Those who would recognize certain signs and hunt us down."

"Who?" Ricardo asked. "What signs?"

"Secret members of the Inquisition for one. And what signs? Why, bodies. Too many bodies, all drained of blood!" They all laughed.

"New Spain is the perfect place for us. There are thousands of peasants dying by the score in mines, on campaigns, of disease. Out here on the borders, no one is even looking much. If a whole village dies, we say a plague struck. We take all the blood we need and no one notices."

At the mention of blood, Ricardo's mouth watered. A hunger woke in him, like a creature writhing in his belly. Each time Diego said the word, his vision clouded. He shook himself to remain focused on the hills before them.

"I know how it is with you," Diego said. "We all went through this."

"Though the rest of us were perhaps not so holy to start with." Again they laughed, like young men riding to a night of revelry. That was what they looked like, what anyone who saw them would think. Not that anyone would see them out here. That was the point, to feed on as much blood as they wished without notice. A land of riches. Diego had not lied.

"It's eating away inside of me," Ricardo said under his breath.

"The blood will still that," said Rafael. "The blood will keep you sane."

"Ironic," Ricardo said. "That you must become a monster to keep from going mad."

"Ha. I never thought of it like that," Diego said.

He is already mad, Ricardo thought.

They rode for hours. They could not go far—half the night, he thought. Then they must go back, to take shelter before dawn. He could feel the night slipping away in his bones. It was the same part of him that now called out for blood.

Rafael said, "The villages nearby know of us. They go to the hills to hide, but we find them. Look toward the hills, take the air into your lungs. You can sense them, can't you?"

The air smelled of dust, heat, sunlight that had baked into the land during the day and now rose into the chill of night, lost in the darkness. The breeze spoke of emptiness, of a vast plain where nothing larger than coyotes lived. When he turned toward the hills, though, he smelled something else. The warmth had a different flavor to it: life.

When they brought him the child, he had known what was there before he saw it. He could feel its life in the currents of the air; sense its heartbeat sending out ripples, like a stone tossed into a body of still water. A live person made a different mark on the world than one of these demons.

"Our kind are drawn to them, like iron to a lodestone," Diego said. "We cannot live without taking in the human blood we have lost. We are the wolves to their sheep."

"And now you hunt. Like wolves," said Ricardo.

"Yes. It's good sport."

"It's a thousand childhood nightmares come to life."

"More than that, even. Come on!"

He spurred his horse. Kicking dirt behind them, the other four followed.

It was just as Diego said: a hunt. The leader sent two of the caballeros to ascend the hill from a different direction. They flushed the villagers from their hiding places, where they lived in caves and lean-tos. Like animals, Ricardo could not help but think. Easier to hunt them, then, when one did not think of them as human. It was like facing the native tribes with Coronado all over again. The imbalance in strength between the two parties was laughable.

On horseback, Rafael and Octavio galloped across the hill, chasing a dozen people, many of them old, before them. Diego and Esteban had dismounted and tied their horses some distance away, waiting on foot for the prey to come to them.

Ricardo watched, and time slowed.

It was as if he played the scene out in his mind while someone told him the story. Diego moved too fast to see when he stepped in front of the path of a young man, grabbed his arm with one hand and took hold of his hair with the other. The boy didn't have time to scream. Diego held the body like a lover might, hand splayed across his chest, holding him in place, while pulling back his head, exposing his neck. He bit, then sank with the boy to the ground while he drank. The boy didn't even thrash. He was like a stunned rabbit.

Each of the others chose prey and struck, plucking their chosen victims from the scattered, fleeing peasants. The creature lurking where Ricardo's heart used to be sang and longed to reach out and grab a rabbit for itself. As he watched, the scene changed, and it was not the caballeros who moved quickly, but the villagers who moved slowly. Ricardo had felt like this once in a swordfight. His own skills had advanced to a point where he had some proficiency, his mind was focused, and he knew with what seemed like supernatural prescience what his opponent was going to do. He parried every attack with ease, as if he watched from outside himself.

This was the same.

It was not himself but the unholy monster within who stepped aside as a woman ran past him, then slipped into place behind her and took hold of her shoulders, moving like the shadow of a bird in flight across the land.

Jerked off her feet by his hold on her, she screamed and fell against him, thrashing, panicked, like an animal in a snare. He held her, embraced her against his body to still her, and touched her face. The coiled hunger within him gave him power. As he ran his finger down her cheek and closed his hand against her face, she quieted, stilled, went limp in his grasp. Her heartbeat slowed. He could take her, drink her easily, without struggle. This was better, wasn't it? Would he have this power if this wasn't what he was meant to do? She was young, almost a girl, her skin firm and unlined, lips full, her eyes bright. He could have her in all ways, strip her, lie with her, and he could make her want it, make her open to him in a way their Catholic religion would never allow, even in marriage. In the ghostly moonlight, she was beautiful, and she belonged to him. He laid her on the ground. She clutched his hand, and confusion showed in her eyes.

He couldn't do it. He sat with her as though she were his ill sister, holding her hand, brushing damp hair from her young face. The creature inside him thrashed and begged to devour her. Ricardo felt the needle-sharp teeth inside his mouth. And he turned his gaze inward, shutting it all away.

I am not this creature. I am a child of God. Still, a child of God, like her. And the night is dangerous.

Quickly, he made her sit up. He laid his hand on her forehead and whispered, "Wake up. You must run." She stared at him blankly, groggily. He slapped her cheek. She didn't even flinch. "Wake up, please. You must wake up!"

Her gaze focused. At last she heard him. Perhaps she didn't understand Spanish. But then, which of a dozen native dialects would she understand?

Fine, he thought. He didn't need language to tell her to run. He bared his teeth—the sharp fangs ripe for feeding, wet with the saliva of hunger—and hissed at her. "Run!"

She gasped, scrambled to her feet, and ran across the hillside and into shadow.

Just in time. The world shifted, the action around him sped up and slowed as it needed to, and all appeared normal again. A still night lit by a waxing moon, quiet unto death.

The caballeros surrounded him. Ricardo could sense the blood on their breaths, and his belly rumbled with hunger. He bowed his head, content with the hunger, with the choice he had made.

They could probably smell on him the scent of resignation.

"Brother Ricardo," Diego said. "Aren't you hungry? Were the pickings not easy enough for you?"

"I'm not your brother," Ricardo said.

Diego laughed, but nervously. "Don't starve yourself to spite us," he said.

"Don't flatter yourself," Ricardo said. "I don't starve myself for you."

The four demons looked down on him, where he sat in the dust, content. They would kill him, and that was all right. The demon they had given him screeched and complained. Ricardo sat rigid, keeping it trapped, refusing to give it voice.

"You're not strong enough to survive this," Diego said. "You don't have the will to refuse the call of our kind."

At this, Ricardo looked at him with a hard gaze. Unbelievably, Diego took a step back.

"I was one of the hundred who returned to Mexico City with Coronado. Don't tell me about my will."

To his left, a branch snapped as Octavio broke a twisting limb off a nearby shrub. "Diego, I will finish him. Turning him was a mistake."

"Yes," Diego said. "But we didn't know that."

"We'll leave him. Leave him here and let the sunlight take him," said Rafael.

Diego watched him with the air of a man trying to solve a riddle. "The Master wants to keep him. The governor will listen to him, and he will keep us safe. He must live. Captain Ricardo de Avila, you must accept what you are, let the creature have its will."

Ricardo smiled. "I am a loyal subject of Spain and a child

of God who has been saddled with a particularly troublesome burden."

Diego looked at Octavio. Ricardo was ready for them.

Together, the thing coiled inside him and his honor as a man of Spain rose up to defend, if not his life, then his existence. Octavio made an inhuman leap that crossed the distance between them, faster than eye could see. The perception that made time and the world around Ricardo seem strange and move thickly, like melting wax, served him now. For all Octavio's speed, Ricardo saw him and wasn't there when his enemy struck.

He could learn to revel in this newfound power.

Ricardo longed for a sword in his hand, no matter that steel would do no good against these opponents. He would have to beat them with wood through the heart. Octavio held the torn branch, one end jagged like a dagger. The other three ranged around him, ready to cut off his escape, and a wave of dizziness blurred his vision for a moment. Despair and hunger. If he'd taken blood, he would have more power—maybe enough to fight them all. As it was, he could not fight all four of them. Not if they meant to kill him.

He ran. They reached for him, but with flight his only concern, he drew on that devilish power. *Make me like shadow,* he thought.

The world became a blur, and he was smoke traveling across it. Nothing but air, moving faster than wind. He felt their hands brush his doublet as he passed. But they did not catch hold of him.

He found a cave. Villagers might have hidden here once. Ricardo found the burned remains of a campfire, some scraps of food, and an old blanket that had been abandoned. The back of the cave was narrow and ran deep within the hillside. It would always be dark, and he could stay there, safe from sunlight.

But would they come after him?

They could not tolerate rivals. Animal, demon, or men fallen beyond the point of redemption, they had claimed this territory as their own. He had rebuffed their brotherhood, so now he was an invader. They would come for him.

Ricardo put the blanket over a narrow crag in the rock, deep in the cave. The light of dawn approached. As he lay down in the darkness, he congratulated himself on surviving the night.

He fell asleep wondering how he would survive the next.

At dusk, he hurried over the hillside, gathering fallen sticks, stripping trees of the sturdiest branches he could find, and using chipped stones he had found in the cave to sharpen the ends into points. It was slow going, and he was weak. Lack of blood had sapped his strength. His skin was clammy, pale, more and more resembling a dead man's. *I am a walking corpse,* he thought, and laughed. He had thought that once before, while crossing the northern *despoblado* with Coronado.

Ricardo had to believe he was not dead, that he would not die. He was fighting for a much nobler cause than the one that had driven him north ten years ago. He'd made that journey for riches and glory. Now, he was fighting to return to God. He was fighting for his soul. But without blood, he couldn't fight at all.

"Señor?" a woman's voice called, hesitating.

Ricardo turned, startled. It was a sign of his weakness that he had not heard her approach. Now that he saw her, the scent of her blood and the nearness of her pounding heart washed over him, filling him like a glass of strong wine. His mind swam in it, and the demon screeched for her blood. Ricardo gripped the branch in his hand, willing the monster to be silent.

The mestiza woman wore a poor dress and a ragged shawl over her head. Her hair wasn't tossed and tangled in flight tonight, but he recognized her. She was the one he'd let go.

"You," he breathed, and discovered that he loved her, wildly and passionately, with the instant devotion of a drunk man. He had saved her life, and so he loved her.

She kept her gaze lowered. "I hoped to find you. To thank you." She spoke Spanish with a thick accent.

"You shouldn't have come back," he said. "My will isn't strong tonight."

She nodded at his roughly carved stake. "You fight the others? The wolves of the night?"

He chuckled, not liking the tone of despair in the sound. "I'll try."

"But you are one of them."

"No. Like them, but not one of them."

She knelt on the ground and drew a clay mug from her pouch. She also produced a knife. She moved quickly, as if she feared she might change her mind, and before Ricardo could stop her, she drew the knife across her forearm. She hissed a breath.

He reached for her. "No!"

Massaging her forearm, encouraging the flow of blood, she held the wound over the mug. The blood ran in a thin stream for several long minutes. Then, just as quickly, she took a clean piece of linen and wrapped her arm tightly. The knife disappeared back in the pouch. She glanced at him. He could only stare back, dumbfounded.

She moved the cup of blood toward him. "A gift," she said. "Stop them, then leave us alone. Please?"

"Yes. I will."

"Thank you."

She turned and ran.

The blood was still warm when it slipped down his throat. His mind expanded with the taste of it. He no longer felt drunk; on the contrary, he felt clear, powerful. He could count the stars wheeling above him. The heat of young life filled him, no matter if it was borrowed. And he could survive without killing. That gave him hope.

He scraped the inside of the cup with his finger and sucked the film of blood off his skin, unwilling to waste a drop. After tucking the mug in a safe place, he climbed to his hiding place over the cave and waited. He had finished his preparations in time.

They came like the Four Horsemen of Revelations, riders

bringing death, armed with spears. They weren't going to toy with him. They were here to correct a mistake. *Let them come,* he thought. Let them see his will to fight.

They pulled to a stop at the base of the hill, within sight of the cave's mouth. The horses steamed with sweat. They must have galloped most of the way from the village.

Diego and the others dismounted. "Ricardo! We have come for you! Fray Juan wants you to return to him, where you belong!"

Ricardo could smell the lie on him. He could see it in the spears they carried, wooden shafts with sharpened ends. The other three dismounted and moved to flank the cave, so nothing could escape from it.

Octavio stepped, then paused, looking at the ground. Ricardo clenched fistfuls of grass in anticipation. Another step, just one more. But how much could Octavio sense of what lay before him?

"Diego? There's something wrong—" Octavio said, and leaned forward. With the extra weight, the ground under him collapsed. A thin mat of grass had hidden the pit underneath.

Almost, Octavio escaped. He twisted, making an inhuman grab at earth behind him. He seemed to hover, suspended in his moment of desperation. But he was not light enough, not fast enough, to overcome his surprise at falling, and he landed, impaled on the half-dozen stakes driven into the bottom of the pit. He didn't even scream.

"Damn!" Diego looked into the pit, an expression of fury marring his features.

Ricardo stood and hurled one of his makeshift spears at the remaining riders. He put all the strength and speed of his newfound power, of the gift of the woman's blood, into it, and the spear sang through the air like an arrow. He never should have been able to throw a weapon so strong, so true.

This curse had to be good for something, or why would people like Juan and Diego revel in it? He would not revel. But he would use it. The bloodthirsty demon in him reveled in this hunt and lent him strength. They would come to an understanding. Ricardo would use the strength—but for his own purpose.

The spear landed in Rafael's chest, knocking him flat to the ground. He clutched at the shaft, writhing, teeth bared and hissing in what might have been anger or agony. Then, he went limp. His skin tightened, wrinkling, drying out, until the sunken cavities of his skull were visible under his face. His clothes drooped over a desiccated body. He looked like a corpse years in the grave. That was how long ago he died, Ricardo thought. He had been living as a beast for years. But now, perhaps he was at peace.

Diego and Esteban were both flying up the hill toward him. Almost literally, with the speed of deer, barely touching earth. Ricardo took up another spear. This would be like fighting with a sword, a battle he understood a little better. They had their own spears ready.

He thrust at the first to reach him, Esteban, who parried easily and came at him, ferocious, teeth bared, fangs showing. Ricardo stumbled back, losing ground, but braced the spear as his defense. Esteban couldn't get through to him. But then there was Diego, who came at Ricardo from behind. Ricardo sensed him there but could do nothing.

Diego braced his spear across Ricardo's neck and dragged him back. Reflexively, Ricardo dropped his weapon and choked against the pressure on his throat, a memory of the old reaction he should have had. But now, he had no breath to cut off. The pressure meant nothing. Ricardo fell, letting his head snap back from under the bar, and his weight dropped him out of Diego's grip. Another demonic movement. But he would not survive this fight as a human.

Esteban came at him with his spear, ready to pin him to the ground. Ricardo rolled, and did not stop when he was clear. *I am mist, I am speed.* He spun and wrenched the spear from Esteban's grip. He was charging one way and couldn't resist the force of Ricardo's movement in another direction. Even then, Ricardo didn't stop. He slipped behind Esteban, who had pivoted with equal speed and grace to face him. But he had no weapon, and Ricardo did. He speared the third of the demons through his dead heart. Another desiccated corpse collapsed at his feet.

Ricardo stared at Diego, who stood by, watching.

"I was right to want you as one of Fray Juan's caballeros,"

Diego said. "You are very strong. You have the heart to control the power."

"Fray Juan is a monster."

"But Ricardo, New Spain is filled with monsters. We both know that."

Screaming, Ricardo charged him. Diego let him run against him, and they both toppled to the ground, wrestling.

How did one defeat a man who was already dead? Who moved by demonic forces of blood? Ricardo closed his hands around the man's throat, but Diego only laughed silently. He did not breathe—choking did no good. He tried to beat the man, pound his head into the ground, but Diego's strength was effortless, unyielding. He might as well wrestle a bear.

Diego must have grown tired of Ricardo's flailing, because he finally hit him, and Ricardo flew, tumbling down the hill, away from his dropped weapons. Diego loomed over him now, with the advantage of high ground.

Ricardo made himself keep rolling. Time slowed, and he knew what would happen—at least what might happen. So he slid all the way to the bottom of the hill and waited. He wasn't breathing hard—he wasn't breathing at all. He hadn't broken a sweat. He was as calm as still water. But Diego didn't have to know that.

The smart thing for Diego to do would be to drive a spear through his chest. But Ricardo thought Diego would gloat. He'd pick Ricardo up, laugh in his face one more time, before tossing him aside and stabbing him. Ricardo waited for this to happen, ready for it.

But he'd also be ready to dodge if Diego surprised him and went for a quick kill.

"Ricardo! You're more than a fool. You're an idealist," Diego said, making his way down the hill, sauntering like a man with an annoying chore at hand.

God, give me strength, Ricardo prayed, not knowing if God would listen to one such as him. Not caring. The prayer focused him.

He struggled to get up, as if he were weak, powerless, starving. Let Diego think he had all the power. He flailed like a beetle trapped on his back, while Diego leaned down, twisted his hands in the fabric of his doublet and hauled him to his feet.

Then Ricardo took hold of the man's wrists and dragged him toward the hole that had swallowed Octavio.

Diego seemed not to realize what was happening at first. His eyes went wide, and he actually let go of Ricardo, which was more than Ricardo had hoped for. Using Diego's own arms for leverage, he swung the man and let go. Diego was already at the edge of the pit, and like Octavio he made an effort to avoid the fall. But with the grace of a drifting leaf, he sank.

Ricardo stood on the edge and watched the body, stuck on the stakes on top of Octavio, turn to a dried husk.

He gathered up their horses and rode back to the church, torn between wanting to move and worrying about breaking them down. They had already made this trip once, and they were mortal. He rode both as quickly and slowly as he dared, and when he reached the village, the sky had paled. He could feel the rising sun within his bones.

Rushing, he unsaddled the horses and set them loose in the pasture. He would need resources, when he started his new life, and they were worth something, even in the dark of night.

He had only moments left to find Juan. Striding through the chapel, he hid a spear along the length of his leg.

"Juan! Bastard! Come show yourself!"

The friar was waiting in the back room where Ricardo had first spoken with him, a respectable if bedraggled servant of God hunched over his desk, watching the world with a furtive gaze.

"I felt it when you killed them," the friar said in a husky voice. "They were my children, part of me—I felt the light of their minds go out."

Don't let him speak. Ricardo's own power recognized the force behind the words, the connection that bound them together. His power flowed from the other.

Ricardo started to lunge, but the friar held up a hand and said,

"No!" The younger man stopped, spear upraised, face in a snarl, an allegorical picture of war.

Fray Juan smiled. "Understand, you are mine. You will serve me as my caballeros served me. You cannot stop it." The Master had a toothy, wicked smile.

Ricardo closed his eyes. He'd fought for nothing, all these years and nothing to show for it but a curse. He was not even master of his fate.

Free will was part of God's plan. What better way to damn the sinful than to let them choose sin over righteousness? But he had not chosen this. Had he? Had something in his past directed him to this moment? To this curse?

Then couldn't he choose to walk away from this path?

He started to pray out loud, all the prayers he knew. *Pater Noster, Ave Maria,* even passages of Psalms, what he could remember.

The friar stared back at him. His lips trembled. "You should not be able to speak those words," Juan said. "You are a demon. One of Satan's pawns. He is our father. The holy words should burn your tongue."

"Then you believe the tales of the Inquisition? I don't think I do. Come, Juan, pray with me." Louder now, he spoke again, and still Juan trembled at the words.

"They're only words, Padre! Why can't you speak them?" Ricardo shouted, then started the prayers again.

The hold on his body broke. He had been balanced, poised for the strike, and now he plunged forward, his spear leading, and drove it into the friar's chest. Juan tumbled back in his chair, Ricardo standing over him, still leaning on the spear though it wouldn't go farther. Juan didn't make a sound.

Juan's skin turned gray. It didn't simply dry into hard leather; it turned to dust, crumbling away, his cassock collapsing around him. A corpse decayed by decades or centuries.

Ricardo backed away from the dust. He dropped the spear. His knees gave out then, and he folded to the floor, where he curled up on his side and let the sleep of daylight overcome him.

Rumor said that the small estancia had once been a mission, but that the friar who ran it went mad and fled to the hills, never to be seen again. A young hidalgo now occupied the place, turning it into a quiet manor that bred and raised sheep for wool and mutton. The peasants who lived and worked there were quiet and seemed happy. The governor said that the place was a model from which all estancias ought to learn.

The hidalgo himself was a strange, mysterious man, seldom seen in society. Of course all the lords in New Spain with daughters had an interest in getting to know him, for he was not only successful, but unmarried. But the man refused all such overtures.

It was said that Don Ricardo had ridden north with Coronado. Of course that rumor had to be false, because everyone knew Ricardo was a man in the prime of his life, and Coronado's expedition to find Cibola rode out fifty years ago.

But such wild rumors will grow up around a gentleman who only leaves his house at night.

The Book of Daniel

Daniel stood at the edge of the pit and prayed. *God of my ancestors, wise in all things, powerful beyond measure, thank you for my life. All praise is yours.*

Daniel's rivals at court stood around the pit, almost daring to smile.

King Darius—a proud king, susceptible to flattery and prone to suspicions—would not face him. He could not look Daniel in the eye as he condemned him, however much Daniel stared at him, trying to meet his gaze. Darius had trusted him, once.

"Put him in," the king said and turned away.

The royal guards shoved Daniel onto the ramp that led into the brick-lined pit of lions. Daniel fell and rolled down. The thick wooden lid closed overhead, and the light was gone.

For a man who had been twice-conquered, Daniel had done well. He stood among the advisers to Darius, King of Persia. Before that, he had counseled Nebuchadnezzar of Babylon. Then Persia invaded. Because Daniel was not Babylonian, he was spared the fate of the conquered. He was an Israelite and already in exile.

The Persian king held court in the great atrium of the palace at Babylon, which until five years ago had been the seat of the kings of Babylonia. Civilizations had risen and fallen on this spot for countless centuries. Cities, palaces, and the fortunes of men like Daniel rose and fell with them.

The atrium of the palace reached several stories high, a tower soaring to heaven, a triumph of empire and ambition. Fountains and artificial streams watered a jungle of vegetation, trees—palms, cedars, poplars—and rare flowers that climbed for the sunlight shining through windows set high in the reaching walls. The splash and trickle of water made a constant sound that blended with the murmur of voices in conversation and with the music from the chimes and lyres of the musicians. Darius nominally conducted business when he held court here, but the setting was pleasant and distracting—a world apart from the dirt and heat outside.

Near the musicians, a court dancer performed, a piece of living artwork. Suza moved like a sapling in the wind, swaying, her limbs curving. Her bare feet touched the floor with the lightest grace. Bangles around her ankles rang at each step. Her gold tunic, tightly cinched, showed the curves of her hips and breasts. Her dark, curling hair—loose and unadorned, scandalous and alluring—fell down her back. She had almond-shaped eyes the color of mahogany.

Much food and wine circulated, carried by slaves in gleaming white tunics, bearing bronze ewers and platters. Supplicants to the king were lulled and diverted. Unfortunately, many of the advisers and administrators were as well. Not to mention the king himself, so noble in his tunic and robe, whiter than the plumage of egrets. His rich headdress sat perfectly on his head, pressing on his curled and oiled hair, even as he leaned back in his throne, half-asleep.

Daniel drank water, to keep his senses clear.

The court was in the midst of hearing an adultery case. Two prominent merchants claimed they had seen the wife of a judge in a dalliance with a young man. The woman was young and beautiful. The rumors flew. Many could believe such a deed of her, no matter that her husband was well respected and their family admired. If found guilty, she would be put to death.

In the marketplace, around the wells and plazas where people gathered and talked, Daniel had heard other rumors: The merchants had made advances toward her, she had rejected them, and now they took revenge on her. When Daniel focused on the merchants, he could smell the sweat of a lie on their skin, even through the smell of spice, flowers, honey, and perfume.

The merchants made a great deal of the story they told the king, dramatically relating how they chanced upon the house's garden, saw the lady send her maids away, watched as the young man in question appeared from his hiding place, and then how the couple sported in the shade of a tree outside her husband's very window. The witnesses did not seem concerned that the identity of this young man remained a mystery.

The husband—a self-made man who seemed uncomfortable in his finery—looked stunned, uncertain, glancing back and forth between the merchants and his wife. The lady stood apart. She was draped in a rich silk tunic and shawl. Two veiled maids stood with her. Her gaze was downcast, but her posture was proud.

The merchants finished and begged the king for his judgment.

Darius glanced at the husband, then at his advisers. He said, "It is difficult to deny the firsthand testimony of such esteemed citizens of our empire. What say my advisers?"

They agreed, bowing and murmuring, that yes, the account told by such respected witnesses was undeniable, the lady must be guilty, yes, yes.

Hands clasped behind his back, Daniel stepped forward, leaned close to Darius's ear and said, "Sire, question them separately. Discover if their testimony remains as sure."

One of the advisers spoke angrily, "Why must you always be contrary, foreigner?"

Lifting a brow, the king said, "You do enjoy making things difficult, Daniel."

"I seek only the truth, Sire." He was out of place in his simple tunic belted with a plain brown sash.

"And if such truth goes against my wishes?"

"Truth is truth, Sire," Daniel said with a careful bow.

From another adviser, a not-so-subtle whisper reached them. "See how arrogant he is, he thinks his truth is greater than the king!"

Daniel met the king's gaze and did not flinch.

Darius looked away and gestured, "You. Come forward."

The first merchant approached the dais and bowed. Did his hands tremble ever so slightly? Darius tipped a finger at Daniel, indicating he should proceed.

In a low voice, so that only the king, the other advisers, and the merchant could hear, Daniel asked, "What kind of tree was it that you saw them under?"

The man shrugged, glancing over his shoulder at his fellow, but Daniel stepped beside him and held his shoulder, to keep him facing forward. The man said, "How should I know? I'm not a gardener."

"Just describe it."

"It . . . it was wide. With many branches spreading out."

"And the leaves?"

"Dark green. Oval."

"Did it have fruit? Lemons, perhaps? Or apples?"

"Yes, yes. Perhaps they were lemons."

"Thank you."

Released, the merchant retreated from the dais. Darius called the second forward. Daniel guided him, so the two merchants could not exchange words.

When asked what tree it had been, the second merchant said, "Why, I'm sure it was a date palm."

The most common tree in all of Babylon, of course.

"Tall?" Daniel said.

"Yes, yes. Very tall."

"And the leaves?"

"Fronds, high off the ground. You know what a palm looks like."

"Thank you."

As the second merchant retreated, Daniel said to the king and the other advisers, "Sire, they are lying."

Darius nodded and announced his verdict. "Their story is invention. They have witnessed falsely against an innocent woman."

Then came an uproar, because the punishment for false witnessing was death. Darius ordered guards to come, the advisers shuffled and grumbled among themselves, and the courtiers sighed in wonder. The husband ran to his wife. When she lifted her face to him, tears covered her cheeks. They embraced, abased themselves before the king, and begged leave to return to their home.

Daniel stood out of the way, smiling wryly at the havoc he'd created.

"That was well done, Daniel, my friend." He looked behind him to find Suza leaning on a marble pillar, her arms crossed, grinning. "But you make enemies. The sycophants hate it when you make them look bad." She nodded at the advisers who huddled in conversation. Occasionally one glanced at him. Daniel could almost taste their envy of the attention he garnered from the king. It was like sand, dry and coarse.

King Darius eyed him as the advisers whispered around him.

"They make themselves look bad. I don't have to do anything."

"They're jealous of your wisdom."

He shook his head. "It is not my wisdom, but God's."

"You always say that." She touched his arm. "Have supper with me at the bazaar tonight."

"I'll be there."

She drifted away, her footsteps ringing.

Pavilions and awnings in a hundred colors spread across the marketplace. Beneath them, merchants sold wares from across the empire: the gold of Egypt, the silk of the far eastern lands, horses from Anatolia, coral and pearls from the coast. A dozen different languages clashed and made music, cheers went up as an acrobat finished a series of backflips in the plaza, a camel brayed across the street. Meat roasted and wine spilled, turning the air heady.

This was truly the most wondrous city in the world. This was truly a wondrous time to be alive. This was the height of civilization. Except for the cruelty of empires and conquerors.

The sensations would have overwhelmed Daniel, if he hadn't been used to them. He could hear conversations a block away, smell a dozen different scents on the air. He'd grown used to the complex barrage of information. It was a part of the curse he'd learned to use.

On the steps leading from one level of houses to the next, he leaned against the wall, eating a handful of dates one by one. He smiled when he saw Suza running toward him, weaving around market crowds and crates of pottery.

He might have guessed Suza was a dancer, even when she wore a loose-fitting tunic the color of dust and hid her hair and striking face under a wrap and veil. She moved with the grace of mist rising from a pool of water, effortless and peaceful.

In the same movement, she stopped and sat beside him. "You've started without me."

"Nonsense. I was saving this one for you," he said, and offered her the last date. She laughed.

They wandered the marketplace in search of delicacies. Suza bought her supper from a woman who roasted spiced pork on a skewer. She offered some to Daniel, who shook his head.

"There's a booth on the next row that's run by a Hebrew family. I'll find food there."

She smirked. "You and your Hebrew law. You understand, I had to offer you some out of politeness, even though I knew you wouldn't accept."

"I know."

They rested at a terrace overlooking the marketplace and watched the sun set over the palace gardens. Suza leaned on the wall, her mood turning somber.

"The full moon rises tomorrow."

And they'd been having such a lovely evening. "Do you think I don't know that?"

"Come with me. I hate for you to be alone on those nights."

"I will stay at home and pray, like always."

"You always *say* you will, but you never do. You can't, any more than the rest of us can."

"I will pray."

"Your devotion to your Hebrew God—it makes you both a hero and a fool. Everyone says so. You're admired for it—but because of it you'll never belong here."

"I *don't* belong here. I belong to my God. I trust in Him."

"There is another tribe you belong to."

More angrily than he intended he said, "It's not a tribe, it's a curse."

She touched his cheek, a fleeting gesture that he barely felt. "I will pray for you to Ishtar. The lion is her beast. So you are hers, whether you like it or not."

She left him. He almost called after her, wanting to explain, to make her understand. But he remained silent.

Persia, Babylon before it, venerable Egypt, and all the kingdoms in the world were empires built on false idols. But what glorious idols.

Bulls with wings and the heads of men, full-bearded and wearing tall headdresses. Human bodies with the heads of cats and jackals, cows and ibis. And lions. Lions with the heads of men. Powerful, animal bodies governed by human reason. They recalled a time when men and animals lived more closely than they did now, when men were known to run as animals in the wilderness and each knew the other's language. Those times were gone, but signs of them lingered.

Some of the offspring, the spawn of mortals and these animal gods, beings who were both and neither, lingered.

The Ishtar Gate opened north from the palace to the road outside the city. Tall enough to block out the sun, the walls, glazed blue and gleaming, marked the Processional Way, wide enough for a pair of chariots to travel abreast. Along the walls, gold lions prowled on blue tiles, row after row of them.

At twilight, Daniel had every intention of staying in his room and praying to God for protection, for self-control, for freedom from the curse. At first dark, but before the full moon had risen, he was walking past the lions stalking around the walls, through the Ishtar Gate and out of the city. Suza was waiting for him.

"I knew you'd come," she said, falling into step beside him.

They did not speak for the next two hours as they walked away from the city to a forest near the Euphrates River. Smells of the city—cooking and crowds—gave way to hot winds and rich vegetation, alive and rotting. They took a wild path that disappeared in a ravine near a village, so they would not be followed. Others came. Daniel recognized some: a palace guard, a priest of Marduk, a prostitute from the bazaar. Those were other lives. Here, those roles meant nothing. Here was the place to run wild.

By not exposing their identities or this place, they ensured that they would be able to run in safety when their beasts broke free on full-moon nights. In the city, they kept each other's secret; they were part of the same tribe of the cursed.

Some relished this time. The palace guard stripped off his tunic and turned to the moon, low on the horizon. His face, awash in silver light, grew longer, a snout formed where his mouth had been, and sharp fangs emerged. Before their eyes he became a wolf. With a gleeful bark, he ran away, claws digging into the earth.

Let me go, set me free—a beast writhed inside Daniel, clawing and scratching to get out.

He shut his eyes. "I hate this," he said, gritting his teeth.

"Fighting it makes it worse," said Suza. She pulled her tunic over her head and dropped it. A sheen of brindled fur was growing on her naked skin.

Around them writhed half men, half beasts, the images of a dozen false idols.

Daniel dropped to his knees.

"Oh Lord my God, I am Your servant, and by Your power I bear this burden. By Your will I carry this curse. By Your mercy I do not fear. Oh God. Help me bear this burden."

Where Suza had been, a leopard stood, stretching her body, flicking her long tail. She jumped, kicking her feet as if for joy, graceful as a dancer. Then she ran.

Bones melting to a different form, skin stretching, a coat of tawny fur sprouting—Suza was right, fighting it made it worse. But he fought. Every month, every full moon, he fought.

And lost. He changed. His lion's roar echoed in the night.

When folk of the city heard the howls of creatures in the dark, they huddled in their houses, safe in their tribes, and prayed to their animal-shaped gods for protection. If the doors stayed barred and the fires stayed lit, they had faith their gods would protect them. People prayed, because it made them feel safe.

The beasts hunted, then returned to the oasis to sleep.

Daniel started from a nightmare, his eyes growing wide all at once, his breathing fast and panicked. There had been blood. He could taste it. Gazelle. He would have to purify himself after this ordeal and pray for forgiveness.

"Hush, Daniel. You're safe." Suza put her hand on his shoulder.

Groaning, he rested his head on a pillow of grass. His body was his own again. Naked, he was tucked in the hollow under a leafy thicket. Dawn was close. The sky was gray and chill.

Suza propped her head on her hand and watched him. Her hair was tangled in a halo around her face, her eyes shadowed and weary, her smile amused.

She smoothed his hair behind his ear. "Good morning."

"At least it's morning."

"You sound surprised."

He stared up at the tangled pattern the tree's branches made. "I'm afraid that one day the lion will not leave me. That I won't wake up."

She kissed his forehead and whispered nonsense sounds of comfort.

He continued, "The others who were captured with me when Babylon invaded Jerusalem, they said, 'Why has God done this to us? Why has He punished us like this?' But I knew. God sent me here to be an example, to show the empires of idols what it is to be a servant of God. To show them the wisdom of God, so that they might understand.

"But this—this, I don't understand. I have faith, I *must* have faith that there is a reason, that God has afflicted me thus for a reason. But I cannot see it."

"Don't look for reason from a god. The gods are petty, they act on whims, and we are their playthings."

"I don't believe that."

"Then perhaps your god did this so that we might meet and become friends. Would we have, otherwise? You a Hebrew and me a Persian, you a respected counselor and me a courtesan?"

She sounded so matter-of-fact, he couldn't help but smile. "I don't know, Suza."

Somehow, as they did every month, they found their clothing, dressed, returned to the city and pretended that they were normal, that they had no affinity for the clawed and fanged statues that populated the city, that watched them from every street.

In his quarters, Daniel prayed, kneeling on bare tile toward the west, toward Jerusalem. The prayer fumbled—on these mornings his faith was weakest. He did not belong to the Hebrew tribe of his forefathers, of his God. He belonged to a tribe he hated, and when he searched for the reasons, his mind was empty. He was used to God answering him with some flash of reason.

He washed and dressed and made his way to the palace of Darius.

The business of the day had already started, earlier than usual. The other advisers were in a flurry, clustered around the king. Not even noon, and they were urging Darius to some action. Across the room, Daniel's keen sometimes-lion's ears heard the whispers:

"Sire, it is dangerous to put faith in people who have no faith in you."

"Sire, this law will curb the influence of foreigners on your glorious empire."

"Sire, it will protect your own power. *You* will be the one whom everyone looks to."

The king had a clay tablet before him, which a moment later he stamped with his seal. A couple of the advisers chanced looks at Daniel. Their smiles were cold.

Then the new law was read aloud. " 'Those who beseech any god shall be put to death. All faithful citizens of the empire shall rightfully seek boons from one being alone, the person of His Most Divine Majesty. All other prayers are unworthy and condemned.' "

Daniel was famous for his piety. The advisers wrote this law and persuaded His Majesty to endorse it for one reason only: to incriminate Daniel.

Suza, clothed in her silk tunic and jewelry, stepped beside Daniel. Her face was still as stone, but her eyes showed fear. "Surely your god will forgive you if you forsake him for this little time, until the king's whim changes."

"Every morning I pray. Every evening I pray. That is right and just. In fact, I feel I must pray now. If you'll excuse me." He would show them true faith, as he believed he came here to do.

"Daniel—"

He returned to his chamber, to the window that faced west over the city, toward the Promised Land, and he prayed.

My faith has brought me this far. I will not falter now, though I face death. Oh Lord, You are great.

He knew he could be seen, knew his enemies would be watching. He almost taunted them. When, no more than a dozen breaths later, the king's soldiers splintered the wood of his door, he was not surprised and did not flinch. He went quietly, prepared to be a martyr.

For defying the king's edict against prayers, he was arrested. By royal decree he was convicted. He was marched under guard down the street, toward whatever death the advisers planned for him. King Darius, carried on his litter and flanked by his advisers, led the procession. Frowning, he kept his gaze above the crowd, to the stone of the walls, and seemed unmoved.

At the gate outside the city, Daniel saw Suza, standing on her toes to better see over the crowd. He decided to look strong, to impart some comfort to her, for he expected to see her upset at his predicament, and was astonished and confused when she was not.

Rather, she wore a smile, thin and puckered as if she was trying to hide it. Her eyes were shining, and she waved to him. He learned later that she had discovered what method of execution was planned for him, and she had no fear at all.

The lid was shut over the pit, the light went out, and the only sensations Daniel could discern were the thick, musky scent of lions and the echoing sound of their breathing. He crouched at the base of the ramp and listened to claws scratch on stone, to the hollow growl as one of them yawned. A dozen of them lived here, fed by victims of the empire's laws and the king's whim.

He blinked. His half-lion eyes became accustomed to the darkness. One of the beasts was approaching him—the king of this pride, a tawny giant of thirty stone with a tangled black mane that flared around his head like a crown. Daniel bowed, ducking his gaze as the massive beast came close enough to breathe on him. He let his lion's instincts fill him and tell him what to do.

Daniel waited, bowing his shoulders in a way that said, *I am the weaker of us, I am not here to fight.* The king's nostrils flared. Daniel held his breath, careful not to meet the beast's gaze in challenge.

Their languages were not so different. It was as if he could hear the lion speak, and he knew how to answer.

"Why are you here?" said the lion.

"I am a traveler seeking rest among your pride."

Daniel felt the lion's hot breath on his skin—dry and fierce like the desert and reeking of old blood.

"You smell like beast. But there is also the scent of man on you."

"The men are all outside."

The lion lifted his head, and gooseflesh rose on Daniel's suddenly cool skin. He kept his head low, but in the corner of his vision he saw the lion's amber gaze judge him. Then, the animal turned and padded back to his place. The other lions had been sitting watchful, but now they rested, stretched out on rocks, cleaning themselves with thick pink tongues.

"Rest here, traveler," the lion bade him from across the pit.

Tension left Daniel's muscles as though lifted by a breeze. Slowly, he stood. The lions paid him no more attention than if he had been one of them. Which, he supposed, he was. A young male stretched out a few boulders away from the king looked at him and invited him to share his place. Daniel did, lying on the rock beside the beast, who returned to cleaning his paws. Daniel was warm here, and safe. He closed his eyes and made a silent prayer.

The next day, the lid was lifted from the pit, and Daniel walked up the ramp. He was cramped and tired—even his lion self preferred the cushion of a bed, or at least a tuft of grass, to the rocks of the pit. But he was alive, praise God for it.

The king and his retinue waited at the rim of the pit, and all gasped when he appeared well and whole, without a scratch.

Darius, reclining on his litter, surrounding by gaping sycophants, could not maintain an indifferent mask. He'd become dumbfounded, barely able to move his mouth to speak. "Daniel! How—how did you survive?"

Daniel gave a wry smile. "I prayed, and my God sent angels to hold closed the mouths of the lions." Later, he would pray for forgiveness for that fib.

His voice filled with awe, Darius said, "Your God is powerful."

"And wise," Daniel said, thinking of all the full moon nights he had asked *why*. Of course God had known why. "God is most wise."

The Temptation of Robin Green

The talking dog always whined when Robin fed the griffin.

"C'mon, Robin, please? The doc'll never know. I *never* get any treats."

"Sorry, Jones," Robin said to the dust-colored mutt in the steel and Plexiglas cell.

"Please? Please please *please*?" Jones's tail wagged the entire back end of his body.

"No, Jones. Sorry."

"But it's not fair. *Those* guys get fed late."

"They have bigger stomachs than you."

"Oh, please, just once, and I'll never ask again!"

But it was a lie; the whining would never stop, and giving in would make it worse. It turned out that a talking dog was even more endearing than the nontalking kind. It took all of Lieutenant Robin Green's army training to turn away from the mutt and move on to the rest of her rounds.

She hit a switch to illuminate a bank of lights in the second enclosure. The occupant had the thick, tawny-furred body of a lion, but its neck and head were those of an eagle: feathered, dark brown, with glaring eyes and a huge hooked bill. It opened its beak and called at her when the light came on, a sound somewhere between a screech and a roar.

A small door at the base of the Plexiglas allowed her to slide a tray of steaming meat into the cell. The griffin pounced on it, snarling and tearing at the meat, swallowing in gulps. Robin jumped back. No matter how many times that happened, it always surprised her.

Next, she took a bundle of hay to a side door that allowed access to a third enclosure and went inside. Technically, entering the enclosures was against regulations, but she had asked for special permission in this case.

"Here you go, kid."

Hoofed footfalls shuffled toward her through the wood shavings that covered the floor. The animal stood about fifteen hands high, had a milk-white coat, cloven hooves, a tuft of hair under its chin, and a silver spiral horn between its eyes.

Robin spread out the hay, feeding some of it to the creature by hand. She and the unicorn got along well, though at twenty-three she didn't like to admit her virginity. She'd fallen back on excuses to explain why she'd never seemed to make time for dates, for getting to know the men around her, for simply having fun: too much to do, too much studying, too much work, too much at stake. She'd always thought there'd be time, eventually. But those old patterns died hard. Colleagues and friends paired off around her, and she'd started to feel left out.

All that aside, now she was glad about it. Otherwise, she'd never have had the chance to hold a unicorn's muzzle in her hands and stroke its silken cheek.

She'd graduated top of her class with a degree in biology and made no secret of her interest in some of the wilder branches of cryptozoology, however unfashionable. She'd gone through the university on an army ROTC scholarship and accepted an active-duty commission because she thought it would give her a chance to travel. Instead, she'd been offered a position in a shadowy military research project—covert, classified, and very intriguing. She'd accepted, transferred to the base in California, where she couldn't talk to anyone about her work because of how classified it was. Not that anyone would believe her if she did talk.

After visiting with the unicorn for half an hour, Robin continued to the next level down: The Residence.

This level of the Center for the Study of Paranatural Biology made Lieutenant Green nervous. It seemed like a prison. Well, it was a prison, though the people incarcerated here weren't exactly criminals. Colonel Ottoman, PhD, MD, et cetera, liked to say it didn't matter since they weren't really human. A lowly research assistant and low-ranking, newly minted officer like Robin, perfectly turned out in her prim uniform with pressed collar and skirt, was not supposed to question such a declaration. Still, she made an effort to treat the inhabitants of the Residence like people.

"Hello? Anyone home?" Colonel Ottoman and Dr. Lerna were supposed to be here, but Robin must have been the first in for the night shift. The day shift had already checked out.

Despite its clandestine military nature, the place was as cluttered as one would expect from any university laboratory. Paper-covered desks and crowded bookshelves lined one wall. Another wall boasted a row of heavy equipment: refrigeration units, incubators, oscillators. Several island worktables held sinks and faucets, microscopes, banks of test tubes and flasks.

One Plexiglas wall revealed a pair of cells. The first cell was completely dark, its inhabitant asleep. Special features of this room included a silver-alloy lining and silver shavings embedded in the walls. The next cell had garlic extract mixed with the paint.

"How are you this evening, Lieutenant?" the occupant of the dimly lit second cell greeted her.

"I'm fine, Rick. Where is everyone?"

"There's a note on your desk."

Her desk was the smallest of the group, and the only one without a computer—she was still using a typewriter, although the colonel had promised to get her a computer on the next requisition cycle. She assumed he'd forget. She found a note in Dr. Ottoman's jagged writing on her desk calendar:

Lt. Green, sorry to leave you alone, special conference came up, Bob and I will be in DC all week. Hold down the fort.

No special instructions regarding the new arrival, just leave it alone.

Col. Ottoman

Just like that. Gone, leaving her alone on the night watch for a whole week. That meant she wouldn't actually have anything to do but feed everyone and keep an eye on the closed-circuit screens.

"Bad news?" Rick said.

"Just inconvenient. Do you know anything about a new arrival?"

"In the aquatics lab."

She started for the next door.

"Ah, Lieutenant. Chores first?" Rick—short for Ricardo, surname unknown, date of birth unknown, place of birth unknown—slouched nonchalantly against the plastic window at the front of his cell. He didn't sound desperate—yet.

"Right."

From the incubator she removed the three pints of blood, "borrowed" from the base hospital, which had been warming since the last shift. She poured them into clean beakers, the only useful glassware at hand, and reached through the small panel in the window to Rick's cell to set the glasses of blood on a table inside. It wasn't really any different than feeding raw meat to the griffin.

Rick waited until the panel was closed before moving to the table. He looked composed, classic, like he should have been wearing a silk cravat and dinner jacket instead of jeans and a cotton shirt.

"Cheers." He drank down the first glass without pause.

She didn't watch him, not directly. The strange, hypnotic power of his gaze had been proven experimentally. So she watched his slender hands, the shoulder of his white shirt, the movement of his throat as he swallowed.

He lowered the beaker and sighed. "Ah. Four hours old. Fine vintage." His mouth puckered. A faint blush began to suffuse his face, which had been deathly pale.

Robin continued the last leg of her rounds. The next room contained aquariums, large dolphin tanks with steel catwalks ringing the edges. Bars reaching from the catwalks to the ceiling enclosed the tanks, forming cages around the water.

Robin retrieved a pail of fish—cut-up tuna, whole mackerel, a few abalone mixed with kelp leaves—from the refrigerator at the end of the work space and climbed the stairs to the top edge of the south tank.

"How are you, Marina?"

A woman lounged on an artificial rock that broke the surface of the water in the middle of the tank. Hugging a convenient outcrop of plaster, she played with her bronze-colored hair. Instead of legs she had a tail: long, covered in shimmering, blue-silver scales, ending in a broad fin that flapped the water lazily.

The mermaid covered her mouth with her pale hand and laughed. It was teasing, vicious laughter. Marina seldom spoke.

"Here you are, when you're hungry." Robin nudged the pail to where the mermaid could reach it through the bars.

Marina's laughter doubled. She arched her back, baring her small breasts, and pushed into the water. Diving under, she spun, her muscular tail pumping her in a fast loop around the rock's chain anchor. On the surface, the rock swayed, causing ripples to spread. Bubbles streamed from her long hair, a silver trail.

Suddenly, she broke the surface and shook her hair, spraying water. Still laughing, her gaze darted across the catwalk to the north tank. Slyly, she looked back at Robin, writhed so she floated on her back, and splashed her tail.

Robin looked at the north tank, which until that night had been empty. A seal, torpedo-shaped, rubbery, its gray skin mottled with black, lay on the artificial rock and stared at her with black, shining eyes. The new arrival. A tag, sealed in a plastic, waterproof cover, hung from the rail by the cage. It read:

> On loan from the British Alternative Biologies Laboratory.
> *HOMO PINNIPEDIA.* Common names: selkie (Scottish), silke (Irish)

A selkie. It used its sealskin to travel through the water, but it could shed the skin to walk on land as a human. The creature raised itself on its flippers and looked at her with interest. Real, human interest shone in those round black eyes.

"Wow," Robin murmured. What were they going to do with a selkie?

She leaned on the railing, watching for a time, but the selkie didn't move. She kept a notebook, a journal for informal observations and such. She could write: "seal, lounging."

She had to walk rounds every two hours, since many of the subjects didn't show up on the video monitors. She was supposed to conduct formal interviews with Rick, since he was obviously most active during the night watch. But Ottoman had collected all the arcane information he could from him—without going so far as staking and dissecting him—months ago, so they usually just chatted. Tonight, though, she found herself leaning in the doorway to the aquatics lab. The lights over the aquariums were dim. The water seemed to glow with its own blue aura.

"It won't change form while you're staring at it," Rick said.

"I'm just curious."

Now, the seal swam, fluidly circling, peering at her through the thick glass, disappearing regularly as it bobbed to the surface for air.

" 'It.' Don't you even know what it is?" Bradley Njalson, the werewolf, had woken up. His deep voice echoed from his bed against the far wall of his cell.

"Yes, oh great biologist," Rick said. "Have you sexed the specimen?"

She'd tried, but the seal deftly managed to keep that part of its anatomy turned away from her. Not that external genitalia would be visible on a marine mammal.

"The tag didn't say," she said. She'd looked for the research files and the reports that had arrived with the selkie, but Ottoman had locked them up before rushing off to his conference.

For all she knew, it was just a seal.

The next night, she spent most of her shift sitting on the top step of the steel catwalk stairs, watching it.

Splashing in the south tank, Marina pulled herself to the bars and watched Robin watching the other tank.

"Marina, what do you know about selkies?"

The mermaid, who'd been collected in Dingle Bay in Ireland several years before, had been humming a song, an Irish-sounding jig. "A mermaid died to save a silke once."

"Can you tell me about it?"

"Ask 'im."

Robin turned to where the mermaid nodded, to where a man hung on to the bars of the selkie's cage, holding himself half out of the water, smiling. Surprised, Robin jumped to her feet.

He was lean, muscular. Slick with water, his pale skin shone. Black hair dripped past his shoulders. His face was solid, unblemished. He didn't grip the bars like a prisoner; he held them loosely, using them to balance as he treaded water. His smile was playful, like she was inside the cage and he was studying her.

Tentatively, she nodded a greeting. "Hello."

He pushed himself away from the bars, gliding back through the water. He was naked and totally unself-conscious. His body was as sculptured and handsome as his face. He had the broad shoulders and muscular arms of an Olympic swimmer, powerful legs, every muscle in his torso was defined. She could have used his body for an anatomy lecture.

He swam to the artificial rock, climbed out of the water, and sat back, reclining. He spread his arms, exposing to best advantage his broad chest, toned abdomen and . . . "genitalia" was too clinical a word for what he displayed. He was posing for her.

Next to him lay a bundle of gray, rubbery skin.

Robin stood at the bars of his cage, looking through them for an unobstructed view. She didn't remember moving there. She took a deep, reflexive breath. Her heartbeat wouldn't slow down.

Marina laughed uncontrollably, both hands over her mouth, tail flapping. Her voice was musical, piercing.

Robin fled the room.

Back in the main lab, she stood with her back against the wall, eyes closed, gasping.

"Let me guess. The selkie—male?" Rick's tone was politely inquisitive.

The flush in Robin's face became one of embarrassment. So much for the biologist and her professional demeanor. "Yes. Yes, he is."

"They have a knack for that."

"A knack for what?"

"Flustering young women out of their wits. I'm sure you know the stories."

Since her posting to the center, Robin had had to question all the myths and ancient tales. They might be just stories; then again. . . . She went to the bookshelves to look up "selkie" in Brigg's *Encyclopedia of Fairies*.

"How do you do it?" Rick asked, moving to the end of his window.

"Do what?"

"Remain so clinical, when confronted with so many contradictions to your assumptions about the world."

"I expand my assumptions," she said.

"What about the magic? Your inability to control your reaction to the selkie. You are so careful, Lieutenant, not to look into my eyes."

The impulse was, of course, to look at him. The voice hinted at rewards she would find when she did. Mystery. Power. She resisted, taking the book to her desk, passing Rick's cell on the way. She looked at the collar of his shirt. "Why are you all so damn seductive?"

"It's in the blood." He grinned. The allure disappeared. He could turn it on and off like a light switch.

Brad laughed, a sound like a growl.

Robin almost wished for the seal back. It had been much less distracting. For the rest of the night, the skin remained folded on the rock, and the man watched her. She turned her back on him to check off her rounds on the charts, and when she looked again he was right there, pressed against the bars. Sometimes, their faces were only inches apart. Sometimes, she didn't shy away, and she could feel his warm breath. He never said a word.

She was attracted to the selkie. That was a statement, an observation, something empirical with explanations having to do with the fact that she was a young woman and he was a young man. A very handsome young man. Hormones were identifiable. Controllable.

So why couldn't she seem to control the way her body flushed every time she entered the aquatics lab? Rick had mentioned magic. But the center was here precisely because magic didn't exist, only biology that had not yet been explained.

Biology. She needed a cold shower.

Wednesday night.

She turned around after setting down Marina's supper and tripped on the catwalk. No, she didn't trip—Marina had reached through the bars, grabbed her ankle, and tipped her over. The mermaid was stronger than she looked. Robin sprawled across the catwalk between the tanks, too surprised to move, lying with the meat of her palms digging into the steel treads.

The selkie was by the bars, right beside her, reaching through. He touched her hand. Even though his hand was damp and cool, Robin thought her skin would catch fire. He took her hand, brought it through the bars, and kissed it, touching each knuckle with his lips.

When she didn't pull away, he grew bold, turning her hand, kissing the inside of her wrist, tracing her thumb with his tongue, sucking on the tip of a finger. She hadn't imagined she could feel like this, all her nerves focused on what he was doing to her. She closed her eyes. Nothing existed in the world but her hand and his mouth.

She was on duty. This was not allowed. She should stand up and leave. Write a report about the cooperative behavior of the selkie and the mermaid. Marina was laughing, quietly now, from behind her rock.

Gradually, Robin slid forward so that her face was at the bars. She shouldn't be doing this. The security cameras recorded everything. The selkie kissed her. His lips moved slowly, carefully tasting every part of her mouth, letting her taste him. His hands cupped her face. If it hadn't been for the bars, she would have let him pull her into the water.

He drew away first. The bars kept her from reaching after him. He swam a few feet away, holding her gaze until he reached the door of the cage, where he lingered, waiting. The message: If she wanted to continue, she'd have to open the door.

Well then, that was it. She lay on the catwalk, her hand still thrust through the bars, dangling in the cool water.

She used the bars to pull herself to her feet. She trembled a little, her heart racing. Nerves, that was all. She couldn't take her eyes off him. She could still feel his lips.

She planned to go straight to the next room. The control box to deactivate the electronic locks on the cages was at the top of the stairs. A single move. That's all it would take. Marina made a sound, part sympathetic, part mocking.

She walked past the control box, into the next room. Her lips pursed, her blood rushed.

"Lieutenant?" Rick said.

Ignoring him, she continued to the side room that held the bank of a dozen TV monitors, showing the view from cameras focused on every enclosure in the center. Jones the dog was gnawing on a rawhide bone. The griffin was scratching the steel wall of its cell. The unicorn stood with a foot cocked, nose to the floor, sleeping. In the aquatics lab, Marina was basking on her rock, brushing her hair with her fingers, probably singing as well. The selkie, still in human form, swam back and forth in front of the door, like he was pacing. Like he was waiting.

She shut off the cameras, rewound the tapes, and erased the evening's footage. All the monitors went to static. She left a note for the day shift complaining that the security system was on the fritz, that she'd tried to fix it and failed.

On her way back to the aquatics lab, Rick called, his voice harsh. "Lieutenant Green, this isn't you. This is the magic. Selkie magic. Stop and think what you're doing."

She paused at the door. She was sure she knew what she was doing. But she'd read the stories, and Rick was right. Male selkies had a predilection for seducing women. This wasn't her, it was the magic.

And she wanted it.

The hand that pressed the button for the lock to the north tank was not hers. Not really.

The door to the selkie's cage opened with a small noise. She kept her back to it, her breath short, her eyes closed with the realization of what she was doing. She'd worked so hard, stayed in control her whole life, and now she did nothing but wait. She gripped the railing by the stairs.

She heard dripping, water rushing off a body climbing onto the catwalk. Still, the touch on her shoulders came as a shock and made her flinch. He must have sensed her anxiety, because he brushed her arm gently, stroking lightly with fingertips until she relaxed. Letting her grow accustomed to him, as if he were taming a wild animal. Then both his hands touched her, moved along her arms to her shoulders. Her shirt grew damp with his touch.

He kissed the back of her neck at her hairline, below the twist she kept her hair up in. His breath was hot on her skin. Her body melted, slumping into his touch. He pulled her back, away from the stairs, slipped his body in front of hers, and pressed her against the cage. She was limp, unseeing. She let him guide her.

He nuzzled her neck. Her nerves tingled with every touch. Overwhelmed, she moaned softly. His hands moved to the buttons of her dress shirt. He had them open before she realized it, and his hands were inside, cupping her breasts, fingers slipping under her bra.

Instead of putting her hands on his shoulders to push him away, like she should have done, Robin clutched at him, her fingers slipping on his slick skin. She dug her nails in for a better grip.

"Hmm," he murmured and pinned her against the bars. It was the first sound she'd ever heard him make.

He pulled her arms away just long enough to take her shirt off. His hand slid easily over her skin, and her bra fell away. His kisses moved from her neck, down to her breasts. She wrapped her arms around his head, holding him close.

She bent, unconsciously trying to pull away from so much

sensation, so much of him, but the bars kept her close to him. She couldn't get away. She didn't want to. Skillfully, more deftly than she could have thought from someone who lived in water and didn't wear clothes, he opened the zipper of her skirt, slipped his hands into her panties. One hand caressed her backside, the other—played. Oh—she struggled to kick her shoes off, to get her skirt and pantyhose off, to give him better access. He helped.

Her clothes gone, they were naked together. Skin pressed against skin. His erection was hard against her thigh, insistent. He paid attention to nothing but her, and she was overwhelmed. Locking her against him, he eased her down to the catwalk.

They were going to do it, right here on the catwalk, her clothes awkwardly spread out to protect her from the steel. Marina softly sang something in Irish that was no doubt very bawdy.

Robin felt like she had saved herself just for this moment.

The next evening, she brought hay to the unicorn's cell.

"Here you go. Come on."

The unicorn stayed at the far end of the room, its head down, its ears laid back, its nostrils flaring angrily.

Robin stood, arms limp at her sides. Of course. She left the hay, closed the door, and continued her rounds.

She found a note in the lab from the day shift explaining that the problem with the security system had been fixed by simply changing out the fuses, and if it happened again she should try it. The officer in charge sounded testy that they'd lost a whole evening's worth of surveillance. Not that anything around here ever changed.

Except that it had, everything had changed, and Robin didn't want anyone to know it. She shut down the cameras again, and removed fuses from half the monitors as well, blinding them.

"Lieutenant," Rick said to her as she removed his pints from the incubator and prepared his supper. "Look at yourself. This isn't like you. He has enchanted you."

"I don't want to hear it," she murmured, sliding his beakers of blood through the slot in the window.

Rick didn't look at them; instead, he pressed himself to the window, palms flat against the plastic, imploring. "He's using you. He doesn't care about you, he's only manipulating you."

She looked at him. Not his eyes, but his cheekbones, his ear, the dark fringe of hair. Anything but his eyes. "Just like you would do, if I opened your door and let you seduce me?"

Which wasn't fair, because Rick had never tried to seduce her, never tried to take advantage of her. Not that she'd ever given him the opportunity. But he'd always spoken so kindly to her. He'd spoken *to* her. Until now, she had never thought of Rick as anything but the elegant man who was supposed to be a vampire, locked in a prison cell.

"I'd never hurt you, Robin."

Now when he looked at her, she flushed. Quickly, she turned toward the aquatics lab.

"Robin, stop," he implored. "Don't go in there. Don't let him use you like this."

She gripped the doorway so hard her fingers trembled. "I've never felt like this before," she murmured.

She hadn't meant for him to hear, but he was a vampire, with a vampire's hearing. He replied, "It's not real. Let it go."

"It feels . . . I can't," she said. Because she had never felt like this before, she had never felt so good, so *much* before, it was like a drug that filled her up and pushed every other worry aside. A part of her knew Rick was right, that if this feeling was a drug, then she'd become an addict in a day and she should stop this.

The rest of her didn't care.

When she reached the aquatics lab, the selkie hung on to the door of the cage, his dark eyes shining in anticipation. As soon as she'd given Marina her supper, Robin pressed the button for the lock.

Friday night.

Colonel Ottoman left a message on the answering machine saying he'd be back Saturday. So this was it, for her and the selkie.

She lay in his arms, on the rock in the aquarium. He played with her loose, damp hair, running his fingers through it. She held his other arm around her middle. He was strong, silent. He wrapped her up with himself when they were together.

She couldn't let it end.

"We'll go away, you and I."

He looked away and laughed silently. He kissed her hand and shook his head.

It was a game to him. She couldn't be sure what he thought; he never spoke. She didn't know if he couldn't or wouldn't.

"Why not?"

He traced his finger along her jaw, down her neck. Then he nestled against the rock and closed his eyes.

She couldn't hope to understand him. Colonel Ottoman was right, they weren't even human.

His sealskin lay nearby, on the rock where he had discarded it. She grabbed it, jumped into the water, and swam to the door. He splashed, diving after her, but she climbed onto the catwalk and slammed the door shut before he reached her.

She clutched the skin to her breast. Glaring at her, he gripped the bars of the locked door.

"Tell me why I shouldn't do this."

He pressed his lips into a line and rattled the door.

She put the skin out of reach of the cage and pulled on the skirt and shirt of her uniform. All expression of playfulness, of seduction, had left the selkie. His jaw was tight, his brow furrowed.

Skin in hand, she ran to the main lab where she found a knapsack stashed under her desk. She needed clothes for him, maybe an extra lab coat . . .

"You know how all the selkie stories end, don't you?" Rick leaned on his window.

"They're just stories."

"*I'm* just a story."

She smirked. "You're no Dracula."

"You've never seen me outside this cage, my dear."

She stopped and looked at him. His eyes were blue.

"Robin, think carefully about what you're planning. He has enchanted you." The vampire's worried expression seemed almost fatherly.

"I—I can't give him up."

"Outside this room, you won't have a choice. You will throw away your career, your life, for that?"

The official acronym for it was AWOL, not to mention stealing from a government installation. Her career, as far as Robin could tell, amounted to studying people in cages. People who defied study, no matter how many cameras and electrodes were trained on them. The selkie had shown her something that couldn't be put in a cage, a range of emotions that escaped examination. He'd shown her passion, something she'd been missing without even knowing it. She wanted to take him away from the sterility of a filtered aquarium and a steel cage. She wanted to make love with him on a beach, with the sound of ocean waves behind them.

"I have this." She held up the knapsack in which she had stuffed the sealskin and left the lab to stash it in her car and find some clothes.

For all its wonder and secrecy, the center was poorly funded—it didn't produce the results and military applications that the nearby bionic and psychic research branches did—and inadequately supervised.

She knew the building and video surveillance patterns well enough to be able to smuggle the selkie to her car without leaving evidence. Not that it mattered when Rick would no doubt give Colonel Ottoman a full report. She waited until close to the end of the shift to retrieve the selkie. He came with her docilely, dressed in the spare sweats she gave him.

Marina sat on her rock and sang, her light voice echoing in the lab.

The selkie lingered for a moment until Marina waved good-bye. Robin pulled him to the next room.

"Sir," Rick, hands pressed to the plastic of his cell, called. The selkie met Rick's gaze unflinching. "I know your kind. Treat her gently."

The selkie didn't react. He seemed to study the vampire,

expressionless, and only looked away when Robin squeezed his hand.

Robin lingered a moment. "Good-bye," she said.

"Take care, Robin."

Impulse guided her again, and she went to the control box for the lock to Rick's cell. She pushed the button; the lock clicked open with the sound of a buzzer. The door opened a crack. Rick stared at the path to freedom for a long moment.

Not lingering to see what the vampire would do next, she gripped the selkie's hand and ran.

She smuggled him in the backseat of her car, making him crouch on the floorboard. Routine did her service now; the shift had ended, and the guard at the gate waved her through.

They'd be looking for her in a matter of hours. She had to get rid of the car, find a place to hide out, wait for the bank to open so she could empty her account. She could leave tracks now, then disappear.

Desperation made her a criminal. She ditched her car, swapping it for a sedan she hotwired. She kept the sealskin under her feet, where the selkie couldn't get to it.

Two more stolen cars, a thousand miles of highway, and some fast-talking at the border, flashing her military ID and spouting some official nonsense, found her in Mexico, cruising down the coast of Baja.

She knew the stories. She should have driven inland.

They stayed in a fishing village. Robin's savings would hold out for a couple of months at least, so she rented a shack and they lived as hermits, making love, watching the sea.

Convinced that she was different, that she was smarter than those women in the stories, she hid the sealskin not in the house, but buried it in the sand by a cliff. She wrestled a rock over the spot while the selkie slept.

He was no less passionate than before. He spent hours, though, staring out at the ocean. Sometimes, he wore the same sweats she'd smuggled him out in. Usually, he wore nothing at all.

She joined him one evening, sitting beside him on still-warm sand, curling her legs under her loose peasant skirt. Her shirt was too big, hanging off one shoulder, and she didn't wear a bra—it seemed useless, just one more piece of clothing they'd have to remove before making love. Nothing of the poised, put-together young army lieutenant remained. That person wouldn't have recognized her now.

He didn't turn his eyes from the waves, but moved a hand to her thigh and squeezed. The touch filled her with heat and lust, making her want to straddle him here and now. He never seemed to tire of her, nor she of him. Wasn't that close enough to love?

She kissed his shoulder and leaned against him. "I don't even know what your name is," she said. The selkie smiled, chuckled to himself, and didn't seem to care that she didn't have a name for him.

He never spoke. Never said that he loved her, though his passion for her seemed endless. She touched his chin, turned his gaze from the ocean and made him look at her. She only saw ocean there. She thought about the skin, buried in sand a mile inland, and wondered—was he still a prisoner? Did he still see bars locking him in?

Holding his face in her hands, she kissed him, and he wrapped his arms around her, kissing her in return. He tipped her back on the sand, trapped her with his arms, turned all his attention to her and her body, and she forgot her doubts.

One night, she felt the touch of a kiss by her ear. A soft voice whispered in a brogue, "Ye did well, lass. No hard feelings at all."

She thought it was a dream, so she didn't open her eyes. But she reached across the bed and found she was alone. Starting awake, she sat up. The selkie was gone. She ran out of the shack, out to the beach.

Sealskin in hand, he ran for the water, a pale body in the light of a full moon.

"No!" she screamed. How had he found it? How could he leave her? All of it was for nothing. Why had he waited until now to speak, when it didn't matter anymore?

He never looked back, but dove into the waves, swam past the breakers, and disappeared. She never saw him again. The next shape that appeared was the supple body of a gray seal breaking the surface, diving again, appearing farther out, swimming far, far away.

She sat on the beach and cried, unable to think of anything but the square of sand where she sat, and the patch of shining water where she saw him last. He'd taken her, drained her, she was empty now.

She stayed in Mexico, learning Spanish and working in the village cleaning fish. She treasured mundane moments these days. Nights, she let the sound of water lull her to sleep.

The army never found her, but someone else did, a few months later.

That night, she sat on the beach, watching moon-silvered waves crash onto the white sand, like her selkie used to. Sitting back, she grunted at the weight of her belly. The selkie hadn't left her so empty, after all. She stroked the roundness, felt the baby kick.

She didn't hear footsteps approach and gasped, startled, when a man sat down beside her.

Dark hair, an aristocratic face, permanently wry expression. He was even graceful sitting in the sand. He wore tailored black slacks and a silk shirt in a flattering shade of dark blue, with the cuffs unbuttoned and rolled up—the kind of clothes she always imagined him in. He flashed a smile and looked out at the water.

"Rick! What are you doing here?"

"Besides watching the waves?"

"So you did it. You left." She was smiling. She couldn't remember the last time she'd smiled.

"Of course. I didn't want to stay to explain to Colonel Ottoman what you'd done. I brought Mr. Njalson along with me."

"Brad's here?"

"He's hunting back on the mesa. Enjoying stretching all four legs."

Robin sighed, still smiling. Of course, Rick could have gotten himself out of there—just as soon as he convinced one of the doctors to look in his eyes in an unguarded moment. Now she wished she'd let them all out a long time before she did.

"I was worried about you," he said, in a tone that made it a prompt, a question rather than a statement.

"I'd have thought you'd have much more interesting and important things to do than look after me."

"I had the time."

"How did you find me?"

He shrugged. "I know the stories. I followed the coast. Asked questions. I'm very patient."

She imagined he would be. He could have left that lab any time he wanted. Maybe he stayed to see what the researchers were up to. To experience something new for a while.

"When are you due?" Rick asked softly.

He startled her back to the moment, and she swallowed the tightness in her throat. "In a month. It'll have webbed feet and hands. Like in the stories."

"And how are you?"

She took a breath, held it. She still cried every night. Not just from missing the selkie anymore. She had another burden now, one she'd never considered, never even contemplated. The supernatural world, which she'd tried to treat so clinically, would be with her forever. She didn't know the first thing about raising a child. She didn't know how she was going to teach this one to swim.

Looking After Family

The funeral was closed casket. With a body that mangled, the mortician couldn't do much to make it presentable. Douglas Bennett was forty-eight years old when he died.

His son shot dead the man who killed him. Not that anyone believed a man could do what had been done to Douglas. The police assumed it was an animal—a bear, or maybe even a wolf—so when they saw the second body with a bullet wound through the head and sixteen-year-old Cormac Bennett holding the rifle, they thought they had a delinquent on their hands. Maybe the kid just snapped out of grief and rage at losing his father.

Then the coroner found Douglas Bennett's blood and skin under the victim's fingernails and human flesh between his teeth. The kid pleaded self-defense through his court-appointed attorney. The DA dropped the charges.

Douglas Bennett's sister, Ellen O'Farrell, took the boy in.

Ellen, her husband David, and their son Ben walked on eggshells around him. He had killed a man, whatever the circumstances might have been, and at his age he could go either way: recover and move on, or spiral down into psychosis. They didn't talk about Douglas and what had happened; they tried to pretend everything was normal. They kept Cormac busy.

Ben didn't want to keep quiet. He was crazy to ask his cousin what it had been like, how it had felt, did he want to do it again, and what had *really* happened? He watched Cormac out of the corner of his eye, hiding behind a light brown flop of bangs. Cormac hadn't said two sentences together in the month he'd been there.

Ben was doing homework at the chrome and Formica kitchen table after supper. His mother was washing dishes in the kitchen. Cormac helped her, drying plates and stacking them on the counter for her to put away. Tall, lanky, he slouched and had a lazy way of moving. His limbs seemed to hang loosely.

David came in from the mudroom attached to the kitchen, wearing his heavy work coat and putting on his cowboy hat. "Cormac? You want to help me put out hay?"

Cormac set the towel on the counter. "Yes, sir."

Ben stood, jostling the table. "I'll help, too."

"No, Ben, you stay and do your homework," his father said.

"But—"

"It's cold, and I don't want you out in it."

He disappeared through the door. Cormac followed, pausing a moment to look back at Ben, who sat and ducked his gaze, blushing, not wanting to get caught staring. His father didn't have to tell him off like a little kid in front of Cormac. But Ben supposed he'd asked for it. He'd known what his father would say.

The numbers on his algebra worksheet seemed to fade and jumble together.

A moment later his mother stood beside him, drying her hands. "He's right, Ben. It's too cold out. You know he really wants you to stay in and study hard."

"Yeah. I know." He didn't care about the cold. He wasn't sick anymore.

"You're going to be the first one in the family to go to college. It means the world to him. And me, too." She squeezed his shoulder and went back to the counter to put dishes away.

He knew, but college was such a long way off, and it wouldn't get him the respect of someone like Cormac.

Ben told his mother he was reading for school, but he turned the light out, sat up by the window in his bedroom, and stared over the nighttime ranch. The moon was almost full and made the patches of snow scattered across the prairie glow silver. The posts and rails of the corral fences were shadows, streaks of dark in the moonlight.

The pickup, its bed empty of hay now, drove around the corner and parked by the barn on the other side of the corrals. His father and Cormac jumped out of the cab and came toward the house. They looked good together. Right. The burly rancher and the tall kid walking beside him. They weren't even related by blood and they looked more like father and son than David and Ben did. Ben was scrawny, not strong enough for ranch work. Not that he'd had a chance to prove himself or grow into the work. Better suited for books, they'd all decided.

He turned on the light, sat on his bed leaning against a pillow, held his book, and tried to look like he'd been that way for the last couple hours. When Cormac came to live with them, they'd squeezed a spare bed into the room. Ben had lost his only private place on the ranch.

Cormac opened the door.

Ben glanced up, he hoped casually. "Hey."

"Hey," Cormac said.

Ben couldn't think of anything to say after that. *So, how are the cows? What's it like being an orphan?* He just watched his cousin over the edge of his book. Cormac pulled off a sweatshirt, unbuttoned the flannel shirt underneath, slung them over the back of a chair. Peeled out of his white T-shirt, dropped it, turned back the covers of his bed, unzipped and shoved down his jeans. Crawled into bed wearing only his briefs. Rolled over with his back facing Ben, who'd lost his chance to say anything.

He couldn't remember what they'd talked about when they were kids. Movies and TV, probably. They'd seen each other every spring—Cormac's family had always come to help with branding the calves—and at Thanksgiving. They were about the same age and hung out with each other then. Ben could remember playing king of the hill, riding ponies, and taking family trips to Grand Lake. But those times were a while ago, and the person sleeping in the next bed seemed like someone different.

He put down his book and turned out the light. Moonlight bled into the room around the edges of the curtain.

Cormac went through the motions. Wake up, wash and dress, function for the day. Sleep at night. The rest was numb. If he didn't think, he didn't have to react.

His aunt and her family were good to take him in, house him and feed him and all. He paid them back by doing chores. It was how he'd been taught. You got more out of life being polite than not. He couldn't forget what he'd been taught. Especially now.

Full-moon night, he went hunting, like he'd been taught. Full moon was when they came out, and there was no one left to do it but Cormac.

The cops told him he shouldn't handle guns anymore, even though he'd been hunting for years, helping with Dad's outfitting business. Too many questions about him and guns. They wanted him to keep his nose clean, they said.

Cormac didn't care.

Uncle David, a little more practical and a lot more knowledgeable about how they led their lives, had let him keep his rifle. For keeping coyotes off the property, he said. Didn't matter, as long as Cormac had access to it. He had the bullets, too. His dad's bullets. The cops hadn't known about those.

Aunt Ellen and Uncle David hadn't asked him about the man he shot. They must have known what it was he'd shot, even if none of them could tell the cops about it. They'd understand about him going out now.

He wrapped up a slice of beef from the fridge and carried it with him in a paper bag.

With all the sense of righteousness in the world, he quietly made his way to the mudroom and loaded the silver bullets into his rifle.

"Hey."

Cormac looked up, too distracted to be startled by Ben's appearance. He stood there, dressed in jeans and a T-shirt, a stripe of moonlight from the window slicing across him, his thin frame, shaggy hair.

"What're you doing?" Ben asked.

"Nothing," Cormac said automatically. He snapped the chamber closed.

"Can I go with you?"

Ben stood with his hands clenched, almost trembling, looking a lot younger than he was. He wanted outside so badly. Folks kept him on a chain, and Cormac wondered why. Ranch kid oughta be tough as nails. He'd slow Cormac down, if he came along. Couldn't be sure he knew anything.

He might go tell Aunt Ellen and Uncle David what he was doing if Cormac left him behind.

After a moment, he said, "Sure."

Ben rushed to grab coat, knit cap, and thick work gloves.

Let him come along. If he couldn't hack the trip, he could always turn around and go back home. Wasn't Cormac's business, as long as he didn't get in the way.

The air was the crystalline freezing that only a clear winter night could produce. Cormac breathed it in and let its sharpness urge him on. Only way to keep warm on a night like this was to keep moving.

Also, he half wanted to see how quickly Ben dropped back and complained about not being able to keep up. But he didn't. His wiry frame gave him a long stride to match Cormac's.

"Your folks are going to kill you for coming outside," Cormac said.

"I don't care. They don't know anything. Haven't had an asthma attack in three years."

They'd walked out of sight of the farmhouse when Ben said, "What're we hunting?"

Cormac looked at him, wondering again how much he knew. Decided he didn't care. If Ben didn't know what was out there, he would by morning. "What killed my dad. Full moon's when they come out."

Ben turned the collar of his coat up around his jaw and walked beside Cormac, determined to keep up with the taller boy's easy stride. Their boots crunched on dry prairie grass and occasional crusts of snow. The air was searing cold, and their breath came out as fog.

God, why did he feel like such a little kid around Cormac?

Eventually, they reached the foothills and the first of the pine trees that became the forest that covered the mountains. The full moon was high, the air crisp and silent. They moved quickly enough that Ben didn't get cold.

He wondered if he should have brought a gun, too.

A song broke the night, a high-pitched note that held long, then sank into nothing.

Cormac stopped Ben with a hand on his arm. "Hear that?"

The sound had made his gut turn and his hair stand up. The thing that made it might have been far away, or watching them from the stand of trees a hundred yards off. Lots of animals lived out here, between prairie and mountain. Deer, elk, fox. Didn't see most of them most of the time. They knew how to hide, but they had ways of letting you know they were there.

"Coyotes?"

Cormac gave him a brief, pained look. "Wolf."

He knew Cormac was right, but he argued anyway. It made sense to argue. "There aren't any wolves around here."

"No, there aren't." He looked around, eyes narrowed, studying the world. Ben looked, too; he didn't know what he was looking for, except the shapes of his own fears. The shadows were so black and stark. He could see far, but the landscape wasn't familiar or friendly. He was the invader here, waiting for the attack that would have to come.

The wolf howl sounded again and was cut short. The tone of it echoed.

Ben wanted to suggest that maybe they go back to the house. But he wanted to see what Cormac was going to do.

There wasn't a wind for them to walk down of. On such a clear, still night, their scent would just float, and every sound they made thundered.

Cormac went to a stunted tree that had ventured onto the plain. It stood about four feet high and had only a few gnarled branches with spiky tufts of pine needles. He opened the paper bag he'd brought and pulled out something wrapped in butcher paper. From the wrapper, he removed a sizable piece of beef, raw and dripping. He must have taken it from the fridge. Mom was going to be livid.

He stabbed the meat through the end of a branch, then crumpled up the paper and stuffed it back in the bag. "Come on," he said, and nodded to a stand of trees fifty yards off. Ben followed, looking over his shoulder at the meat, wondering what would come to the bait.

They hunkered down in the shadow of the trees and waited. Now, Ben started to get cold. It seeped into his hands and feet first, then numbed his ears and nose. Cormac sat as still as a rock, not complaining, so Ben didn't dare thump his feet and clap his hands to warm them. He felt a cough tickling his lungs and swallowed it. He didn't need to cough. He wasn't going to catch pneumonia.

He couldn't stop his teeth from chattering. He tightened his jaw and wondered how Cormac could stand it. But then, Cormac had a reason for being here and the will to stay. Some family gossip said an animal had killed Cormac's father. But Cormac had shot dead the man who murdered him. So which was it?

"How long we going to wait?" Ben finally asked in a tense whisper.

"All night. Don't worry, it's not that cold. You won't freeze."

"I'm not worried," Ben said. "Just bored."

"Be quiet."

"You're crazy, you know that?"

"Shh!" He never took his gaze off the tree with the meat.

Ben tried to see inside his cousin's thoughts. "Is all this 'cause of your dad? I thought you already got what killed him. Don't see much point in this unless you just like shooting things."

What Ben really wanted was for Cormac to break. To get angry, shout, scream, cry, anything. His face never changed. His cold gaze kept staring out.

Then Cormac licked his lips. "My dad taught me how to do this. We went out every full moon. It's what he did. He taught me, and now I have to do it myself."

He put his gloved hand in his pocket, took it out fisted around something. He held his hand open to Ben. A bullet lay in Cormac's palm. Ben picked it up, held it to the moonlight, rolled it between his fingers. It shone, luminous and otherworldly. Silver.

Cormac was either crazy or he was right.

The part of hunting that most people couldn't stand was the waiting. Dad's business had been taking people into the back country, equipping them, guiding them, holding their hands so they could bag an elk or eight-point buck and take the trophies and stories back to their corporate boardrooms. High-end outfitting. They didn't have to like their clients—Cormac didn't, most of the time. Self-centered, heads up their butts. Treated Cormac and his dad like they were backwoods hicks. And they didn't understand waiting. Sometimes the best way to find your quarry was to sit still and wait for it. Know where they like to go, then park there and make yourself part of the landscape. The rich playboys wanted their kills *now*. They'd paid their money and couldn't understand why the animals didn't just walk up to them and bare their necks.

The attitude showed a severe lack of respect for the animals. They didn't understand—they couldn't, with only five days in the wilderness, with someone else pitching the tents and cooking their meals—that the smarter the animal, the harder the kill. The greater the challenge.

Dad taught him that these were the smartest animals out there. Hunting them was an art. Cormac could wait for it.

His cousin surprised him. Didn't fidget, didn't complain. Showing him the bullet had shut him up. At least he was smart. Seemed to be patient, too. Might make a good hunter.

Ben must have thought he was clever, trying to see through him like that. His words couldn't touch Cormac, though. Wasn't anything he hadn't already thought of. He didn't have nightmares about what happened, because he'd already seen his fears with his waking eyes. He'd already killed them. Nothing else could get him now. Especially not Ben.

This—this was just what he was supposed to do. His mission,

handed down from father to son for four generations. Sacred trust, Dad had called it.

Cormac kept his gaze soft. Wouldn't do any good to focus on the bait; his vision would close down to that one spot and he wouldn't see anything approach. He relaxed and took in as much of the land around him as he could, all the hills and trees, all the shadows that something could hide in, watching for that flicker of movement. The moonlit world was bright, but a kind of filtered brightness. The colors were all drained to black, white, charcoal, and deep blue.

Then, there it was. A rustle of movement, something four-legged gliding like fog. That hadn't taken long at all—the moon was still high.

It was a big one, two hundred pounds or so, three foot at the shoulder. Male. Dark gray, well camouflaged. Big and confident.

He waited. He'd been patient this long; a few more moments wouldn't matter. Wait until it had the bait, until it was occupied.

He braced the rifle under his arm and sighted down the barrel. There, under the ear, middle of the skull. He had him.

Something exploded. A gunshot, not his. Splinters flew out. Someone had shot the tree they'd sheltered by. Ben skittered sideways and curled up on the ground with his arms over his head.

Cormac looked out, followed the path from where bits of the tree were blown out, up the hill.

A figure dressed for winter hunting moved toward them, holding his own rifle ready to fire a second shot, right at Cormac.

He wasn't scared. It occurred to him that Ben had the right idea, huddling on the ground for protection. But Cormac found himself staring at the mouth of that weapon and not caring. He'd seen worse. He'd stared down worse. This was nothing. He stood his ground.

The wolf looked up and watched them with interest.

"Put your gun down!" the stranger shouted. His expression twisted with anguish.

"Why should I?" Cormac breathed, in and out, wondering if he was going to have to kill this guy to get to the wolf.

"I won't let you hurt him."

He kept moving closer, and Cormac knew he could shoot him. It was self-defense. His second shooting in as many months. The sheriff was going to love this. "That's close enough. Stop there."

He did. He looked a little like Cormac himself, young and desperate. Probably not much older. Mirror image. Not quite.

"What business is this of yours, if I shoot that thing on our property?"

"I can't let you do that. He's mine. My pet."

Not likely, not in a million years. Not that big, not that intelligent. The wolf still watched them. A real wolf would have run away by now. But this one knew what was happening, and Cormac grew angry that the stranger with the rifle would lie so blatantly.

"Do you know what it is?"

"Yes. Yes I do. He's my brother. I look after him."

Christ, did he think that changed anything? Didn't matter if he went around twenty-nine days out of the month on two legs, nicest guy in the world. Didn't matter at all, because that one day he was a killer. They gave men the chair for being killers. Cormac was just part of that process, in a roundabout way.

The wolf growled and started moving toward him. Cormac swung around to aim at it, ready to blow it away, this other guy be damned.

"No, Michael," the stranger said. "Stay back. Don't make it worse, please."

The wolf stopped and wagged its tail. Brothers. Cormac wouldn't have believed it.

Dad never taught him what to do in a mess like this. Monster was a monster, he'd always said. That was so perfectly clear when he'd been attacked last month. When he'd been killed.

And what if Dad had survived the attack? What if he'd turned into one of those things? What would Cormac have done, shot him?

"He hasn't hurt anyone," the stranger said. "Just let us go. Lower your gun and we'll walk away. I'm telling you, he hasn't hurt anyone!"

"How am I supposed to believe that?" Cormac's voice shook, tight with tears that he hadn't cried, not once.

"It's true. He listens to me. He's never hurt anyone."

He saw his father, his face ripped to shreds, throat torn open so the vertebrae of his neck were visible, blood pouring from arteries.

"But he might. Someday. If you're not around to stop him." Do it. He had the shot. For his father.

"You fire and I'll shoot you!"

He thought that Cormac actually cared, that he actually still had some life in him. "I'll get my shot off same time you shoot me. Your brother'll die, too."

"And I'll shoot your friend here right after."

Cormac looked at Ben, who was sprawled at his feet. Ben caught his gaze, begging him with his eyes. Even now he didn't complain, didn't shout or cry or anything. But he had those eyes, with fear locked down inside him.

Ben locked it down tight. His voice didn't waver when he said, "If you kill that wolf, he'll turn into a person, won't he? Like the guy that killed your dad."

Cormac nodded, wondered what he was going to do. Wondered if Ben's fear was right: that he would just as soon let his cousin die.

"Cormac, you have to let them go. He's just looking after his family. Like you."

Cormac almost lost it then, because Ben was wrong. Cormac wasn't looking after anything. He didn't care, didn't they see that? This was pure, meaningless revenge, because Ben was right, he'd already got the one that had killed his dad. And if he'd been faster, been less afraid, more ruthless, he might have been able to save his father. He should have been able to save him.

That would always be true, no matter how many monsters he killed. This wasn't about looking after family. Cormac should have done better, should have known better. Dad should still be alive. He'd know what to do.

Ben knew what to do.

Cormac lowered his rifle.

A heart-stopping moment later, the stranger lowered his. Cormac wouldn't have blamed him if he'd shot them all. That would have been the safest, most ruthless thing to do. "Come on, Michael," he said and backed away.

The wolf picked up the meat and trotted off. His brother followed him to the trees.

Ben got to his feet. His breaths wheezed a little, and Cormac remembered he'd mentioned asthma. Kid shouldn't have come along. Cormac shouldn't have let him. He should have helped him up off the ground. He thought about it too late.

Maybe he'd remember next time.

The wolf and the stranger disappeared into the trees, and Cormac's heart clenched. He'd missed his shot. His father would be disappointed.

At first, Ben wondered how he was going to keep his cousin from shooting—push the rifle away, yell at him, chase off the wolf, anything. He'd start a fight with Cormac, he didn't doubt that and didn't doubt that he'd lose badly—and that would get Cormac in trouble all over again with his folks. Wolves were endangered, he knew that much about them. Shooting one would bring down a lot of grief on Cormac, which he didn't need since his father died.

Then the stranger showed up, and he was the only one who'd walk away from this, Ben was sure.

Ben wondered at the story behind the pair: How did the brother get this way, and how long had they been doing this? How could someone be so devoted to a brother that he'd follow him into this?

How could Cormac be so devoted to his father that he'd follow him into this?

Ben had no doubt Cormac would let it happen. He only cared about killing the wolf, even if it meant they all died for it. Ben wondered if he could make a run for it. His lungs were already hurting. The stranger had hit the tree from farther off. He'd shoot Ben easy. No running away from that, even if his lungs could take it.

Cormac looked at him. His gaze was stony as ever, and the hard look didn't seem right on a smooth-faced kid. Ben didn't know if he stared back at a cold killer, or the cousin who shared his room. They couldn't possibly be the same person. Cormac had to pick one or the other.

Pick me, Ben pleaded silently. He didn't remember what he said—probably begging for his life like a snot-nosed kid.

Then it was over. The guns were lowered, and the stranger and the wolf—his brother—went away.

Ben started to get up. Hours must have passed, and he didn't think he'd ever be able to stand again, he was so stiff with cold. He managed it, his muscles creaking, his hands shaking.

"I should have shot him," Cormac said, clenching his rifle.

The pain of memories filled Cormac's eyes. Now that he'd seen the kind of reaction he'd wanted, Ben wished he could make it stop. Cormac was the strong one.

"Come on." Ben put his hand on Cormac's shoulder to turn him around. "Let's go home."

They walked in silence until the house came into view. No lights were on. They hadn't been discovered.

Off-handed, Cormac said, "Know how to shoot?"

Ben considered him. Something was different. He couldn't say how. Cormac still had that cold, rigid stance that made everyone so careful around him. But Ben didn't think times in the house would be so quiet and strained anymore.

"Course I do. Dad taught me." Couldn't live on a ranch with rifles and not know how to shoot. Everybody knew that.

"Maybe we could go hunting sometime."

Ben looked sharply at him.

He shrugged. "You know, coyotes. Or deer or something."

"Real hunting?"

"Yeah, sure. I mean, *I* know you can go out in the cold, even if your folks don't."

Ben bit back a grin. Couldn't let Cormac think he was excited or anything.

The moon set behind the hills.

God's Creatures

Cormac waited in the cab of his Jeep, watching each car that pulled into the rest area on I-25 north of Monument. So far, none of them looked like the one he was waiting for. A lot of truckers stopped here, with a few road-trippers thrown in, all shapes and sizes. McNeill would stand out, when he made his appearance.

Forty-five minutes after he was due, the aggressively souped-up pickup truck veered off the freeway and came up the lane. It had oversized tires, lights on the roll bar, a gun rack—empty for now—in the back window and a Confederate flag sticker on the bumper. McNeill was that kind of asshole.

Cormac stepped out of the Jeep; McNeill saw him and swerved to park a couple of spots down. The guy climbed out of his truck and dropped to the ground. He was tall and stocky, wearing worn jeans and a flannel shirt over a white tee. He shoved his hands in his pockets and pretended he wasn't cold in the winter air, but he was shrugging and tense, trying to keep warm. Cormac waited for him.

"You're supposed to be keeping your head down," Cormac said flatly, prodding on purpose, knowing it would piss McNeill off.

"What? My head's down." He looked around, frowning, appearing smug because there weren't any cops in sight. "What's your problem?"

"Registration sticker on your plate's expired. That's like waving a flag at the cops," Cormac said, nodding toward the back end of the truck.

"And I don't give a fucking cent to an illegal government." He pulled himself straighter, like he was daring Cormac to make a big deal out of it.

Yeah, McNeill was one of those. Didn't seem to care that the cops wouldn't get you on the weapons stockpiles or the conspiracy charges. They nailed you on back taxes and traffic violations. You covered your ass on the little things as the price of doing business. But that was why McNeill was a go-between and Cormac did the heavy lifting.

"What's the job?" Cormac asked.

He'd gotten a call two days ago. A rancher he'd worked with before had had some trouble—Cormac's kind of trouble. They both knew McNeill, who spent a lot of time traveling around the state, so he sent McNeill with the details you didn't talk about over the phone and the down payment. McNeill didn't know what exactly Cormac did. He probably assumed he was some kind of hit man.

Which was mostly true.

McNeill went back to his truck and returned with a manila envelope, which he handed to Cormac. He only took a brief look inside, finding a page of description and a business-sized envelope, thick with cash. There'd be ten hundred-dollar bills. He wasn't going to count it out in the open, but he did pull out a bill and hand it to McNeill for payment.

"Thanks," McNeill said, shoving the hundred in his pocket. "Good luck, man."

Cormac had already turned back to the Jeep.

He arrived at Joe Harrison's ranch in Lamar early the next morning. The old man was waiting for him on the front porch of the ramshackle house. The two-story building was probably close to a hundred years old. It needed a new roof and a coat of paint at the very least. But with a place like this, any extra money the family earned went right back into the ranch. The barns and fencing would get repairs before the house did.

"Thanks for coming," Harrison said as Cormac left the Jeep, and walked down to shake his hand. The rancher was in his sixties, his face furrowed and weathered, tough as leather from spending his life raising cattle out here. The kind of guy who was more at home with barbed wire and baling twine than a comfortable chair and a TV set.

"Let's take a look," Cormac said.

Harrison opened a gate in the fence, and they rode in Cormac's Jeep, straight across the prairie for about three miles. Harrison navigated by landmarks, pointing to show Cormac the way.

"There, it's right there," Harrison said finally, and Cormac stopped the Jeep.

Harrison led him to a spot where stands of scrub oak followed the contour of the hills, bordering the open plains. A carcass lay here, partly sheltered by the wind, flattening the grass. About a week old, Cormac guessed. The steer, a typical rust-and-cream-colored Hereford, had been savaged, its gut ripped open from sternum to tail, its face and tongue torn out, its throat flayed. Scavengers had been through since then—scraps of hair and bone radiated out from the remains. Most of what was left was leathery skin and hair over a ribcage and a leering, ragged skull.

"The second one's about a mile that way," Harrison said, pointing again. "And we had another one just last night."

They returned to the Jeep and drove east a mile or so. Cormac didn't need directions this time; he spotted the vultures circling overhead. When he pulled up near the spot, a pair of coyotes ran off, then hunkered down in the long grass, waiting to return to their meal in peace.

The other carcass had been dried out and picked over; it hadn't smelled like anything. The rotten, bloody stink of this one hit Cormac as soon as he left the Jeep.

"The others looked just like this one?" Cormac asked Harrison, who nodded. The rancher winced, turning his face away from the stench.

This one had been gutted like the other. Savaged, but not eaten. Guts and organs spilled out, pink flesh glistened on bones. The scavengers had had a meal handed to them. The weather was too cold for flies, which would have been swarming.

This was why Harrison had called him. They weren't dealing with a predator that killed because it needed to eat. This was a pure killer, and it was only a matter of time before it attacked someone. Cormac had seen this pattern before. A beast like this might start out with the best of intentions. It might flee to distant wilderness where it would kill a few rabbits or maybe a deer with no harm done. But then it would start to slide. It couldn't stay away from civilization forever. It would still have the bloodlust, but it wouldn't bother fleeing. Inhibitions would fail; it would struggle to keep from hurting anyone, but someday it would slip. It would attack livestock. Then it would finally give in to instinct and kill the human beings it hated because it was no longer one of them.

Cormac had to find the thing before that happened. Full moon was still a week off, but that didn't matter when one of them went bad. They could change anytime they wanted, and did mostly when they lost control.

"You have any idea who's doing this? Anybody notice any strangers around here? Someone who might be camping out? Or has someone in town started acting funny?"

"If I had any idea who it was I wouldn't need to call you," Harrison said, frowning.

Cormac stepped around the kill, looking for tracks, for the pattern of wolf pads as big as a man's face, with the matching puncture marks of claws. The winter had been dry so far, the ground was rock hard. He might not have found anything among the carpet of dead grasses, but werewolf claws were sharp and he found the little holes in the ground, as far apart as his spread hand. He threw his keys to Harrison. He'd left his rifles in the vehicle, but had a semiautomatic handgun in a shoulder holster, hidden under his leather jacket. "I'll meet you back at the house."

"What did you find?"

"Give me the afternoon, I'll let you know."

Harrison drove off in the Jeep, and Cormac followed the tracks.

The wolf could have run for miles. Cormac might be hiking all day—or at least as long as he could keep following his quarry. But for the first couple of miles the trail was clear; he found prints from one stride to the next, and on. The thing was headed in a straight line. Straight for home.

He reached the edge of the property, where Harrison was waiting at the Jeep. Cormac waved at him and kept going. The immense wolf tracks followed the ranch's dirt driveway, then paralleled the highway, back toward town.

So it was someone from town. Not some recluse cut off from civilization. That made it worse. This was civilization gone amok. A werewolf could only follow instinct, which would drive it back home, wherever that might be. A monster might kill its own family and not even know what it did. Cormac had to find it first.

Brick-dry prairie along the highway gave way to empty, weed-grown lots, dirt roads, then cracked pavement, then sidewalks. Weeds gave way to lawns and welcoming rows of houses with porches, screen doors, and family cars outside. This all gave Cormac a sense of foreboding, because he was still following the same tracks, sparse now but sure in their direction: the puncture marks of claws in garden soil, torn up tufts of grass. He'd lose the trail on pavement, but find it again after hunting along the margins of lawns. The trail was straight enough that he wondered if he'd find a man at the end of it, staring back at him with a wolf behind his eyes.

What he found, when the prints and claw marks ended, was an oblong of pressed earth against an old brick building—the kind of shape a person might have made if he'd curled up and went to sleep right there. The building was big, three stories, probably built around the turn of the last century. It might have been a schoolhouse. Why had the wolf come here?

There were no human footprints to follow—the distinctive claw marks had disappeared. Finally, he lost the trail.

He expanded his search, took in the area—the tall brick building seemed to be the center of a complex. One of the other buildings was definitely a school, like the kind built in the 1960s—low, one story, a flat roof, a grid of windows. Construction paper artwork hung in the windows in one classroom.

Across a lawn stood another antique building, this one with a high, peaked roof—a steeple with a cross on top. He went around to the front and read the stone marker there: Saint Catherine's.

This was a Catholic church and school.

He preferred the jobs where the wolf was an outcast who fled to wilderness—no witnesses.

At the end of this, he'd have to kill someone. There'd be a body, and the cops didn't take "He needed killin'" as an excuse. He could try to tell them the thing was a werewolf, but the end result wouldn't be much different. Prison, psych ward, same thing.

The fewer people saw him lurking around, the fewer people he talked to, the better. He needed to keep it so that the people who did spot him wouldn't be able to point the cops at him. When the body turned up, Harrison wouldn't turn him in—Harrison understood.

Cormac walked along the street, passing the school's grounds and trying to get a feel for the place. He only walked by once, normal, like he had someplace else to be. Several buildings made up the complex, including a couple of homey brick blocks that seemed to be dorms. Around back was a sports field, and a group of girls in matching gray sweatshirts and green sweatpants played soccer. Maybe aged fifteen to seventeen. So, a girls' boarding school, high school. It was a Saturday; they wouldn't be in class. There looked to be a couple of adults out with them, women in sweatpants and jackets. During the week there'd be teachers as well, and priest and staff for the church. They'd live on campus, too. In fact, behind the church he spotted what must have been the rectory, a small, square clapboard house attached to a meeting hall.

The werewolf could be any of them. A hundred possibilities, at least. He didn't know where to start.

When he was done with his quick survey, he cut back a couple of blocks, made his way to the highway again, and returned to Harrison's ranch. Dusk was falling.

Joe Harrison must have seen him coming through a window, and met him on the porch.

"You get it? Is it dead?" Harrison said.

Cormac didn't nod or shake his head, didn't say yes or no. "I'm working on it. Wondered if you could tell me anything about the Catholic school up the highway."

"Saint Catherine's? It's a reform school. All girls. Full of troublemakers."

"Really? I didn't see any fences."

Harrison chuckled. "Look around. Where are they going to run off to?"

"I tracked your killer there," Cormac said.

"You think it's one of them kids?" The rancher donned an eager, hungry look.

Cormac frowned, hoping it wasn't. He didn't want to have to go shooting a kid. "I guess I'll have to find out."

Harrison shook his head. "Wouldn't that just figure?"

"You know about any rumors, any suspicions about anyone there? Hear about anything odd?"

"They're Catholics," he said with a huff, as though that explained everything. "You know somebody's always talking about the priest there, if you want rumors."

Cormac rubbed the back of his neck and looked to the distance, to the flat horizon. The sky was deep blue, turning black with the setting sun. "That's not a lot of help."

"I'm just telling you what you asked for. Hey, how long's this thing going to take? When am I going to be able to let my herd graze again?"

"I'll let you know when it's done. By the full moon for sure."

"That's a week away."

"Sure is. But I'll finish when I finish." He turned away.

"I wish Douglas was here working on this," Harrison called after him.

Douglas was Cormac's father. Harrison had known him—that was how he'd known to call Cormac.

Cormac didn't slow down. "Yeah. Well. You got me instead."

He kept watch on the ranch through the night; the werewolf might return to where it had found easy pickings before. Harrison had penned up the cattle since last night's attack, and the animals crowded the corrals, milling and murmuring unhappily. Cormac kept walking the plains around the ranch house, covering half a dozen miles over the course of a couple of hours. He didn't see anything. He didn't even get that crawling feeling on his neck, like something was watching him. It was just another cold night.

In the morning, he reclaimed his Jeep and found a ratty motel at the edge of town, where he talked the desk clerk into letting him have a room early. The clerk gave some bullshit about the rooms not being clean, but Cormac only counted three cars in the lot and at least two dozen rooms. Places like this didn't have check-in times he told the guy and paid cash in advance.

He brought his weapons case into the room and looked over his collection one more time. A revolver, two semiautomatics, a shotgun, and a pair of rifles. The revolver was mostly to show off. He wore it when he needed to cop attitude, when a potential client expected the tough guy, the Old West gunslinger. And the boxes of ammunition for each of them: nine-millimeter silver rounds for the semis, silver filings in the shotgun shells, and so on. If he couldn't take down the quarry with this, he likely couldn't take it down at all. He'd never needed more than this. He also had a bowie knife with silver inlay. The bone handle was worn. His father had told him it had belonged to *his* grandfather. His family had been doing this a long time, apparently.

He couldn't be sure; his father hadn't finished telling him all the stories when he'd died, when Cormac was sixteen. Harrison was right; it ought to be his father out here doing this.

After a quick shower and a change into some slightly less grungy clothes, Cormac went to church.

He hadn't been to church—any kind of church—since he was in high school and living with his aunt and uncle. They were some flavor of born-again Christian, and services had involved sitting on hard metal folding chairs in a plain room—rented office space—listening to fire-and-brimstone lectures. He hadn't been back since he'd gone out on his own. He'd never been to a Catholic church at all. He used the tools, of course, holy water and crosses, when he had to. But they were just tools. Any God he believed in wasn't like the one most preachers talked about.

The service had already started when he arrived. He stepped softly inside and found a seat on the bench in back. No one seemed to pay any attention to him. The church smelled of old wood, melted wax, and incense. The architecture was maybe a hundred years old, lots of dark wood, aged and smooth. The benches—pews—might have been mahogany, but there were pale scuff marks around the edges, where generations of bodies had banged into them. Pale stained glass decorated the tall windows along the walls.

He had a good view of the congregation: a hundred or so girls in front, identical in pressed uniforms; a bunch of plain folk from the town; the priest in a white cassock, standing in front, leading a prayer; and nuns, maybe a dozen, in prim black dresses, sitting in the rows with the girls. Their heads were bare—short and simple haircuts for the most part, no veils—which surprised him. He'd expected them to look like they did in the movies, with the weird hats and veils.

There were altar girls instead of altar boys. Probably students from the school. Cormac didn't know there was such a thing as altar girls.

During communion, everyone stood, filed down the central aisle, faced the priest with hands raised, accepted the host, and marched back to their seats. Cormac was able to look at nearly every person there. Sometimes, he could spot a werewolf in human form just by looking. The way they moved, the body language—more canine than human, hunched over, glaring outward, walking like they had a tail raised behind them. The gleam in their eyes, like they'd kill you as soon as look at you. Ones who were losing control, like Harrison's cattle killer, had a harder time hiding it.

He didn't spot anyone who made him suspicious.

The service ended, the priest and altar girls processed out as the congregation sang, accompanied by one of the nuns playing a piano that sounded tinny in the big space. The congregation followed, filtering down the central aisle and two aisles to the sides. Cormac made his escape as part of the crowd. He lingered at the corner of the church building, watching. He still wasn't getting a sense off anyone. In his experience, werewolves didn't do well in crowds. They sometimes lived in packs of their own kind, but didn't cope well around normal human beings. They saw people as prey. A werewolf wouldn't go to church and be part of a crowd like this—unless his absence would be out of the ordinary and noted. He'd followed the tracks back to town—this wolf was trying to hang on to normal. Maybe he was here and hiding really well. Maybe Cormac would have to stir things up a bit to flush him.

But not right here. Not right now.

He was about to walk away, back to his Jeep and the next part of his plan, when he caught sight of someone coming toward him. One of the nuns; he felt a completely irrational moment of fear. Too many stories about nuns in the collective unconscious; he wasn't even Catholic. It wasn't a mistake—she'd broken from the lingering crowd and come toward him.

Tall, solid, with short gray hair and soft features, jowly almost. She might have been as old as the priest, and had the air of an aunt rather than a grandmother. Stern, maybe, rather than kind. Someone who had spent a lifetime bullying girls at a reform school, smacking knuckles with rulers and all. He was letting stereotypes get the better of him again.

He supposed he could have just ignored her and walked away. What was she going to do, run after him? The last thing he wanted to do was raise suspicions. It wouldn't cost him anything to find out what she wanted.

"Good morning," she said, when she stopped in front of him, hands folded before her, pressed to her skirt.

"Hi," he said, then waited for her to say what she wanted.

"We like to welcome visitors who might be new to the parish," she said. "I wondered if I could answer any questions for you, about the parish or the town."

He probably shouldn't have been instantly suspicious of anyone who showed him the least bit of friendliness. Some people might accuse him of paranoia. But the woman wasn't smiling.

"I'm just passing through, ma'am," he said.

"Oh? Where are you headed?"

He couldn't blame her for looking a little confused there. Lamar wasn't really on the way to anywhere else.

"Denver, eventually," he said.

"Ah. Well then. I hope your travels are safe."

Cormac left. She continued watching him; he could just about feel it.

Back at his motel room, he slept for a few hours, getting ready for another long night. He dreamed; he always dreamed, vague images and feelings, a sense of some treasure just out of reach, or some danger just within reach. That if he was just a little faster, just a little smarter, he could make everything—his life, his past—better. He usually woke feeling nervous. He'd gotten used to it.

Later that afternoon, just before business closing time, he found a butcher shop in town and bought a couple pounds of a low-grade cut of beef, bloody as he could get it. At an ancient Safeway, he picked up a five-pound bag of flour.

Around 10:00 P.M., well after sunset, when most folk were heading to bed—when someone else might be trying to sneak out—he returned to the school. At the edge of the campus, along the trail of claw prints he'd followed back from the ranch, he staked out the bait.

A wind blew in from the prairie, almost constant in this part of the state, varying from a whisper of dry air to tornado-spawning storms. Tonight, the breeze was occasional, average. Cormac marked it and moved across it, away from the meat he'd hung from a low branch on a cottonwood. The wind would only carry the meat's scent, not his. The hunter scattered flour on the ground underneath the meat, forming a thin, subtle layer. If the wolf ran away, this would make it easy to track.

He went across the street and found a place near a dusty, unused garage, a hundred yards or so away, to hunker down. He let his gaze go soft, taking in the whole scene, keeping a watch on the bait and the paths leading to it.

Time passed. The moon rose, just a few days from full. However much the werewolf might resist the urge, might control himself until then, at the full moon he would be forced to come out. Then Cormac would have him.

Midnight came and went, and the wolf never showed up to take the bait. It must have satiated the bloodlust on the cattle. It was being careful, now.

After a couple more hours of waiting with no results, he dismantled the trap—took down the meat and brushed his boot across the flour until it was scattered and ground into the dust and lawn. Covering his own tracks.

He returned to the rattrap motel to try to get some sleep, and to come up with the next plan.

The sky was black. It was that time of night when streetlights—and even this town had a few—seemed to dim, unable to hold back the dark. In just a couple of hours, the night would break, the sky would turn gray, and the sun would rise pink in the east. He'd stayed up and watched it happen enough nights he could almost set his clock by the change in light. But right now, before then, the night was dark, cold, clammy; 3:00 A.M. had a smell all its own.

He switched off the headlights as he slipped into a parking space in front of his room. The motel was a one-story, run-down strip, a refugee from 1950s glory days, with peeling white paint and a politically incorrect sign out front, showing a faded screaming Indian holding a tomahawk: The Apache. All lights were out, the place was dark, not a soul awake and walking around. No witnesses.

Cormac set foot on the asphalt and hesitated. He listened to instinct; when his gut poked him, he trusted it. Something wasn't right. Something was out there. Slowly, he pulled the rifle from under the Jeep's front seat.

There wasn't any place to hide out here; the land around the motel was flat as a skillet, with no trees, only a few buildings, and the motel itself. The two-lane highway stretched out to either direction straight and empty. Cormac didn't hear footsteps, breathing, a humming engine, nothing. He didn't see a flicker of movement except for grasses touched by a faint breeze. He had no sign that anything was out there, except for the tingling hairs on the back of his neck screaming at him that something inhuman was watching.

It thumped onto the roof of the Jeep, slamming the metal, rocking the whole vehicle. Cormac ducked, hitting asphalt, as the oversized wolf skittered across the steel and leapt to the ground in front of him.

The door to the Jeep was still open; Cormac jumped inside, scrambling backward, and slammed it shut as the wolf crashed into it on its next attack. Its front claws scraped against the window, digging against the slick surface, snapping at the glass with open jaws and spit-covered teeth.

The damned werewolf had tracked him. No—it hadn't even needed to track him. The Apache was the cheapest motel in town. It just had to lie in wait.

It hadn't made a sound, not a growl or a snarl. It had just pounced, ready to rip him apart. On its hind legs now, it was as tall as the Jeep, larger than a natural wild wolf, because it weighed as much as its human form—conservation of mass. A wild wolf might be around a hundred, hundred twenty pounds. A big werewolf would be close to two hundred. This one was maybe a hundred sixty, hundred eighty. However large it was, however shocking it was to see a wolf as tall as his Jeep, this wasn't the largest he'd ever seen. Not a two-hundred pounder. It was thin, rangy. It had speed rather than bulk. Its coat was mostly gray, edged with beige and black. Prairie colors.

The werewolf backed off a moment, then sprang at the Jeep again, crashing full force into the window. The glass cracked.

Cormac couldn't stay in here forever. And he wasn't going to get a better shot than this. He fired.

The rifle thundered in the closed space of the Jeep, rattling Cormac's ears to numbness. The glass of the driver's side window frosted with a million cracks radiating from a quarter-sized hole in the middle. The wolf had vanished.

He couldn't hear a damn thing, and he wasn't willing to bet he'd blown the thing's head off that easy; he couldn't spot any blood. He looked around, but couldn't see much, lying back across the front seats, peering out the remaining windows, mostly into sky.

Struggling to his knees, he broke out the driver's side window with the muzzle of his rifle, dropping a rain of glass outside, and looked out. Shards of glass glittered across the asphalt. He didn't see the wolf. Definitely didn't see blood. Which meant it had ducked and run. Making his life harder.

He made a quick three sixty, looking out every window, hoping to see where it had fled. Werewolves were fast, but he should have seen something, a flash of movement, the lupine form dashing madly to safety. Otherwise, it was still here, hiding low and out of sight next to the Jeep. He wasn't going to go outside until he knew.

Even if he did manage to kill the thing in a head-to-head fight, facing it down meant risking getting bitten or scratched, which was as good as dead as far as Cormac was concerned. No sense in taking stupid risks, that was the trick.

He started the engine and backed away. Right away he heard a *thunk* against the side, and saw what he was hoping for—the wolf scrambling away from the vehicle, turning tail and running away across the parking lot.

The other trick was realizing werewolves didn't generally take stupid risks, either. Instinct told them to run when a hunt stopped being easy.

Cormac shoved open the door, stepped out, took aim with the rifle, and fired. The wolf disappeared around the side of the building.

"Damn," he murmured. He'd have known right away if he'd even clipped the wolf. All he had to do was clip it. The silver in the bullet only had to touch the monster's blood to poison it, killing it in a matter of moments. That wolf hadn't slowed down. Cormac had just plain missed. He could kick himself. He didn't miss very often, even when his target was running.

But he'd flushed the thing into the open. That was something. The game wasn't over yet.

The engine in the Jeep was still running, and Cormac got in

and headed back toward the Catholic school. Maybe he could run the thing down. Not to mention, he didn't want to be around when the cops arrived to investigate the gunfire. Assuming they did. He glanced in the rearview mirror; the motel was still dark. No lights had turned on. He had to smile—small town on the plains, random gunfire in the middle of the night, and nobody bats an eye. They probably thought it was some kid out shooting street signs. Good enough.

He couldn't hope to follow the wolf in the Jeep—the beast traveled overland, in a straight line. Cormac had to stick to streets. But that was okay. The sun had started rising. Monday morning, the school would be busy, just starting its day. Good. Easy for Cormac to tell who was missing, then.

He was too close to identifying the wolf to worry too much about his low profile. Parked in his Jeep, he watched the campus come to life, girls in their uniforms spilling from the dorms in clumps—packs, almost—hanging around on the lawns, filing into the classrooms.

Then came his turn. He kept the rifle under the seat, automatically felt for the handgun under his jacket, and headed toward the newer school building, where most of the activity was. He scanned the faces quickly, efficiently, recognizing many of them from the church service yesterday. His wolf was around a hundred and seventy pounds, and he searched his mental catalog for anyone he'd seen who fit that description. That ruled out most of the students. But a number of the adults were that size. It would all depend on who was missing, who was away, sleeping it off.

He entered the school and made his way down the main corridor, knowing he was out of place here; his skin crawled as people looked at him, stared at him, identified him as a stranger. Wasn't anything he could do about that, so he concentrated on the job at hand. He walked up and down the hallway once, glancing through the windows in classroom doors, marking faces, noting rooms that didn't have a teacher in them, making a mental checklist of other staff members he ought to be looking for—administrators, even janitors. He hadn't seen anything definitive, nothing that worked on his gut feeling. In a sense, he was trying to prove a negative here, trying to prove an identity by its absence. He had to make sure. He couldn't be wrong when he pulled the trigger.

The building had a lobby, and he waited there while the last of the morning crowd came in and made their way to their classes. A few of the nuns were also teachers—he noted them. He also noted that he didn't see the nun who'd spoken to him yesterday. But maybe she wasn't a teacher. He also hadn't seen the priest. At least, not until he went back outside, where the man was waiting for him on the sidewalk out front.

Out of his cassock now, the man wore plain black trousers and a black shirt with a clerical collar. As Cormac left the building, the priest caught his gaze and started toward him. Cormac could have avoided him, but he'd just as soon hear what the guy had to say. He looked to weigh about a hundred and seventy.

Cormac waited, and the priest stopped in front of him. "You must be the visitor Sister Hilda told me about. I'm Father Patrick." He didn't offer his hand. Neither did Cormac, who only nodded a greeting. The priest didn't seem to mind that Cormac didn't say his name. "You seem to be looking for something," he said.

Cormac kept it straightforward. "There's a wild animal been killing cattle out east of here. I tracked it here. You see anything? Hear anything?"

"And here I was, hoping you were looking for redemption."

In spite of himself, Cormac chuckled. "No. Not yet, anyway."

"Maybe someday, then."

In fact, Cormac was pretty sure he wouldn't make it that far. It didn't bear thinking on. "So I take it you haven't seen anything? If the thing's bedding down around here, you ought to be worried. All these kids around."

Father Patrick gave him a quizzical look. "It's that dangerous?"

"Yeah, it is. I think it'll kill anything in front of it."

"You make it sound like a monster," Father Patrick said.

"Yeah, that's about right."

"And why is it up to you to hunt it? You aren't with the Department of Wildlife, I suspect."

"No, sir. Look, I won't take up any more of your time—"

"Not at all." The priest made a calming gesture with a hand. Like a saint in a religious painting. "But I would ask you to consider letting this go. I'd hate to have to call the police about a trespassing violation."

Cormac just smiled. He'd heard shit like this a hundred times before. "I'll get out of your hair, then." He started to turn away.

"Also consider, that even a monster is a creature of God, and God does take care of His own," the priest said.

Cormac looked at him. "You believe in a God that creates monsters? Monsters who murder?"

"We don't get to choose God. We don't get to make God. God makes us."

He knows, Cormac thought. Or maybe—but he couldn't have been the werewolf, the timing was off. He wouldn't have had enough time to shift back to human, dress, and appear so calm and put together. At least, Cormac was pretty sure he wouldn't have had enough time.

"You know who it is," Cormac said. "You know *what* it is. Then you know it's a devil, a demon—"

"And we're all God's children," Father Patrick said firmly. "I'm going to make that phone call now."

Cormac walked away.

It could be the priest. If he'd been a werewolf a long time, if he had the experience, maybe he could shape-shift that quickly and appear so calm just an hour after attacking Cormac, after getting shot at. But Cormac wasn't sure that made any sense.

Something screwy was going on here. Cormac didn't care what the old man said, he had to take care of it. He had to make the kill soon, because the full moon was still a couple days away and he had a feeling that would be too late. That monster this morning wasn't a creature of God; it was a pure cold killer. A child of Satan. Didn't matter what kind of fancy theology you dressed it up in.

Someone was lounging on the hood of his Jeep. One of the

students—an honest-to-God Catholic schoolgirl in a knee-length plaid skirt, cardigan, crisp shirt, and maroon tie, the knot hanging loose, about halfway down her chest. Her black hair—dyed, probably—was in a ponytail, with loose wisps hanging around her face. She was looking away at something and seemed to be chewing gum.

This place was too damn crowded, and too many people had seen him already.

Cormac was practically in front of her when she decided to look at him.

He made the automatic assessment: she was older, maybe seventeen, and full grown. "Big boned" was the polite way of describing her sturdy frame. Not quite big enough to be the wolf from last night. But he had to acknowledge the rather predatory look to her. She definitely didn't seem afraid of him.

"What's your story?" he said, resting his hands on his hips.

"I was framed," she said. "They weren't my drugs."

Chuckling, he looked away. "You out here scuffing up my Jeep for a reason?"

She gave the Jeep a long, pointed look. Pale mud caked the wheel wells, the paint job had gone from olive green to pale green over the years, and rust spots had broken out across the hood, where the paint had been dinged by rocks and hail. Not to mention the shot-out window.

"I heard you talking to Father Patrick. And . . . I don't know. I shouldn't even be here." She slumped away from the Jeep and started to walk away.

"Hold on there," Cormac said. "What have you seen?"

She glanced nervously toward the school and bit her lip—a physical expression of the tension he'd been feeling since he arrived. So it wasn't just him. "The other kids tell ghost stories. They talk about hearing noises—howling, banging on the windows. When I first got here, I thought it was just the usual thing; they're always trying to scare the new girl. But they don't go out at night. This is my third boarding school and I've never been to one where kids didn't break curfew. But here, they don't. They're scared."

"You know that for sure?"

"Yeah. And it's not just them. No one goes out at night. It's the kids who double-check the locks on the doors and windows. We've all heard the noises. The sisters say it's bears or coyotes. But I don't think that's what it is."

"And what do you think it is?"

She ducked her gaze. "It's crazy."

Cormac gave a wry smile. "People always say that to me. Listen, something killed some cattle on a ranch ten miles or so out, and it wasn't coyote or bear. I tracked the thing back here. I think it may be living around here, and I think it's not going to stay happy just killing livestock."

The fearful look in her eyes showed shock, but not surprise. He had a feeling he could have said the word "werewolf," and she wouldn't have been surprised.

"I'll get it," Cormac said. "Whatever it is."

"Okay. Good," she said. Her smile was nervous. "I should get back—"

"Hey," he said, before she could scurry away. He had a bad idea and hated himself for even thinking it. "Would you mind doing something for me?"

He asked the girl to walk across the campus at midnight. That was all. Back and forth between the dormitory and the old school building, across the longest stretch of lawn, slowly and leisurely. She'd looked at him like he was crazy, and Cormac hadn't wanted to defend himself. He wasn't crazy, just driven. And he lived in a different world than most folks, a world where monsters like vampires and werewolves existed.

Which was, in fact, one definition of crazy.

Cormac had promised he would be there, that he wouldn't let anything happen to her. And that he would fix whatever the trouble was. He tried to tell himself that even if something did happen to her, it was a small price for getting rid of the werewolf. He didn't ask for her name on purpose.

He was nervous. He'd never worked with live bait before. Not intentionally.

He left the Jeep, plastic sheeting taped over the driver's side window, at the motel. It would be too hard to hide, and the werewolf would recognize it right off. Easier to sneak around on his own. But without the Jeep he didn't have an escape route.

It was all in the setup. No reason he'd need an escape route, unless this went south. Really far south.

The open lawn separated the campus's buildings from the street. A few trees, towering cottonwoods for the most part, with some maples scattered around and a few clumps of shrubs made up the landscaping. Not a lot of cover available. A long sidewalk led from the street to the church doors, and a couple of tall, well-trimmed shrubs served as a sort of gate at the end of the sidewalk. Cormac settled here with his rifle. The spot offered a view of the lawn, and was downwind from most of the campus. The werewolf wouldn't be able to smell him.

He arrived early and waited there for more than an hour. All the lights in all the buildings went off at 10:00 P.M., except for a porch light over the door of the church. A faint light was visible within as well, over the altar, filtered through stained glass. Cormac supposed the door to the church was unlocked, if tradition held. Maybe that would be his escape route. Ironic.

Midnight came, and he didn't see anything. The girl might have decided not to help him after all. He couldn't blame her. He'd give it another half hour, then go looking for the monster himself. He had to be able to flush the werewolf out somehow. Quietly, he flexed his legs and arms, stretching in place to keep the blood flowing, to keep warm.

There she was. He recognized the dark figure by the shape of her ponytail. Out of the uniform, she wore torn jeans and hugged a short leather coat around herself, hunched over, as if cold or fearful. She stomped down the walk aggressively, like she had something to prove. Cormac might have wished for her to be more skittish—to move like a prey animal. But she was alone, obviously nervous. That would have to do to attract the wolf.

She made her way quickly across the open space, taking the concrete sidewalk from the dorms to the school building. She moved more quickly than he'd have preferred, just short of jogging, looking nervously around her the whole time.

The werewolf wasn't going to go for such obvious bait, Cormac decided. But he wondered. It was losing control, that much was clear. Killing livestock was the first step. Attacking people was the next. It had to know it was losing control—so why stay here? The town was rural, but this spot was full of tempting targets—a hundred kids, easy pickings. He had to conclude that the monster just didn't care. Or the thing thought it could handle itself—and it was wrong.

Even if the werewolf was too smart to go after such an obvious target as the girl, Cormac was pretty sure the monster still had a bone to pick with him, so to speak. One way or another, the werewolf would make an appearance.

The girl was two-thirds of the way to the school building when he saw it, a shadow pouring across the lawn. It wasn't stalking; it had already targeted her and was running, ready to strike. Wolves hunted by running, smashing into their prey, which they knocked over as they anchored their jaws and teeth in its flesh. The girl wouldn't even see it happen. She might have enough time to scream.

No hesitation, Cormac stood, braced, aimed, and fired, all in the same motion, as reflexive as breathing.

The wolf fell and cried out.

Cormac walked toward it and fired again. The wolf flinched again. It rolled over itself in a chaos of fur, biting at its own flank, whining in pain.

The girl had stopped, frozen in fear or panic, hands to her face. Then she stepped forward, arm outstretched as if to comfort the monster.

"Get inside! Get inside right now!" Cormac yelled at her. She ran inside the dorm and slammed the door.

The silver ought to be traveling through the wolf's veins, ought to be poisoning its heart and killing it in slow agony. The beast looked to the sound of Cormac's voice and snarled, lips pulled away from gleaming teeth, hackles bristling. Then the wolf turned and ran.

A last burst of adrenaline, a final gasp before death. This thing wasn't going to go down so easy after all. But it was only a matter of time.

Cormac jogged after it as it ran, trailing drops of blood, to the church.

The wolf had slowed to a stumbling trot, limping badly, to the front steps of the church, where Father Patrick was waiting for it.

Cormac watched dumbfounded as the priest guided the injured wolf inside and closed the door behind them. He ran up the steps and stopped himself against the door, rattling the handle. Locked, the son of a bitch.

On the plus side, it was an old lock on an old wooden door, a latch and not a deadbolt. He stood back, put his shoulder to it and rammed hard, and again. The wood splintered. The third time, the latch ripped out of the wood and he was inside.

A shaded electric light illuminated the altar area of the church, at the far end of a long aisle. Father Patrick and the werewolf had made it about halfway there. A trail of blood dripped unevenly along the hardwood floor from them to the door. Cormac stepped around it, hesitating at the last pew.

The wolf was gone. Father Patrick held Sister Hilda's body on his lap. Two bloody wounds were visible on her naked back, blackened from the poison. Dark streaks of silver-poisoned blood crawled up her back and down her legs, along the veins.

Cormac's hands flexed, ready to raise the rifle and aim at Father Patrick.

"She smelled you. Sunday, after Mass. She knew what you were. She told me. Told me to be careful." His voice was stretched to breaking, but he held the tears back. He didn't look at Cormac but kept his gaze on the woman. "She controlled it for forty years. She took orders to help her control it, and it worked. The routine, the structure of this life—it worked for so long. I helped her, helped take care of her. But she was losing the fight, she knew she was losing. I suppose I should thank you for doing this before she hurt anyone. She isn't a killer. And she's with God now. This wasn't her fault."

What a story. And of course it wasn't her fault, it was never anyone's fault, was it?

"This is just God playing tricks, is it?" Cormac said, his voice flat, his patience thin. He just wanted to get out of here.

"God sends us obstacles," Father Patrick said. "It's up to us to overcome them. Like she did."

He'd killed a monster, Cormac reassured himself. He'd done the right thing, here. He knew it.

"I have to ask—are you infected, too? Has she ever bitten you?" Cormac asked. He'd shoot the man right here if he said yes, if he even hesitated, if he gave the slightest hint that the werewolf had bitten him.

The priest shook his head and murmured, "No."

There were ways of telling for sure. Slice his skin with a regular knife and watch if it healed fast. Slice it with the silver-inlaid knife and watch if he died from it. But Father Patrick didn't have the wolfish look in his eyes. He didn't have the rage, the tension like he was holding something back. Cormac believed him and left him alone.

Cormac retreated from the school without saying anything to the girl. He'd already done a piss-poor job of covering his tracks; no need to make it worse. At dawn's light, he checked out of the motel and showed up on Harrison's doorstep.

He knocked on the front door and waited for Harrison to answer, which he did after a couple of minutes. His wife was looking over his shoulder, until he barked at her to leave them alone.

"Did you finally get it?" the rancher asked.

"Yeah, I got it."

"Who was it?"

"It doesn't matter. But you won't have any more problems."

"And where's your proof that you got it?"

"Talk to Father Patrick over at the church. He'll tell you."

Harrison frowned, plainly not happy with that idea. "Just a minute, then."

He went inside, leaving Cormac standing alone on the porch.

Didn't even invite him in for morning coffee. Mrs. Harrison would have invited him in, which was maybe why Mr. Harrison had ordered her away. Folk didn't like having Cormac around much more than they liked having the monsters. Two sides of the same coin in some ways, Cormac supposed. Though Sister Hilda never killed anyone, did she? And Cormac had. Over and over.

Harrison returned with a fat envelope to round out the job. He didn't hand it to Cormac so much as reluctantly hold it out, making Cormac take it from him.

"You can let your herd out, now," Cormac said, instead of thanking a man like Harrison.

"Well. I'm glad the bastard's gone. I hope it died painful, I hope—"

"Shut up, Harrison," Cormac said, exhausted on a couple of levels. "Just—just shut up."

Tucking the blood money in his jacket, Cormac walked back to his Jeep, feeling the rancher's gaze on his back the whole time.

He drove away from Lamar, away from the morning sun, as fast as he could.

WILD RIDE

Just once, he wouldn't use a condom. What could happen? But it hadn't been just once. It could have been any one of the half-dozen men he'd drifted between over the last two years. His wild years, he thought of them now. He'd been so stupid. They all had said, just once, trust me. T.J., young and eager, had wanted so very much to please them.

"I'm sorry," the guy at the clinic said, handing T.J. some photocopied pages. "You have options. It's not a death sentence like in the old days. But you'll have to watch yourself. Your health is more important than ever now. And you have to be careful—"

"Yeah, thanks," T.J. said, standing before the counselor had finished his spiel.

"Remember, there's always help—"

T.J. walked out, crumpling the pages in his hand.

Engines purred, sputtered, grumbled, clacked like insects, and growled like bears. Motorbikes raced up the course, a barren, cratered landscape of tracks, channels, hills, and ridges. Catching air over hills, leaning into curves, biting into the earth with treaded tires, kicking up clods, the swarm of bikes gave the air a smell like chalk and gasoline. Hundreds more idled, revved, tested, waited. Thousands of people milled, riders in fitted jackets of every color, mechanics in coveralls, women bursting out of too-small tank tops, and most people in T-shirts and jeans. T.J. loved it here. Bikes made sense. Machines could be fixed, their problems could be solved, and they didn't judge.

He supposed he ought to get in touch with his partners. Figure out which one had passed the disease on to him and who he might have passed it on to. Easier said than done. They'd been flings; he didn't have phone numbers.

"Look it, here he comes." Mitch, Gary Maddox's stout, good-natured assistant, shook T.J.'s arm in excitement.

Gary's heat was starting. T.J. looked for Gary's colors, the red and blue jacket and dark blue helmet. He liked to think he could pick out his bike's growl over all the others. T.J. had spent the morning fine-tuning the engine, which had never sounded better.

They'd come up to one of the hills overlooking the track to watch the race. T.J. wanted to lose himself in this world, just for another day. He wanted to put off thinking about anything else for as long as possible.

The gate slammed down, and the dozen bikes rocketed from the starting line, engines running high and smooth. Gary pulled out in front early, like he usually did. Get in front, stay in front, don't let anyone else screw up his ride. Some guys liked messing with the rest of the field, playing mind games and causing trouble. Gary just wanted to win, and T.J. admired that.

Mitch jumped and whooped with the rest of the crowd, cheering the riders on. T.J. just watched. Another rider's bike, toward the back, was spitting puffs of black smoke. Something wrong there. Everyone else seemed to be going steady. Gary might as well have been floating an inch above the dirt. That was exactly how it was supposed to be—making it look easy.

"Ho-*leee*!" Mitch let out a cry and the crowd let out a gasp as one of the riders went down.

T.J. could tell it was going to happen right before it did, the way the rider—in the middle of the pack to the outside—took the turn too sharply to make up time, gunned his motor a little too early, and stuck his leg out to brace, a dangerous move. His front tire caught, the bike flipped, and it might have ended there. A dozen guys dropped their bikes one way or another every day out here. But everything was set up just wrong for this guy. Momentum carried the bike into the straw bale barrier lining the track—then over and down the steep slope on the other side. Bike and rider finally parted ways, the bike spinning in one direction, trailing parts. The few observers who'd hiked up the steep vantage scattered in its path. The rider flopped and tumbled in another direction, limp and lifeless, before coming to rest faceup on a bank of dirt.

For a moment, everyone stood numb and breathless. Then the ambulance siren started up.

Red flags stopped the race. Mitch and T.J. stumbled down their side of the hill to get to the rider.

"You know who he is?"

"Alex Price," Mitch said, huffing.

"New on the circuit?"

"No, local boy. Big fish, little pond kind of guy."

The rider hadn't moved since he stopped tumbling. Legs shouldn't bend the way his were bent. Blood and rips marred his clothing. T.J. and Mitch reached him first, but both held back, unwilling to touch him. T.J. studied the rider's chest, searching for the rise and fall of breath, and saw nothing. The guy had to have been pulverized. Then his hand twitched.

"Hey, buddy, don't move!" Mitch said, stumbling forward to his knees to hold the rider back.

T.J. thought he heard bones creaking, rubbing against each other as the rider shuddered, pawing the ground to find his bearings. Next to Mitch, he tried to keep the rider still with a hand on his shoulder. Price flinched as if shrugging him away, and T.J. almost let go—the guy was strong, even now. Maybe it was adrenaline.

The ambulance and EMTs arrived, and T.J. gratefully got out of the way. By then, the rider had taken off his own helmet and mask. He had brown hair a few inches long, a lean tanned face covered with sweat. He gasped for breath and winced with pain. When he moved, it was as if he'd slept wrong and cramped his muscles, not just tumbled over fifty yards at forty miles an hour.

At his side, an EMT pushed him back, slipped a breathing mask over his face, started putting a brace on his neck. The second EMT brought over a backboard. Price pushed the mask away.

"I'm *fine,*" he muttered.

"Lie *down,* sir, we're putting you on a board."

Grinning, Price laid back.

T.J. felt like he was watching something amazing, miraculous. He'd *seen* the crash. He'd seen plenty of crashes, even plenty that looked awful but the riders walked away from them. He'd also seen some that left riders broken for life, and he'd thought this was one of those. But there was Price, awake, relaxed, like he'd only stubbed a toe.

Price rolled his eyes, caught T.J.'s gaze, and chuckled at his gaping stare. "What, you've never seen someone who's invincible?"

The EMTs shifted him to the board, secured the straps over him, and carried him off.

"Looks like he's gonna be okay," Mitch said, shrugging away his bafflement. T.J. stared after Price and that mad smile in the face of destruction.

Invincible, T.J. thought. There wasn't any such thing.

At the track the following weekend, T.J. was tuning Gary's second bike when Mitch came up the aisle and leaned on the handlebars. "He's back. Did you hear?"

The handlebars rocked, twisting the front tire and knocking T.J.'s wrench out of his hand. T.J. sighed. "What? Who?"

"Price, Alex Price. He's totally okay."

"How is that even possible?" T.J. said. "You saw that crash. He should have been smashed to pieces."

"Who knows? Guys walk away from the craziest shit." Mitch went to the cab of the truck at the front of the trailer and pulled a beer out of the cooler.

It was true, anything was possible; Price might have fallen just right, so he didn't break and the bike didn't crush him. Every crash looked horrible, like it should tear the riders to ribbons, and most of the time no one was hurt worse than cuts and bruises. In fact, how many people even looked forward to the crashes, the spike of adrenaline and sense of horror, watching tragedy unfold? But something here didn't track.

T.J. tossed the wrench in the toolbox, closed and locked and lid, and set out to find Price.

Today was practice runs; the atmosphere at the track was laid-back and workmanlike. Not like race days, which were like carnivals. He went up one aisle of trucks and trailers, down the next, not sure what he was looking for—if he was local, Price probably didn't ride for a team, and wouldn't have sponsors with logos all over a fancy trailer. He'd have a plain homespun rig. His jacket had been black and red; T.J. looked for that.

Turned out, all he had to do was find the mob of people. T.J. worked his way to the edge of the crowd that had gathered to hear Price tell the story. This couldn't have been the first time he told it.

"I just tucked in and let it happen," Price said, a smile drawing in his audience. He gave an "awe, shucks" shrug and accepted their adoration.

T.J. wanted to hate the guy. Not sure why. He wasn't quite his type—lean instead of burly, grinning instead of brusque. Or maybe it was the matter of survival. Price had survived, and T.J. wanted to. Arms crossed, skeptical, he stood off to the side.

Price looked friendly enough, smiling with people and shaking all the hands offered to him, but he also seemed twitchy. He kept glancing over his shoulders, like he was looking for a way out. T.J. worked his way forward as the crowd dispersed, until they were nearly alone.

"Can I talk to you privately?" T.J. said.

"Hey, I remember you," Price said. "You helped, right after the crash. Thanks, man."

T.J. found himself wanting to glance away. "I just want to talk for a second."

"Come on, I'll get you a beer."

Price led him to the front part of the trailer, which was set up as a break area—lawn chairs, a cooler, a portable grill. From the cooler he pulled out a couple of bottles of a microbrew—the good stuff—and popped off the caps by hand. Absently, T.J. wiped the damp bottle on the hem of his T-shirt.

"What's the problem?" Price asked.

T.J. wondered if he really came across that nervous, that transparent. He was trying to be steady. "The crash last week. What really happened?"

Price shrugged. "You were there. You saw the whole thing."

T.J. shook his head. "Yeah. I saw it. You shouldn't be standing here—your legs were smashed, your whole body twisted up. Everyone else can write it off and say you were lucky, but I'm not buying it. What really happened?"

He expected Price to deny it, to wave him away and tell him he was crazy. But the guy looked at him, a funny smile playing on his lips. "Why do you want to know? Why are you so worked up over it?"

So much for playing it cool. "I need help."

"Why do you think I can help you? What makes you think I can just hand over my good luck?"

He was right. T.J.'s own panic had gotten the better of him, and he'd gone grasping at soap bubbles. Whatever he'd seen on the day of the crash had been his own wishful thinking. He'd wanted to see the impossible.

"You're right. I'm sorry. Never mind." Ducking to hide his blush, he turned away, looking for a place to set his untasted beer before he fled.

"Kid, wait a minute," Price called him back, and T.J. stopped. "What's your name?"

"T.J."

"What would you say if I told you you're right?"

"About what?"

"I'm invincible. I can't be killed. Not by a little old crash, anyway. Now—what are you looking to get saved from? What are you so scared of?"

Now that he'd said it, T.J. didn't believe him. Price was

making fun of him. And how much worse would it be if T.J. actually told him? He turned to leave again.

"Hey. Seriously. What's wrong? Why are you so scared of dying that you need my help?"

T.J. took a long draw on the beer, then said, "I'm HIV positive." It was the first time he'd said it out loud. It almost hurt.

"Rough," Price said.

"Yeah." T.J. kicked his toe in the dirt. What did he expect Price to say to him? What could anyone say? Nothing.

"Hey," Price said, and once again T.J. had to turn back, obeying the command in his voice. "What are you willing to do to turn that around? You willing to become a monster?"

"You talk to some people, I already am," T.J. said, putting on a lopsided smile.

"You know about the Dustbowl?"

"Yeah."

"Stop by tonight, seven or seven thirty. If you're really sure."

"Sure about what?" he asked.

"Just show up and I'll explain it all." He walked away, past the trailer to the cab of the truck. Meeting over.

It seemed like an obvious trap—he'd show up and walk into a beating. The Dustbowl was one of the bars up the road; some of the riders liked to hang out there. Not Gary—he was serious about riding and didn't need to show how tough he was off the track. T.J. had stayed away; the place had an uncomfortable vibe to it, a little too edgy, though it was hard to tell if the atmosphere was just for show. He preferred drinking at one of the larger bars, where he didn't stand out so much.

He didn't know whether to believe there really was something different about Price, something that had saved him from the awful wreck, or if Price was making fun of him. He could check it out. Just step in and step back out again if he didn't like the look of the place. Make sure Mitch knew where he was going in case something happened and he vanished.

That would solve his problems real quick, wouldn't it?

He hitched a ride from the track with some friends of Mitch's who were on their way into town. T.J. must have sounded convincing when he said he was meeting somebody and that everything was okay. The sun was close to setting, washing out the sky to a pale yellow, and summer heat radiated off the dusty earth. The air was hot, sticky, making his breath catch.

The Dustbowl was part of a row of simple wooden buildings set up to look like an Old West street but without disguising the modern shingles, windows, and neon beer signs. At one end was a barbecue place that T.J. had heard was pretty mediocre but cheap. The place smelled like overcooked pork, which made his stomach turn.

Walking into the bar alone, he felt like an idiot. Not just a loser, but a loser looking for trouble. The bullies would be drawn to him. He had to shake off the feeling—if he looked scared, of course he'd get picked on. He straightened, rounded his shoulders, and took a deep breath to relax. He had to look at ease, like he belonged.

Feeling a little more settled in his skin—he tried to convince himself that everyone in the half-filled room wasn't staring at him—he went to the bar, ordered a Coke, and asked if Alex Price was here.

"He might be in back," the bartender said. "That guy's nuts—did you see his crash last week?"

"Yeah," T.J. said. "I had a front-row seat. It was bad."

"And he gets up and walks away. Crazy." Shaking his head, the bartender moved off.

T.J. put his back to the bar and looked around. TV screens mounted in the corners showed baseball. Tables and chairs were scattered, without any particular order to them. A waitress in a short skirt delivered a tray of beers to a table of what looked like truckers, but he hadn't seen any rigs parked outside. No sign of Price. He'd give it the time it took to finish the Coke, resisting the urge to upend it and down the whole thing in a go.

Halfway through, a woman came through a door in back and sauntered along the bar toward him. She was petite, cute, with softly curling brown hair bouncing around her shoulders and a size-too-small T-shirt showing off curves.

"Are you the guy looking for Alex?" she said.

"Yeah."

"Come on back, he's waiting for you." She gave him a wide smile and tipped her head to the back door.

And if that didn't look like a bad situation . . . "There a reason he can't talk to me out here?"

"Not scared, are you? Come on, you can trust me." She sidled closer, gazing up at him with half-lidded eyes and brushing a finger up his arm.

He never knew in these situations if he should tell her she was wasting her efforts or let her have her fun. He let it go and went with her. He was good enough in a fight—he just wouldn't let anyone get between him and the door. It would be okay.

She led him through a hallway with a concrete floor and aged walls. A swinging door on the left opened to a kitchen; doors on the right were labeled men's and women's restrooms. At the end of the hall was a storage closet. Through there, another door opened into a huge garage—four, maybe five cars could fit inside. Nobody out front would hear him if he yelled. He tried not to be nervous.

A tall, windowless overhead door was closed and locked. A few cardboard boxes and a steel tool closet were pushed up against the walls. Right in the middle sat a steel cage, big enough to hold a lion. A dozen or so people were gathered around the cage. Alex Price stood at the head of the group, drawn straight and tall, his arms crossed.

Oh, this did not look good. T.J. turned to go back the way he'd come, hoping to make it a confident walk instead of a panicked run.

The woman grabbed his arm. "No, no, wait, we're not going to hurt you." Her flirting manner was gone.

T.J. brushed himself out of her grip and put his back to the wall. She gave him space, keeping her hands raised and visible. None of the others had moved. Their gazes were curious, amused, watchful, suspicious—but not hateful. Not bloodthirsty.

Price just kept smiling. "The cage isn't for you, kid," he said. "Remember when I asked you if you're willing to become a monster?"

T.J. shook his head. "I don't understand."

"I can cure you, but it won't be easy."

"It never is," T.J. said. He met Price's gaze and held it, refusing to be scared of this guy. "I still don't understand."

"We're a pack," he said, nodding at the people gathered around him. "We've talked it over, and we can help you. But you have to really want it."

"Pack," T.J. said. "Not a gang?"

"No."

The people only looked like a group because they were standing together; they didn't look anything alike—three were women, a couple of the men were young, maybe even younger than T.J. A couple wore jeans and T-shirts, a couple looked like bikers, like Price—leather jackets and scruff. One guy was in a business suit, the tie loosened, his jacket over his arm. One of the women wore a skirt and blouse. They were normal—shockingly normal, considering they were standing in an empty garage behind a bar, next to a large steel cage. T.J. felt a little dizzy.

"He's not going to believe anything until we show him, Alex," the woman with the curling brown hair said. She had a sly, smiling look in her eyes.

"Believe what?" T.J. said, off balance, nearing panic.

"You want to do it?" Price said to her.

"Yeah. Sure." She looked at T.J., then quickly grabbed his hand and squeezed it. Her skin was hot—T.J. hadn't realized that his hands were cold. She whispered, "I want to help. I really do." Then she went to the cage.

This was a cult, he thought. Some weird, freaky religious thing. They had some kind of faith healing going on. Did Price really think a miracle had saved him?

T.J. stayed because *something* had saved Price.

Without any self-consciousness, the woman took off her clothes, handing them to the woman in the skirt. One of the others opened the cage. Naked, she crawled in and sat on all fours, and seemed happy to do so, as the cage door was locked behind her.

"Ready, Jane?" Price said, reaching a hand into the cage. The woman licked it, quick and doglike.

As if this couldn't get any stranger. T.J. inched toward the doorway. He ought to run, but the same horrified fascination that kept him from looking away from the crash kept him here.

"Don't go," Price said. "Wait just another minute."

The woman in the cage bowed her back and grunted. Then, she blurred. T.J. blinked and squinted, to better see what was happening.

Her skin had turned to fur. Her bones were melting, her face stretching. She opened her mouth and had thick, sharp teeth that hadn't been there before. This wasn't real, this wasn't possible, it was some kind of hoax.

T.J. stumbled back, launching himself toward the door. But Price was at his side, grabbing his arms, holding him. T.J. could have sworn he'd been on the other side of the room.

"Just wait," Price said, calmly, soothing, as T.J. thrashed in his grip. "Calm down and watch."

In another minute, a wolf stood in the cage, long-legged and rangy, with a gray back and pale belly. It shook out its fur, rubbed its face on its legs, and looked out at Price. T.J. couldn't catch his breath, not even to speak.

"That's right," Price said, as if he knew the word T.J. was trying to spit out.

And that was the secret. That was how Price had survived. Because he was one of those, too. Every one of them standing before him was like her.

He tried to convince himself he wasn't afraid of them. "It's crazy. You're all crazy." He hated that his voice shook. He still pulled against Price's grip—but Price had a monster's strength.

"You're not the only one who's stood there and said so," Price said.

"What are you saying? That's the cure? Become like that?"

"We're all invulnerable. We don't get sick. We don't get hurt. Oh, we still age, we'll all still die someday. The silver bullet part is real. But when nobody else believes in this, what are the odds anyone's going to shoot you with a silver bullet?"

"And the full moon thing is real, too?" T.J. said, chuckling, because what else could he do?

"Yes," Price said.

"No, no," T.J. said, giving himself over to the hysteria.

Price spoke softly, steadily, like he'd given this speech before. "All you have to do is stick your hand in the cage. But you have to ask yourself: If you're not brave enough to deal with your life now, then why would you be brave enough to stick your hand in the cage? You have to be brave enough to be a monster. You think you're that brave? I'm not sure you are."

Of course he'd say it like a dare.

T.J. had spent the last few weeks in a constant state of subdued panic. Trying to adjust his identity from healthy to sick, when he didn't feel sick and didn't know what being sick even meant. Here he was being asked to do it again, change his identity, his whole being. He'd spent his whole life changing his identity, announcing it, feeling good about it, then feeling it slip out from under him again. He thought he'd done the right thing when he told his parents he was gay. They'd kicked him out, just like he'd known they would. He'd been ready for it—happy to leave, even, bag already packed and bike filled with gas and ready to go. But from one day to the next he'd gone from closeted son to outed and independent—free, he'd thought of it then.

He went to the clinic and got tested because he'd had a raw, nagging feeling that he'd done it all wrong and was paying a price for all that freedom. From one day to the next he'd gone from healthy to not. Now, Price was offering him a chance to do it again, to change himself in the space of a minute to an animal, a creature that shouldn't exist, with sharp teeth behind curling lips.

The wolf's eyes, golden brown, stared at him, gleaming, eager. The woman—still flirting with him.

He could face one horror, or the other. Those were his choices. That was what he had brought on himself.

But wouldn't it be nice to be invincible, for once?

"It can't be that easy," T.J. whispered.

"No, it's not. But that's why we're here," Price said. "We'll help you."

"How do you know it'll cure me?"

"Jane had an inoperable brain tumor. Now she doesn't."

If he asked for time to think about it, he would never come back. What did he have to lose? Wasn't he dying anyway? He stepped toward the cage.

It was going to hurt. He repeated to himself, *invincible,* and he glanced at the people gathered around him—werewolves, all of them. But none of them looked on him with anger or hate. Caution, doubt, maybe. But he would be all right. It would be like a shot, a needle in the arm, a vaccination against worse terrors.

Price stood behind him—to keep him from fleeing? The others gathered around to watch. All he had to do was reach. The wolf inside the cage whined and turned a fidgeting circle.

"You can still back out. No shame in walking out of here," Price said, whispering behind him.

It didn't look so monstrous. More like a big dog. All he had to do was reach in and scratch its ear. T.J. rested his hand on the top of the cage. The bars were smooth, cool, as if the steel had absorbed the chill from the concrete underneath.

Kneeling, T.J. slipped his hand down to the side, then pushed his arm inside. The wolf carefully put her jaws around his forearm. He clenched his hand into a fist, and by instinct he lunged away. The wolf closed her mouth on him, and her fangs broke skin.

He thrashed, pulling back, fighting against her. Bracing his feet against the bars, he pushed away. That only made his skin tear through her teeth, and she bit harder, digging in, putting her paws on him to hold him still so that her claws cut him as well as her teeth. Behind him Price grabbed hold, securing him in a bear hug, whispering.

The pain was total. He couldn't feel his hand, his arm, the wolf's gnawing, but he could feel his flesh ripping and the blood pouring off him, matting in the fur of her snout. All that infected, tainted blood.

He looked away and clamped his jaws shut, trapping air and screams behind tightly closed lips.

By the time Price pulled T.J. away from the cage, he'd passed out.

When he woke up, he was in a twin bed in what looked like a sunny guest room. The decorations—paisley bedspread, out-of-date furniture set—lacked personality. The woman who had been a wolf sat on a chair next to the bed, smiling.

He felt calm, and that seemed strange. He felt like he ought to be panicking. But he remembered days of being sick, sweating, swearing, fighting against blankets he'd been wrapped in, and cool hands holding him back, telling him he was going to be fine, everything was going to be fine. All the panic had burned out of him.

He pulled his hands out from under the sheets and looked at them. His right arm was whole, uninjured. Not even a scar. He remembered the claws tearing, the skin parting.

He took a deep breath, pressing his head to the pillow, assaulted by smells. The sheets smelled of cotton, stabbed through with the acerbic tang of detergent—it made his eyes water. A hint of vegetation played in the air, as if a window was open and he could smell trees—not just trees, but the leaves, fruit ripening on boughs, the smell of summer. Something was cooking in another part of the house. He'd never smelled so much.

The woman, Jane, moved toward him and her scent covered him, smothered him. Her skin, the warmth of her hair, the ripeness of her clothes, a hint of sweat, a touch of breath—and more than that, something wild that he couldn't identify. This—fur, was it fur?—both made him want to run and calmed him. Inside him, a feeling he couldn't describe—an instinct, maybe—called to him. *It's her, she did this.*

He breathed through his mouth to cut out the smells, to try to relax.

"Good morning," she said, wearing a thin and sympathetic smile.

He tried to speak, but his dry tongue stuck. She reached to a bedside table for a glass of water, which she gave him. It helped.

"I'm sorry I hurt you," she said. "But that's why we do it like this, so the choice has to be yours. Do you understand?"

He nodded because he did. He'd had the chance to walk away. He almost had. He wondered if he was going to regret not walking away.

"How do you feel?" she said.

"This is strange."

She laughed. "If that's all you have to say about it, you're doing very well."

Her laughter was comforting. With each breath he took, he felt himself grow stronger. It was like that moment just past being sick, when you still remembered the illness but had moved past it.

"I'm starving," he said—the hunger felt amazing. He wanted to eat, to keep eating, rip into his food, tear with his claws—

And that was odd.

He winced.

"Oh, Alex was right bringing you in," Jane said. "You're going to do just fine."

He hoped she was right.

He had to know for sure, so he went back.

A different guy was working at the clinic, which was just as well. "Have you ever had an HIV test before?" the staffer said.

"Yeah. Here, in fact. About eight months ago."

"Oh? What was the result? Is there a reason you're back? Let me look it up."

T.J. gave the guy his name, and he looked it up. Found the two positives, and T.J. wanted to snarl at him for the look of pity he showed.

"Sir," he said kindly—condescendingly. "With a result like this you should have come back sooner for counseling. There's a lot of help available—"

"The results were wrong," T.J. said. "I want another test. Please."

He relented and took T.J. into the exam room, went through the ritual, drew the blood, and asked T.J. to wait. The previous times, it had taken a half an hour or so. The guy came back on schedule, wearing a baffled expression.

"It's negative," the staffer said.

T.J. exalted, a howl growing in his chest.

The staffer shook his head. "I don't understand. I've seen false positives—but two false positives in a row? That's so unlikely."

"I knew it," T.J. said. "I knew it was wrong."

He gave the guy a smile that showed teeth and walked out.

On his first full moon, on a windswept plain in the hills of central California, he screamed and couldn't stop as his body broke and changed, shifting from skin and reason to fur and instinct. The scream turned into a howl, and the dozen others of the pack joined in, and the howls turned into a song. They taught him to run on four legs, to smell and listen and sense, to hunt, and that if he didn't fight it the change didn't hurt as much. In the morning, the wolves slept and returned to their human forms, but they remained a pack, sleeping together, skin-to-skin, family and invincible. They taught him how to keep the animal locked inside until the next full moon, despite the song that called to him, the euphoria of four legs on a moonlit night. He'd never felt so powerful, not even when he left home. He was so sure he'd done the right thing then, and now.

He'd called Mitch and told him that he'd been sick with the flu and staying with a friend. When he returned, the track had changed.

It had become brilliant, textured, nuanced. The dust in the air was chalk, sand, earth, and rubber. The exhaust was oil, plastic, smoke, and fire. And the crowd—a hundred different people and all their moods, scents, and noises. A dozen bikes were on the track; each engine had a slightly different sound. He sneezed at first, his nose on fire, before he learned to filter, and his ears burned before he figured out how to block the chaos. He didn't need to take it all in, he only had to focus on what was in front of him. But he could take it all in, whenever he wanted.

The world had changed. Terrifying and brilliant, all of it. He was free, clean, powerful.

Alex had given T.J. a ride. Before T.J. left the truck, Alex touched his arm, calming him. The animal inside him that had been ready to run wild.

"You going to be okay?" Alex said.

"Yeah," T.J. said, breathing slowly as he'd been taught, settling the creature.

"I'm here if you need anything. Don't wait until you get into trouble. Come find me first," he said.

If the pack was a new family, then Alex was its father, leader, master. That was another thing T.J. hadn't expected. He'd never really had a father figure to turn to.

Over the last week he'd learned what the price for invincibility was: learning to pass. Moving among people, thinking all the time how easy it would be to rip into them and feast, imagining their blood on his tongue but never being able to taste. Because if he tried it—if any of them ever actually lost control—the others would rip his heart out. That was how they'd stayed secret for centuries: Never let the humans know they were there. Closeted again, ironically.

So he worked on Gary's bikes and thought about the engine, belts, carburetor, and transmission, and remembered that the people around him were his friends and didn't deserve to die by a wolf's claws. He wanted to keep his old life. It was worth working to keep. That was the trick, Alex and Jane taught him. You can keep your old life. It won't be the same, but it'll still be there.

He'd actually get to live to enjoy it, now. It was a relief. Made him want to howl.

Something fell on him, knocking the wrench out of his hand. He sprang to his feet, hands clenched, turning to snarl at whomever had done it, interrupted him—*attacked.* Then he closed his eyes and took a deep breath.

Mitch was waving him over. A dirty rag lay on the ground next to the wrench—that was all that had hit him.

"Gary's last race is up, you coming to watch?" Mitch said.

His wolf settled. T.J. put away his tools and followed Mitch to the straw bales ringing the track.

"You okay? You seem a little jumpy lately," Mitch asked.

He didn't know the half of it. "I'm okay. I probably need more sleep."

"Don't we all," Mitch said.

It gave him a sense of déjà vu, watching Gary and Alex ride in the same race. This time, though, the PA system was too loud, the crowd of spectators pressed too close, and he didn't know who to watch, Gary or Alex. Gary was his friend, the guy who paid him under the table to keep his bikes running, who'd given him a break when T.J. needed one so desperately. But Alex was . . . something else entirely. Something bigger than T.J. had words for. Alex was the way he felt howling at the full moon.

The crowd buzzed, because this was Alex's first race after the spectacular crash. It had only been a few weeks, but it seemed much longer, months or years ago. Gary won the race; Alex didn't crash again. The incident faded from memory in that moment, but T.J. realized he saw the crash as a turning point—it had changed his life.

He and Mitch raced to the finish line to meet up with Gary. This was another of T.J.'s favorite things about the track, racing, bikes—the crowds gathering after the race, offering congratulations and condolences, dissecting what had happened, arguing, handing out cold beers and drinking as they wheeled bikes back to their trailers. This had been the last race of the day; the party spilled onto the track. Someone blasted AC/DC on a radio, and people started dancing.

Last race of the season. Gary was moving to the pro circuit, to a track out east, and had asked T.J. to come with him. The three of them made a good team. It was a huge opportunity, to go from scraping by as a bush-league mechanic to working for a team with a real shot. But a weight seemed to tie him down. Like a collar and leash.

Gary lounged back on the seat of his bike, enjoying the attention he was getting. T.J. found himself drifting toward Alex. To an observer, it would have looked like the natural movement of the crowd, people circling, clusters gathering and breaking apart. But T.J. had Alex's black jacket in the corner of his eye, and even amid all the sweat, dirt, spilled gas and oil, he could smell the animal fire of another werewolf. A pack should stay together. Alex, helmet in the crook of his arm, caught his gaze and smiled.

"Good race," T.J. said, as he might have said even if they hadn't been werewolves and Alex the alpha of his pack.

T.J. suddenly wanted to be out of there—his wolf was prowling, making him nervous and awkward. He edged back to Gary and Mitch, suddenly wanting to be near his human friends.

Alex stopped him with a hand on his arm that sent a flush over him. Staticky, warm, asexual, comfortable. He could rub his face across the man's coat. The feeling could get addictive.

"What's wrong?" Alex asked.

"Gary's leaving. He asked me to go with him."

"You can't do that, you know," Alex said. "Your family is here. Stay, come work for me," Alex said.

And how would he tell Mitch and Gary? "I like Gary," T.J. said. "He's been good to me. He's a good rider."

"I'm a good rider."

T.J. certainly wasn't going to argue with that. Shaking his head, he started to walk away.

"T.J."

He struggled. He had two voices, and both wanted to speak. But his wolf side was slinking, hoping for Alex's acceptance. "I don't have to do what you say."

"You sure about that?"

If he didn't walk away now, he'd never be able to. It was like that last dinner at home—if he didn't say it now, he never would, and then he'd curl up and disappear. So he turned and walked away, even though some sharp instinct wanted to drag him back. Claws scraped down the inside of his skin; he tried to ignore it.

Back with Mitch and Gary, rolling the bike to Gary's trailer, he started to relax.

"Saw you talking to Price," Mitch said. "I didn't think he swung your direction." He was teasing but amiable. T.J. gave him a searing look.

Gary and Mitch left, and T.J. stayed behind. The circuit was over, racing done for the season, and the track settled into a lethargic rhythm of local practice. Guys screwing around on backyard bikes. T.J. scrounged up mechanic jobs when he could and worked cheap. Alex rented him the guest room in the outbuilding behind his rural ranch house—the room where he'd woken into his new life. Just until he got back on his feet. Whenever that was. Months passed.

He drank at the Dustbowl with the rest of the pack, spent full moon nights with his new family, and that was the life that stretched before him now. But at least he was healthy.

No, truth spoke back at him—he'd traded one disease for another.

He'd taken a shower and was lying on the narrow bed, not thinking of anything in particular, when Alex knocked on the door. He could tell it was Alex by the knock, by the way he breathed.

"We're leaving for the Dustbowl."

Part of T.J. sprang up, like a retriever wagging its tail and grinning. Another part of him wanted to growl. He didn't feel much like socializing. "I think I'm going to stay in tonight."

"I think you ought to come along."

Alex's commands never sounded like commands. They were requests, suggestions. Strong recommendations. He spoke like a parent who always had your best interests at heart.

T.J. started to give in. It was his wolf side, he told himself. The wolf wanted to make Alex happy so the pack would stay whole, and safe.

But he wondered what would happen if he said no.

He sat up. "I don't really feel like it."

Sure enough, the door slammed open, rattling the whole frame of the shack. T.J. flinched, then scrambled back when Alex came at him. He tripped over the bed, ended up on his back, with the alpha werewolf lunging on top of him, pinning his shoulders, breathing on his neck.

T.J. lay as still as he could while gasping for breath. He kept his head back, throat exposed, hardly understanding what was happening—his body seemed to be reacting without him, showing the necessary submission so that Alex wouldn't hurt him. He flushed with shame, because he thought he'd be able to fight back.

Alex got up without a word and stalked out of the room. T.J. moved more slowly, but followed just the same.

T.J. sat in the corner, away from the others, staring out, turning over thoughts that weren't his. He could run or he could fight. And what happened to safety? To peace? All he had to do was sit back and take it. Not argue. Not rock the boat, not stick his neck out.

He couldn't stop staring, which in the body language of these creatures meant a challenge. He dropped his gaze to the bottle of beer, which he hadn't been drinking.

Jane pulled up a chair next to his and sat, then leaned on his shoulder, rubbing her head against his neck, stroking his arms. Trying to calm him, make him feel better.

"You know I'm gay, right?" he said.

Pouting, she looked at him. "We just want you to be happy. We want you to feel like you belong. You do, don't you?"

He closed his eyes. "I don't know."

"It doesn't matter as long as you're safe. You know if anyone came through here and gave you trouble, Alex would go after them, right?"

He almost laughed. Like she knew anything about it. "That isn't the point."

He'd raised his voice without realizing it, glaring at her so that she leaned away, a spark of animal flashing in her eyes. Heavy boots stepping across the floor inevitably followed, along with a wave of musk and anger, as Alex came to stand beside Jane. It was the two of them, bad cop and good cop, keeping the pack in line. Like they were one big happy family.

T.J. should have gone with Gary.

He stood, putting himself at eye level with Alex—also a sign of challenge. "I'm leaving," he said. Alex frowned. His mouth had been open to speak, but T.J. had done it first. The rest of the pack was here—they'd fallen silent and gathered around, the happy family. T.J. recognized a gang when he saw one.

Alex laughed—condescending, mocking. As if T.J. were a child.

As far as their wolf sides were concerned, he supposed he was. He thought back to Alex throwing him to the floor, felt that anger again, and tamped it down tight. The alpha was trying to get a rise out of him, goad him into some stupid attack so he could smack him right back down. T.J. wouldn't let him. All he had to do was stare.

"You'll be on your own," Alex said. "You won't like that. You'll never make it."

T.J.'s mouth widened in a grin that showed teeth. He shouldn't taunt Alex. He ought to just roll over to show his belly like the others. But he shook his head.

"I've done it before," he said. "I can do it again."

The wolf rose up, standing in place of the scared kid he used to be.

They could all jump him. He looked at the door and tried not to think of it, pushing all his other senses—ears, nose, even the soles of his feet—out, trying to guess when the rest of them would attack. He'd run. That was his plan.

"You don't really want to leave," Alex said, still with the laugh hiding in his voice.

T.J. looked around at all of them, meeting each person's gaze. The others looked away. They'd all come here by accident, through werewolf attacks, or by design—recruited and brought to the cage. T.J., on the other hand, had come to them alone, and he could leave that way. Maybe they didn't mind it here, but one of these days, T.J. would fight back. Maybe he'd win against Alex and become the alpha of this pack. Maybe he'd lose, and Alex would kill him. But they could all see that fight coming.

Which was maybe why they let him walk out the door without another argument. Rather than feeling afraid, T.J. felt like he'd won a battle.

He hadn't been brave enough to live out his old life. But he'd been brave enough to stick his hand in that cage. Maybe, eventually, he'd be okay.

Winnowing the Herd

Nobody was wearing perfume or fancy aftershave. It wasn't that kind of crowd. But I did smell patchouli, three different kinds of bathing products from the Body Shop, a recently changed baby, more patchouli covering up the smell of pot, and a shedding German shepherd.

The German shepherd belonged to Frank from marketing. He'd left the dog at home, cleaned up, didn't have a German shepherd hair on him, and probably didn't even realize he smelled like dog.

". . . so I told him, no. Absolutely not. I mean, we're an NPR affiliate, why would we want to advertise a gun show? We'd be a laughingstock . . ."

I nodded politely and made appropriate noises of sympathy. I'd met the German shepherd once. His name was Spirit, or Shadow, or something. He hadn't liked me much. That was because I could rip out his throat in a white-hot second, and he knew it.

". . . you guys in programming have no clue what we go through."

I shrugged with mock apology. "I guess not. Hey, is that a meat tray?"

Ozzie's wife, Cherie, was bringing out another platter to the lobby from the break room. Ozzie was the KNOB station manager. The staff appreciation party was Cherie's idea. Ozzie didn't appreciate his staff.

At second sniff, it wasn't a meat tray. No, it was more hummus. All the party platters were vegetarian—crackers with hummus, pita bread with hummus, ten kinds of vegetables with three kinds of dips, something made of tofu. Not just vegetarian, but vegan. Not even a chunk of Brie in sight. None of it smelled like food to me.

The beer was free so no one complained.

I hoped my sigh wasn't too audible. For lack of anything that might have bled before being cooked, the only things that smelled edible were my coworkers.

This was one of those optional-but-not-really parties. Time to play nice, even though Ozzie was under pressure to make budget cuts and everyone was on the verge of stabbing each other in the back to make sure they weren't the ones who were cut. Frank had been making lots of noise about how much work he did and how little anyone realized it. Ann the programming director appealed to noble sensibilities: We were a public service, not a business, and programming should be the last thing to go. Who needed advertising? And every two-bit night-shift DJ was desperate to show how indispensable they were.

So, if the station was under budget pressures, why were we spending all this money on a party that didn't even have any meat? I moved through the evening smiling vaguely at little ironies.

Perry. That was who I'd go after first. If I were going to go after anyone, which I wasn't, because I had better control than that. Perry was the receptionist/secretary/bookkeeper. Small, delicate, big eyed, slouching warily in her baggy sweater. She wrote romance novels at her desk on the sly. She'd totally freeze in the face of an attack. Easy prey.

"Kitty? What do you think?"

"Hm?" I turned to find Ike and Sean staring at me.

"Weren't you listening?" Ike said.

"Sorry. What?"

"Who would you rather meet: Iggy Pop or Bowie?"

I narrowed my eyes. "That's a trick question, isn't it?"

KNOB ran a "diverse music" format when it wasn't running NPR, which meant the average DJ was as likely to follow up Ella

Fitzgerald with the Chieftains as with the Clash. More than one programming meeting had degenerated into too-serious arguments about the merits of Velvet Underground versus They Might Be Giants.

I had to get out of here. I should have skipped the party, mandatory or no.

"Hey, Kitty, can I get you a beer?"

"No thanks," I said and sipped my cup of water. I knew better than to get even a little tipsy the night before a full moon.

"So, any big plans this weekend?" Sean was talking to me. Ike had disappeared.

I had originally been scheduled to work tomorrow, Saturday night. I'd had to make a big stink about getting the night off. Called in way too many favors. But since I actually liked the night shift and had traded with people countless other times, I'd had a lot of favors to call in. In the end everyone knew I'd wanted Saturday off and everyone wanted to know why.

They all figured I had a hot date. I was the station's resident single twenty-something, always a topic of speculation.

"I'm going camping."

Sean stared blankly. "In March? Isn't it a little cold?"

"Yeah, but it's a full moon," I said with a straight face. He had no response to that.

I grabbed a handful of crackers to nibble, to give me something to do. Just another half an hour, then I'd leave. Frank and Bill the tech guy stood by the food table, chatting.

"I think the food's great. Takes courage, standing up for a vegetarian lifestyle like this," Frank was saying. "I didn't know Ozzie was a vegetarian."

"He isn't," Bill said. "Neither is Cherie for that matter."

Frank looked taken aback. "Really? Huh."

"Maybe she thought, it's public radio, everyone here must be vegetarian."

"So, is anyone here actually a vegetarian?" I said.

Frank shrugged. Bill said, "Ike is."

"He looks it." Ike was thin, gangly, pale. Vegetarianism only worked if you knew how to do it. Otherwise, it made you look sick. He probably tasted like tofu. Ike was the last person in the room I'd go after. If I ever went after people. Which I didn't. I said, "You know, cows were bred to be eaten. Same with chickens, pigs—all the major meat animals. To not eat them is to deny them their purpose in life. Don't you think?"

Frank paused, scoop of hummus dip halfway to his lips. "I guess I never thought of it that way."

Bill said the only thing he could in the face of such a declaration. "Can I get you a beer or something?"

"No thanks, I'm fine."

He drifted off to the cooler anyway, and Frank turned back to the bowl of hummus, away from me.

Sheep. They were all a bunch of sheep.

I didn't usually feel this way. Usually, I could get through an entire day of work without making little baaing noises in my head in reference to my colleagues. I didn't always walk into a room and automatically winnow the herd in my mind.

Human: The other white meat.

The later the party went, the more everyone smelled like beer, the more people laughed, and the more I paced like a caged predator. I made myself sit in a chair and watch. Perry had left. So, I'd go after Ann next, because Ann needed getting. She was telling Beth from programming a complicated story about her partner's, i.e., longtime live-in boyfriend's, reprehensible behavior at her cousin's wedding, which was really a disguised rant about his not proposing to her years ago and thus depriving her of her own wedding. Being a freethinking liberal feminist, Ann was not supposed to complain about such things.

"He's an animal!" Beth said commiseratively.

These people had no idea. Try dating people who sprouted three-inch claws on a regular basis.

It was all pretense, one way or another. The reason I wasn't kissing Ozzie's ass or worrying about my job was because if I lost this job, I'd have an excuse to run away and never come back. So maybe that was why I kept up the pretense. For the challenge. Because I wanted to believe that civilization was worth the effort.

"Kitty! What was that shit you were playing the other night?"

I blinked, startled, and searched the room for the heckler. Ozzie, aging hippie ponytail and all, was standing on the other side of the sofa, hands on hips, glaring at me. The cluster of people seated on the sofa and nearby chairs fell silent, watching with big eyes like they'd just seen a car wreck.

What shit? was not the ideal response to that question. "Can you be a little more specific?"

"A couple nights ago. That spoken word stuff. That totally suicidal spoken word stuff."

I composed myself and said, "That was poetry. I found a recording of Sylvia Plath reading her poems. You know—literature."

With a scowl, he pulled a crumpled wad of cash from his pocket, smoothed out a couple of ones, and handed them to Bill, who grinned.

They'd had a bet going on one of my sets? Crazy.

Ozzie pointed at me. All ready to take his loss out on somebody. "Well, we can't have that."

Have what—literature? I raised my brows, inquiring.

He continued. "Suicidal shit on the radio. We might be held liable for—for something." He made a vague gesture.

My God, if the Plath estate were held liable for every suicidal teenager who got ahold of *The Bell Jar* . . .

I rolled my eyes. "It was two in the morning. Can you prove to me anyone was even listening?"

"Kitty, we can't have that kind of attitude here."

The air quivered. I wasn't being nice. I wasn't playing the game. I might as well have acquired a bull's-eye on my chest. My colleagues stared at me, nearly salivating. Like a pack of wolves moving in for the kill.

I supposed I should have been flattered that *someone* had listened to my shift.

"Can we talk about it at the next programming meeting?" I said. Nicely.

"Yeah, sure."

Ozzie didn't deserve to be alpha of this pack.

I stared at him. Hard. Almost, a growl started in my throat. I pursed my lips, to stop them from curling and baring my teeth.

My shoulders tensed, like hackles rising. Frank's German shepherd would have recognized the challenge. Ozzie almost did. His eyes went a little wide, but then he took a long draw from his beer and skulked off to the break room. He may not have understood that he was avoiding a challenge, but that was what he was doing.

I turned my lips into a wry smile as people nervously restarted conversations and stole twitchy glances at me.

"Baa-a-a-a-a-a-a!" I yelled in a staccato voice, hands cupped around my mouth. And they all just looked at me, before turning back to their beers and conversation.

I could eat them all. But I had a bad taste in my mouth. Time to blow this Popsicle stand. I grabbed another handful of crackers, waved a half-assed good-bye, and stalked out the door. It was early enough I could still find someplace to serve me a nice, rare steak.

Kitty and the Mosh Pit of the Damned

It felt good to get away from the radio station.

At least that was what I kept telling myself as I tried to make my way to the back of Glamour, a nightclub that attracted a young and dissolute crowd. I was here for a concert. I squeezed along the wall, pausing every couple of steps as people surged back, threatening to crush me. I dodged full cups of beer and lit cigarettes. The dance floor was shuffle-room only. The crowd was way past fire-code capacity.

A few hundred hot-blooded beating hearts surrounded me. It was all I could do to keep from drooling. A deeply buried part of me sensed the sweat, the heat, and thought, *Easy prey.* I could smell ten different brands of perfume and aftershave. Someone nearby was high on pot; I could smell it on his breath. Another had done X in the last hour; I could smell it in her blood.

This part of me had to sprout fur and claws every full moon. Between moons, I was careful to keep my claws to myself.

I finally reached the secondary bar with the majority of my self-control intact. Red track lighting backlit a couple rows of liquor bottles, casting shadows over the usual detritus of napkins, lime slices, dirty glasses, and taps. I checked for spills on the black Formica, and finding a dry spot, hopped up to take a seat.

The bartender started to glare, but when he saw me, he leaned his elbows on the counter.

"Kitty, hiya." Jax was about six feet tall and a hundred thirty pounds on a heavy day. He was shaved bald, and, living the nocturnal lifestyle he did, his skin was pale.

"Hey. When's Devil's Kitchen up?"

"Five minutes. Your timing is great."

"What are the chances they'll stick around after the show to talk to me?"

"When I tell them Kitty Norville wants to talk to them? They'll stick around like duct tape."

I was still getting used to the fame thing. My call-in radio talk show for the supernaturally challenged went national less than a year ago, but a lot had happened in that time. I'd revealed my werewolf identity on the air, for one. The episode put my ratings through the roof and made me one of the first lycanthrope celebrities in the country.

Fame opened doors and I had to take advantage of it when I could. I wanted to get Devil's Kitchen on my show for an interview.

The concert started late. The crowd, sensing the minutes ticking on some internal group chronometer, pressed closer to the stage. The angry edge tingeing the air intensified. Lots of black, lots of chains, and shouting.

The room went dark, all the lights cutting off at once, and the taped music went dead. Crammed bodies that had been governed by the beat of the music milled, uncertain. Then, the stage lit up. White spots glared straight down on amps and mike stands. A drum machine started up, followed by an electrified bass line, manic and terrible, like coming war.

Spirits from shadow, the band appeared. A bald guy with a ripped T-shirt and denim overalls played bass—Danny Spense. He came on stage and played like he was digging his own grave, with a kind of intense desperation, focusing only on his hands clutching the instrument, wincing in anguish.

Lead guitar, Kent Hayden, had a fascist look, slick-backed black hair, black T-shirt and jeans, fingerless leather gloves. He stared at the crowd impassively while his fingers danced on the frets of his instrument.

Together, they set up a textured rain of sound, melody struggling to escape chaos.

Eliot Ray, lead singer, leapt to the fore, grabbing the mike and pressing his mouth to the foam. He wore work boots, cutoff shorts, and a three-sizes-too-big T-shirt with the sleeves ripped off. He shut his eyes and wailed, but it was controlled, playing with the rhythm and song; it was, after all, music. I forgot to pay attention to the lyrics.

The crowd in the pit surged toward the stage, screaming. Fists pounded the air, a hundred bodies jumped in time with the beat.

Near me, Jax leaned on the bar, as enthralled as I was. Nobody wanted to buy drinks now.

Shouting into his ear over the music, I asked him, "How much security you guys have tonight?"

"Every bouncer on staff—and each of 'em brought a buddy. Ambulance waiting around the corner."

Over the last year, Devil's Kitchen had started headlining the club circuit. Their recent East Coast tour had made news: They'd left a trail of injured concertgoers in their wake. Every show they did, someone was hospitalized with injuries way beyond the usual cuts and cracked ribs of the mosh pit. It became part of the show in a way—a new kind of extreme sport, like rock climbing in Afghanistan. The more publicity they got about the casualties, the more popular their shows became. People had started following them from show to show like they were some kind of postapocalyptic version of the Grateful Dead.

They attracted a dangerous crowd. Part of this was the music they played, heavy as granite, sharp as razors, drawn from the old European industrial scene and punk they'd cut their teeth on as kids. Most of it was the band's reputation for putting people in the hospital. Not that any of the spike-haired heroin-thin manic kids currently in the mosh pit thought that *they* were in danger of getting hurt. But they sure wouldn't mind watching someone else break a bone.

I had some theories about the band and the kind of energy they generated. They, or maybe just one of them, were vampires.

Maybe not the standard bloodsucking undead, but some kind of psychic variety, feeding on danger, aggression, and bloodshed. What better venue to generate such emotions?

Eliot had more energy than any one person had a right to, leaping from one end of the stage to the other, bent over with the mike stand clutched in both hands one minute, stretched to his full height the next. He was fun to watch. I was screaming just as loud as anyone at the end of each song.

A couple of kids had started crowd surfing in the mosh pit, people passing them overhead from one end to the other. Then, one would get swallowed, disappearing in the crowd and another would spring up to take his place, riding on the upstretched arms of his friends.

They must have been four songs into the set when the first fight broke out. I didn't notice exactly when it happened; the surge and lurch in the crowd seemed like part of the natural flow. Then, a body slammed against a railing. The guy bent, his arms limp and flailing, and slid down to the floor. Four or five other guys suddenly locked together, grappling, and a space of a foot or two cleared around them. In the press of people trying to get away, more punches and body slams crashed. Eliot kept screaming into the mike, and a swarm of bouncers descended on the crowd.

A half-dozen people, men and women, with bloody cuts streaming over their faces were dragged past me. The music faded, reverb whining over the speakers and echoing in my ears.

"We're taking a break," Eliot said. Kent and Danny were unplugging their instruments. "Round two, ten minutes. Don't move." They disappeared behind the stage.

All that blood. My shoulders tensed, hackles rising. I had to get out of here.

I jumped off the bar and ran, climbing stairs to the catwalk circling the pit, dodging the press of onlookers. The pit was a war zone, half the mob still thrashing to the taped music now playing, the other half trying to pick fights, struggling against bouncers and friends who held them back. At the other end of the walkway, I slipped over the rail and hopped to the back of the stage.

"Jesus fuckin' Christ, it's not even ten minutes into the show and they're already killing each other! That's a record even for us. I can't do this anymore."

"Come on, it's what they're paying for. You don't think they're actually coming for the music, do you?"

The green room was a piece of the club's storage area that had been curtained off and decorated with a minifridge and sofa. I stood at the edge of the curtain's opening and listened.

"Shit like this is not supposed to happen every show!" The angry voice—I could tell he was stalking back and forth across the space by the stomp of his boots—belonged to Eliot.

"So what're you going to do?" said the other one. "Quit in the middle of a gig? What kind of riot do you think that'll start?"

Eliot threw something and kept pacing.

"Just chill, Eliot. You're not going to quit, so stop bitching." I was guessing that was Kent. Calm and pragmatic. The third, Danny, hadn't spoken. "We're going to go back and play. The crowd'll fight like they always do. Then we'll go home. We're not paid to worry about what those jerks do to each other. Not our problem."

"Just once," Eliot said between deep, careful breaths, "I'd like to get through an entire gig without stopping because of a fight."

He threw back the curtain on his way out and ran smack into me. It was my fault; the possibilities presented by this conversation—dissention within the band, the fact that they, or at least not all of them, knew what was going on—so intrigued me that I missed him stomping toward me. We stared at each other, startled. His jaw clenched, and he looked like he was about to yell a string of obscenities.

I forestalled this by smiling. "Hi. You must be Eliot Ray. I'm Kitty Norville." I stuck out my hand for him to shake.

He looked at my hand, looked at me, his snarl twitching. "Kitty Norville? The fuckin' talk show chick?"

"Yeah."

The snarl melted into a smile, and he shook my hand. "Cool. I'm a big fan."

"Thanks." I looked over his shoulder. Kent stood with his

arms crossed. Danny sat on the couch, shoulders hunched. "I'm real interested in talking to you guys. Maybe after the show? Would that be possible?"

"You want to talk to us?" Eliot threw a grin at the others. "Now we really are famous, if Kitty Norville wants to talk to us. You're, like, the Barbara Walters of freaky shit."

Kent, frowning, shoved past Eliot and me. "You'll have to set it up with our manager." He stalked toward the stage door.

"Sorry about that. I think he's got a thing against werewolves."

"Werewolves or nosy people? So—this kind of thing happens every show?" I nodded toward the chaos still rumbling from the main part of the club.

His expression tightened; he looked like he was going to yell again. But he just ducked his gaze and scuffed his boot on the concrete floor. "Yeah."

"You ever think it might be caused by something—oh, external? Like someone's manipulating things to cause the violence?"

"You mean—not our fault?"

I shrugged noncommittally. "Not specifically. It's just something to think about."

Danny was staring at me from the sofa. I couldn't read anything in his expression. Just a hard, interested stare. It made me twitch.

"Come back after the show," Eliot said. "We'll talk."

"No calling the manager?"

"Our manager doesn't know dick."

"Thanks."

The show must go on. The bouncers had cleared away the injured and the survivors were hungry for more. It was a wall of emotion, of anger and hate. More fights were waiting to break out. All my instincts said to get the hell out of here—I couldn't hold my own in a fight, not with this many people. Even if I sprouted claws and fought like a wolf. I returned to the safety of Jax's bar.

Jax was nervous, too, standing tense and clutching the edge of the bar, white-knuckled.

"This is really weird," I murmured.

"This is totally fucked up," Jax said, without a trace of sarcasm.

So, Eliot didn't know anything. Moreover, he was upset about the violence. There was more to him than his image suggested. Kent seemed perpetually anxious. Who wouldn't be, with kids beating each other up over his music? And Danny—who knew what was going on in his head?

The lights went dark. The smoke came up, and the band was back, pounding its way through another set. The crowd slammed to the music as if there hadn't been a break. It was like they were on a switch, still one moment, and in the next ramming each other and screaming. Like throwing a bloody carcass in the middle of a pack of wolves. Except a pack of wolves is more organized and has manners.

About fifteen minutes into the set, with the volume and mayhem of the crowd increasing the whole time, Eliot stopped singing. The musicians carried on a few more bars, unaware that his voice was missing from the feedback. Then, Eliot jumped off the stage.

It wasn't unusual for punk and metal musicians to dive into the mosh pit. But when the others finally stopped playing, I knew something was wrong. Eliot was beating people, grabbing them and shoving them out of the way, hitting them to get their attention and forcing them back.

He was clearing a space in the middle of the floor. The body of a young man lay there, twisted and bloody.

When people saw this, they moved voluntarily. This left a circle of empty floor, the body in the middle, and Eliot crouched beside it, touching the man's neck, feeling for a pulse.

Somehow, there was silence when he straightened, scanning the crowd with a hooded gaze, his mouth twisted in a snarl.

"You people are fucking maniacs! He's *dead*. Do your puny little brains even understand what that *means*?" He looked like he might scream, his fists clenched and his whole body tensed. But he just shook his head, like he was shaking free of an insect. "I'm done," he said. "I'm outta here."

He stalked off toward the hall that led to the front of the club.

"Eliot!" Kent lurched to the edge of the stage. "You can't go. We have to keep playing."

Eliot turned, and this time he did shout. "Why? Look at that—" He pointed at the dead boy on the floor. "What are we doing that can justify that?"

Kent said, "The—the music. You know, we have to stay true."

"This isn't about the fucking music!" Eliot brought his fists to his temples, like he was going to start pulling his hair. Danny looked on, his bass hanging limp in one hand.

Kent said, "Just calm down—"

Eliot marched to the stage, reaching it in a few large strides. He grabbed Kent's guitar and, swinging it by the arm, smashed it against the floor, over and over. Still plugged into the amp, the thing squealed like a living thing, doubling over in hissing feedback. I curled up and covered my ears. Most of the clubbers did the same. Jax didn't flinch.

Kent screamed, covering his ears and staring at the broken instrument as if it had been his child. "God, Eliot—do you know what you've done?"

Eliot stood, splintered guitar in his hand. His feet were apart, his shoulders hunched, and he was breathing hard, a grimace on his face challenging Kent to fight him.

The floor had cleared of moshing kids by this time. I'd assumed most of them had fled the club, not wanting to be questioned about the death. But none of them had left. Two hundred kids huddled around the edges of the floor, clinging to the railings, staring at the unfolding drama with hungry eyes. Pasty-faced Goth chicks leaned forward; leather-clad metalheads bounced in place, like a single guitar chord would get them started again. Paramedics were stalled at the front hallway, unable to push through the crowd.

Straightening, Eliot dropped the instrument and brushed his hands. "I quit."

He started his exit one more time, but someone blocked his way.

A tall, lithe man with silver hair and sharp features stood in front of Eliot, barring his way. I thought I would have noticed someone pushing his way through the crowd. Surely I would have noticed him if he'd already been here. He was taller than anyone else in the room. Or maybe he just seemed taller.

I crouched on the bar, legs tucked under me, balanced on my hands, ready to run.

Jax cracked his knuckles and frowned at the stranger.

"Who is he, Jax?"

"Bad news."

"Vampire?" Vampires didn't come to Glamour—too many groupies. And I thought I knew most of the vampires in town.

"Does he smell like a vampire?"

I straightened a little, lifting my face to the air. I could smell the fresh blood pooling on the floor. My nostrils flared. Vampires smelled dead, preserved, cold-blooded. In a crowd of pounding hearts, I could spot a vampire across the room with my eyes closed. This guy didn't smell like a vampire. I closed my eyes and took a deep breath, mentally filtering out the blood, sweat, and anger of the crowd.

"He smells . . . different," I said, confused. I couldn't put a name to any of the things I smelled in the current the stranger left in the air. "Midsummer. Starlight. He smells like—" I opened my eyes and looked at Jax. My nose tingled, taking in more scents. "He smells like you."

Jax glared at me.

Jax had been part of the local club scene for as long as I'd known the local club scene existed. He told stories about him and his droogs picking fights with skinheads when he had a blue mohawk, when moshing was slamming, before punk had splintered into Goth and industrial and rave, and before alternative was mainstream.

He wasn't a vampire, wasn't a were-creature. It had never occurred to me to wonder if he was anything other than the bartender punk veteran he appeared to be.

The drama unfolded.

"Who are you?" Eliot said.

"You've no right to question me. Step aside," he said in a rich, arrogant voice.

Wrong thing to say to Eliot. He bristled, shoulders bunching and tensing for a fight. Unconcerned, the stranger tilted his head, raised an inquisitive brow—

And backhanded Eliot clear across the floor. He landed hard and slumped like a sack of wheat.

Claws scratched at the inside of my hands. I was scared, and the Wolf wanted out.

The stranger knelt by the dead mosher, dipped his finger in the kid's blood, and tasted it. Then he stood, faced Kent, and spoke with chilling calm.

"Kent Hayden. You were doing so well. And now—silence?"

"Temporary," the guitarist said desperately. "Eliot's temperamental. I'll get him back, we'll start again. We have another gig tomorrow—"

"You said the band was with you. You said you spoke for all when we made our bargain."

"Kent? What bargain?" Danny ventured, his voice cracking.

The stranger only spared him a glance, saving most of the power of his stare for Kent, who was wilting under the pressure. "You know the one. Everyone knows it: The Devil's bargain at the crossroads."

The deal with the Devil . . . you'd sell your soul to play great music . . . music to die for.

"That explains it," I murmured. "All the weirdness—Kent Hayden sold his soul to the Devil—" And got more than he bargained for, evidently. This guy was after more than souls. He wanted blood.

Jax said, "Technically, he's not a devil. He just acts like one."

"So what are *you*?"

He shrugged. "Same coin, different side. Kitty—distract him. I need to sneak in the back and get the nail gun."

"Nail gun—what?"

"Cold iron. Just make a distraction."

Cold iron—as opposed to hot iron? "How?"

"Keep him talking. You're good at that." He pushed through the crowd toward the back door.

Jax was already halfway around the crowd. He didn't want the stranger to see him. So . . . I had to do something. But if that guy tried backhanding me like he had Eliot, I was going to Change. When it came to self-defense, I couldn't hold it back.

Off we go, then. I reached into my pocket and turned on my mini–tape recorder. Just in case.

I slipped through the crowd, ducking low and shoving until I reached the rail around the dance floor. On the other side of the rail another layer of people blocked my way. I stood on the rail and screamed.

"Eliot!" I jumped, and everyone got out of my way as I hit the floor running. What was the good of being a werewolf with superhuman strength and agility if you couldn't show off every now and then?

I skidded to a stop next to the singer. Eliot was starting to recover, pulling himself upright by gripping the rail. He held a hand on his forehead and winced.

"You okay?" I said.

"I think so."

"What are you?" the stranger said, sounding like twilight: clear voice, hinting at darkness. He was looking at me, his arms crossed.

"Radio talk show host. Can I get an interview?"

"What are you *really*?"

The air around him shimmered a little, like he was shivering with repressed emotion, a taste of coming action. I was afraid. I wanted to growl, to make him back off. But I didn't think a warning like that would have any effect on him. My skin flushed, my heart raced. *Keep it together.*

His lips thinned into a smile. He knew very well what I was.

Something touched my shoulder and I flinched. Eliot drew back his hand, startled.

"Are *you* okay?"

I was crouched on the floor, balancing on one hand, ready to spring. All I had to do was sprout fur and I was gone. I lowered my head and took a breath.

I looked at Kent, standing at the edge of the stage like he might jump off and try to run for it.

"What was the deal, Kent? What exactly did you agree to?" I asked.

Kent stammered. He couldn't look at the gleaming man before him. "F-fame," he said. "I wanted fame."

Eliot laughed, a thin, almost hysterical noise. "Shit, Kent—you made the wrong bargain! You were supposed to sell your soul to become a great musician. But you sold it for fame? You, of all people. You were supposed to be for real."

"I was tired," Kent said. "I worked, I practiced—and I still wasn't good enough. What happens then? What was I supposed to do?"

"Take the easy route, of course," the stranger said.

"You have a contract signed in blood?" I said. I tried to remember every story I knew about Devil's bargains, Faustian deals, the whole nine yards. There was always a loophole, right? Always a way to get out of it.

I always liked the version of Faust where he gets dragged screaming into hell.

"Of course," the stranger said, drawing a tied roll of paper from inside his waistcoat.

"I didn't sign that contract," Eliot said.

"Me neither," Danny said, raising a hand.

"Kent—did you sign in blood?" I said.

"Yes."

"You see? He, at least, belongs to me now." The smarmy bastard grinned.

For all my experience, for all that I liked to think I knew, I didn't know what to do with a soul-stealing demon. If that was really what this guy was.

"We'll keep playing!" Kent went to a second guitar case sitting at the back of the stage. In moments he was plugging the instrument into the amp. "We don't need Eliot. Come on, Danny. We can keep going!"

Danny dropped his bass, which moaned.

I moved closer to the stage, so I was standing between Kent and the stranger. "Let me see if I understand this: You promised him fame, in exchange for his soul"—I pointed to the stranger, then to the guitarist—"They'd have fame, just as long as the band kept performing, no matter what." The body still lay in front of us. I got a better look at him: the kid, male, with a short mohawk and a nose ring, must have been about eighteen. "But if the band stops, you"—I pointed back at the stranger—"get their souls." No arguments so far. "So what you really want isn't their souls. You wanted the violence. The bloodshed. You get that, they get fame."

He inclined his head, smiling a crooked, amused smile.

"The music is a catalyst. The music covers up the real source. The violence comes from you. What are you?"

"An agent of chaos." He raised his left hand and snapped his fingers.

In the far corner of the dance floor, the restless energy that had been pressing against the crowd burst. Someone fell, or tripped, or shoved himself against a wall of bristling moshers. They reacted instantly by beating on the assailant. His friends came to the rescue, and a full-blown fight erupted. Half a dozen bouncers waded in and were overwhelmed. The shouts of the crowd were deafening.

"Stop it!" Behind me, Eliot screamed with berserker fury. "Make it stop!"

Fists curled into hammers, he rushed the guy.

In a real fight with a normal human, Eliot would have pounded into the guy, pummeling his head, overpowering him with sheer brutal fervor. But the stranger wasn't human. He merely held out his hand and swept Eliot aside. Eliot went tumbling back the way he'd come. He lay still.

The stranger looked at me, and I held my place. The fights were still going on around us, the crowd moshing without music, keeping its own violent rhythm, slaves to this being's power. I was hemmed in.

"I can make you fight," he said, his voice low and taunting. "I can make you Change, turn on the crowd, and rip out the throats of everyone here."

I believed him and knew I'd do better to let him smack me unconscious. So I did.

At least, I tried. I rushed him, much like Eliot had. I didn't know what I was hoping for. Jax said to distract him, so I did. I thought if he knocked me out at least he couldn't make good his threat. Maybe he was bluffing, but I couldn't take a chance on him making me hurt people.

I forgot one thing: I was a lot tougher than Eliot. As a lycanthrope, I could take more abuse, I healed faster. The blow that had knocked him unconscious knocked me to the floor and pissed me off. Rather, it pissed off my Wolf. She'd been itching for a chance to run loose all night. So now, in the name of self-defense, she took it.

The claws sprouted, and I lost it.

. . . the fur is free, the claws are free. Blood on the air smells sharp. But sharper is the figure of a creature. He glows, shining and dangerous. Hackles rise and finally she can growl, loud and fierce. She braces, backed against the wall. Time to fight. Find his throat. Muscles tense, and like a spring she's away, launched from a standstill, flying at him. Teeth bared, claws ready to rip.

And he flings her away. His fist catches her under her ribs and she yelps. She sprawls on the floor, splay-legged and ungraceful. He's so much stronger, no way can she win.

But she scrambles to her feet and tries again.

Someone shouts. Familiar voice. Her ears prick and she turns, just as the enemy kicks her hard with a boot like steel. Hits the wall, vision flashing. Shakes her head and looks for the next blow.

Another figure is there. Shimmering and strong. Raises a hand—he's holding something. And the thing flashes with power, over and over. And the enemy falls, screaming.

She huddles, hackles as stiff as they can go, not sure which of them to hate.

The newcomer looks at her. She growls. If she could run away she would but she can't, so she'll fight.

—Kitty, it's me. It's Jax.

The familiar voice. In another life she knows that voice. But he smells like the enemy.

—Kitty, come back now. Change back.

In spite of herself, she listens. She blacks out.

I woke up not knowing how much time had passed. Time moved strangely for the Wolf. What was it they said, seven canine years for every human one? I was comfortable, and that was good. Warm, head resting on a friendly lap.

And that, so incongruous with my last memory, was disconcerting. I sat up and found myself wrapped in a heavy leather trench coat. Eliot was there, holding an ice pack to his head with one hand. His other hand rested on my shoulder. It was his lap I'd been using as a pillow.

"You okay?" he asked.

I didn't really want to know how I ended up like this. I settled back, snuggling more firmly into the trench coat. I was, of course, completely naked under it.

I smiled at Eliot. "I think you just passed the lycanthrope equivalent of the drunk test."

"Huh?"

"The drunk test: If you get throwing-up drunk in front of a guy, and he's still there when you wake up, he's a keeper." I shrugged, indicating my postlupine state. "If you turn into a wolf in front of him, and he's still there when you wake up . . ."

His blank expression took on a more thoughtful quality, lips pursed and brows raised. "Hm. How about that?"

I looked around. The club had been cleared. Somehow, they'd gotten everyone out. The kid's body was gone. The stranger was lying spread-eagle on the floor. I buttoned up the coat and inched closer to get a better look.

He'd been nailed to the floor—long iron nails driven through his hands and ankles. Another dozen nails protruded from his chest. He was gasping for breath, but not dead. The wounds smoked, but they didn't bleed.

Jax stood over him, holding a nail gun. He was talking to him, the words angry and spitting. It was a language I'd never heard before. Then Jax grabbed his collar and pulled him to his feet. The nails popped out of the floor. The stranger yelped and cowered where Jax put him.

Next, Jax went to the stage. Danny was pressed against the wall of amps. Kent still stood at the edge of the stage, trembling. He'd dropped the guitar. Jax took his collar and hauled him off stage.

In English he said, "I'm sending him back Underhill. You're going with him. He was right—you signed the contract. You belong to him."

"But—but—but—" Kent didn't get out more than that. Jax shoved him at the stranger, who gathered him in an embrace. Kent started screaming.

"Tithe to hell, man," Jax said.

The stranger disappeared, taking Kent with him.

The room was very quiet after that.

I stared at Jax. When I became a werewolf, I'd had to reevaluate what I previously considered to be fable, folklore, mythology. Fairy tale. Things that could never exist before became possible, and I had to wonder where the truth of the stories lay. I filed through my mental catalog of folklore for a hint of Jax.

"What are you?" I said, more than a little awestruck.

He gave me a wry look—not unlike the stranger's crooked grin—with narrow, knowing eyes. When he answered, it was in that odd language, complex and musical.

I sighed. I should have known better than to expect a straight answer. At least I could guess now why vampires didn't show up here. Someone tougher was guarding the place. Glamour.

My clothes were in a pile nearby. I reached for my jeans and the tape recorder in the pocket. Still going. I stopped, rewound, and played.

Nothing. Static. Not even the screaming of possessed moshers. Damn.

So there was only one thing left to ask. "Any chance you'd do an interview on my show?"

Jax smirked. "Not a chance in hell, Kitty."

Kitty's Zombie New Year

I'd refused to stay home alone on New Year's Eve. I wasn't going to be one of those angst-ridden losers stuck at home watching the ball drop in Times Square while sobbing into a pint of gourmet ice cream.

No, I was going to do it over at a friend's, in the middle of a party.

Matt, a guy from the radio station where I was a DJ, was having a wild party in his cramped apartment. Lots of booze, lots of music, and the TV blaring the Times Square special from New York—being in Denver, we'd get to celebrate New Year's a couple of times over. I wasn't going to come to the party, but he'd talked me into it. I didn't like crowds, which was why the late shift at the station suited me. But here I was, and it was just like I knew it would be: 10:00 P.M., the ball dropped, and everyone except me had somebody to kiss. I gripped a tumbler filled with untasted rum and Coke and glowered at the television, wondering which well-preserved celebrity guest hosts were vampires and which ones just had portraits in their attics that were looking particularly hideous.

It would happen all over again at midnight.

Sure enough, shortly after the festivities in New York City ended, the TV station announced it would rebroadcast everything at midnight.

An hour later, I'd decided to find Matt and tell him I was going home to wallow in ice cream after all, when a woman screamed. The room fell instantly quiet, and everyone looked toward the front door, from where the sound had blasted.

The door stood open, and one of the crowd stared over the threshold, to another woman who stood motionless. A new guest had arrived and knocked, I assumed. But she just stood there, not coming inside, and the screamer stared at her, one hand on the doorknob and the other hand covering her mouth. The scene turned rather eerie and surreal. The seconds ticked by, no one said or did anything.

Matt, his black hair in a ponytail, pushed through the crowd to the door. The motion seemed out of place, chaotic. Still, the woman on the other side stood frozen, unmoving. I felt a sinking feeling in my gut.

Matt turned around and called, "Kitty!"

Sinking feeling confirmed.

I made my own way to the door, shouldering around people. By the time I reached Matt, the woman who'd answered the door had edged away to take shelter in her boyfriend's arms. Matt turned to me, dumbstruck.

The woman outside was of average height, though she slumped, her shoulders rolled forward as if she was too tired to hold herself up. Her head tilted to one side. She might have been a normal twenty-something, recent college grad, in worn jeans, an oversized blue T-shirt, and canvas sneakers. Her light hair was loose and stringy, like it hadn't been washed in a couple of weeks.

I glanced at Matt.

"What's wrong with her?" he said.

"What makes you think I know?"

"Because you know all about freaky shit." Ah, yes. He was referring to my call-in radio show about the supernatural. That made me an expert, even when I didn't know a thing.

"Do you know her?"

"No, I don't." He turned back to the room, to the dozens of faces staring back at him, round-eyed. "Hey, does anybody know who this is?"

The crowd collectively pressed back from the door, away from the strangeness.

"Maybe it's drugs." I called to her, "Hey."

She didn't move, didn't blink, didn't flinch. Her expression was slack, completely blank. She might have been asleep, except her eyes were open, staring straight ahead. They were dull, almost like a film covered them. Her mouth was open a little.

I waved my hand in front of her face, which seemed like a really clichéd thing to do. She didn't respond. Her skin was terribly pale, clammy looking, and I couldn't bring myself to touch her. I didn't know what I would do if she felt cold and dead.

Matt said, "Geez, she's like some kind of zombie."

Oh, no. No way. But the word clicked. It was a place to start, at least.

Someone behind us said, "I thought zombies, like, attacked people and ate brains and stuff."

I shook my head. "That's horror movie zombies. Not voodoo slave zombies."

"So you do know what's going on?" Matt said hopefully.

"Not yet. I think you should call 911."

He winced and scrubbed his hand through his hair. "But if it's a zombie, if she's dead an ambulance isn't—"

"Call an ambulance." He nodded and grabbed his cell phone off the coffee table. "And I'm going to use your computer."

I did what any self-respecting American in this day and age would do in such a situation: I searched the Internet for zombies.

I couldn't say it was particularly useful. A frighteningly large number of the sites that came up belonged to survivalist groups planning for the great zombie infestation that would bring civilization collapsing around our ears. They helpfully informed a casual reader such as myself that the government was ill prepared to handle the magnitude of the disaster that would wreak itself upon the country when the horrible zombie-virus mutation swept through the population. We must be prepared to defend ourselves against the flesh-eating hordes bent on our destruction.

This was a movie synopsis, not data, and while fascinating, it wasn't helpful.

A bunch of articles on voodoo and Haitian folklore seemed mildly more useful, but even those were contradictory: The true believers in magic argued with the hardened scientists, and even the scientists argued among themselves about whether the legends sprang from the use of certain drugs or from profound psychological disorders.

I'd seen enough wild stories play out in my time that I couldn't discount any of these alternatives. These days, magic and science were converging on one another.

Someone was selling zombie powders on eBay. They even came with an instruction booklet. That might be fun to bid on just to say I'd done it. Even if I did, the instruction book that might have some insight on the problem wouldn't get here in time.

Something most of the articles mentioned: Stories said that the taste of salt would revive a zombie. Revived them out of what, and into what, no one seemed to agree on. If they weren't really dead but comatose, the person would be restored. If they were honest-to-God walking dead, they'd be released from servitude and make their way back to their graves.

I went to the kitchen and found a saltshaker.

If she really was a zombie, she couldn't have just shown up here. She had come here for a specific reason, there had to be some connection. She was here to scare someone, which meant someone here had to know her. Nobody was volunteering any information.

Maybe she could tell me herself.

Finally, I had to touch her, in order to get the salt into her mouth. I put my hand on her shoulder. She swayed enough that I thought she might fall over, so I pulled away. A moment later, she steadied, remaining upright. I could probably push her forward, guide her, and make her walk like a puppet.

I shivered.

Swallowing back a lump of bile threatening to climb my throat,

I held her chin, tipping her head back. Her skin was waxen, neither warm nor cold. Her muscles were limp, perfectly relaxed. Or dead. I tried not to think of it. She'd been drugged. That was the theory I was going for. Praying for, rather.

"What are you doing?" Matt said.

"Never mind. Did you call the ambulance?"

"They should be here any minute."

I sprinkled a few shakes of salt into her mouth.

I had to tip her head forward and close her mouth for her because she couldn't do it herself. And if she couldn't do that, she surely couldn't swallow. None of the information said she had to swallow the salt, just taste it. In cultures around the world salt had magical properties. It was a ward against evil, protection against fairies, a treasure as great as gold. It seemed so common and innocuous now. Hard to believe it could do anything besides liven up a basket of French fries.

Her eyes moved.

The film, the dullness went away, and her gaze focused. It flickered, as if searching or confused.

Fear tightened her features. Her shoulders bunched, and her fingers clenched into claws. She screamed.

She let out a wail of anguish, bone-leaching in its intensity. A couple of yelps of shock answered from within the apartment. Her face melted into an expression of despair, lips pulled back in a frown, eyes red and wincing. But she didn't cry.

Reaching forward with those crooked fingers, she took a stumbling step forward. My heart racing, my nausea growing, I hurried out of her way. Another step followed, clumsy and unsure. She was like a toddler who'd just learned to walk. This was the slow, shuffling gait of a zombie in every B-grade horror movie I'd ever seen. The salt hadn't cured her; it had just woken her up.

She stumbled forward, step by step, reaching. People scrambled out of her way.

She didn't seem hungry. That look of utter pain and sadness remained locked on her features. She looked as if her heart had been torn out and smashed into pieces.

Her gaze searched wildly, desperately.

I ran in front of her, blocking her path. "Hey—can you hear me?" I waved my arms, trying to catch her attention. She didn't seem to notice, but she shifted, angling around me. So I tried again. "Who are you? Can you tell me your name? How did this happen?"

Her gaze had focused on something behind me. When I got in front of her, she looked right through me and kept going like I wasn't there. I turned to find what had caught her attention.

A man and woman sat wedged together in a secondhand armchair, looking like a Mack truck was about to run them down. The zombie woman shuffled toward them. Now that I was out of the way, she reached toward them, arms rigid and trembling. She moaned—she might have been trying to speak, but she couldn't shape her mouth right. She was like an infant who desperately wanted something but didn't have the words to say it. She was an infant in the body of an adult.

And what she wanted was the man in the chair.

A few steps away, her moaning turned into a wail. The woman in the chair screamed and fell over the arm to get away. The man wasn't that nimble, or he was frozen in place.

The zombie wobbled on her next step, then fell to her knees, but that didn't stop her reaching. She was close enough to grab his feet. Those clawlike hands clenched on his ankles, and she tried to pull herself forward, dragging herself on the carpet, still moaning.

The man shrieked and kicked at her, yanking his legs away and trying to curl up in the chair.

"Stop it!" I screamed at him, rushing forward to put myself between them.

She was sprawled on the floor now, crying gut-wrenching sobs. I held her shoulders and pulled her back from the chair, laying her on her back. Her arms still reached, but the rest of her body had become limp, out of her control.

"Matt, get a pillow and a blanket." He ran to the bedroom to get them. That was all I could think—try to make her comfortable. When were those paramedics going to get here?

I looked at the guy in the chair. Like the rest of the people at the party, he was twenty-something. Thin and generically cute, he had shaggy dark hair, a preppy button-up shirt, and gray trousers. I wouldn't have picked him out of the crowd.

"Who are you?" I said.

"C-Carson."

He even had a preppy name to go with the ensemble. I glanced at the woman who was with him. Huddled behind the armchair, she was starting to peer out. She had dyed black hair, a tiny nose stud, and a tight dress. More like the kind of crowd Matt hung out with. I wouldn't have put her and Carson together. Maybe they both thought they were slumming.

"Do you know her?" I asked him, nodding at the zombie woman on the floor.

He shook his head quickly, pressing himself even farther back in the chair. He was sweating. Carson was about to lose it.

Matt returned and helped me fit the pillow under her head and spread the blanket over her. He, too, was beginning to see her as someone who was sick—not a monster.

"You're lying," I said. "She obviously knows you. Who is she?"

"I don't know, I don't know!"

"Matt, who is this guy?"

Matt glanced at him. "Just met him tonight. He's Trish's new boyfriend."

"Trish?" I said to the woman behind the armchair.

"I—I don't know. At least, I'm not sure. I never met her, but I think . . . I think she's his ex-girlfriend. Beth, I think. But Carson, you told me she moved away—"

Carson, staring at the woman on the floor, looked like he was about to have a screaming fit. He was still shaking his head.

I was ready to throttle him. I wanted an explanation. Maybe he really didn't know. But if he was lying . . . "Carson!"

He flinched at my shout.

Sirens sounded down the street, coming closer. The paramedics. I hoped they could help her, but the sick feeling in my stomach hadn't gone away.

"I'll meet them on the street," Matt said, running out.

"Beth," I said to the woman. I caught her hands, managed to pull them down so they were resting on her chest. I murmured at her, and she quieted. Her skin color hadn't gotten any better. She didn't feel cold as death, but she felt cool. The salt hadn't sent her back to any grave, and it hadn't revived her. I wasn't sure she could be revived.

A moment later, a couple of uniformed paramedics carrying equipment entered, followed by Matt. The living room should have felt crowded, but apparently as soon as the door cleared, most of the guests had fled. God, what a way to kill a party.

The paramedics came straight toward Beth. I got out of the way. They immediately knelt by her, checked her pulse, shined a light in her eyes. I breathed a little easier. Finally, someone was doing something useful.

"What happened?" one of them asked.

How did I explain this? *She's a zombie.* That wasn't going to work, because I didn't think she was one anymore. *She* was *a zombie* didn't sound any better.

"She was going to leave," Carson said, suddenly, softly. Responding to the authority of the uniform, maybe. He stared at her, unable to look away. He spoke as if in a trance. "I didn't want her to go. She asked me to come with her, to Seattle—but I didn't want to do that, either. I wanted her to stay with me. So I . . . this stuff, this powder. It would make her do anything I wanted. I used it. But it . . . changed her. She wasn't the same. She—was like that. Dead almost. I left her, but she followed. She kept following me—"

"Call it poisoning," said one paramedic to the other.

"Where did you get this powder?" I said.

"Some guy on the Internet."

I wanted to kill him. Wanted to put my hands around his throat and kill him.

"Kitty," Matt said. I took a breath. Calmed down.

"Any idea what was in this powder?" one of the paramedics said, sounding like he was repressing as much anger as I was.

Carson shook his head.

"Try tetrodotoxin," I said. "Induces a death-like coma. Also causes brain damage. Irreparable brain damage."

Grimacing, the paramedic said, "We won't be able to check that until we get her to the hospital. I don't see any ID on her.

I'm going to call in the cops, see if they've had a missing persons report on her. And to see what they want to do with him."

Carson flinched at his glare.

Trish backed away. "If I tried to break up with you—would you have done that to me, too?" Her mouth twisted with unspoken accusations. Then, she fled.

Carson thought he'd make his own zombie slave girlfriend, then somehow wasn't satisfied at the results. She probably wasn't real good in bed. He'd probably done it, too—had sex with Beth's brain-damaged, comatose body. The cops couldn't get here fast enough, in my opinion.

"There's two parts to it," I said. "The powder creates the zombie. But then there's the spell to bind her to you, to bind the slave to the master. Some kind of object with meaning, a receptacle for the soul. You have it. That's why she followed you. That's why she wouldn't stay away." The salt hadn't broken that bond. She'd regained her will—but the damage was too great for her to do anything with it. She knew enough to recognize him and what he'd done to her, but could only cry out helplessly.

He reached into his pocket, pulled something out. He opened his fist to reveal what.

A diamond engagement ring lay in his palm.

Beth reacted, arcing her back, flailing, moaning. The paramedics freaked, pinned her arms, jabbed her with a hypodermic. She settled again, whimpering softly.

I took the ring from Carson. He glared at me, the first time he'd really looked at me. I didn't see remorse in his eyes. Only fear. Like Victor Frankenstein, he'd created a monster and all he could do when confronted with it was cringe in terror.

"Matt, you have a string or a shoelace or something?"

"Yeah, sure."

He came back with a bootlace fresh out of the package. I put the ring on it, knotted it, and slipped it over Beth's head. "Can you make sure this stays with her?" I asked the paramedics. They nodded.

This was half science, half magic. If the ring really did hold

Beth's soul, maybe it would help. If it didn't help—well, at least Carson wouldn't have it anymore.

The cops came and took statements from all of us, including the paramedics, then took Carson away. The paramedics took Beth away; the ambulance siren howled down the street, away.

Finally, when Matt and I were alone among the remains of his disaster of a party, I started crying. "How could he do that? How could he even think it? She was probably this wonderful, beautiful, independent woman, and he destroyed—"

Matt had poured two glasses of champagne. He handed me one. "Happy New Year, Kitty." He pointed at the clock on the microwave. 12:03 A.M.

Crap. I missed it. I started crying harder.

Matt, my friend, hugged me. So once again, I didn't get a New Year's kiss. This year, I didn't mind.

Life Is the Teacher

Emma slid under the surface of the water and stayed there. She lay in the tub, on her back, and stared up at a world made soft, blurred with faint ripples. An unreal world viewed through a distorted filter. For minutes—four, six, ten—she stayed under water, and didn't drown, because she didn't breathe. Would never breathe again.

The world looked different through these undead eyes. Thicker, somehow. And also, strangely, clearer.

Survival seemed like such a curious thing once you'd already been killed.

This was her life now. She didn't have to stay here. She could end it any time she wanted just by opening the curtains at dawn. But she didn't.

Sitting up, she pushed back her soaking hair and rained water all around her with the noise of a rushing stream. Outside the blood-warm bath, her skin chilled in the air. She felt every little thing, every little current—from the vent, from a draft from the window, coolness eddying along the floor, striking the walls. She shivered. Put the fingers of one hand on the wrist of the other and felt no pulse.

After spreading a towel on the floor, she stepped from the bath.

She looked at herself: She didn't look any different. Same slim body, smooth skin, young breasts the right size to cup in her hands, nipples the color of a bruised peach. Her skin was paler than she remembered. So pale it was almost translucent. Bloodless.

Not for long.

She dried her brown hair so it hung straight to her shoulders and dressed with more care than she ever had before. Not that the clothes she put on were by any means fancy, or new, or anything other than what she'd already had in her closet: a tailored silk shirt over a black lace camisole, jeans, black leather pumps, and a few choice pieces of jewelry, a couple of thin silver chains and dangling silver earrings. Every piece, every seam, every fold of fabric, produced an effect, and she wanted to be sure she produced the right effect: young, confident, alluring. Without, of course, looking like she was *trying* to produce such an effect. It must seem casual, thrown together, effortless. She switched the earrings from one ear to the other because they didn't seem to lay right the other way.

This must be what a prostitute felt like.

Dissatisfied, she went upstairs to see Alette.

The older woman was in the parlor, waiting in a wingback chair. The room was decorated in tasteful antiques, Persian rugs, and velvet-upholstered furniture, with thick rich curtains hanging over the windows. Books crammed into shelves and a silver tea service ornamented the mantel. For all its opulent decoration, the room had a comfortable, natural feel to it. Its owner had come by the decor honestly. The Victorian atmosphere was genuine.

Alette spoke with a refined British accent. "You don't have to do this."

Alette was the most regal, elegant woman Emma knew. An apparent thirty years old, she was poised, dressed in a silk skirt and jacket, her brunette hair tied in a bun, her face like porcelain. She was over four hundred years old.

Emma was part of her clan, her Family, by many ties, from many directions. By blood, Alette was Emma's ancestor, a many-greats grandmother. Closer, Alette had made the one who in turn had made Emma.

That had been unplanned. Emma hadn't wanted it. The man in

question had been punished. He was gone now, and Alette had taken care of her: mother, mentor, mistress.

"You can't bottle-feed me forever," Emma replied. In this existence, that meant needles, IV tubes, and a willing donor. It was so clinical.

"I can try," Alette said, her smile wry.

If Emma let her, Alette would take care of her forever. Literally forever. But that felt wrong, somehow. If Emma was going to live like this, then she ought to live. Not cower like a child.

"Thank you for looking after me. I'm not trying to sound ungrateful, but—"

"But you want to be able to look after yourself."

Emma nodded, and again the wry smile touched Alette's lips. "Our family has always had the most awful streak of independence."

Emma's laugh startled her. She didn't know she still could.

"Remember what I've taught you," Alette said, rising from her chair and moving to stand with Emma. "How to choose. How to lure him. How to leave him. Remember how I've taught you to see, and to feel. Remember to only take a little. If you take it all, you'll kill him. Or risk condemning him to this life."

"I remember." The lessons had been difficult. She'd had to learn to see the world with new eyes.

Alette smoothed Emma's hair back from her face and arranged it over her shoulders—an uncharacteristic bit of fidgeting. "I know you do. And I know you'll be fine. But if you need anything, please—"

"I'll call," Emma finished. "You won't send anyone to follow me, will you?"

"No," she said. "I won't."

"Thank you."

Alette kissed her cheek and sent her to hunt alone for the first time.

Alette had given her advice: Go somewhere new, in an unfamiliar neighborhood, where she wasn't likely to meet someone from her old life, therefore making her less likely to encounter complications of emotion or circumstance.

Emma didn't take this advice.

She'd been a student at George Washington University. Officially, she'd taken a leave of absence, but she wasn't sure she'd ever be able to continue her studies and finish her degree. There were always night classes, sure . . . but it was almost a joke, and like most anything worth doing, easier said than done.

There was a place, a bar where she and her friends used to go sometimes when classes got out. They'd arrive just in time for happy hour, when they could buy two-dollar hamburgers and cheap pitchers of beer. They'd eat supper, play a few rounds of pool, bitch about classes and papers they hadn't written yet. On weekends they'd come late and play pool until last call. A completely normal life.

That was what Emma found herself missing, a few months into this new life. Laughing with her friends. Maybe she should have gone someplace else for this, found new territory. But she wanted to see the familiar.

She came in through the front and paused, blinked a couple of times, took a deep breath through her nose to taste the air. And the world slowed down. Noise fell to a low hum, the lights seemed to brighten, and just by turning her head a little she could see it all. Thirty-four people packed into the first floor of this converted townhouse. Twelve sat at the bar, two worked behind the bar, splashing their way through the fumes of a dozen different kinds of alcohol. Their sweat mixed with those fumes, two kinds of heat blending with the third ashy odor of cigarette smoke. This place was hot with bodies. Five beating hearts played pool around two tables in the back, three more watched—these were female. Girlfriends. The smell of competing testosterone was ripe. All the rest crammed around tables or stood in empty spaces, putting alcohol into their bodies, their blood—Emma could smell it through their pores. She caught all this in a glance, in a second.

She could feel the clear paths by the way the air moved. Incredibly, she could feel the whole room, all of it pressing gently against her skin. As if she looked down on it from above. As if she commanded it. There—that couple at the table in the corner was fighting. The woman stared into her tumbler of gin and tonic while her foot tapped a nervous beat on the floor. Her boyfriend stared at her, frowning hard, his arms crossed, his scotch forgotten.

Emma could have him if she wanted. His blood was singing with need. He would be easy to persuade, to lure away from his difficulty. A chance meeting by the bathrooms, an unseen exit out the back—

No. Not like that.

A quartet of boisterous, drunken men burst into laughter in front of her. Raucous business-school types, celebrating some exam or finished project. She knew how to get to them, too. Stumble perhaps. Lean an accidental arm on a shoulder, gasp an apology—and the one who met her gaze first would be the one to follow her.

Instead, she went to the bar, and despite the crowd, the press of bodies jostling for space, her path there was clear, and a space opened for her just as she arrived because she knew it would be there.

She wanted to miss the taste of alcohol. She could remember the taste of wine, the tang on the tongue, the warmth passing down her throat. She remembered great dinners, her favorite Mexican food, overstuffed burritos with sour cream and chile verde, with a big, salty margarita. She wanted to miss it with a deep and painful longing. But the memories turned her stomach. The thought of consuming anything made her feel sick. Anything except blood.

The glass of wine before her remained untouched. It was only for show.

She never would have done this in the old days. Sitting alone at the bar like this, staring into her drink—she looked like she was trying to get picked up.

Well, wasn't she?

When the door opened and a laughing crowd of friends entered, Emma turned and smiled in greeting. Even before the door had opened, she'd known somehow. She'd sensed the sound of a voice, the tone of a footstep, the scent of skin, a ripple in the air. She couldn't have remembered such fine details from her old life. But somehow, she'd known. She knew *them*.

"Emma!"

"Hey, Chris." Finally, her smile felt like her old smile. Her old friends gathered around, leaned in for hugs, and she obliged them. But the one who spoke to her, the one she focused on, was Chris.

He was six feet tall, with wavy blond hair and a clean-shaven, handsome face, still boyish but filling out nicely. He had a shy smile and laughing eyes.

"Where've you been? I haven't seen you in weeks. The registrar's office said you took a leave of absence."

She had her story all figured out. It wasn't even a lie, really.

"I've been sick," she said.

"You couldn't even call?"

"Really sick." She pressed her lips in a thin smile, hoping she sounded sad.

"Yeah, I guess." He took the cue not to press the question further. He brightened. "But you look great now. Really great."

There it was, a spark in his eye, a flush in his cheek. She'd always wondered if he liked her. She'd never been sure. Now, she had tools. She had senses. And she looked great. It wasn't her, a bitter voice sounded inside her. It was this thing riding her, this creature inside her. It was a lure, a trap.

Looking great made men like Chris blush. Now, she could use it. She knew how to respond. She'd always been uncertain before.

She lowered her gaze, smiled, then looked at him warmly, searching. "Thanks."

"I—I guess you already have a drink."

The others had moved off to claim one of the pool tables. Chris remained, leaning on the bar beside her, nervously tapping his foot.

Compared to him, Emma had no trouble radiating calm. She was in control here.

"Let me get you something," she said.

For a moment—for a long, lingering, blissful moment—it felt like old times. They only talked, but the conversation was long and heartfelt. He really listened to her. So she kept talking—so much so that she almost got to the truth.

"I've had to reassess everything. What am I going to do with my life, what's the point of it all." She shrugged, letting the implications settle.

"You must have been really sick," he said, his gaze intent.

"I thought I was going to die," she said, and it wasn't a lie. She didn't remember much of it—the man, the monster's hand on her face, on her arms, pinning her to the bed. She wanted to scream, but the sound caught in her throat. However frightened she'd been, her body responded to his touch, flushed, and this made her ashamed. She hoped that he would kill her rather than turn her. But she awoke again and the world was different.

"You make it sound like you're not coming back."

"Hm?" she murmured, startled out of her memory.

"To school. You aren't coming back, are you?"

"I don't know," she said, wanting to be honest, knowing she couldn't tell him everything. "It'd be hard, after what's happened. I just don't know." This felt so casual, so normal, that she almost forgot she had a purpose here. That she was supposed to be guiding this conversation. She surprised herself by knowing what to say next. "This is going to sound really cliché, but when you think you aren't going to make it like that, it really does change how you look at things. You really do try to live for the moment. You don't have time to screw around anymore."

Which was ironic, because really, she had all the time in the world.

Chris hung on her words. "No, it doesn't sound cliché at all. It sounds real."

"I just don't think I have time anymore for school. I'd rather, you know—live."

This sounded awful—so false and ironic. *Don't listen to me, I'm immortal,* part of her almost yelled. But she didn't, because another part of her was hungry.

When he spoke, he sounded uncertain. "Do—do you want to get out of here? Go to my place maybe?"

Her shy smile widened. She'd wanted him to say that. She wanted him to think this was his idea. She rounded her shoulders, aware of her posture, her body language, wanting to send a message that she was open, willing, and ready.

"Yeah," she said, touching his hand as she stood.

His skin felt like fire.

Chris took her back to his place. He lived within walking distance, in a garden-level unit in a block of apartments. A nice place, small but functional, and very student. It felt like a foreign country.

Emma watched Chris unlock the door and felt some trepidation. Nerves, that was all. Anticipation. Unknown territory—to be expected, going home with a new guy for the first time.

Chris fumbled with the key.

There was more to this than the unknown, or the thrill of anticipation. She stood on the threshold, literally, and felt something: a force outside of herself. Nothing solid, rather a feeling that made her want to turn away. Like a voice whispering, *Go, you are not welcome, this is not your place, your blood does not dwell here.*

She couldn't ignore it. The voice fogged her senses. If she turned away, even just a little—stepped back, tilted her head away—her mind cleared. She didn't notice when Chris finally unlocked the door and pushed his way inside.

She didn't know how long he'd been standing on the other side of the threshold, looking back at her expectantly. She simply couldn't move forward.

"Come on in," he said, giving a reassuring smile.

The feeling, fog, and voice disappeared. The unseen resistance fell away, the barrier was gone. She'd been invited.

Returning his smile, she went in.

Inside was what she'd expected from a male college student: The front room had a ripe, well-lived-in smell of dirty laundry and pizza boxes. Mostly, though, it smelled like him. In a moment, she took it all in, the walls and the carpet. Despite how many times the former had been repainted and the later replaced, the sense that generations of college students had passed through here lingered.

The years of life pressed against her skin, and she closed her eyes to take it all in, to feel it eddy around her.

"Do you want something to drink?" Chris was sweating, just a little.

Yes. "No, I'm okay."

Seduction wasn't a quick thing. Though she supposed, if she wanted, she could just take him. She could feel in her bones and muscles that she could. He wouldn't know what hit him. It would be easy, use the currents of the room, slow down the world, move in the blink of an eye—

No. No speed, no fear, no mess. Better to do it cleanly. Nicer, for everyone. Now that they were alone, away from the crowd, her purpose became so very clear. Her need became crystalline. She planned it out: a brief touch on his arm, press her body close, and let him do the rest.

Fake. It was fake, manipulative. . . . She liked him. She really did. She wished she'd done this months ago, she wished she'd had the nerve to say something, to touch his hand—before she'd been attacked and turned. Then, she hadn't had the courage, and now she wanted something else from him. It felt like deception.

This was why Alette had wanted her to find a stranger. She wouldn't be wishing that it had all turned out different. Maybe she wouldn't care. She wanted to like Chris—she didn't want to need him like this. Didn't want to hurt him. And she didn't know if she'd have been so happy to go home with anyone else. That was why she was here. That was why she'd gone to that particular bar and waited for him.

That doesn't matter, her instincts—new instincts, like static across her skin, like the heat of blood drawing her—told her. The emotion is a by-product of need. *He is yours because you've won him. You've already won him, you have only to claim him.*

She reached out—she could feel him without looking, by

sensing the way the air folded around his body—and brushed her fingers across the back of his hand. He reacted instantly, curling his hand around hers, squeezing, pulling himself toward her, and kissing her—half on cheek, half on lip.

He pulled back, waiting for a reaction, his breath coming fast and brushing her cheek. She didn't breathe at all—would he notice? Should she gasp, to fool him into thinking she breathed, so he wouldn't notice that she didn't? Another deception.

Rather than debating the question, she lunged for him, her lips seeking his, kissing forcefully. Distract him. In a minute he wouldn't notice anything. She devoured him, and he was off balance, lagging behind as she sucked his lips and sought his tongue. She'd never been this hungry for someone before. The taste of his skin, his sweat, his mouth, burst inside her and fired her brain. He tasted so good on the outside, she couldn't wait to discover what the inside of him tasted like, that warm blood flushing just under the surface. Her nails dug into his arm, wanting to pull off the sleeves of his shirt, all his clothes, to be closer to his living skin. She wanted nothing more than to close her teeth, bite into him—

She pulled back, almost ripping herself away. Broke all contact and took a step back, so that she was surrounded by cool air and not flesh. She could hear the blood rushing in his neck.

This wasn't her. This wasn't her doing this. She couldn't do this.

Chris gave a nervous chuckle. "Wow. That was . . . Emma, what's wrong?"

She closed her eyes, took a moment to gather herself, drew breath to speak. It would look like a deep sigh to him.

"I'm sorry," she said. "I can't do this."

She couldn't look at him. If he saw her eyes, saw the way she looked at him, he'd know about the thing inside her, he'd know she only wanted to rip him open. How could she explain to him, without explaining?

"I had a really nice time . . . but I'm sorry."

Holding the collar of her jacket closed, she fled before he could say a word in argument.

Alette had had to force her to drink blood the first time. Emma hadn't wanted to become this thing. She'd threatened to leave the house at dawn and die in the sunlight. Alette persuaded her to stay. A haunted need inside her listened to that, wanted to survive, and stayed inside, in the dark. Still, she gagged when the mistress showed her the glass tumbler full of viscous red. "It's only your first night in this life," she said. "You're too new to hunt. But you still need this." Alette had then stood behind her, embraced Emma and locked her arms tight with one hand while tipping the glass to her mouth with the other. Emma had struggled, fought to pull out of her grasp, but Alette was deceptively powerful, and Emma was still sick and weak.

Emma had recognized the scent of the blood even before it reached her lips: tangy, metallic, like a butcher's shop. Even as she rebelled, even as her mind quailed, part of her reached toward it. Her mouth salivated. This contradiction was what had caused her to break down, screaming that she didn't want this, that she couldn't do this, kicking and thrashing in Alette's grip. But Alette had been ready for it, and very calmly held her still, forced the glass between her lips, and made her drink. As much spilled out of her mouth and down her chin as slid down her throat. Then, she'd fallen still. Helpless, she'd surrendered, even as that single sip returned her strength to her.

Eventually, she could hold the glass herself and drain it. She even realized she should learn to find the blood herself. She thought she'd been ready.

Alette found her in the parlor, sitting curled up on one of the sofas. "What happened?"

Emma hugged her knees and stared into space. She'd spent hours here, almost until dawn, watching dust motes, watching time move. This was fascinating—the idea that she could see time move. Almost, if she concentrated, she could reach out and touch it. Twist it. Cross the room in a second. She would look like she was flying. She'd almost done it, earlier tonight. She'd have taken him so quickly he wouldn't have known . . .

Alette waited patiently for her to answer. Like she could also spend all night watching time move.

"I don't know." Even after all that had happened, her voice sounded like a little girl's. She still felt like a child. "I liked him. It was . . . it felt good. I thought . . ." She shook her head. The memory was a distant thing. She didn't want to revisit it. "I got scared. I had him in the palm of my hand. He was mine. I was strong. And this *thing* rose up in me, this amazing power—I could do anything. But it wasn't me. So I got scared and ran."

Poised and regal, Alette sat, hands crossed in her lap, the elegant noblewoman of an old painting. Nothing shook her, nothing shattered her.

"That's the creature. That's what you are now. How you control it will determine what your life will look like from now on."

It was a pronouncement, a judgment, a knell of doom.

Alette continued. "Some of our kind give free rein to it. They revel in it. It makes them strong, but often leaves them vulnerable. If you try to ignore it, it will consume you. You'll lose that part of yourself that is yours."

In her bones, in the tracks of her bloodless veins, Emma knew Alette was right, and this was what she feared: that she wasn't strong, that she wouldn't control it. That she would lose her self, her soul to the thing. Her eyes ached with tears that didn't fall.

How did Alette control it? How did she manage to sit so calm and dignified, with the creature writhing inside of her, desperate for power? Emma felt sure she wouldn't last long enough to develop that beautiful self-possession.

"Oh my dear, hush there." Alette moved to her side and gathered her in her arms. She'd seen Emma's anguish and now sought to wrap her in comfort. Emma clung to her, pressing her face against the cool silk of her jacket, holding tight to her arms. For just a moment, she let herself be a child, protected within the older woman's embrace. "I can't teach you everything. Some steps you must take alone. I can take care of you if you like—keep you here, watch you always, hold the creature at bay and bring you cups of blood. But I don't think you'd be happy."

"I don't know that I'll ever be happy. I don't think I can do this."

"The power is a tool you use to get what you need. It should not control you."

Not much of the night remained. Emma felt dawn tugging at her nerves—another new sensation to catalog with the rest. The promise of sunlight was a weariness that settled over her and drove her underground, to a bed in a sealed, windowless room. At least she didn't need a coffin. Small comfort.

"Come," Alette said, urging her to her feet. "Sleep for now. Vanquish this beast another night."

Her mind was still her own, and she still dreamed. The fluttering, disjointed scenes took place in daylight. Already, the sunlit world of her dreaming memories had begun to look odd to her, unreal and uncertain, as if these things could never really have happened.

At dusk, she woke and told herself all kinds of platitudes: She had to get back on the horse; if at first you don't succeed. . . . But it came down to wanting to see Chris again. She wanted to apologize.

She found his phone number and called him, half hoping he wouldn't answer, so she could leave a message and not have to face him.

But he picked up. "Hi."

"Hi, Chris?"

"Emma?" He sounded surprised. And why wouldn't he be? "Hey. Are you okay?"

Her anxiety vanished, and she was glad that she'd called. "I'm okay. I just wanted to say I'm so sorry about last night. I got scared. I freaked. I know you'll probably laugh in my face, but I want to see you again."

I'd like to try again, an unspoken desire she couldn't quite give voice to.

"I wouldn't laugh. I was just worried about you. I thought maybe I'd done something wrong."

"No, no, of course you didn't. It's just . . . I guess since this was my first time out since I was sick, my first time being with anyone since then . . . I got scared, like I said."

"I don't know. It seemed like you were really into it." He chuckled nervously. "You were really hot."

"I was into it." She wasn't sure this was going to sound endearingly awkward or just awkward. She tried to put that lust, that power that she'd felt last night, into her voice. Like maybe she could touch him over the phone. She held that image in her mind. "I'd like to see you again."

The meaning behind the words said, *I need you.*

Somehow, he heard that. She could tell by the catch in his breath, an added huskiness in his voice. "Okay. Why don't you come over."

"I'll be right there." She shut the phone off, not giving him a chance to change his mind, not letting herself doubt.

Emma could screw this up again. There was a gnawing in her belly, an anxious thought that kept saying, *This isn't right. I'm using him, and he doesn't deserve that.* She was starting to think of that voice as the old Emma. The Emma who could walk in daylight and never would again.

The new Emma, the voice she had to listen to now, felt like she was about to win a race. She had the power here, and she was buzzed on it. Almost drunk. The new Emma didn't miss alcohol because she didn't need it.

It felt good. Everything she moved toward felt so physically, fundamentally good. All she had to do was let go of doubt and revel in it.

That near ecstasy shone in her eyes when Chris opened the door. For a moment, they only looked at each other. He was tentative—expecting her to flee again. She caught his gaze, and he saw nothing but her. She could see him, see through him, everything about him. He wanted her—had watched her for a long time, dreaming of a moment like this, not thinking it would happen. Not brave enough to make it happen. Assuming she wasn't the kind of girl who would let him in.

And yet here she was. She saw all of this play behind his eyes.

She touched his cheek and gave him a shy smile. "Thanks for letting me come over."

Gazing at him through lowered lids, she pushed him over the edge.

He grabbed her hand and pulled her against him, bringing her lips to his, hungry, and she was ready for him, opening her mouth to him, letting him devour her with kisses and sending his passion back to him. He clutched at her, wrinkling the back of her shirt as if he were trying to rip through it to get to her skin, kneading, moving his hand low to pin her against him. These weren't the tender, careful, assured movements he might have used if he were attempting to seduce her—if he'd had to persuade her, if she had shown some hesitation. These were the clumsy, desperate gropings of a man who couldn't control himself. She made him lose control. If she could now pick up those reins that he had dropped—

She pulled back her head to look at him; kissed him lightly, then slowly—staying slow, forcing him to match her pace. She controlled his movements now. She unbuttoned his shirt, drawing out every motion, brushing the bare skin underneath with fleeting touches. Lingering. Teasing. Heightening his need, feeding his desire. Driving him mad. He was melting in her arms. She could feel his muscles tremble.

Taking hold of his hands—she practically had to peel them off her backside—she guided them to her breasts and pressed them there. His eyes widened, like he'd just won a prize, and she smiled, letting her head fall back, feeling the weight of her hair pull her back, rolling her shoulders and putting her chest even more firmly into his grasp. Quickly, he undid the buttons of her shirt, tugged aside her bra, and bent to kiss her, tracing her right breast with his tongue, taking her nipple between his teeth. For all that had happened, for all that she'd become, her nerves, her senses, still worked, still shuddered at a lover's touch. Her hands clenched on his shoulders, then tightened in his hair. She gasped with pleasure. She wanted this. She wanted this badly.

She pulled him toward the bedroom. Didn't stop looking at him; held his gaze, would not let him break it. Her own veins were fire—controlled fire, in a very strong furnace, directed to some great purpose, a driving machine. She needed him, the blood that flushed along his skin. His very capillaries opened for her. She did not have a heartbeat, but something in her breast cried out in triumph. He was hers, to do with as she pleased.

She ran her tongue along her top row of teeth, scraping it on needle-sharp fangs.

He tugged at her shirt, searching for more bare skin. She shivered at his touch on the small of her back. His hands were hot, burning up, and for all her desire, her skin felt cold, bloodless.

She would revel in his heat instead.

She pushed his shirt off his shoulders and let it drop to the floor, then wrapped herself around him, pulling as much of that skin and heat to her as she could.

"You're so warm," she murmured, not meaning to speak at all. But she was amazed at the heat of him. She hadn't felt so much heat since before . . . before she became this thing.

He kept his mouth against her, lips working around her neck, pressing up to her ear, tasting every inch. Her nerves flared at the touch.

And suddenly, finally, she understood. It wasn't just the blood that drew her kind to living humans. It was the heat, the life itself. They were bright sunlight to creatures who lived in darkness. They held the energy that kept her kind alive and immortal—for there would always be people, an endless supply of people, to draw that energy from. She was a parasite and the host would never die.

Neither, then, would she.

With new reverence, she eased him to the bed, made him lay back, and finished stripping him, tugging down his jeans and boxers, touching him at every opportunity, fingertips around his hips, along his thighs. She paused to regard him, stretched out on his back, naked before her, member erect, whole body flushed and almost trembling with need. She had brought him to this moment, with desire burning in his eyes. He would do anything she asked, now. She found herself wanting to be kind—to reward him for the role he'd played in her education, in bringing about the epiphany that so clarified her place in the world.

This exchange would be fair. She would not simply take from him. He would have pleasure as well.

She rubbed her hands down his chest, down his belly. He

moaned, shivered under her touch but did not interfere. She traced every curve of his body: down his ribs, his hips. Stretched out on the bed beside him, she took his penis in her hand. Again, their mouths met. His kissing was urgent, fevered, and she kept pace with him. He was growing slick with sweat and smelled of musk.

She laughed. The sound just bubbled out of her. Lips apart, eyes gleaming, she found joy in this. She would live, she would not open the curtains on the dawn. She had power in this existence and she would learn to use it.

"Oh my God," Chris murmured. He froze, his eyes wide, his blood suddenly cooled. In only a second, she felt the sweat on his body start to chill as fear struck him. He wouldn't even notice it yet.

He was staring at her, her open, laughing mouth, the pointed canine teeth she'd been so careful to disguise until this moment, when euphoria overcame her.

In a moment of panic like this, it might all fall apart. An impulse to run struck her, but she'd come too far, she was too close to success. If she fled now she might never regain the nerve to try again.

"Shh, shh, it's all right," she whispered, stroking his hair, nuzzling his cheek, breathing comfort against him. "It's fine, it'll be fine."

She brought all her nascent power to bear: seduction, persuasion. The creature's allure. The ability to fog his mind, to erase all else from his thoughts but his desire for her, to fill his sight only with her.

"It's all right, Chris. I'll take care of you. I'll take good care of you."

The fear in his eyes ebbed, replaced by puzzlement—some part of his mind asking what was happening, who was she, what was she, and why was she doing this to him. She willed him to forget those questions. All that mattered were her, him, their joint passion that would feed them both: his desire, and her life.

He was still hard against her hand, and she used that. Gently, carefully, she urged him back to his heat, brought him again to that point of need. She stroked him, first with her fingertips, then with her whole hand, and his groan of pleasure gratified her. When he tipped back his head, his eyes rolling back a little, she knew he had returned to her.

The next time she kissed him, his whole body surged against her.

She twined her leg around his; he moved against her, insistent. But she held him, pinned him, and closed her mouth over his neck. There she kissed, sucked—felt the hot river of his blood so close to his skin, just under her tongue. She almost lost control, in her need to take that river into herself.

Oh so carefully, slowly, to make sure she did this right and made no mistakes, she bit. Let her needle teeth tear just a little of his skin.

The flow of blood hit her tongue with a shock and instantly translated to a delicious rush that shuddered through her body. Blood slipped down her throat like honey, burning with richness. Clenching all her muscles, groaning at the flood of it, she drank. Her hand closed tight around his erection, moved with him, and his body responded, his own wave of pleasure bringing him to climax a moment later.

She held him while he rocked against her, and she drank a dozen swallows of his blood. No more than that. Do not kill, Alette's first lesson. But a dozen mouthfuls would barely weaken him. He wouldn't even notice.

She licked the wound she'd made to hasten its healing. He might notice the marks and believe them to be insect bites. He would never know she'd been here.

His body radiated the heat of spent desire. She lay close to him, gathering as much of it as she could into herself. She now felt hot—vivid and alive. She could feel his blood traveling through her, keeping her alive.

Stroking his hair, admiring the lazy smile he wore, she whispered to him. "You won't remember me. You won't remember what happened tonight. You had a nice dream, that's all. A vivid dream."

"Emma," he murmured, flexing toward her for more. Almost, her resolve broke. Almost, she saw that pulsing artery in his neck and went to drink again.

But she continued, "If you see me again, you won't know me. Your life will go on as if you never knew me. Go to sleep. You'll sleep very well tonight."

She brushed his hair with her fingers, and a moment later he was snoring gently. She pulled a blanket over him. Kissed his forehead.

Straightening her bra, buttoning her blouse, she left the room. Made sure all the lights were off. Locked the door on her way out.

She walked home. It was the deepest, stillest hour of night, or early morning. Streetlights turned colors but no cars waited at intersections. No voices drifted from bars and all the storefronts were dark. A cold mist hung in the air, ghostlike. Emma felt that she swam through it.

The stillest part of night, and she had never felt more awake, more alive. Every pore felt the touch of air around her. Warm blood flowed in her veins, firing her heart. She walked without fear along dark streets, secure in the feeling that the world had paused to notice her passage through it.

She entered Alette's townhouse through the kitchen door in back rather than the through the front door, because she'd always come in through the back in her student days when she studied in Alette's library and paid for school by being Alette's part-time housekeeper. That had all changed. Those days—nights—were finished. But she'd never stop using the back door.

"Emma?" Alette called from the parlor.

Self-conscious, Emma followed the voice and found Alette in her favorite chair in the corner, reading a book. Emma tried not to feel like a kid sneaking home after a night of mischief.

Alette replaced a bookmark and set the book aside. "Well?"

Her unnecessary coat wrapped around her, hands folded before her, Emma stood before the mistress of the house. Almost, she reverted to the teenager's response: "Fine, okay, whatever." Monosyllables and a fast exit.

But she felt herself smile broadly, happily. "It was good."

"And the gentleman?"

"He won't remember me."

"Good," Alette said, and smiled. "Welcome to the Family, my dear."

She went back to the bar once more, a week later. Sitting at the bar, she traced condensation on the outside of a glass of gin and tonic on the rocks. She hadn't sipped, only tasted, drawing a lone breath so she could take in the scent of it.

The door opened, bringing with it a cold draft and a crowd of college students. Chris was among them, laughing at someone's joke, blond hair tousled. He walked right by her on his way to the pool tables. Flashed her a hurried smile when he caught her watching him. Didn't spare her another glance, in the way of two strangers passing in a crowded bar.

Smiling wryly to herself, Emma left her drink at the bar and went out to walk in the night.

You're on the Air

Jake leaned his elbows on the counter by the cash register and stared out over vacant aisles. His shoulders were bunched, his back slouched. This was way bad for his posture. Like he cared.

The store had been empty for hours. Half an hour ago somebody had pulled up to the gas pumps outside and paid by credit card. Really, they didn't need him here minding things. Put a vending machine outside for the stoners and the store would make a profit.

Then again, it was just as well they hired him for the graveyard shift. What else would he do for money?

Graveyard shift. That was funny.

He didn't do much these days. Slept during daylight hours, got up, grabbed a bite, came to work. Went home and was asleep again by dawn. He hadn't seen the sun in . . . he couldn't remember how long it had been. He only had these glaring white fluorescent bulbs. They hummed like insects.

The radio, a beat-up model sitting on the shelf behind him, crammed between cartons of cigarettes, scratched a folk rock song, which faded, and a voice cut in.

"Good evening, and welcome to *The Midnight Hour.* This is Kitty Norville, your ever-cheerful hostess."

Oh, *score.* It was Friday. He'd forgotten. He turned up the volume. This was his favorite show.

"Tonight it's all vampires, and all calls. I want to hear from you . . ."

Jake couldn't understand why anyone would want to become a vampire. And yet, they called into Kitty's show all the time. Wannabes. They had no clue.

"I'm ageless," said the underage caller breathlessly. "Ageless as the *grave.*"

"Okay, this is not the kinderbat poetry hour," Kitty said, which made Jake laugh, which was the reason he listened to the show. "You'll want—oh, I don't know—public access television for that."

"Whoa, what a wicked cool idea," the kid said.

If that ever happened, Jake would find the kid and beat the crap out of him himself. Thankfully, Kitty switched calls. "Please, someone with sense call me so we can discuss Byron or something. Next caller, hello."

"I knew him, you know."

Jake perked up. That cool assurance in a voice usually meant a vampire. A real one.

"Knew who?"

"Lord Byron, of course."

"*Really,*" Kitty drawled, clearly disbelieving. "You know, there are about as many vampires who say they knew Byron as there are reincarnation freaks who say they were Cleopatra in a past life. Which would mean Byron had, like, *hundreds* of obnoxious simpering twits trailing after him wherever he went. When he really only had Keats and Shelley."

The guy huffed. "How very droll."

"I'm sorry, you just hit one of my buttons, you know?"

"You've never considered that perhaps one of those vampires who say they knew Byron might be right?"

The call went on for a few more moments, and Jake's attention faded. He was thinking about what he wanted to say to this guy. More than anything he wanted to talk to another vampire—a powerful one, a reasonable one. Someone who could explain to him what was supposed to be so great about being a vampire. There had to be more to it than beating up winos who didn't even notice the parasites on their necks, all for a pint of stolen blood.

He'd changed—he could feel this humming in his muscles, like he *ought* to be stronger. Like if he tilted his head a little bit he ought to be able to see into other dimensions. So maybe he did have powers, but what was he supposed to do with them when he spent all his time hiding? He never talked to anyone anymore except to say, *Here's your change.*

There had to be a way to dig out of this hole he was in.

"What's on your mind?"

"Destiny," the vampire said.

What the hell did that even *mean,* Jake thought.

"Right, the *big* question. Like, why are we here, what's the point to life, that sort of thing?"

"I'm curious to hear what you think about it."

"That's my line." Kitty sounded put out.

"Are you going to tell me?"

She sighed, a hiss over the radio. "All right. I'll bite. Here's what I think, with the caveat that I may be wrong: I think we're here to make the world a better place than we found it. I think we don't always deserve the cards that we're dealt, good or bad. But we are judged by how we play the cards we're dealt. Those of us with a bum deal that make it harder to do good—we just have to work a little more is all. There's no destiny. There's just muddling through without doing too much damage."

Jake admired Kitty: She was so down-to-earth and practical and yet inspiring, all at the same time. All she really wanted was for people to stop feeling sorry for themselves, get off their asses, and make their lives better. She made it sound like anyone could do it.

It was almost enough to inspire him get off his ass and make his life better.

"Hmm, that's very nice," the vampire said, and the condescension in his voice made Jake fume, gritting the back of his teeth in frustration. Easy for *him* to be arrogant.

On a whim, he picked up the phone and dialed. Kitty was

always telling her listeners to *do* something—here he was, doing something.

"All right. I *know* you're just trying to bait me. Why don't you come out and say what you want to say."

The caller's attitude got even worse.

"You talk about us, vampires and lycanthropes, like we're afflicted. Like we have a handicap. And I suppose if your goal is to *pass* as human, to *blend in* with society, then it is a handicap. But have you ever thought that *we* are the chosen ones? Fate marked us, and we became what we are. We are superior, marked by destiny, and one day we will rule the world . . ."

Jake gripped the edge of the counter until the plastic cracked. He let go, startled. Cheap crap. And the guy on the radio was *still talking.* This was the glorified stereotype, the reason why some people actually *wanted* to be vampires. This was all those stories of elegant men and women, hundreds of years old, stalking the night like predators—such a sexy picture that made. Made it sound like you'd actually get something good out of the transformation.

The guy didn't say anything about what happened when you got your throat ripped out in the back alley of a convenience store. Jake never saw what did it—a piece of shadow broke away from the night and swallowed him, and he remembered thinking this was it, he was done, and he'd always meant to go back to college and finish that last semester, and now he never would and what a waste it all was. He'd woken up freezing cold, in a dark room, and had assumed it was hell, and you didn't just go to hell for being bad—you went there for being *nothing.* But no, it wasn't hell, not like that. The thing that attacked him transformed him, saved him, because he thought it would be funny, and then abandoned him.

Oh, please let his call get through so he could rant at this guy.

The phone rang. Three rings, four rings. She wouldn't even pick up the phone. But at least it wasn't busy . . .

After five rings, someone answered. "You've reached *The Midnight Hour.*"

Then it happened so fast. He talked to a guy, a screener, gave his name, what he wanted to talk about, "That guy who said he knew Byron made me so *mad*," was what he thought he said. The screener told him to turn his radio off—and the show, Kitty's voice, piped through the phone.

Oh my God, oh my God—

"Well, thank you for the public service announcement." Her voice dripped with her trademark sarcasm. "I'm cutting you off now, you've had a little too much ego tonight. Next call—ooh, I think I might have a debate for us here. Hello, Jake? You're on the air. What do you have for me?"

If he still had a heartbeat, it would be racing. As it was, he was afraid he was going to swallow his tongue. He had to remember to breathe so he'd have air to speak. He sucked in like a bellows and almost choked.

"Um, Kitty? Oh, wow. I mean—" *Stupid!* He was an idiot. *Get it together.* "Hi."

"Hi. So you have a response to our esteemed vampire caller."

Remember how angry he was. He had to get this off his chest. "Oh, do I ever. That guy is so full of . . . crap. I mean, I really want to know where I can get in on some of this vampire world domination action. 'Cause I'm a vampire and I'm stuck working the night shift at a Speedy Mart. *I'm* not top of any food chain." His blood—borrowed blood, weak blood—ran hot, burning to the tips of his ears. He probably looked almost human right now.

"You're not part of a Family?"

He almost laughed. "If it weren't for your show I wouldn't even know about Families." He wouldn't know what he was missing. He would just think that he'd been dealt the shittiest hand imaginable: working the night shift at Speedy Mart for all eternity.

He felt calmer, getting it out. He'd kept this a secret. This was the first time he'd said out loud, *I'm a vampire.*

Kitty said, "I know this is personal, but I take it that you were made a vampire under violent circumstances, against your will."

"Got that right. And if destiny had anything to do with it, I'd sure like to know why."

"I wish I had an answer for you, Jake. You got one of the bad cards. But since you and I both know there's no destiny involved, you have a choice on what to do about it." Her voice was friendly, comforting. He wasn't going to get reamed for being whiny. *You have a choice.* But what could he *do*?

"I really just wanted to tell the other side of the story. My side. That guy wasn't speaking for all vampires. Thanks for listening."

"That's what I'm here for. I'm going to move on to the next call now, okay? Good luck to you, Jake."

And the line clicked off. Just like that, it was over. Good luck. Was luck anything like destiny?

The bell on the door rang, and two women came into the store. They were college-aged, dressed in sweats, their hair up in ponytails. They giggled and looked a little dazed. They were probably on a road trip, driving all night, and stopped for sodas and snacks to keep them awake. Sure enough, one headed for the refrigerator section and the other to the chips aisle.

He tried to say hello to them as they walked past, but they didn't hear him. Or they ignored him. Either way, he felt like an idiot.

He could hear their heartbeats from across the store, and sense the warm trail their bodies left in the air as they moved. Fresh blood. Beautiful. He tried not to stare.

He wasn't going to attack them for blood or anything. He appreciated the company too much for that. Maybe they'd smile at him when he rang them up. Maybe he could think of something clever to say—without sounding creepy. Have an actual conversation. *So, where are you girls headed?* No, that was creepy. Stalkerish. *Nice night we're having . . .*

He leaned on the counter and tried to look friendly.

That was another thing: Vampires were supposed to be so seductive, having this uncanny ability to lure anyone they wanted into their clutches. But he looked at these girls and clammed up, got all nervous and sweaty-palmed, like any other geeky kid. He wouldn't be seducing anyone.

Maybe he was too new a vampire. He'd only been at this a few months. Maybe he just needed to practice. Smile. Work on the smile. And saying hi—warmly, but not too eagerly. The girls were still in the back of the store, giggling over something. He tried to see them in the convex security mirrors, but no luck.

Man, this sucked. How much of a loser was he when becoming a vampire didn't even make him cool?

He tapped a hand on the counter, adding another crack, and told himself to stop fidgeting.

The bell rang again, making him flinch. He straightened from the counter and looked. A man walked in, and the hairs on Jake's neck tingled, all his muscles tensing. The guy wore a heavy coat with the hood pulled over his head—in the heat of summer. His hands were shoved deep in his pockets. The right one had a bulge larger than just the guy's hand. Jake didn't need hyperaware senses to know what that meant.

He came straight to the cash register.

The girls in the back were quiet for the moment. If they stayed like that for just a few more minutes, Jake could clear the register and get the robber out of here before they got hurt.

The man moved in front of the register, standing with his back to the security camera that was trained on the door. He put the gun on the counter, kept his hand on it, finger on the trigger.

"Gimme all your cash." He wore sunglasses and kept his eyes downcast.

Jake already had the register open and scooped the cash into a plastic grocery bag. He stole a glance to the mirror in the corner—the girls were moving, coming up the aisle toward the register. They didn't see what was happening.

He finished and quickly slid the bag to the guy. A smart thief would have grabbed it and run, happy to get away with whatever he could. The cameras wouldn't have gotten a good look at him, and corporate headquarters wasn't going to sweat a hundred bucks when no one got hurt.

But no. He had to stand there and look in the bag. "Is that all?"

"That's all they let me have, man."

"—trust me, it's not going to kill you to drink regular Coke just this once—"

The girls stopped at the end of the aisle, just a few feet from the counter and the man with the gun. The first one, the blonde, looked up, eyes wide, and put her hand on the brown-haired one's arm. Equally startled, the thief looked at them.

Reflexively, the robber's hand clenched on his weapon. He brought the gun up, swung it around.

For Jake, time slowed. He *knew* the guy was going to shoot. It was as if Jake could hear the nerves firing along his arm. That humming in his muscles moved to his skin. His brain wasn't in control; his panicked adrenal gland was. The bullet would hit the blond girl. Also controlled by instinct, she had moved in front of her friend, putting herself in the line of fire to protect her.

Jesus, Jake was a freakin' *vampire.* He ought to be able to handle this.

He jumped over the counter.

At least, he tried, imagining that he could plant his hands and make an elegant leap, swinging his legs and flying toward the gunman feetfirst, knocking him out and saving the day. But he was suddenly a lot more powerful than he thought he should have been, and his whole body turned into a flailing projectile, tumbling toward the assailant. He was *flying.* Never mind that he couldn't stop. Could he look like any more of a dork . . .

It happened so fast the guy didn't even look at him. One moment Jake was behind the counter, the next he was crashing into him, knocking him into a display of neon-blue washer fluid.

"What the fu—?" the guy said.

The gun went off—two, three times. Jake felt an impact, and the girls screamed.

That humming strength buzzed through him again, and he was on his feet, looking at his stomach where he was sure he'd been shot. His hand even snagged on a bullet hole in his shirt; but there wasn't any blood, and even the sensation of impact faded to nothing. Because he was a *freaking vampire.*

He put his hands on his hips, stared down at the guy, and laughed.

The guy screamed, a guttural sound of denial. Still on his ass, he scuttled away from Jake, slipped, and a half-dozen bottles of washer fluid fell on him. His sunglasses came off and skittered on the floor tiles.

Jake was on him in a second, his hands gripping the guy's collar, pinning him to the floor. With a sense of amazement, he parted his lips, baring his teeth. His fangs.

I could break his neck. Drink him 'til he's dry.

The guy started crying. His lips were moving, but his words were unintelligible. He tried to bring his hands up, to ward Jake away, but he could only bat weakly at him.

Pathetic. And Jake had thought himself a loser.

He called back to the girls, "There's some duct tape behind the counter. Could one of you bring it here? And call 911."

If he'd been alone, he might have done more to the guy. But this was good enough. This made him a hero. A vampire superhero.

The blond girl approached, offering him the roll of duct tape. "That was incredible, what you did. I thought for sure he'd shot you. You must know some kind of funky martial arts." Her friend was on the phone, her voice shaking and hands trembling.

Jake taped together the guy's wrists, then his ankles. Not that he seemed inclined to run off. That look Jake had given him must have come straight out of a nightmare.

Jake stood, crossing his arms to cover the bullet hole in his T-shirt. "It was mostly instinct." He looked bashfully at his shoe. He didn't forget to smile.

The smile she gave back was warm and beckoning. The other girl hung up the phone and hurried around the counter to hold her friend's arm. They both looked up at Jake with the same earnest admiration.

He'd seen girls look at rock stars that way. And they were looking like that at *him*.

He'd just beat up an armed robber. He could do *anything*.

"Hey, you two look really shaken up. You should sit down, at least until the cops get here." He slipped between them, put his arms around their shoulders, and guided them to the plastic chairs sitting against the wall by the coffeemaker near the counter. They clung to him, leaning against his body. They were so warm. And *fresh.* He breathed deeply, taking in the scent of them. He sat on the middle chair; they perched on either side of him and didn't let go. *Score.*

"I don't think I can keep driving tonight," said the brown-haired one.

"That's okay," Jake said. "Stay here as long as you need to." At least until dawn.

Now, how to play the cards he'd been dealt tonight?

Long Time Waiting

Manitou Springs, Colorado, 1900

Amelia's scrying brought her to a cottage perched on the hill overlooking the road. Tucked in the woods, the place was meant to be charming, but the blue paint had faded to gray and the shadows of the surrounding trees fell across it strangely.

The feeling of doom that had brought her here grew stronger. *I am too late.* For the thousandth time she rebuked herself; she should have heeded the warning on that crossroads tomb . . .

Dismounting, she tossed her horse's reins over the porch railing and charged inside.

Lydia Harcourt, nineteen, lay in the foyer, sprawled on her side on the hardwood floor. A pool of blood had spread around her, a scarlet carpet. Her blue cotton dress was stained and spattered with it. Her throat had been cut so deeply, the head lolled back at an angle that caused it to stare inhumanly over her shoulder. The wound exposed muscle, bone, torn vessels, and windpipe. One would think the girl had been mauled by an animal, but the cut was too clean. A single swipe of a claw, not the work of teeth and limbs. The blood was still wet, shining in the light coming through the window. This hadn't happened long ago, but the perpetrator was gone, vanished into air quite literally, same as last time. Last month, she'd tracked the demon to a village in Juarez, where it had slaughtered a herd of cattle. She had known it was only a matter of time before it chose a human target, and one likely to most infuriate Amelia.

Nothing in the place was broken, no struggle had taken place, no one in the neighborhood had been alerted by screams. Lydia might have simply fallen where she stood.

"Damn," Amelia whispered. She cursed herself for having the ability to know what was happening, to mark it and track it, but not the speed to catch the thing. As if the demon knew this, it seemed to taunt her.

She opened the satchel she wore over her shoulder.

Chalk. A red candle. A bundle of sage. Flint and steel. A round mirror the size of her hand. The body had not yet stiffened. A trace of warmth still lingered in the blood. If Amelia hurried, she might be able to catch the trail of the demon. Keep such slaughter from happening again.

She set the candle near the girl's head and lit it. Next, she drew a circle in chalk. To contain the girl and all the blood, she had to draw it clear to the walls. She paused a moment to take direction, found north, and drew the proper symbols, the ancient signs that communed with the stars overhead and the elements on earth, that opened doors between worlds.

Lydia watched her with eyes like frosted glass.

"Rest easy, my dear," Amelia murmured. "Soon you can tell me what you know, and I'll stop the thing that did this."

She lit the sage, set it smoldering. Placed the mirror by the candle. It reflected golden light back into the room. Amelia knelt before it, and watched Lydia.

The smoke from the incense set Amelia's eyes watering. Closing them in a moment of dizziness, she drew a breath. Her mind was entering another state. Opening passages, picturing a great ironbound block of a door that separated the world of the living and the world of the dead.

"Lydia Harcourt, I need to speak with you," she said, and imagined the door cracking open.

Fog appeared in the mirror.

"Lydia. Can you hear me?" Amelia breathed slowly to keep her heart from racing. If she panicked now, she'd lose the trail and would never vanquish this creature. She focused all her attention on the room, the door, the body, the dead eyes.

"Lydia, please. I know it's difficult. I want to help. Can you hear me?"

The eyes blinked.

Amelia's heart jumped, and she steadied her breathing. The dead eyes swiveled to look up at her, and something stared out of them. Amelia found the courage to look back.

"Lydia. I know you can't speak. But I need you to remember what happened. Think of who did this to you, live through it one more time, just once. I'll see it in the mirror here. Then I can find what did this. Punish it. Do you understand? Can you do this for me?"

The eyes blinked.

"Oh my dear, thank you." Amelia brushed a strand of the girl's chestnut hair off her forehead, as if she could still feel comfort. But who could say what she felt, with the door open? Even if it was only a crack. "Follow the light. Show me in the mirror."

The mirror presented an image of fog. Figures began to emerge. A dark form had the shape of a man, tall and stout, but it was featureless. When it reached, the fingers were as long as its arm, and it had claws, extending, curling. In the mirror, Lydia showed a picture of herself, her mouth open to scream as one of the claws raked across her neck.

"Lydia, you must try to remember. Where did it go?"

The shadow in the mirror took on red eyes. Again and again, the claw tore through her throat, and she fell before she could make a sound. That was all she had, all she could give Amelia. The corpse, its gaze still locked on her, blinked again, and a tear slid from the outside corner of its eye, down its cheek.

Amelia sat back and clenched her hands in her lap. What was she doing here? Abusing the dead for no good purpose. She fancied herself a wizard, an arcane scholar, a demon hunter. She'd traveled the world to learn what she knew. It all should have been good for something.

She touched Lydia's face and closed her eyes. "Sleep, Lydia. Leave this world. May the next treat you better." In her mind, she closed the door, slid shut the bolt. The mirror was a mirror again. She snuffed the candle with her finger.

Then she heard footsteps on the porch. Perhaps Lydia had had time to scream after all.

The rumble of a carriage and horses came up from the road beyond. More steps on the porch. Her heart in her ears, Amelia was too shocked to move, so when the men opened the door, they found her kneeling by the body with blood on her hands and the occult circle drawn around her.

Cañon City, Colorado, Four Months Later

Doors, passages, worlds. A skillful magus could travel between them by his thoughts alone, or so Amelia had read. In the East she had seen orange-clad monks who could stop their own breathing by meditation and seemed to be dead, but they awoke safely.

Did she believe a person could travel between life and death? Pass through that iron door and return unharmed?

The bricks of the prison where she was housed were old enough, at least by this country's standards. Their roots stretched into the earth. They had seen forty years of life and death. They had passages and portals the wardens did not know about. Lying on her canvas cot at night, she traveled them. She bound together a bit of candle and a lock of hair and burned them until neither remained.

Would it work?

The iron door was open wide, gaping like a mouth.

They had cut her dark hair short and put her in a poor cotton dress, a bleached gray prison uniform. They had let her keep her boots, thank God. These boots had traveled the world and were well broken in, comfortable. At least her feet were not sore. The boots would walk her to the scaffold. She could travel between worlds, but not escape a steel-barred prison. A sore irony.

The day was blustery, a wind pouring from the mountains, carrying dust and the promise of rain. For now the sky was hazy, washed out by an arid sun. A crowd of spectators had gathered, all men in proper suits and hats, hairy mustaches making their frowns seem fiercer, more judgmental. They were all no doubt horrified at what she'd done. What they thought she'd done. The bastards had no idea. They would truly be horrified if they knew what lived in the world, dime-novel monsters they could not believe.

She stood on the platform. A man tied her hands in front of her. A noose hung. Part of her wanted to look away, but part of her studied it. She had seen men hanged, but had never seen a noose from this angle, so close. The knot had been tied correctly. She had never seen a woman hanged.

Her thoughts were scattered, her mind already partway gone. Not through the door, but into a little room she had built beside the door with hair, candle, and incantation. She would fool that iron slab. Doors and rooms existed between life and death.

The candle, the hair. The light, her life.

How had it come to this? part of her wailed. Her parents had been right, she should have stayed home, married the unremarkable suit they'd put in front of her. Too late, the scientific part of her mind reprimanded. She followed this path of her own free will and she must continue on. When the path seemed to end, you blazed a new trail through the wilderness.

"Amelia Parker, you have been tried and convicted for the murder of Lydia Harcourt and sentenced to death according to the laws of the state of Colorado."

She cleared her throat and tried not to sound nervous. Her voice came out halting anyway. "Lady Amelia Parker. I'd prefer my title entered into the records, if you please." Her throat closed, and she swallowed. Just a little longer. Stay focused on that room beside the iron door.

"*Lady* Amelia Parker, do you have any last words?"

"None whatsoever. Thank you."

"Then may God have mercy on your soul."

Closing her eyes, she left the scaffold. It was a strange feeling. She merely thought, *Breathe out.* Breathe it all out. Focus on the small symbols she had built, make them real, go there. Light, life, the room beside the door. Then she was watching a slim waif of a girl standing on the scaffold. It was her, pale and despairing. She'd hardly eaten for days and it showed. The prison dress hung limply on her. Hood over her head, rope around her neck. Still she could see. Was pleased the body did not tremble. But the executioners had to guide it into place, as if the person was no longer truly conscious.

The floor dropped with a creak and a snap, and everything went dark.

Cañon City, Colorado, The Present

Cormac took another step forward in line and tried not to think too hard. This place was built on routine, rhythm. If he let himself fall into it, the days flew by. He'd be out of here in no time, if he could keep up the rhythm and not let anything—anyone—knock him out of it. He made sure not to get too close to the guy in front of him—big guy, beefy shoulders, white, tattoo-covered—and tried not to think of the guy behind him—shorter, wiry, which probably meant he was quick—breathing down his neck. Cormac didn't look at anyone, didn't meet anyone's gaze. Let himself be carried by the rhythm. He'd pick up his tray, his plastic utensils, find a place to sit where he wouldn't have to talk to anyone, and eat to keep himself going for another day. Try not to think about the way the orange jumpsuit didn't fit right across his shoulders, or the way this place smelled like fifty years of bad cooking.

He had his tray in hand when a shove hit his shoulder. Because he'd been expecting it, the tray didn't go flying.

He didn't have to look to know it was the guy behind him, the scrappy freak who'd tried to stare him down before at meals or out in the yard. It wasn't an accident, though if Cormac confronted him the guy would say it was. More than that, he wouldn't apologize; he'd turn it around, accuse Cormac of trying to start something, then he really would start something—a fight to knock him a few pegs down the pecking order. Cormac had seen this play out a dozen times. The black guys had their gangs, and they picked on the Latino gangs who picked on the white gangs who picked on everybody else, spouting some kind of superiority shtick, which was a riot because they were all locked up in the same cinder-block box wearing the same prison jumpsuits. Even their tattoos blurred together after a while. Cormac didn't try to keep score.

He turned his head just enough to look at the guy, whose eyes were round, whose lips were snarly. The collar of his jumpsuit was crooked. He was bristling, teeth bared, like he was getting ready to jump him. But Cormac didn't react. Just looked at the guy, frowning. Cold. The big mistake these jokers made was thinking Cormac cared about his rep, cared about the pecking order, wanted or even needed to join up for protection, for friendship, for some sense of belonging. Like they were all some pack of wolves, he thought with some amount of irony.

They stood like that for maybe a full minute until the next guy behind muttered, "Hey, move it." Cormac only turned back around when the scrappy freak ducked his gaze. No need to get excited, no need to say a word. You just had to keep to yourself. He wasn't here to make lifelong friends or be the boss of anyone.

No one else bothered him as he picked up his tray and went to an empty table at the far end of the cafeteria. Prison guards stood at the doorways, watching. Cormac didn't pay them any more attention than he did to his fellow prisoners. There was no point to it.

He hadn't been trying to earn a reputation over the last few months, but he seemed to have one anyway. No one else sat with him; the others gave him plenty of room. He didn't talk, didn't try to make friends. That cold stare was enough to keep trouble away. So he ate greasy chicken and mashed potatoes with watery gravy in silence.

He didn't want to think too hard about it, but keeping stock of his surroundings was too much a habit to quit: noting where the people around him were, how they carried themselves, where the exits were, what dangers lay in wait. The hunter's instincts. He should have been grateful—those instincts were keeping him safe here. But they also made him edgy. Maybe it was the feeling of being trapped, that he couldn't go anywhere in this place without being watched, without the chance that one of those uniformed, frozen-faced guards might decide to take him down for no reason at all. He hadn't seen open sky in weeks. Even the yard was ringed with concrete and barbed wire.

He set down his fork and flattened his hand on the table, just for a moment, until the tension went away. He was doing all right. He just had to keep putting one foot in front of the other.

And he had to get rid of the tightness in his spine that said someone was watching him. That something around here was just a little bit . . . off.

The inmates told ghost stories.

"There's a warden fifty years ago who hung himself," the guy in the next cell, Moe, was saying. "Can you believe that? A warden. Hung himself on the top floor. That knocking sound? That's him. Walking around."

"Shut *up,*" hollered another inmate in another cell.

"You've heard it," Moe insisted.

"It's pipes. It's old fucking pipes," Cormac's cellmate Frank said.

"You know the story, you know it's true."

The pipes acted up once a week or so, and every time Moe had to talk about the ghost of the warden who hanged himself. Cormac thought it was just the pipes.

Trouble was, inmates told lots of stories, and something here wasn't right. That tingling at the back of his neck made him reach for a gun on his belt. Easy enough to brush it off, to tell Moe to shut up. But something dripped off the walls here. Of course a prison was going to be tense, all these angry guys penned up together.

But Cormac knew what was really out there. A prison filled with ghosts wasn't the worst of it.

"I'm going to beat you if you don't shut it!"

"I'm just telling you. I'm *warning* you!"

This would go on for another minute before Moe finally shut up. Wasn't anything anyone could do about it.

Cormac pressed his pillow over his ear and tried to think himself away from this place. To a meadow up in Grand County, miles from anywhere. Tucked on the side of a valley, east facing so it got the first sun of the morning. Green grass, tall trees, blue sky, and a creek running down the middle of it. His father had taken him hunting there when he was a kid, and he never forgot it. Camping, waking up before dawn when a layer of mist clung to the grass. Drinking strong coffee heated over a campfire. He went back there, when he needed to get out of his own head.

The nameplate sitting on the desk read "Dr. Ronald Olson." Cormac sat in the not-so-comfortable chair across the desk from an unassuming man in an oxford shirt and corduroy jacket. He even had glasses. He was maybe in his fifties, and his hair was thinning. He looked soft rather than weathered. Cormac classified him as prey.

"How are you doing today?" Olson asked.

Cormac shrugged. This was just another hoop to jump through. Play nice for the camp counselor. He doubted the guy could tell him anything about himself he didn't already know. Both his parents had died violently when he was young, his whole life had been filled with violence, he'd fallen back on violence as a solution to every problem, and that was what landed him here.

He didn't know if Olson expected him to try to manipulate him, play some kind of mental hide-and-seek, Hannibal Lector–style. Cormac didn't want to work that hard for so little payoff. But Olson was free to think Cormac was a puzzle he could pick apart and solve.

"How are you adjusting?"

"It's just a place," Cormac said, shrugging again. "One day at a time."

"Any problems? Anything you'd like to talk about? It can be a shock, going from the outside to this."

Cormac smiled and looked away. "Am I supposed to get pissed off because I can't run out to McDonald's and get a hamburger? That's a waste of energy."

"That's an admirable stoicism. Are you sure you aren't in denial? That can be dangerous as well."

Cormac had a feeling the two of them looked at dangerous in completely different ways. He resisted an urge to glance at the clock, to see how much time they had left. He hadn't asked for this—the guy had gotten hold of Cormac's file and decided he must be crazy.

"I figure I keep my head down and get out of here just as quick as I can."

"Goal oriented. That's good."

Now Cormac wondered if the guy was for real. He shifted, leaning forward just a little. "There's one thing you could maybe tell me about."

"Go on."

"You hear many ghost stories around here? Do guys come in here telling about . . . things. Noises, spooky stuff."

Olson's smile seemed condescending. "I suppose every prison has its share of ghost stories. Some inmates have active imaginations."

"There seem to be a lot of them around here. Like the guys have passed them down over the years. They say some warden hanged himself and now his ghost walks around, that a serial killer came in slitting inmates' throats, that sort of thing."

"You believe that?"

"The one about the warden? No. Not that one."

"But you believe . . . something."

"People tell stories because there may be something to some of it." He wasn't trying to rattle the guy; wasn't sure much would rattle a prison therapist. That wasn't a game Cormac wanted to start. But there had to be something to the constant chill that had settled in his spine.

Olson leaned forward to study a page in an open folder, Cormac's file, as if he hadn't already memorized it and was working from a script.

"In your deposition, you claimed your victim wasn't human," he said.

"I didn't say that. I said she wasn't *all* human."

"Then what else was she?" He didn't ask like someone who was really interested in the answer. He asked like a psychologist who expected his patient to say something damning. Hell, how much more damned could he be?

"It's hard to explain," he said.

"You think something like that is going on here? Something that's hard to explain?"

This isn't about me, Cormac wanted to yell at the guy. But he settled back, didn't look away, didn't give an inch. "Maybe it's just being in jail."

"I just have a couple of more questions for you. Your parents both passed away when you were quite young. What do you remember about them?"

Cormac stared at the guy, his expression unchanging. "I don't remember anything."

Of course Olson didn't believe him; Cormac hadn't expected him to. They stared at each other, waiting for the other to break.

Olson glanced at his watch and said, "I think that's enough for today. Until next week, then." He smiled kindly. A guard took Cormac back to his cell.

Part of the general population, he was allowed out of his cell for meals, showers, time in the yard, and his work detail washing dishes. He'd put in for a better job, but that would take time, a review. He had to prove that he wasn't going to cause trouble. He was trying to do just that. The days ticked on, hour by hour. Best not to count the time, but there it was.

His half of the cell was starting to look like it belonged to him—his small shelf displayed a growing collection of books, a small stack of letters he'd gotten, a couple of magazines. Frank had been here longer and had a radio and pictures of his two kids on display. None of those details could disguise the bars, or the fact that their bedroom was also a bathroom, with a stainless steel toilet and sink mounted in the corner. This was a cage in a zoo.

Yet another night after lights out he lay on the top bunk, staring at the shadowed ceiling, waiting for sleep to pull him under. He could almost hear the shadows shifting across the walls, moving through the building, claws scratching on concrete. The place was old, haunted. A prison had been on this spot for almost a hundred fifty years. If any ghosts had taken up residence during that time, he was stuck with them.

"Hey," said Frank from the bottom bunk. Cormac didn't answer, but Frank continued. "You got a girl waiting for you on the outside, don't you?"

It was an odd question. Cormac kept staring up. "What makes you say that?"

"The way you stare, like you're looking somewhere else. Guys only stare like that when they're thinking about a girl. Not just a hot piece of ass, but someone they really like."

Cormac's thoughts flashed on a face and a name. The girl he liked. The one who wasn't waiting for him on the outside.

He rolled over on his side and didn't say a word.

Ghosts haunted the place. She built up her walls and they left her alone. She waited.

The first one who went mad was a veteran of the Great War who'd returned home to few prospects and been caught stealing an automobile. She had thought perhaps the chaotic visions swirling in his mind would prepare him for her. She was wrong. She slipped in quietly, tentatively, like dipping fingers in the surface of a pool of water to test the temperature. She whispered words, told him what would happen, that it wouldn't hurt—she didn't think it would. She hoped it wouldn't. But it did. Her presence pushed an already disturbed mind past breaking. He woke from sleep screaming and wouldn't stop. Said he heard voices.

Madmen who speak of the voices they hear was such an awful cliché. And yet.

She tried to be more careful. Her second attempt was a family man convicted of fraud. A stable, quiet man who'd committed a nonviolent crime and had much to keep him levelheaded. When he heard the voice, the whisper, and felt her tendrils in his mind, the spirit that wasn't his own moving through his flesh, he split his skull trying to fight his way out of the cell.

And so it went. No matter how carefully she chose her targets, how gently she pressed against their thoughts, she broke minds, searching for one that would fit her. She was waiting for a certain quality of mind: intelligent, astute, observant, patient. So many of the minds that passed through here were troubled, ill, wracked by demons of their own making that had nothing to do with the supernatural. Weak, prone to violence, which was what brought many of them here in the first place. She waited a long time.

She might have given up entirely, let what was left of her fade to shadow, but the murders followed her. The curse of the demon should have ended with her death. But she hadn't really died, had she?

She needed a body to resume the hunt, to finally destroy the curse. So she kept trying, kept making morbid sacrifices.

If she'd had any fear in her state, any feeling beyond the instinct to seek out what she needed, she'd have been afraid. She would lose herself in this place. The spell would never work to completion. She'd never find the vessel. She would fade, become simply another voice calling purposelessly to madmen. Another shade to the miasma seeping from the stones.

Then, one of the minds recognized her.

He'd been primed, and he had the instincts. He recognized the irregular, the uncanny. Magic. He didn't even know it. He'd lived with it so long, he only noticed it as a tickling in his mind.

He was violent, here for killing. But it was a controlled, chilled violence of necessity and will. In some ways, his ability to kill was less understandable than the ones who lashed out in the heat of violence and caused mayhem. They lost control and that was reason enough.

This man approached it like a job, with no more passion than he might mend a shirt or dig a hole. She was drawn to him and horrified—her, horrified! What was he?

Human, nothing more. She could see by the glow of him.

Most of all, though, she felt he was a hard mind. Resilient. He might hear a voice, but wouldn't break from it like the dozen before him had. She was sure of it.

After breakfast the next day, an alarm sounded. Lockdown. Cormac lay on his bunk, waiting for news. The grapevine would start feeding rumors soon enough. Probably it was just someone trying to get out. It happened more often than he would have thought, inmates packing themselves into crates to be shipped out or squeezing through barbed wire. He didn't understand how that could look like a good idea to anyone, even someone who spent twenty-three hours a day in a ten-by-ten cell. People succeeded more often than he would have thought, but seldom for very long. The guy who packed himself into a crate was found when they unloaded the truck at its destination. He was hauled back with a few more years added to his sentence.

The gamble wasn't worth it. Just a few years, keep his nose clean, get out. That was the plan. He'd still have a life when he got out of here. Maybe even more of one than when he arrived. He could stare at the ceiling for a few years and not go crazy.

Moe, the flighty guy in the next cell over, said, "They found Brewster."

Frank stood by the bars in the corner to talk to him. "Found him where?"

"Dead, throat cut, blood everywhere. Right in his cell."

"So Gus did it?"

Cormac listened, almost amused. Gus must have snapped. The guy was half Brewster's size, but he could have managed it.

"No, that's the thing, Gus's pissing his pants. They don't think he did it."

That piqued Cormac's attention.

"They were locked in together, what else could have happened?" Frank said.

"All I know is he got cut up, but they didn't find a knife, and Gus is pissing himself. Says he didn't even see what happened."

Frank chuckled. "Yeah, that's a good story. That'll get him off the hook for sure."

"It's just like what happened with that serial killer, the one from the thirties, remember?"

"I thought that happened in the sixties," Frank said.

"Maybe it was a vampire," Cormac said. "Turned to mist, come in through the bars."

Frank stared at him. He was young but worn down, a stout white guy with a dozen tattoos scattered piecemeal across his back and arms. He'd spent more of his adult life in prison than out of it.

From the other cell Moe said, "What'd he say?"

"You're not serious," Frank said. "Can they do that?"

One thing was for sure, the world had gotten a whole lot more interesting over the last year, since the NIH went public with data proving that vampires and lycanthropes were real. Cormac loved throwing out bombshells like that. He loved that people acknowledged the existence of monsters without knowing anything about them. It made terrifying them so easy.

"But it probably wasn't that," Cormac said. "Vampire wouldn't have left all that blood lying around."

"Jesus Christ," Frank muttered. "Now how am I supposed to sleep?"

Cormac knew that vampires didn't turn into mist. They moved quickly, with faster-than-the-eye reflexes, and that was probably how the mist stories started. They couldn't break into a locked cell. But if Gus had nothing to do with the murder, then *something* had gotten in and killed Brewster.

It was just the rumor mill. He'd wait for more reliable information before drawing conclusions.

That night, Cormac woke up sweating, batting at a humming in his ear. The place had bugs. Rolling to his side, he settled his arm over his head, and tried to imagine he was outdoors, camping at the edge of his meadow, his father sleeping a few feet away, his rifle beside him. Any sign of trouble, Dad would take care of it.

Cormac hadn't thought much of his father in years, until he ended up here. Here, he thought about everything. What would his father think of him now? Would he be surprised his kid ended up in prison?

The breathing and snores of the dozens of other men on the block echoed and kept Cormac rooted to this place. Best not to let his mind wander too much. Had to stay here. Pay attention. He shouldn't have thought of his father.

A voice plucked deep in his mind, a buried place carefully covered over, where not even his dreaming self went. That place had lain quiet as a matter of survival.

What are you?

A shadow stirred, rustling, looking for the light. Cormac shut the door on it.

Olson would see him next week and ask, *Anything troubling you? Anything you want to talk about?* That shadow would start to rattle around the inside of his mind, but Cormac would just shake his head no. *Nothing to talk about.* Except that the inside of his skull itched. Again Olson would ask, *What's on your mind?* And Cormac would say, *Let me tell you about my father, who died when I was sixteen. Let me tell you how, and what I did to the monster that killed him.*

The buzzing wasn't a fly; the legs crawled on the interior surface of his skull. He suddenly wanted nothing more than to take the top of his head off and scratch.

It was just this place getting to him. Well, couldn't let that happen. Had to hold on, stay sane. He had too many reasons to stay sane and get out of here in one piece. He never thought he'd say that. Never thought he'd have anything to live for except the next job, the next hunt.

He drifted off and again woke up sweating. This time it was light out, sun coming in through distant skylights. Cormac still felt like the bugs had gotten to him.

He thought of all the things that could slice up a man in a locked cell. A guy could do himself in like that if he put his mind to it, and it wasn't too hard to think of how captivity could drive a man—the right kind of man—to it. That was the simplest explanation and the one the warden would probably settle on. Let the psychologists hash it out.

While Cormac had been joking about vampires turning to mist and coming in through the bars, other things could appear from nowhere, things that didn't have physical bodies, demons with knifelike claws that fed on blood, curses laid from afar. Ghosts that tickled the inside of your mind. If he'd been in charge of an investigation and the physical evidence couldn't explain it, that would be the first trail Cormac followed: Did Brewster know anyone who could work that kind of magic, who also had it in for him? Without seeing the body for himself, Cormac didn't have much to go on. They'd probably find some reasonable, nonsupernatural explanation.

Two guards didn't come to work the next day.

Yard time was cut short. Half the block didn't get time at all, which set up an afternoon of trouble. Guys yelled from their cells, hassling guards during counts, which happened half a dozen times a day. The warden even added a count, which started up a rumor that somebody was missing and probably cut up the same as Brewster.

That couldn't have been the case, because when a count turned up short the whole facility went into lockdown, and that hadn't happened since the body was found. Lockdown then had only lasted a day, but that made two days now that the routine had been trashed. Without routine, inmates floundered.

At dinner, Cormac took his tray to his usual corner in the dining hall. A couple of tables over, his neighbor, Moe, was tugging on another guy's arm. Big guy, bald, tattooed arms, glaring across the room with murder in his eyes. Cormac followed the gaze to a group of black men who seemed to be minding their own business. Moe was trying to get the guy to sit back down.

Cormac took his tray and moved another table down, farther away from them, and put his back to the wall. Sure enough, the shouting started, the big guy broke away from Moe's grasp and lunged toward one of the black guys, who lunged right back at him. The fight turned into a full-blown melee in seconds, two gangs pounding into each other, surrounded by a ring of more men screaming them on.

This was what passed for entertainment around here.

Cormac kept quiet and wolfed down as much of his dinner as he could, because sure enough, guards swarmed into the place, clubs drawn to beat the crowd into submission and drag the worst offenders to the hole. They cleared the whole room. When a guard approached Cormac, he raised his hands, lowered his gaze, and went back to his cell without argument. The prison went into lockdown yet again, which mean a lot more staring at ceilings and grumbling.

"He said it was voodoo," Moe said right after lights out, in a hissing voice that managed to carry down the row. The guy had somehow managed to extricate himself from the worst of the mess and got out of any kind of punishment. "Hal said that Carmell knew voodoo and made a voodoo doll of Brewster and ripped it to pieces. That's what got Brewster."

Somebody muttered at him to shut up.

"Voodoo doesn't work like that," Cormac said. He shouldn't be encouraging the guy.

"It don't work at all," Frank said.

"You know so much about it, how does it work?" Moe said.

Cormac sighed. Maybe a scary enough story would shut him up—or make it worse. "That voodoo doll thing is Hollywood. Saturday morning cartoons. Real voodoo, you want something done you have to make a sacrifice. Usually a blood sacrifice for something big. You'd slaughter somebody in order to do the curse, not as the curse itself."

Now there was a thought that halfway made sense. It wasn't a murder, but a blood sacrifice. That still didn't explain who or why.

The others shut up for at least half a minute.

"Christ, you're worse than him," Frank grumbled.

Moe perked up with what seemed to be a new theory. "Hey, if it wasn't Carmell, maybe it was you. You seem to know all about this shit."

"Forget I said anything," Cormac said, rolling to his side and pulling his pillow over his head.

"Maybe it was Satanists. I heard this story about a cult of Satanists here like twenty years ago—"

In winter, the creek froze solid, but in spring it ran white and frothing with snowmelt, lace waterfalls tumbling over sheer boulders. He could watch it for hours and stay calm.

Elk came down into the meadow to graze early, an hour or so after dawn when the sun began to peek over the mountaintops. Dad would stake out the herd, choose his target, and fire. Never missed. This was where he'd taught Cormac to do the same. He didn't bring his clients here. He'd run an outfitting service, worked as a private guide for hunting parties made up of folks with more money than sense. Got them their big stuffed trophy heads and stories for their fancy cocktail parties. But this place was different. This place was for family.

As Cormac watched, the elk vanished. Like someone turning off a TV.

A woman appeared before him, gray, ghostlike.

Terrifyingly out of place, she stood on the dewy grass, hands folded demurely before her, chin tipped up. Her clothing was old-fashioned: a dark skirt that draped to the ground, a high-collared neckline with tight little buttons going all the way up, lace around the wrists of her long sleeves. Her black hair was twisted at the base of her neck, and she wore a hat, a flat thing with a brim and a few feathers curling down the side.

Cormac had an urge to unwrap that hair to see how long it was.

She opened pale lips to speak. The inside of Cormac's skull itched.

Shivering, he opened his eyes to darkness. Twisting, he looked over his shoulder through the bars, fully expecting to see the woman standing outside the cell. His instincts told him someone was standing there. But deep into night, the place was still. Nothing moved. No one stood there, the pressure at the back of his neck notwithstanding.

"Goddamn," he whispered. He scratched his head, fingers scraping through his rough hair. The itching faded, but didn't go away. The skin on his back crawled.

This place was doing its best to make him crazy, but he'd be damned if he let it.

Moe's cellmate's screaming woke the block in the morning, at dawn.

Cormac hadn't slept well and was already awake. He jumped off the top bunk and pressed himself to the bars, trying to see next door. Frank was right beside him.

In the next cell over, Moe's cellmate, Harlan, was throwing himself against the bars, reaching through them, lunging like he could push his way through. His breaths came in full-throated screams, over and over.

Cormac smelled blood, and the only way he could smell it from ten feet over was if there was a whole lot of it. Looking down, he saw a dark puddle pushing out, oozing on the floor from the cell to the walkway outside. Harlan must have been standing in it.

A pair of guards came, annoyed looks on their faces, as if they were fully prepared to beat the shit out of the guy. When they reached the cell, their expressions changed. They radioed the control room to open the door, and as soon as the bars slid away, Harlan fell out and ran smack against the railing opposite before the guards caught him and hauled him upright. He was gibbering, unable to stand on his feet. He kept looking back into the cell, eyes wide and horrified. His socks left bloody footprints on the concrete.

It had happened again.

Cormac thought they might move him and Frank to another cell while they investigated Moe's death, but they didn't. They didn't have anywhere else to put them while the block was under lockdown. Harlan had been dragged to the infirmary.

Frank paced. The prison equivalent of cabin fever was getting to lots of them. Some of the guys were shouting about cruel and unusual punishment, that none of them should have to stay here until the warden figured out why men were dying. Someone had started an Ebola rumor—the disease had infected the prison and was now spreading. Or that the government was using the inmates in experiments. None of that was right. Cormac wondered if that ghostly woman carried a knife under her skirt.

He leaned against the bars, arms laced through, to watch as much of the investigation as he could. The lead investigator, a burly middle-aged guy in a blue Department of Corrections uniform, stepped carefully around the pool of blood. A photographer snapped his camera, recording the crime scene.

An hour or so later, the guards brought the body out on a stretcher. They didn't cover it up at first, and Cormac got a pretty good look. Moe's throat had been slit from ear to ear, torn maybe, though the edges weren't clear through the blood. He didn't seem injured or cut in any other way. Cormac was willing to bet the same thing had happened to Brewster.

The investigator noticed him watching. The guy had probably been around long enough to have seen a few wild crime scenes and was probably already cooking up some story about how Gus and Harlan had gone crazy and killed their cellmates in exactly the same way. He studied Cormac, taking in details, probably figuring he knew everything about him from those few seconds of looking. Gruff-looking thirty-something hanging on the bars of a prison cell. What else did he need to know?

"You see anything?" the investigator said. "Hear anything unusual from over here?"

Cormac made a shrugging motion with his hands. "I was laying on my bunk. I didn't hear anything until Harlan screamed."

The investigator smirked. "Does that mean you didn't hear anything, or you 'didn't hear anything.' " He put up finger quotes the second time.

Why the hell did the guy bother asking if he wasn't going to believe him? "I figure he must have woken up and seen Moe already like that."

"Then who do you think killed Moe?"

"Don't know. Bogeyman?"

Now the guy looked disgusted. "What are you in for?"

"Manslaughter."

"So you killed somebody but you didn't mean to?"

"Oh, I meant to all right. I'm here on a plea bargain."

The investigator walked away in a huff.

"Christ, man." Frank eased up against the bars next to Cormac. "It's like I watch you trying so hard to stay out of folks' way but you just can't help aggravating them."

"I just told the truth."

"Yeah, right," Frank said, laughing. The laughter sounded wrong and put Cormac even more on edge.

He wasn't much surprised when a guard came for him and went through the process of pulling him out of the cell. Frank, standing facing the wall, hands on his head, was still laughing, quietly, like he thought Cormac had brought this on himself.

He expected to be put in a closet and worked over by the smug inspector, but the guard led him to Olson's office. The doctor looked busy, gathering manila folders and setting them aside, indicating for Cormac to sit while he did. He slouched into the chair opposite the desk.

"Thank you for coming," Olson said.

Cormac chuckled. "Seriously?"

Olson granted a thin smile. "That we're sitting in a prison is no reason not to be polite."

"I didn't think I was up for another session yet," Cormac said.

"You're not, but I wanted to talk to you. What have you been hearing about recent events?" He had finished filing and now leaned forward, arms on his desk, his full attention on Cormac.

"My cell's right next to Moe's," he said. "Kind of hard to avoid it."

"Do you think his cellmate did it?"

"What—both his cellmate and Brewster's, going batshit and turning killer in the same way? Neither one of them's a killer."

"But if they didn't, what did?"

" 'What did?' Not who?" Cormac said.

Olson paused, considering, gathering his words. "I'm sure you're hearing more rumors than I am. People are saying what killed him couldn't have been human. It was too brutal."

For a prison full of medium- to high-security inmates, that was saying something. "So what else could it have been?" Cormac said, straight-faced, disingenuous. "Some kind of monster?"

"You've had a long association with monsters."

Cormac wondered how much he'd have to say before he got a referral to the psychiatric ward. Deciding to play out a little line, he said, "Some of my best friends are werewolves."

"Yes, so your file says."

Nothing flustered this guy. Olson was starting to look less like prey.

Olson continued. "An autopsy on Brewster's body showed no fingerprints, no fibers, no sign of a struggle. His throat seemed to have spontaneously opened, the cut reaching all the way to his backbone. Gus is in the infirmary, under sedation. He hasn't been able to communicate since the guards found him with Brewster's body. No weapon was found, and Gus didn't have any blood on him. Because of that he's not being considered a suspect. Now Harlan is in the same state. I suspect Moe's autopsy will reveal the same set of mysteries."

"Why are you telling me this?" Cormac said.

"I'm asking for your advice. Do you have any idea what could have done this?"

Cormac's first impulse was to blow him off. Olson was part of the establishment that locked him in here. Bureaucrats like him didn't have room for the bizarre, couldn't understand that the woman he'd killed was a wizard, powerful and evil, and he'd had no choice but to destroy her. As Frank had observed, Cormac could piss people off just by sitting in one place and looking at them funny. Olson couldn't force him to help. Why should Cormac volunteer?

"There's so much shit out there that could have done this," Cormac said.

"Vampire? Werewolf?"

"Maybe. But you've got the same problem with them—how'd they get through the locked door?"

"So what *can* murder someone behind a locked door? What should we be looking for?"

"Something without a body," Cormac said. "Some kind of curse or magic. Ghost, maybe. Demon."

He could see Olson trying to process, trying to keep an open mind, his mouth pursed against arguments. Finally he said, smiling wryly, "You're getting into issues of physics, now. A physical action requires a physical presence. Doesn't it?"

Cormac couldn't tell if he was being rhetorical or asking a genuine question. "There are more things in heaven and earth," he murmured.

"Hamlet," said Olson. "You like to read, don't you? You have a friend who sends you books."

"I thought this wasn't about me. This is about your bogeyman."

"Do you have any ideas?"

A werewolf had transformed on live TV late last year. Congress had acknowledged the existence of vampires, werewolves, and psychics and brought them to testify in Washington. Cormac had known his whole life that these beings were real, and now the rest of the world was catching up. That didn't stop a lot of folks from pulling the shades down. If Olson were one of those, this whole thing could be a setup. A trap. Get him in here, get him talking crazy, giving them an excuse to pin the deaths on him and lock him up good and tight. No visitors, no parole. Then he really would go crazy.

Cormac said, "Are you serious about this? Are you serious about looking for something that a lot of people don't even believe exists?"

"I wouldn't be asking if we had a logical, mundane explanation for what's happening here."

Not that Cormac had a choice but to trust him. Like so much of his life right now, the decision was out of his hands. "This place has been around a long time. Has anything like this happened here before? Rumor, ghost story, anything."

Olson glanced away briefly, nervously. "It's hard to tell. There've been so many attacks over the prison's history—"

"But have there been any cases of somebody getting their throat cut in a locked cell?" Any sightings of a dark-haired woman in Victorian clothing?

"In fact, there have," Olson said. "A handful over the last

hundred years. But they were isolated—never more than one at a time. In every case another inmate was charged with the murder. Are you saying they may be connected?"

Cormac was both shocked and thrilled at the news—he hadn't expected Olson to answer. This meant there was a thread tying these deaths together. Which meant there was a way to hunt the thing doing it.

This thing had been killing here a long time, but that didn't bother Cormac. He was even a little amused—even inside prison walls where he ought to be safe, this shit just kept following him around.

"Even if you don't know what's doing this, you can try to protect the place. Put up crosses above the doorways, at the ends of hallways. Get a priest in to throw some holy water around, do an exorcism."

"Seriously?" Olson said. "That works?"

"It's not a sure thing."

"That's the trouble with this, isn't it? It's never a sure thing."

Cormac had to grin. "That's why it never hurts to cover all your bases."

When he arrived at the visiting room, he saw that Kitty had joined Ben this time. The joy—or relief—at seeing them both was a physical pain, a squeezing of his heart, though he kept his face a mask. He wanted to melt into the floor, but he only slumped into his chair and picked up the phone.

"Hey," he said, like he always did.

"Hey," Ben said back, and Kitty smiled. They sat close together so they could hold their phone between them. Cormac had gone to live with Ben's family after his father died, and now he was the closest thing he had to a brother. Kitty was . . . something else entirely. The two of them had gotten married a month or so back. Ben had sucked her into the family. She couldn't escape now.

Kitty was cute. Really cute, and not just the way she looked with her shoulder-length blond hair, big brown eyes, and slender body. She burst with optimism, constantly chatting, always moving, and usually smiling. She and Cormac never should have met much less become friends. She represented a lot of lost chances. A lot of things he should have done, and maybe some he shouldn't have. But he wasn't sure he'd want to change any of it. Better to have her as a friend than not at all.

She was better off with Ben. He was man enough to admit that.

Small talk got real small when he didn't have anything new to say. What was he supposed to tell them, when the same thing happened every day? But this week was different, and he wondered: How much should he tell them? Wasn't like they could do anything to help.

Then Kitty mentioned her own demon, derailing the whole routine of their usual visits. It seemed she was in the middle of an adventure, and he couldn't do a thing about it. He didn't know whether to throttle her or laugh. He ended up just shaking his head. He'd come to her rescue, all she had to do was say the word, any time. Except for now. He hoped they didn't get themselves killed before he could get out of here to help them. He hoped whatever was haunting this place left him alone until then.

He'd developed an inner clock—they were running out of time, and he had a bad idea.

"Can I talk to Kitty alone for a minute?" he said to Ben. Ben wouldn't understand—he'd try to fix everything, and he couldn't, not this time. Kitty didn't know him well enough to be suspicious.

Ben left, not looking happy about it.

Alone now, Kitty seemed almost accusing. "What is it? What can you say to me that you can't say to him?"

His lip curled. "You really want me to answer that?" She looked away; so did he. "I don't want him to worry. Kitty, do you believe in ghosts?"

He liked her because nothing ever seemed to shock her. "Of course I do."

He leaned forward. "Can you do some of that research you're so good at?"

"Yeah, sure."

"I need to know the names of any women who were executed

here. Let's say right around 1900, give or take a decade. And any history you can find on them."

She narrowed her gaze, and he wondered if he'd said too much. Now they were both going to worry, because she wouldn't keep this secret from Ben. "Are you being haunted or something?"

"I don't know. It's a hunch. It may be nothing." That last was a lie.

"Is everything okay?"

He hoped she didn't tell him to get some sleep, that she didn't see the stress written on his face. He tried to smile, failed. "Hanging in there. Sometimes by my fingernails. But hanging in there."

He played the visit over in his memory, like he did every time, even though he knew he shouldn't. He made himself sick, worrying that maybe this was the last time they'd visit, maybe they'd skip next week, maybe they'd decide they didn't need him—they wouldn't do that, they weren't like that. But he had a hard time not imagining it, so he dwelled, reflecting on every word they spoke, every loose strand of Kitty's hair, just in case they didn't come back.

Noises here echoed. The hollered complaints kept up even after lights out, and the warden and his guards couldn't do anything about it. They'd have had to put every damn inmate into solitary. Cormac was betting that nobody even knew why they were leaning out, as far as they could, faces pressed to bars and yelling. They were scared and had to do something. Nothing was right and as far as they could tell the folks in charge weren't doing anything about it. The idea that they didn't know what to do was worse than the usual apathy.

Cormac could take care of any problem that bled. But this—without the help of someone like Olson or the warden, he couldn't do anything. He lay on his bunk, staring at the ceiling, trying to block out the noise. Trying not to think too hard about what might be lurking in these walls.

No priests came in to perform an exorcism. Cormac wasn't surprised. He made a cross of his own, borrowing scraps of pine from the wood shop and lashing them together with a shoelace, and hung it over the door of his and Frank's cell. Things got worse.

The dream was a form of escapism, he recognized that. The images kept him from wanting to break things, and that was good. Here, he remembered being safe, when everything was right. Almost everything. Enough of it was right that he didn't think about the rest, the vague memory of a woman who'd died when he was young. He should have loved her, but anymore she was a shadow. A face in a few old snapshots. She didn't enter into calculations of whether he was happy. But sometimes he wondered, *What if.* What if she had lived. Would having a mother have kept him from all this?

He sat on a rock overlooking the stream, squinting into a searing blue sky. Crystals embedded in the granite dug into his hands. He could even smell the sunbaked pines, meadow grasses cooled by the running water, snow-touched air coming down from the peaks. If he had to pick an opposite smell from the prison, this would be it. Clean and natural instead of antiseptic and institutional. Bright instead of sheltered.

He saw the woman again. Not at all ghostly this time, she walked obliquely up the hill toward him, watching where she stepped, lifting her heavy skirt with gloved hands. Some ten paces away, she stopped, smoothed her skirt, and folded her hands before her. She had color in her cheeks and wore a gold cross on a chain. Donning a small, bemused frown, she regarded him as if she had walked a long way to get here, but hadn't found what she expected. Her gaze was cynical.

She didn't look like a murderer or a demon. She looked far too real to be a ghost.

They could stay here, staring at each other for hours. If this had been real, he would have asked her what she was doing here. Or she would have spoken. This was a dream, his imagination, and so they simply stared. Trouble was, he'd never have imagined anyone like her. Nothing in his conscious mind could account for her. His mother had had auburn hair, not so dark as this woman's.

He finally asked, "Who are you?"

The woman's frown disappeared, but her smile was not comforting. She wanted something from him.

"I should be asking you that," she answered. She had a crisp British accent, clipping her words like she was in a hurry.

He looked to the distance. He could wait. She wouldn't stand there staring at him forever, and he was willing to bet his stubborn would outlast hers. Then again, how long had she been lurking here?

"Why won't you let me in?" she said next.

This was getting a little too obvious to be a stray bit of psychoanalysis bubbling up from his subconscious. He didn't *want* to be talking to his subconscious, his feminine side or whatever. Or maybe he was reading too much into it. A woman he didn't know was standing here, asking him a question that had an obvious answer. Why not just answer her? Why not treat it as real?

"I don't know you," he said, looking at her. "I don't know what you want."

"That's wise, I suppose, and I ought to respect that. But you see, Mr. Bennett, I've been waiting such a long time. I need you. More than anyone I've met I think you'd understand that."

For the first time, she looked uncertain, clasping her hands together, ducking her gaze. Cormac thought, *It's an act.* She was trying to soften him up.

"Wrong sales pitch," he said. "Is that what you told Moe and Brewster? Is that how you killed them?"

Clenching her hands into fists, she said, "I did not kill them. I could have saved them, if you'd only listened to me."

He felt the thunder of a sudden storm in the core of his bones, and his skull screamed in pain. She'd done something, he hadn't seen what. Like banging on a door—*Let me in.*

With the flashing light of a migraine, he jerked awake, nearly toppling out of his bunk. He sat up, clutching his sheets like they would anchor him and gasping for breath. Sweat chilled his skin.

"Jesus, fuck, what is it?" Frank, half out of his bunk, clutched the bed's frame and looked up at him.

Cormac felt the remnant of a scream in his throat. Closing his eyes tight, he swallowed and forced his breathing to slow. Everything was fine. He wasn't in pain. Nothing was happening. Except for that almost constant itching in his brain. He scratched his head hard, ripping at his hair. The cell block was dark, quiet.

"I don't know," Cormac said. "Must have been a nightmare."

"You're not getting killed?"

"No. Doesn't look like it."

"There's no blood? Look around—you don't see blood?"

Although he felt silly doing it, he checked himself—and was relieved when he didn't find any blood. "I'm in one piece."

"Jesus Christ, man, don't ever do that again. You have another nightmare I'll beat it out of you, understand?"

Cormac didn't argue because he couldn't blame him; he'd have told Frank the same thing if the roles were reversed. His cellmate was still muttering as he rolled back into bed.

Lying back, Cormac didn't try to sleep. He stared at the ceiling, a field of thick, institutional gray paint full of cracks and shadows. How many hundreds of eyes had stared up like this over the years? What did that do to a building? Cursing himself, he looked away. That was how far gone he was, attributing malevolence to a building.

Somehow, this woman, this demon, whatever she was, had dug into his brain and found his meadow, his refuge. The chink in his armor.

She thought she could get control of him through that weakness. Fine. He just wouldn't go there anymore.

Her overriding goal, the purpose of her being—however truncated it had become—became more imperative than ever.

She found herself in a bind she had not expected. Not that she'd even known what to expect. Hacking her way through a jungle of unknown size and density was the least of it, really. But she was hacking and had faith that if she continued long enough, she would persevere. She had lasted this long, hadn't she? At some point, time had no meaning. Science had discovered that fossils could lie in the earth undiscovered for millions of years. So would she.

Once she found her proper vessel, though, she assumed it would simply let her in. The paradox presented itself: A mind pliant enough to recognize her and not go mad would also have the ability to resist her. A mind that recognized her would know better than to let her in. So it was with this man. The door between them remained closed, barred with iron, stubbornly locked.

How much simpler it would be if she could persuade him! She called through the door, picked at the lock, tried battering it down with her will, which was all she had left. And he resisted.

She found another entry, however—a wedge he himself provided: the meadow. A magnificent, beautiful scene she would not have thought his troubled mind capable of conjuring. He himself didn't seem to recognize that the memory of the place was filled with sadness and regret, the safety of a world and home he believed he had lost forever.

She hadn't been able to delve farther, to learn where this memory had come from or the circumstances that tainted the air of his refuge, that he didn't even seem to notice or refused to acknowledge.

She must win him over. The rituals of thought had become second nature over the century. The focusing of the mind, visualizing action, making action real. When nothing was real, the world became nothing but thought. She focused on the single cell, the single bed, where a man lay and put himself to sleep with thoughts of a meadow. She became tendrils, thin lines of energy melding into the patterns of his mind. Think of the meadow, put herself there, approach the man sitting on the rock. Listen to the birds in the trees, the water of the brook tumbling over smooth stones—

But the meadow wasn't there anymore. It had lain so close to the surface before, almost as if he could transform this prison into his mountain vista through force of will. Now, he'd managed to lock her out.

There she was again, back at the start, battering at the door.

Oddly, she found herself admiring him.

"You can't keep me out forever!" she shouted. "I'll drive you mad! I've done it before, to men better than you!"

A smug satisfaction barred the door. The emotion roiled off him.

Time for a different approach—send a quiet thought, so quiet he would think it was his own. A bit of intuition granted from the supernatural. Surely he believed in such things.

"I can help you." She didn't even imagine her voice, did not give the words form. Merely let the thought linger. "I know this murderer, this demon. I have hunted it. I can help you."

Create the thought, set it drifting, let him find it. That was all. She felt one impression out of the thought snag him: hunted.

The request for a visit surprised Cormac; this wasn't Ben and Kitty's day for it. He wasn't sure this was a visiting day at all, and he didn't need another anomaly making him twitch.

He sat, looked through the glass, and saw Detective Jessi Hardin of the Denver Police Department sitting across from him.

"Christ," he muttered, looking away, rubbing his cheek.

"Hello," she said. "You look terrible, if you don't mind me saying."

"What do you want?"

"I have to be blunt, Mr. Bennett," she said. "I'm here looking for advice."

Cormac had picked up some bad habits when he was young. The way he looked at cops, for example. They were the bad guys. They wanted to take your guns, they put bugs on your phones, they followed you, they worked for a government that wanted to suck you dry. They were fucking Commies—never just "Commies," it was always "fucking Commies." That's what he learned from his uncle when he was a teenager. That's what he learned from his dad, before he died.

He had to remind himself that the outlook was paranoid. Cops were just doing their jobs like anyone else. They weren't the bad guys—usually. He had to work to not think of Detective Hardin as an enemy. But she wouldn't be here unless she wanted something from him, and he remained suspicious. What his family had taught him: Cops weren't your friends, they weren't going to help you, they'd take you down the minute you did something wrong—the way they defined wrong. He learned to avoid the cops; he definitely never learned to respect them. Especially not after they sent Uncle David to prison. He didn't go to prison because he was wrong, but because he got caught. Same as Cormac.

Hardin didn't have a whole lot of respect for Cormac, either, to be fair. She'd have locked him up herself if she'd had the chance. She came from the overworked and driven mold of detective, her suit jacket worn and comfortable rather than fashionable, her dark hair pulled back in a functional ponytail. She didn't wear makeup, and the frown lines around her mouth were more prominent than the laugh lines around her eyes. The nicotine from cigarettes stained her fingers. She always seemed to be leaning forward, like she was listening hard.

"Not sure I can help you," he said.

"You mean you're not sure you *will*. Maybe you should let me know right now if I'm wasting my time. Save us both the trouble."

"Did Kitty tell you to talk to me?"

"She said you might know things."

"Kitty's got a real big mouth," Cormac said.

Hardin was still studying him, glaring through the glass in a way that was almost challenging. Maybe because she felt safe, because she knew he couldn't get to her here. Except she'd looked at him like that outside the prison, the first time he'd run into her.

"How did you two even end up friends?" Hardin said. "You wanted to kill her."

"It wasn't personal."

"Then, what? It got personal?"

He considered a moment, then said, "Kitty has a way of growing on you."

That got Hardin to smile. At least, one corner of her lips turned up. "I have a body. Well, half a body. It's pretty spectacular and it's not in any of the books." She pulled a manila folder out of an attaché case, and from there drew out a pair of eight-by-ten photo sheets. She held them up to the glass, and he leaned forward to see.

The first showed a crime scene, lots of yellow tape, numbered tent tags laid out on the ground, a ruler set out for scale. The place looked to be a small, unassuming backyard, maybe one of the older neighborhoods in Denver. The focus of the photo was a small toolshed, inside of which stood a set of human legs, standing upright. Just the legs, dressed in a pair of tailored feminine slacks and black pumps. He might have guessed that this was part of a mannequin, set up as a practical joke. But then there was the second photo.

This showed the top of the legs—which had clearly been separated from their owner. A wet vertebra emerged from a mass of red flesh, fat, and organs. The tissue all seemed scorched, blackened around the edges, bubbling toward the middle, as if someone had started cauterizing the epic wound and stopped when the job was half done. The wound, as wide as the body's pelvis, was red and boiled.

He'd seen a lot of gory, horrific stuff in his time, but this made his stomach turn over. In spite of himself, he was intrigued. "What the hell? How are they even still standing? Are they attached to something?"

"No," she said. "I have a set of free-standing legs attached to a pelvis, detached cleanly at the fifth lumbar vertebra. The wound is covered with a layer of table salt that appears to have caused the flesh to scorch. Try explaining that one to my captain."

"No thanks," he said. "That's your job. I'm just the criminal reprobate."

"So you've never seen anything like this."

"Hell, no."

"Have you ever heard of anything like this?"

"No." She'd set the photos on the desk in front of her. He found himself leaning forward to get another, closer look at the body. The half a body. "You have any leads at all?"

"No. We've ID'd the body. She was Filipina, a recent immigrant. We're still trying to find the other half of the body. There has to be another half somewhere, right?"

He sat back, shaking his head. "I wouldn't bet on it."

"You're sure you don't know anything? You're not just yanking my chain out of spite?"

"I get nothing out of yanking your chain. Not here."

Wearing a disappointed scowl, she put the photos back in her attaché. "Well, this was worth a try. Sorry for wasting your time."

"I've got nothing but time."

"If you think of anything, if you get any bright ideas, call me." She looked up at the guard who had arrived to escort Cormac back to his cell. Hardin had a parting shot. "And get some sleep. You look awful."

It was almost nice that she cared.

He could have sworn he heard banging on the bars of the cell, as if someone was hanging on the door, rattling it, trying to get his attention.

You have to let me in! You have to trust me!

Not even bothering to tell her no, he put his hands over his ears, squeezed shut his eyes, ignoring her. That didn't stop the noise.

I know what it is! Listen to me! I'll prove it to you. Those photographs—I know what did it!

He woke up, covered in sweat, a foreign word on his lips and knowledge he didn't know he had flitting at the edge of his mind. He'd had a nightmare—another one, but this one was different. Images of a tropical country full of brown-skinned people. A village wailing in despair because so many women had suffered miscarriages over the last few months, losing babies before they were even born. The vampire has taken them, the vampire has drunk them. Which didn't make sense to Cormac. Vampires drank blood, not babies.

This one takes babies. It travels by separating from its legs and can be destroyed by salt.

He knew what it was. She'd told him. The word was on the tip of his tongue.

When he asked for an extra phone call that week in order to talk to a cop in Denver, the warden gave it to him. Apparently Hardin had left the request in advance, like she had a hunch that he'd get a sudden attack of memory. But this wasn't memory, it was—

He didn't want to think about it.

He called collect and waited for the operator to put him through. She answered, sounding surly and frustrated, then rushed to accept the charges when she heard his name.

"Hello? Bennett?"

"*Manananggal,*" he said. "Don't ask me how to spell it."

"Okay, but what is it?"

"Filipino version of the vampire."

"Hot damn," she said, as happy as he'd ever heard her. "The victim was from the Philippines. It fits. So the suspect was Filipino, too? Do Filipino vampires eat entire torsos or what?"

"No. That body *is* the vampire, the *manananggal*. You're looking for a vampire hunter."

"Excuse me?" she said flatly.

"These creatures, these vampires—they detach the top halves of their bodies to hunt. They're killed when someone sprinkles salt on the bottom half. They can't return to reattach to their legs, and they die at sunrise. If they're anything like European vampires, the top half disintegrates. You're never going to find the rest of the body."

She stayed silent for a long time, so he prompted her. "Detective?"

"Yeah, I'm here. This fits all the pieces we have. Looks like I have some reading to do to figure out what really happened."

She was *really* not going to like the next part. "Detective, you might check to see if there've been a higher than usual number of miscarriages in the neighborhood."

"Why?"

"I used the term 'vampire' kind of loosely. This thing eats fetuses. Sucks them through the mother's navel while she sleeps."

"You're kidding." She sighed, because he clearly wasn't. "So, what—this may have been a revenge killing? Who's the victim here?"

"You'll have to figure that one out yourself." He could hear a pen scratching on paper, making notes.

"Isn't that always the way? Hey—now that we know you really were holding out on me, what made you decide to remember?"

"Look, I got my own shit going on and I'm not going to try to explain it to you."

"Fine, okay. But thanks for the tip, anyway."

"Maybe you could put in a good word for me," he said.

"I'll see what I can do."

Maybe she even would.

He was curious. Itchingly curious. But if he let her in, he'd never get her out again. She already had her foot in the door, and now she was pushing. The bars of the cage rattled, claws scraped the inside his skull, worse than ever, a coarse rasp working on him, over and over. He could beat his head against a wall to make it stop.

Kitty came through. He could tell by the smug, triumphant look on her face when she put a manila folder on the desk in front of her, before she and Ben even sat down on their next visit.

"You found something," he said.

"I did." She grinned.

He tried not to laugh; it would annoy her. "Which means, I assume, that the demon problem is all fixed and everything's okay."

"Would I be smiling if it weren't?" she said.

"Sorry," Ben said. His cousin leaned back in his chair, smirking at Kitty just as much as Cormac was. "We forgot to tell you. The genie is bottled and everything's okay."

Cormac pointed. "See, I know when the problems are solved even when you don't tell me, because you just stop talking about them. And did you say *genie*?"

"Can I tell you about your executions now?" Kitty said quickly, clearly not wanting to explain the adventures they'd been having without him. She opened the folder, and he leaned forward, trying to see. "If you take in the twenty or so years before and after 1900, there were about a half-dozen women executed. There was only one woman executed in 1900."

"What was her name?" Cormac said.

"Amelia Parker. Her story's a little different." The pages looked like photocopies, text from books, a couple of old newspaper articles. She lectured. "Lady Amelia Parker. British, born 1877, the daughter of a minor nobleman. By all accounts, she was a bit of a firebrand. Traveled the world by herself, which just wasn't done in those days. She was a self-taught archeologist, linguist, folklorist. She collected knowledge, everything from local folk cures to lost languages. She has her own page in a book about Victorian women adventurers. She came to Colorado to follow an interest in Native American culture and lore but was convicted of murdering a young woman in Manitou Springs. The newspaper report was pretty sensationalist, even for 1900. Said something about blood sacrifice. There were patterns on the floor, candles, incense, the works. Like something out of *Faust*. The newspaper's words, not mine. She was convicted of murder and hanged. Right here, in fact. Or at least, in this area, at the prison that was standing here at the time."

Bingo. He hadn't expected Kitty to hit the jackpot like this. The fuzzy, old-fashioned photo of the young woman on one of the photocopies even looked like his ghost—black hair, serious frown. Everything fit. Cormac leaned forward. "The victim. How did she die? Did it say what happened to her?"

"Her throat was cut."

They were connected. The murders and his ghost were connected. It was a revelation, she'd been a murderer in life, and kept murdering in death—but no. *Hunted.* He remembered the words, the thoughts she'd flung at him. She was *hunting.* And she'd been wrongly executed. No wonder she was still around.

"What is it?" Kitty asked, probably seeing the stark shock on his face. The wonder in his eyes. "You know something. This all makes sense to you. Why? How?"

Finally, he shook his head. "I'm not sure. May be nothing. But she's got a name. It's not all in my head."

"What isn't?"

He met her gaze. "She didn't kill that girl. She was trying to find who did. *What* did."

She blinked back at him. "What do you mean 'what'?" Ben's lips were pursed, his gaze studious. So much for not making the two of them worry about him.

"Never mind," he said, leaning back and looking away. "I'll tell you when I know more."

"Why is she important?" Kitty said. "She's been dead for over a hundred years."

His smile quirked. "And you really think that's the end of it? You've been telling ghost stories for years. Are you going to sit here now and tell me it isn't possible?"

Ben leaned forward. "She just doesn't like the idea that someone else is having adventures without her."

Kitty pouted. "I'll have you know I'm looking forward to a good long adventure-free streak from here out."

As long as he'd known Kitty, she'd been getting in trouble. She couldn't keep her mouth shut, or she had to swoop to the rescue like some kind of superhero. She was a lightning rod for trouble. *She'd* been the werewolf caught shape-shifting on live TV. Cormac and Ben had been there to clean up after that mess.

"A month," Cormac said finally. "I bet you don't go a month without getting into trouble."

"How are we defining 'trouble'?" she said. "Are we talking life-or-death trouble or pissing-off-the-boss trouble? Hey, stop laughing at me!"

Ben said, "I'm not taking that bet."

Kitty straightened the papers and closed the folder. "I could try to mail this to you, but I'm not sure it would get past the censors."

"Just hang on to it for me," he said. Like the rest of his life. Just hold on.

They said their farewells, and they both wore that pained and pitying look on their faces, the one he'd put there because they could walk out and he couldn't. At the door they hesitated—they usually did—glancing back one more time. He almost stopped them, standing and reaching, calling back. He'd have to shout through the glass because they'd put the phone down. He could feel the guard at his back, but he had the urge to do it anyway. Press his hands to the glass and tell Kitty everything: *I have to tell you what's going on, the murders, the ghost, my meadow and what it means and why I can't go back, I want to tell you everything—*

But he didn't say anything. Just like he always didn't say anything. Without a word, without a flicker in his expression, he stood when the guard told him to and allowed himself to be marched back to his cell.

It sounded like claws scraping on concrete, an insect mash of legs running straight up the wall without rhythm. Like a million other nightmare noises that anyone's imagination might trigger, that would freeze the gut.

But Cormac hadn't been asleep. He was on his back, staring at the gray ceiling, refusing to sleep, refusing to let her in when the noise rattled by outside the cell. He remained still, wondering what would make a noise like that. The sound of a thousand souls that didn't know where to go.

Cormac rolled to his stomach, propping himself up just enough to look out, letting his eyes take in the patterns of light and shadow that made up the prison's weird internal twilight. Resting on his pillow, his hands itched for the feel of a weapon. This was like hunting; he could lie still for hours waiting for the prey to come to him. But here, when he was weaponless, behind bars, which one of them was prey? Did he think he could just stare it down?

He kept his gaze soft, not letting himself stare at any one thing, which would reduce his peripheral vision. So he saw it, when a clawed black hand reached across the ceiling, brushed his throat . . .

He half jumped, half fell from the top bunk, stumbling to the floor in a crouch. Pressing himself to the bars, he looked in the direction the thing must have gone

"Hey! Dude!" Frank hollered. "What did I tell you about your fucking nightmares?"

"Quiet!" hissed the guy in the next cell over. Not Moe's old cell but the one on the other side.

Cormac had his face up to the bars, but he couldn't see anything to the sides. He couldn't see a damn thing from here, though he could still hear claws on concrete, maybe even a voice, growling. He didn't know where it was coming from. If he could just get out of here—

A light shone, the deep orange glow of coals in a forge, across the prison block, inside one of the cells. It flared, turned black—like an eclipse of the sun, a moment of dark terror—then collapsed. All of it without a sound.

He could see it, a demon's claw scraping across a man's throat, and in his mind he heard a voiceless, inhuman laugh of triumph. Another inmate dead.

"No!" he screamed at the block, the sound echoing.

Hands grabbed the back of his T-shirt, twisted, and yanked him back. Cormac led with his elbow, striking hard, hitting flesh and bone—a man's chest. Frank wheezed, falling back, and Cormac followed through, swinging his body into a punch. Frank's head whipped back, but he stayed on his feet and came right back. Deceptively powerful, his blows pounded in like rocks, hitting Cormac's cheek and chest. He was dazed, but he shook it off. He should have explained, but it was too late, and this was more his speed anyway.

Ducking another blow, Cormac delivered his own, tackling Frank in the middle, shoving him against the bunk frame.

Lights came on in the cell block, an alarm siren started, and the door to the cell rolled open. Guards came in, swinging batons. Cormac didn't have a chance against them. They dragged him away, though he kept lunging forward, into the fight. Blows landed on his shoulders, kidneys, gut. He fell, then was hauled up again by his arms.

Waking from his fog, he saw the guards surrounding him. He was totally screwed.

Frank was yelling. "I don't know, man, he's gone crazy! It's not my fault, he jumped out of bed screamin' and he just went crazy!"

Frank's protests didn't matter; the guards dragged both of them out, hauling them in different directions. Cormac tried to get his feet under him—they were keeping him off balance on purpose.

Again, his instinct was to lash out. He locked it down, tried to keep still, tried to speak.

"There's another body. Another guy's been killed, I saw it, I saw what did it. I need to talk to Olson. To Detective Hardin. Somebody. Let me talk to somebody!"

It wasn't their job to listen to him; they were dumb brute enforcers. But the walls were closing in around him. All he really wanted to do was scream.

Another inmate was already screaming. The newest body had been discovered.

The cell in administrative confinement—solitary—had a solid door with a wire mesh–reinforced glass window at face height, a single bed, a toilet and sink, and no room to pace. This was what he'd been so desperate to avoid. They'd put him in smaller and smaller boxes until he couldn't move, couldn't breathe, couldn't think. Only thing left to do now was lie on the bunk and sleep. Escape to that meadow, breathe deep and imagine he smelled pines and snowmelt.

No. This had all started with her, that thing, lost spirit or demon, whatever she was. Everything had been fine until she appeared and started scraping the inside of his skull. His head ached. The walls were collapsing.

He leaned on the wall opposite the bunk, refusing to even lie down. His jaw ached in a couple of places. Bruises bloomed. In a strange way the fight had felt good, and the bruises felt real. It had felt good to finally hit something. To strike back. He hadn't had a chance to strike at anything in so long. He could take his gun to the range, unload a couple boxes of ammo. Feel a hot gun in his hand. That cleansing noise.

Put the gun against his own skull next and make it all stop.

He paced. Three steps one way, three steps the other. Stopped, sat down against the wall. He had to pull his knees up to keep from hitting them on the edge of the bunk. But he wouldn't lie down. He couldn't.

He couldn't tell the difference between exhaustion and the

pain of insanity gnawing at him. But he'd beat this thing. Beat it to a bloody pulp.

He closed his eyes.

A storm rode over the mountains and into the valley.

He didn't want to be here—it meant he was weak. He'd let his guard down, and now she'd found him, battering at him with wind and thunder—that rattling of the bars again, even though there weren't bars anymore. On a slope, he ducked toward a tree at the edge of the valley with his arms over his head, trying to wait it out.

Her shouts were the wind. "Let me in, damn you! I must speak with you! You stubborn fool, let me in! I *will* speak!"

It was a cosmic wail. He, who could wait out statues, couldn't stay silent against it.

"I can't help you!" He turned to the sky, screaming a year's worth of frustration. Maybe a lifetime's. "Leave me alone!"

"Let me speak!" She was a ghost, a stuck record, a moment in time. She was drawing him into her loop, driving him mad. He would never again leave this room or crawl outside his mind.

"No." The only word he could throw at her, his voice faltering to a whisper. The blowing wind made him deaf.

"Listen, just listen to me! What must I do to make you listen!" she howled. The wind blasted through the forest; trees groaned.

"Try *asking*!" he shouted to the sky.

Then, like a whisper through pine boughs, a breath against his cheek, "Please talk to me. Please."

His legs gave out, bringing him heavily to the ground, sitting on grass that was damp with rain. This was all in his mind. He shouldn't feel the wet soaking into his jeans. He shouldn't smell the clean, earthy damp in the air.

"Okay," he said.

And she was there, standing a few paces away, clutching her hands together. Still poised, back straight and chin up, as if refusing to admit that saying "please" had cost her pride. Like she didn't want him to see the pleading in her gaze. The wind-touched strands of her dark hair, curls fallen loose from her bun and resting on her shoulder. He might touch the curl and smooth it back into place.

He looked away from her and across the valley. The stream ran full, frothing over rocks. The green seemed even greener. It was high summer here, and he relaxed. Maybe because he could see her now he knew where she was, what she was doing. He could keep an eye on her.

She'd wanted so badly to talk, but she just stood there, like she was waiting for punishment. Waiting to be hanged. If she really was a ghost, if she really had been executed, she would have been hanged. He didn't want to think about that.

"Well?" he said finally. "After all that, you going to say anything?"

She glanced at the hem of her skirt and wrung her fingers. "I've not engaged in conversation in a very long time, and even then I was not a paragon of courtesy. I'm sure I'm more than a little mad."

That made two of them. "Amelia Parker," he said. "You're Amelia Parker. What the hell's going on?"

She blinked at him. "You know my name? How?"

"I looked it up. You could have just *told* me, instead of this garbage you've been pulling. You want to explain?"

"It's difficult," she said, glancing behind her.

"Try me. I have a pretty open mind," he said.

"Yes, I know. That's how I found you. I needed an open mind."

He glared at her. "For what? So you could break it into pieces?"

"No, so I could . . . so I could control it. I need a body, Mr. Bennett."

"Let me guess: It's harder than you thought it'd be."

"Yes. Minds . . . they tend to twist up into knots in spite of my intentions."

"You've tried this before?"

She didn't answer.

"Jesus," he muttered.

She swallowed, wetting her lips to speak—which made no sense, because she was a ghost. Cormac could almost smell the soap on her skin. The contradiction was making him dizzy.

"I was hanged for murdering a young woman, but I didn't do it. I'm innocent. I know what *did* do it, and it's here now. I hunted this thing a hundred years ago, Mr. Bennett, and while I'm not inclined to believe in an omnipotent God, I believe I have survived—or rather that this small part of me has survived—so that I can stop it now. But I need help."

Put like that, it did seem like fate. How much did she know about him, besides his name? Had she done enough digging in his psyche to learn that he was also a hunter? That she couldn't have picked a better body for her purpose?

He said, "Olson—the psychologist here—said this has happened before. Half a dozen bodies over the last hundred years or so, with their throats cut in locked cells. Just like the girl you were hanged for. You say you didn't do it, but you seem to know a lot about it."

"I hunted it. Tracked it to Lydia Harcourt, where they found me. Then it followed me here."

"Why? Why you? You were supposed to be dead, why'd it stick around?"

"I know I can stop it—"

"Where'd it come from in the first place? Do you know?"

"—but I need hands, a voice. I'm so close—"

"I'm not giving you my body," he said, turning away. "Why not tell me where this demon came from?"

Her brow furrowed, and she seemed to grapple with something. Guilt? Shame, even? "I suppose I ought to have taken it as a lesson not to meddle. Yet I keep on meddling, don't I?" Her smile was pained.

"What happened?"

"A scene from a boys' adventure novel. I'm sure you've had a few of your own. Something had been buried at a crossroads—imprisoned, rather. I should have heeded the warning carved into the headstone. But there was a promise of treasure."

"This is all about a pot of gold?" he said, disbelieving.

"No. A Sumerian cuneiform tablet meant to be buried alongside. I thought I could secure the demon, prevent its escape, obtain the tablet that promised tremendous knowledge. I was wrong."

"The tablet was bait, wasn't it?" Cormac said. "It didn't really exist."

Bowing her head, she hid a sad smile. "The thing bound itself to me. Cursed me. It always stayed just out of reach. I could watch it kill and never stop it. Even now."

He could almost feel sorry for her. He considered the saying about the road to hell.

She paced a few steps down the slope, across his field of vision, looking at the scene, his private valley. Hilltops emerged through misty, breaking clouds. The air was cool on his skin, a different kind of cool than a prison cell in winter. This felt like living rather than being in storage.

"You've gotten better at this," she said, gazing around, squinting against the breeze and surveying the valley as if it were real. "What is this place? It's somewhere in the Rocky Mountains, I should think."

Don't open the door, he thought. After a hesitation, he said, "My dad used to take me here when I was young."

"What was he?"

"A hunter," Cormac said, remembering, and flinching at the memory.

"And you?"

"Same," he said.

"You were sent here for murder, yes?"

He considered his words. Picked at the grass, which felt real, waxy between his fingers. "I killed a skinwalker. She was a monster and needed to die."

"Who are you to decide that?"

"She was trying to kill my friends."

"Ah." She paced a few more steps; her fingers were no longer wringing, but her expression had turned thoughtful, almost resigned. "The friends who come to visit you?"

"That's none of your business," he said.

"I'm sorry—it's hard not to pry. I can tell they're good people."

"Don't touch them."

"I won't," she said and paced a few more steps. "So you hunt monsters."

"Yes. I do."

"Then you understand. You must let me in, you must let me do battle with this thing."

"Do battle yourself," he said.

"I need physical form to work my spells."

"Then tell me what to do. I'll do it, I'll get rid of it."

"I spent a decade learning what I know, I can't just *tell* you."

"Then I guess that's it."

"Is it because I'm female? You don't think I'm capable?"

He chuckled. "I hadn't noticed."

"Then why are you being so stubborn?"

She'd keep picking away at him, like a swarm of gnats. "Look. My mind, this place—it's all I have in here. It's all that's left until I get out. You can't have it."

"You would sacrifice everyone here because of that?"

The situation wasn't that bad. Couldn't be that bad. Somebody would notice before the whole cell block was wiped out. Somebody would do something. Except for a tiny suspicion he had that maybe she was right.

He started awake. Aching from his shoulders to his hips, he straightened from where he'd slumped against the painted cinderblock wall and stretched out the kinks. He hadn't meant to fall asleep. He hadn't meant to even talk to her.

A wave of shouting echoed down the corridor. Hundreds of angry male voices raised in frustration, turned fierce, animal.

He was blind and stupid inside this box. He could look out the window—to the opposite wall, more institutional cinderblock. He couldn't talk to anyone—he didn't even know the time of day. His stomach told him it was late. Somebody should be bringing a meal soon. But the shouting told him that the whole place had been turned upside down. This wasn't right.

Standing, he rammed his shoulder into the door, pounded it a couple of times, hit the intercom button, called for a guard. The shouting outside was like an ocean, like a war.

No one would come to his call. No one would be bringing food. Of all the things that could have happened here, of all the things that could make serving time harder than it already was, he hadn't expected this. If it wasn't a riot, it was close to it. A cold knot grew in his gut, something he thought he'd built walls against a long time ago, so he'd never have to feel it again. He hadn't felt like this since his father died.

He was afraid.

His father taught Cormac as much as he could before he died, because that was what their family did. Cormac's grandfather, his father, and his father, who'd fought in the Civil War and then come west, part of the great migration of fortune seekers. At least that far back. The family didn't have any stories for how they'd learned about werewolves, vampires, and the rest of it. Maybe the line stretched farther back than that. Cormac had always known that monsters were real. When he was twelve, his father started taking him hunting. At first it was the normal kind, deer and elk, living off the land, all that crap. Then they'd tracked and killed a werewolf. His father trailed a wolf where there shouldn't have been any—wild wolves had been hunted to extinction south of Montana fifty years before Cormac was born. More than that, the creature was bigger than any wolf had a right being. They'd tracked it, baited it, Douglas Bennett had shot it dead, and brought his son to watch the body transform. It turned into a naked, bloodied human as they watched, a scruffy guy maybe thirty years old, rangy and dangerous looking even as a corpse. They weren't like us, Douglas had said, and it was us or them. That had been the order of the universe, laid out by the center of his universe.

When he was sixteen, they tracked another werewolf. This one turned the hunt back on them.

They'd gotten word a month before—wolf kill in Grand County, a couple of head slaughtered out of a herd of cattle. A lot of ranchers would have written off the loss and not thought about it again. Maybe set traps or poison. But too much about this didn't sit right—the care with which the prey had been chosen specifically not to draw too much attention, stragglers that weren't as likely to be missed. The fact that wolves hadn't been seen in the area in seventy years. There'd been a light snow and the prints were clear in the damp earth. Douglas Bennett had a reputation for being able to handle problems like this.

Douglas and Cormac spent the week before the full moon checking the lay of the land, where the lycanthrope had struck last time, where it might be likely to strike this time. There was always a chance that it would head out for new hunting grounds before then and they wouldn't find anything. But the creatures were territorial—it'd probably stick around. They asked the ranchers in the area to keep their cattle penned for the full moon and the nights on either side. Except for one fat cow, which they slaughtered as the sun was setting. Then they hunkered down to wait.

The blind, made up of deadwood and laid over with sap-drenched scrub oak, was twenty paces downwind from the carcass. Cormac's father sat on a piece of decayed log, his rifle resting across his lap. His hand lay across the stock, the finger on the trigger guard. He could fire a shot in half a second from that position. Cormac copied him, sitting behind him and a little to the side. Studied the way he held his rifle and tried to do the same. Admired the quiet way he sat, not fidgeting even a little. He barely seemed to breathe. Cormac struggled to stay quiet, though his heart was racing. His breath fogged in the chill air. This prey wasn't like any other, his father said over and over. It had the mind of a person under all that fur and monstrous instinct. You could see it, when you looked into its eyes. His father told him he could fire the killing shot this time. If he sat quietly.

The carcass smelled of blood and rot. The blood had poured out and soaked most of the clearing where it lay. The moon blazed down and painted it black and silver. Cormac caught himself bouncing his foot and stopped it, glancing at his father to see if he'd noticed. He hadn't seemed to. Cormac blushed, wanting so badly not to make a mistake. He hunched inside his army surplus jacket, thankful for his layers of clothing. He adjusted the sleeves, pulling them over his bare hands. He didn't wear gloves; neither did his father. Gloves interfered with the trigger.

A werewolf's natural instinct was to hunt people. A smart werewolf might avoid attention by keeping away from people; but eventually he'd drift back to civilization. He might have a pack to keep a rein on him, but if that pack ever fell apart, then it would scatter and a dozen werewolves, without leadership, would wreak destruction. Best to get them before that happened.

Nobody knew about the threats that lurked not just in the wild, but in cities, everywhere. Wild and inhuman, all the old nightmare stories grew out of truths that most people had forgotten. Didn't want to remember. Folk didn't want to consider that there was something modern technology couldn't solve. It was up to people like the Bennetts and all who'd come before them to protect, to stand guard, with silver bullets and wooden stakes, protecting humanity against evils they didn't know they needed protecting from.

Cormac had learned all of this from his father, as his father had learned from his. He felt proud, part of an unbroken tradition. They were warriors, and no one even knew.

His father pointed with the barest movement of his left hand, no more than a finger lifted from the barrel of the rifle, replaced just as subtly. Cormac wouldn't have seen the wolf as quickly. It didn't make a sound—the clearing was as quiet as ever, but a huge beast, a furred canine as big as a Great Dane, two hundred pounds easy, stepped carefully from the trees across from them. Dark gray and silver, it might have been a shadow come to life. Its fur made it indistinct, its outline hard to see. A few paces from the cow, it paused, raised its head, its eyes sparking gold in the moonlight. Cormac couldn't breathe.

His father's hand had closed around his rifle stock, but he didn't yet raise the weapon. This was going to be Cormac's shot.

Cormac worked to keep his breathing steady. He had one shot, had to make it good. Couldn't move too fast or the creature would see it. Best thing was to let it start in on the bait, distracting it. With silver bullets, they didn't have to get a good target. They only had to break skin and the silver would poison it.

His father leaned out of the way, giving Cormac a clear shot. He watched the wolf, large and unnatural, pause, nose leading, searching the carcass. Any second now, he'd aim and shoot, all in a heartbeat. He could do this.

Then the wolf was gone.

Its coloring blended with the wooded clearing, but Cormac had been watching carefully, he'd followed the thing's movements, he knew where it was. He imagined putting the bullet into it—a good clean shot that meant they wouldn't have to track it. But it had just vanished.

"Where'd it go?" Cormac whispered in a panic.

"Hush," his father breathed. He raised his rifle in a clean movement. Didn't take aim yet; just looked out, waiting.

Somehow, it had sensed them. Maybe smelled them on the cow or noticed the knife cut in the animal's throat, showing that its death wasn't natural, that this was bait and not scavenging. Maybe it had simply backed up the way it had come and slipped into the woods, avoiding the hunters. Cormac started to feel disappointed.

Then his father hissed, "Get back, get back. Cormac—" Douglas threw his arm and hit Cormac, shoving him out of the way as the creature leapt.

His father was strong, and Cormac fell hard and rolled, reaching to stop himself while keeping hold of his rifle. Turning onto his belly, he scrambled to look.

Another thing that made werewolves and wild wolves different: A wild wolf would have run away from the hunters, disappearing into the trees, finding safety in speed. This one attacked.

The thing planted front paws on Douglas Bennett's shoulders and shoved. Douglas fired, the mouth of his rifle flashing, but the shot did nothing, flying uselessly into air. The man screamed while the monster clawed and bit, shaking its head, ripping at flesh like this was an unfortunate rabbit. Douglas kicked and bucked, his hands on the wolf's head, fingers digging at its eyes and twisting its ears. The wolf kept on, lips curled back from red-stained teeth. Emanating from deep in its throat, its snarls sounded like the revving of a broken engine. And still Cormac's father screamed. Full-lunged, tortured, gasping screams.

"Dad!" It happened in a heartbeat. He couldn't breathe, he couldn't think. His scream was an echo of his father's.

He raised his rifle, took half a second to aim. Fired. Later, he'd never know how he managed to hold the weapon steady, to exhale and squeeze the trigger rather than blasting off in a panic.

He got it. That perfect shot in the wolf's head. The blast knocked the wolf away from Douglas, and it lay still.

"Dad?" He dropped the rifle and ran, sliding to the ground next to his father's prone form. His voice sounded suddenly high-pitched and weak, no better than a child's. He was five years old again. "Dad?"

His father reached, clutching at his son with bloody hands. Looking at him, Cormac's gut jumped to his mouth, but he didn't vomit.

Douglas's face was gone, gory meat instead of nose, eyes, lips. His throat was gone, turned into frayed tubes and tendons and a hint of backbone, glistening in moonlight. A wheezing breath whistled and gurgled. Somehow, Douglas pulled another through the mangled windpipe, and his hand closed on Cormac's arm, bunching his jacket in rigid fingers. He didn't breathe again, and the fingers went slack a moment later.

Cormac knelt there for a long time, holding his father's hand. A pool of blood was creeping under him, soaking into the ground. The air reeked. He'd never get that smell out of his nose.

A couple of feet away, a naked man sprawled on his side. He had stringy, shoulder-length hair, black going to gray. He was burly, powerful, the muscles on his arms and back well defined. He was weathered, older, maybe in his fifties. Blood and fragments covered his face.

"Dad?" He swallowed, trying to get his throat to open up. But his father didn't move.

Cormac didn't know what to do. The truck was a couple of miles away and had a CB he could use to call for help. He was pretty sure he had to get help, though he wasn't sure what anyone would make of the situation when they saw this. He couldn't tell them it was a werewolf.

He squeezed his father's hand one more time, placed it gently on the body's chest, found his rifle, checked it to make sure it was loaded and ready for another shot—just in case—and set out for the truck.

He radioed an emergency channel, told them where to go, then went back to wait with his father. To chase coyotes and ravens away from the body. A forest service ranger, county sheriff's deputy, and EMTs arrived to find him standing guard, still holding the rifle, covered in blood.

Slumped against the front corner of the cell, he stared at his hands.

It wasn't your fault.

Everybody said that. But they didn't know, they hadn't been there. They were just words, didn't mean anything. "Leave me alone," he muttered. But he could *feel* her, as if she'd put a hand on his shoulder. He batted the imaginary hand away.

He heard shouting, ringing—inmates banging on the bars of their cells, echoing, thunderous. He couldn't see anything out the window but the wall across from him. Pressing his ear to the crack along the door, he tried to make out what was happening. Not that it helped. Not that it gave him a clue what to do next. Not that he could pick his way out of this door. He couldn't do a damn thing about anything.

Cormac had once felt that he'd been part of an unbroken tradition, a long line of warriors, secret and proud. It had all fallen apart. The line would end with him. He'd made his father's legacy worthless. No better than dust. Nothing more than blood on his hands.

He was trapped, helpless in the face of a threat his father hadn't taught him how to handle.

You aren't helpless.

He tried to shut out the voice. "Leave me alone," he muttered.

It's a prison riot. I've seen it before. Too many guards stopped coming to work after the murders. The prison is understaffed and the inmates are frightened.

"What am I supposed to do about it?"

The demon will take advantage of it. There will be slaughter.

"I'm safest here."

Not if the rioters unlock the doors.

The locks were electronic, connected to both individual and master switches. They'd have to take over the whole prison to do that. Which it sounded like they were on the way to doing.

He put his hands over his ears, shut his eyes, tried to block out the world. "Get out of my head. You're driving me crazy."

She scratched at the inside of his skull, like fingernails on a chalkboard. With the pain came a promise—that it would stop if she would just let him in. Open wide the door to his mind. He was almost there.

I won't hurt you, she said, and he imagined the young woman in the meadow, proud and calm. *If I tried to dominate you we'd both go mad. I see that now.*

"I can't trust you."

You don't trust anyone. He could see the scowl on her refined face.

He almost laughed because it was true. Mostly true.

You're strong, Cormac. I'll need that strength, to do what must be done. We both will.

He wasn't strong. He just faked it real well. He saw his father's blood on his hands and felt like a child.

Cormac—

Don't use my name, he almost shouted at her. The noises outside grew louder, closer. The sound of the riot had changed, from defiance to triumph. A celebration, chaotic and fierce. It didn't sound human anymore.

Then the lock on the door clicked and slid back with a metallic *thunk*. Cormac felt the vibration of it under his hand.

He thought of weapons, whether he could break off part of the bedframe, use the sheets as some kind of garrote, or find anything he could throw. Even a shoe. He had nothing but his hands.

Best to stay out of the way, then. Maybe he could get outside.

Participating in a riot wasn't going to get him anything but more years to his sentence. The door was unlocked, but he didn't have to walk out. On the other hand, he sure as hell didn't want to get stuck in this hole with no place to run if the mob came after him.

Carefully, he slid the door open, keeping his back to the wall. Waiting, he listened.

A man ran past, a young guy Cormac didn't know. His orange jumpsuit was torn, hanging off his shoulder, one leg shredded, and he bled from a wound on his temple. He was trying to hold his jumpsuit up while looking over his shoulder as he ran. Not that he had any place to go but in circles.

A second later, a mob of about a dozen followed, screaming in fury. A few of the men held makeshift weapons—a broken two-by-four as a club; a toothbrush handle, melted and sharpened, as a shiv.

Cormac waited until they'd passed and the corridor was empty again.

The cells in solitary were in a long corridor off the main block. From there, the sounds of riot swelled. Bullies used the chaos to take advantage. A prison riot was a thousand angry men trying to show they couldn't be kept down. It was all a big lie.

To get to a corridor that would take him to the yard, where he could hunker down to wait out the riot in relative safety, he had to go through the central bay of the main block. He crept along the wall, looking ahead and behind, trying not to move too quick, careful not to get noticed. This wasn't hunting; this was stumbling across a mama bear with her cubs and hoping you didn't catch her eye. It was the most nerve-racking thing he'd done in his life. Any minute now, the goon squad would arrive and the tear gas would start flying. He had to get out.

He'd meant to take a quick look, just to get the lay of the land, then slip out. But the scene froze him.

They'd killed at least two guards, it looked like. A mob of maybe a hundred or so was crowded together in the main block, passing the bodies overhead, ripping apart the blue uniforms—and more, when hands couldn't get a grip on fabric. On the fringes of the crowd, inmates turned on each other, clawing and fighting. Others cheered them on. Another group of a dozen moved along the cells, slamming open doors and pulling out the few people who hadn't rushed to take part. The established gangs had splintered. No longer organized by race, affiliation, or anything visible. They'd become opportunistic, chaotic.

Good God, Amelia said. *This isn't right.*

"I thought you'd said you had seen prison riots," Cormac whispered.

This is something else.

Rage, fear, a million emotions that made a guy crazy when he was lying in a prison cell at night and the quiet closed in on him. What did that taste like to a demon who gained its power from fear and blood?

There!

He could almost imagine the woman pointing. He liked to think he'd have seen it on his own, eventually, but he wasn't sure. Human in shape but somehow otherworldly, the figure lurked, slinking across the edge of the ceiling, no brighter than a shadow, no more real than the phantom hints of movement anyone might catch in the corners of their vision and discount as imagination. The little voice that whispered sometimes, *Take it, steal it, break it.* Or, *Kill him, you know you could kill him.*

A lot of the guys in here probably listened to that voice more often than most people.

Cormac could not have said the thing had eyes, but somehow he knew that it looked at him. That it saw him and didn't like him. The thing had clawed hands and feet that clicked on beams as it traversed the ceiling. The claws glinted like steel, sharp as knives. There must have been dozens of them, like the thing was holding bouquets of daggers.

Cormac stood at the end of the corridor, watching the creature run toward him, a figure made of oil, and wondered what to do. Running wouldn't help. Doing so would only rile it. Like a gang of bullies. But he also couldn't fight it.

It's looking for me, she said. *I told you, I've been hunting it for a century. It knows me.*

"And you think you can kill it? Get rid of it?"

I can.

"I don't believe you." He believed in bullets. He believed in being stronger than anything else on the range.

Cormac, we must stop this.

He shook his head. He'd worked too hard to hold on to himself to let his identity—his soul—go now. He'd kept such fierce control, all so he wouldn't lose it and do damage that he couldn't recover from. Now, he nearly laughed, because it had all been for nothing. The thing drew power from blood, and it would kill them all, slicing them to pieces.

"I can't let go," he murmured.

You can. You can keep your core. I'll keep you safe, I can do that, I promise you. But I need you!

He felt how easy it would be to let go. He understood how it was that a psychotic gunman could walk into a crowded room and open fire. It was because they had let go, given themselves over to something that wasn't them.

Please trust me. He felt something, someone, take his hands and squeeze. Soft hands, but firm, as if he and a woman were about to jump off a cliff together. He suddenly wanted to kiss her. Not an abrogation, then. A merging. He wasn't giving himself over. He was loaning. Sharing.

He hoped she was right.

He couldn't feel his muscles suddenly. His nerves were fire, but he couldn't move. Closed his eyes, tipped his head back, thought of a meadow, opened a door, and felt Amelia step into the place where he was—

—and she looked out of his eyes, living eyes, for the first time in over a hundred years. Her body flared—his body. It was powerful, brilliant. Already rangy and athletic, he had kept himself fit, even locked behind bars. She wanted to shout, to sing. Tipping her head back, she felt the smile on her face, and hair on her jaw, odd and tingly, scratchy. This anatomy was most certainly not her own, feeding her a confusing flood of sensations that must have been *maleness*.

Time for that later.

With a body came life, and with life came power, and that was what she had traveled all this way for, waited for all this time, so she could face down the darkness, raise her hand, curl her fingers into a fist as if holding a ball, and shout a word of Latin in a strange, deep, male voice that wasn't hers.

A crackling purple sphere of light came to life in her hand.

He felt it, the power burning through him, and it was like dying, because he couldn't move, react, or change the outcome, and he didn't want to because he felt closer to the source. To God, maybe.

Amelia was using his body to create something astonishing.

The demon approached, arms raised for a killing blow.

She lifted her hand and the light crackled and snapped, sending out tendrils of static, like some mad scientist's machine. The demon paused as if confused, its claws extended midreach.

"Back!" she shouted, startled again that it wasn't her voice, but his, the vessel's. Cormac. She had chosen well—he burned with so much life. The man watched through her eyes, which looked through his.

Respect him. He wasn't simply a tool to be used at will. That had been her mistake. No more.

Her power struck it. It might have been their combined wills as much as anything that forced the demon to fold back on itself. It shrank, screaming—the sound of static dissipating, of a star contracting. The shadow turned red.

It lashed out with fire. The wave of heat scalded—please, let his body be strong enough!—but she stood her ground, raised her other hand and built a shield, an unseen wall painted on air with a gesture and a word of power. The demon beat itself against the shield—it buckled, and she stumbled back before she could brace herself. She was still not used to the bulk, solidity, and sheer inertia of this male body. Cormac was a man who relied on brawn more often than not. Perhaps she would do well to learn to use such brawn.

If they got through this, and did not go mad after.

His muscles strained against the force. What this must look like to an observer: A great clawed shadow pushed against nothing as if throwing itself against a door, and a man dressed in an orange jumpsuit braced and leaned forward as if trying to keep the door closed. She couldn't stand this for much longer.

But she had an ally. She needed to call up power again. To do that, she needed life, energy that a bodiless soul and a shadow creature couldn't draw on.

She turned inward and cried, "Cormac!"

And he *shoved.* Imagined every muscle in his body working at once. Wondered what it might be like to have light pour from his soul and illuminate the world.

Spheres of energy formed in both his hands. She brought Cormac's callused fists together, aimed them at the beast. She couldn't contain the power, couldn't guide it. Could only force it away from her and hope for the best.

Colored light bathed the world, at least the space of it in front of her. She closed her eyes, ducking away from it, and still it burned.

The demon took the full force of it. The light chipped away at its form, tearing off pieces until it became pockmarked, full of holes, and the holes grew larger, and it screamed. Then there was nothing but light, and the light itself disappeared.

She blinked—or he did. She was having difficulty with pronouns. They looked around together.

An amplified voice filled the cavernous room, barely audible. Prisoners milled, confused, staring perplexed at bloodstained hands. Projectiles flew in from far corridors, people scurried out of the way, and white smoke began to fill the air. Someone shouted.

Tear gas, Cormac supplied. Then he collapsed, and Amelia fainted for the first time in her life.

A soft hand lay across his brow. A woman's hand, smelling clean, like soap and lavender. He opened his eyes and saw Amelia sitting at his bedside.

Taking stock: He wasn't in a cell, but in a soft, single bed, part of a row of them lined up, heads against the wall. Several of the other beds were occupied by sleeping, bandaged figures. Prison infirmary.

He didn't feel hurt. Only tired. He also didn't want to try and move.

Amelia smiled at him. "Good morning."

He was confused. He was here, awake, and she looked solid. He could feel her, flesh against flesh.

"Are you real?" he said.

She tipped her head, acknowledging the question. "A bit. Partly. I'm not sure." The smile faltered.

"I can smell you." He reached for her hand. She gazed at his for a moment, almost startled. Then took hold of it. Then disappeared.

A man in a white lab coat walked to the bed. "Good, you're awake. How do you feel?"

His fist was clenched at his side, as if he had grabbed at something that had slipped away. That was it, then. She'd done what she came here to do. Stuck around long enough to say good-bye. And now she was gone.

He tried to tell himself that was okay.

The doctor checked his chart, then picked up Cormac's wrist and counted against the numbers on his watch.

"I'm a little tired," he answered finally. It was his body she'd used to battle the demon. Of course he was tired.

"You have second-degree burns on your face and hands," the doctor said. "There was a fire—you're probably lucky to be alive. You're sedated to help you rest and to keep the pain down, but in a week or so you should be back to normal."

He remembered the fire, the riot, and the demon—but what

did the people in charge think had happened? So he asked, feigning amnesia.

"The warden's still trying to figure that out," the doctor said. "Now, get some rest."

Cormac felt like something was missing. He'd lost something.

At night, the infirmary never got completely dark. A nurse was on duty in the next room, and light from the hallway filtered in. A piece of monitoring equipment made a faint clicking noise. Red status lights peered out. Cormac stared at the ceiling, wondering. He could live a million years and never understand what had happened. Maybe she wasn't a ghost but an angel. Trying to give him purpose in the world.

So. Now what?

Lift your hand. It was a woman's voice, speaking from a distant meadow.

"Amelia," he said.

I'm still here. Lift your hand. I want to show you something.

He uncurled his right fist, the one without the IV needle in it, and raised the arm a few inches. It glowed. Faint, blue, with a nimbus of static. Without his bidding, his fingers, snapped, and the glow dissipated in a crackle of energy. A wizard's spell.

She was still with him, her power still flowed through him.

We're bound, you and I. And I thank you for it.

He settled more firmly on the pillow. He hadn't realized he'd been fighting the sedative, holding himself taut. But now, he was floating. He had stopped worrying.

He was ready to go after two days, even if it meant returning to solitary. He still didn't know what the fallout from the riot—and his part in it—was going to be. If the powers that be would blame him for something and add a decade or so to his sentence. Hardly seemed to matter because he'd won. They'd won.

But two days on his back was plenty. He didn't even hurt much. The aggravating itching was all on the outside, now—the burns were healing. At least they'd let him take a couple of books from the prison library. He was in the middle of another of Kitty's recommendations: *Middlemarch,* by a guy named George Eliot.

George Eliot was a woman. Can't you find something modern? This was stale when I read it as a girl. Cormac smiled.

When Olson entered the infirmary, Cormac scowled, preparing the arguments to get him out of here. The counselor didn't seem to notice and pulled over the chair at his bedside. "You're looking much better."

When had he been here before? Cormac wondered. Thinking of Olson looking over his unconscious form made him twitch.

Cormac frowned and looked at the ceiling. "You're going to ask me what happened, and you won't believe what I tell you."

Olson made a thin, wry smile. "Actually, I think I might. We have surveillance footage of most everything that happened. We've collected the evidence we need in a few assault and murder cases we'll be prosecuting. You're not involved in any of them, if you're worried. But you did . . . something, didn't you?"

"That didn't actually show up on film, did it?" Most of this stuff didn't record too well in any form, or it would have come out a long time ago.

Olson narrowed his gaze, a perplexed expression. "I can't exactly say what I saw. I saw you. You did something—and it all ended. I was hoping you could explain it to me."

Cormac stared. Where did he even start? There are more things in heaven and earth . . . "I don't know how to explain."

"Just tell me," Olson said. "Tell me everything."

Cormac did. Everything except Amelia. He made vague explanations about a demon haunting the place, hungry for blood, gathering power, and about how he'd picked up a spell that banished it. He tried to make it sound matter of fact, like he hadn't even been sure it would work and he'd have been just as happy to mind his own business. It all sounded crazy and Olson wasn't buying any of it, he was sure.

"What would have happened?" he said at the end of it. "If you hadn't done what you'd done to stop it?"

Cormac shrugged. "I don't know. I suppose you folk would have dropped in your tear gas and knocked everyone out anyway. The riot would have died down eventually."

"But that thing would still be on the loose."

The statement didn't require commentary. Cormac kept quiet, lying calmly, book folded across his stomach. Olson's smile was grim, tired and his eyes shadowed. He probably had a lot more patients after the last week. He straightened his jacket as he stood to leave.

Cormac said, "What happens to me now?" He had a flare of hope that they'd be so grateful they would just open the doors and let him leave. He could call Ben, *Come get me, please.* The hope burned, no matter how unrealistic the thought was. But maybe they'd shave a few months off. He was pecking away at his time, day by day.

"You'll go back to your cell when the doctor okays it. A regular cell, not the hole. Things go back to normal." He shrugged. "I'll put in a good word with the parole board. We'll see what we can do."

He walked away.

About a year later, lying on his bunk, staring at the ceiling for the last time, he was scared again.

Maybe it was more accurate to say he'd been scared his whole life. Fear had become background noise that he never noticed. He'd built up this front, these walls, trying to convince everyone he wasn't afraid. Sometimes the walls cracked. He was starting to notice now that he was scared of being normal, scared of being dependent—scared of being scared, even. He could observe it, acknowledge it. But he wasn't going to take down the walls. They kept him upright.

He noticed fear when it slipped over the wall: his lack of control during the riot, his fear of having friends because they might leave. And now.

He was getting out tomorrow.

Hardin and Olson had both spoken for him to the parole board.

Ben had put up a hell of a case, showing that Cormac had family, a place to stay, potential work waiting for him—legitimate work, even. It had gone so smoothly. Despite all the help, Cormac hadn't expected it to. He'd expected to have the parole hearing go wrong, but it hadn't. He was getting out more than a year early as a result. Surprise.

When he had a job to do, he wasn't afraid. The job kept him focused, and the scary usually came so fast he didn't have time to think, only react. His reactions were fast enough to match, most of the time. If they hadn't been, he wouldn't still be around.

Right now, he had to wait, which wore him down. He should have been excited. Happy. Anticipating. But transition was hard, and the world he was about to enter was a different one than he'd left two years ago.

No, tell the truth: The world was the same. He'd changed. He wasn't sure he could handle it anymore.

Closing his eyes, he let out a sigh and thought of his meadow. His muscles unclenched, and he fell into sleep.

In a bright and magnificent summer, wildflowers covered the meadow, purples, yellows, blues, reds dotting the grasses like a painting on a postcard. The sky was too blue, it couldn't possibly be so blue in life. But he knew if he hiked out to the valley and looked, it really would be that blue, and he'd stare up at it marveling at how his memory hadn't done the scene justice. The air smelled fresh, clean, as if a thunderstorm had just passed, scrubbing the world, making it new.

Amelia was there, standing close. He could touch her with a straightened arm, if he wanted. He almost did. Her face was calm. The storms were long gone, but he couldn't seem to tell what she was thinking.

He moved toward the set of boulders overlooking the stream where he was used to sitting, watching elk, or sunrises, or just the water playing.

"You want to sit down?" He gestured. She nodded, and he picked a smooth, flat stone with room enough for both of them.

He expected her to be awkward in the long skirt and formal clothing, but she wasn't. She moved like she was used to it, even in wilderness like this. Tucking her skirt just so, she perched on the boulder, back straight, and folded her hands before her.

"You'll be fine," she said. Even her smile was serious, like she couldn't quite stop thinking about tragedies of past and present.

He shook his head, only able to think, *What am I going to do with myself? What can I possibly do?* He couldn't imagine what guys who'd been in here ten, twenty, thirty years must feel like, when the world outside really had changed in their absence. What would it be like to disappear into prison before cell phones and come out to find you had to learn a new technology? A new language even? He'd only been out of the world a blink.

But still, the world looked different to him, and he wasn't sure how he'd live. Tomorrow, the gates would open and he'd walk out a free man.

"Except that you're saddled with me," she said.

"No. Both of us walk free. That's the plan."

She put her hand on his arm and squeezed. She wasn't wearing the thin leather gloves anymore, and he wondered where they'd gone.

The weight of her touch was strange—she wasn't real, she didn't exist. But here she was, with her hand on his arm, her skin warm against his, and he didn't quite know what to do next. If this had been real, if she had been real, he might have turned away. Walked away to avoid the contact entirely. But this wasn't real, so it didn't matter. He could do anything. So he put his opposite hand on hers, just resting it there. He waited for her to flinch, to pull her hand away, to argue. But she didn't.

They sat like that until morning, watching the meadow.

AUTHOR'S NOTES

The character Kitty started as a short story. At the time, around 1998, I wrote mostly short stories, and I didn't think the idea of a werewolf talk radio host would get any bigger than that—it seemed like a gimmick. I should have known better. I've heard some writers talk about a character "taking over" a story, and I didn't really understand that and it hadn't happened to me until Kitty came along. When I wrote the first short story ("Doctor Kitty Solves All Your Love Problems"), it turned out three times longer than I was expecting, had too many characters, and had too much going on. So I cut it down to two characters—Kitty and Cormac—and saved everything else for the next story, "Kitty Loses Her Faith." I still had more ideas and more characters. At that point, I realized I could fill a novel. But what would it be about?

I went clubbing with friends one night and was out on the dance floor when Peter Murphy's "I'll Fall with Your Knife" came on. I had a vision of Kitty, brimming with newfound confidence, on her own and celebrating. And there was my novel—Kitty learning to stand up for herself.

I still had more ideas. It turns out a werewolf talk radio host is a great platform from which to launch all manner of stories. Ten novels later . . . yeah. Wasn't expecting that.

I still write short stories, because while some ideas need the space of a novel to tell them, others don't. Novels have dozens of characters, at least a couple of plots, lots of settings, time passing, and so on. Sometimes, though, an idea has just a couple of characters, just one problem, one setting, and one moment in time. I had characters I wanted to know more about, but couldn't explore their histories in the novels. Because the novels are in first-person point of view, I can only write about what Kitty knows or discovers, and the other characters aren't always keen to tell her their secrets. Short pieces let me explore Kitty's world, and I can often bring those discoveries back to the novels and make them richer.

Looking back at these stories, I see a record of me trying to work out my own mythology of the supernatural, vampires and werewolves and the like, as protagonists rather than monsters. I'm trying to answer questions like, How do vampires approach sex? How do supernatural beings find each other and interact? How do they make their ways in the world? What do they do for jobs? I write about vampires and werewolves in the "real world," and I find that I've been most interested in the "real world" part of that theme. These stories are about vampires and werewolves (and were-lions and selkies and so on), but they're also about people coping. I think when you cast supernatural beings as heroes, especially if you give them traditional monstrous strengths and weaknesses, part of their stories are necessarily going to be about coping with what they are and their places in the world.

On a day-to-day basis, putting a few hundred words on the work in progress, sorting through correspondence and promotion and all the business aspects of being a full-time writer, I feel like I never get enough done. But gathering these stories together and looking back—damn, I've been busy! I had no idea! I've made this whole world! The only thing better than building up a whole world is having people want to read about it. So, to Kitty's fans and readers: Thank you. Most of these stories wouldn't exist without you and your interest in Kitty's world.

In the tradition of the playlists I've matched a song with each story that I think captures the feeling or tone of the story or character.

(This collection doesn't include the first two Kitty short stories that appeared in *Weird Tales* in 2001 and 2003. Those stories, "Doctor Kitty Solves All Your Love Problems" and "Kitty Loses Her Faith," became part of the first novel, *Kitty and The Midnight Hour.*)

"Il Est Né" (Taverner Consort, "Il Est Né")

This story originally appeared in *Wolfsbane and Mistletoe*, an anthology of werewolf holiday stories edited by Charlaine Harris and Toni L. P. Kelner. Half the fun of some of these stories is seeing what the characters are up to between books. This fits neatly into Kitty's arc, right before the events of *Kitty Takes a Holiday*: She's taking what she's learned so far and using that knowledge to help others.

"A Princess of Spain" (Sally Potter, "Pavanne" from *Orlando*)

I wrote this for an anthology called *The Secret History of Vampires,* edited by Darrell Schweitzer and Martin H. Greenberg. The theme: What turning points in history featured vampires manipulating events behind the scenes? My favorite historical turning point happened early in the sixteenth century, in England, with the death of Henry VII's eldest son, Arthur. Henry VIII wasn't originally meant to be king of England. An England without Henry VIII—without the Protestant Reformation in England, without Queen Elizabeth and the naval triumph over the Spanish Armada—is a very different England indeed. It's an incredible tipping point, and I think its most fascinating player is Catherine of Aragon, who married Arthur before she married Henry and who was an unsuspecting and mostly unwilling lynchpin. The question of whether or not her marriage to Arthur was ever consummated is still hotly debated, as it was when Henry VIII pursued his divorce from her.

"Conquistador de la Noche" (Procol Harum, "Conquistador")

Rick is probably the most interesting character from the novels who gets the least amount of time in the spotlight. So many secrets, so much history, and I never really get a chance to talk

"Looking After Family" (Vangelis, "Movement V" from *El Greco*)

Of all these stories, this one may be the most revealing, and one of the most important in its effect on the novels. In the course of writing the first couple of novels, the relationship between Cormac and Ben developed slowly. Ben appeared on the scene in the first book because I needed a lawyer character. By the second book, I wanted the two of them to have the kind of close friendship that meant they would take a bullet for each other. So they became cousins who grew up together—brothers, for all intents and purposes. At that point, I needed to know what had happened to get them into that situation, and how they came to trust each other. I needed to know how Cormac learned to hunt supernatural beasts, what happened to his family, what traumas drive him. I wanted that background to be realistic, concrete, and visceral.

In some ways, I see this as Cormac and Ben's origin story. We get to see them as teens and get to see a little of how they became the men they are. In my own mind, I'm constantly referring back to this story as something of a benchmark for them. This is where they came from.

"God's Creatures" (Curtis Eller's American Circus, "Sweatshop Fire")

I wrote this for P. N. Elrod's anthology *Dark and Stormy Knights*. Cormac was the obvious choice for a story on such a theme. I wanted to show what a typical day in the life of a werewolf hunter like Cormac might look like.

I was raised Catholic, and bringing these stories together I can see signs of that in many of them. That background definitely influenced my decision to set this story where I did. Saint Catherine's is loosely based on St. Scholastica, a Catholic school in Cañon City, Colorado, where two of my great aunts, who were Benedictine nuns, taught. As far as I know, neither one of them was a werewolf.

"Wild Ride" (Cake, "The Distance")

Another origin story—T.J.'s this time. T.J. only appeared in one of the novels (or maybe a couple of others, depending on what counts as an appearance), but he's still one of the more significant characters in the series because of his impact on Kitty.

The metaphors regarding lycanthropy as disease and HIV and lycanthropy as identity and homosexuality are pretty clear-cut. I'm not the first person to make them. In fact, I've used a rough outline of the history of AIDS awareness to model what might happen if lycanthropy were ever identified as a disease: A long period of great confusion, ignorance, and fear at every level, with activism and advocacy coming from the communities most affected by the issues.

My terrible secret is that I first made T.J. gay so readers wouldn't expect a romance between him and Kitty. Once I'd done that, though, I had a great opportunity to include a nonstereotypical tough gay character in the first novel. I also had the opportunity to make some of those metaphors explicit, which they are in this story.

I originally wrote this one for *Running with the Pack*, edited by Ekaterina Sedia.

"Winnowing the Herd" (Too Much Joy, "William Holden Caulfield")

And this story gives us a glimpse of what Kitty's life looked like before the books started.

I read two stories in a row, "Gestella" by Susan Palwick and "Laika Comes Back Safe" by Maureen F. McHugh. These are both gut-wrenchingly depressing stories in which werewolves stand in as metaphors for horrible tragedies. I wanted to write a literary-type story, like these, in which the werewolf did not die horribly and wasn't depressing, so I recruited Kitty and sent her to the KNOB staff party, where we get her interior monologue about the proceedings.

This takes place before *The Midnight Hour* and before Kitty was outed.

"Kitty and the Mosh Pit of the Damned" (Dead Kennedys, "Holiday in Cambodia")

This started with the title. My friends have learned over time that if we're all sitting around, maybe or maybe not drinking, and we start throwing around crazy ideas that in most groups would be forgotten by morning, I'm as likely as not to grab them and run with them. It's one of the great things about being a writer—I have a viable outlet for crazy ideas. Like a mosh pit of the damned.

Here, we get to see the kinds of things Kitty does between books. I'm a little sad that Jax has never made an appearance in the novels. But he inhabits this story so well it seems to be where he's meant to live.

"Kitty's Zombie New Year" (Big Brother and the Holding Company, "Piece of My Heart")

My big goal with this one was to insert zombies in the Kitty universe, and to do it *my* way. I'm not a fan of the brain-eating shambling undead zombies. It's like the same joke over and over and over again. Yeah, I'm familiar with all the commentary, the metaphors of decay and violence, that it's not really about the zombies but about the survivors and their relationships, and so on.

But let me tell you about the movie *The Serpent and the Rainbow,* based on the book by Wade Davis, and the real source of zombie stories and even the word "zombie": Zombie-ism as a form of mind control and slavery, and the possible existence of a neurotoxin concoction that induces a coma and brain damage in its victims, used to create zombie slaves. Tell me that isn't a million times creepier than the shambling brain-eaters.

"Life Is the Teacher" (Oingo Boingo, "Flesh 'n Blood")

When I was invited to submit a story to the anthology *Hotter Than Hell,* edited by Kim Harrison, I knew I couldn't write a Kitty story. The editor was looking for serious, sexually charged fiction, and that tone was all wrong for Kitty. I tossed around a few ideas and settled on writing about Emma and exploring what happened to her after the events of *Kitty Goes to Washington.*

I had two goals with this story. First, I wanted to delve a bit into how vampires and sex work in my universe. I also wanted to see if I could tell an erotic story in which the main character never actually takes off her clothes. Horror and erotica writing have a lot in common in that sometimes it's what you don't show that counts.

"You're on the Air" (3 Doors Down, "Kryptonite")

In *Kitty and the Silver Bullet*, Kitty gets a call from a vampire who's had really bad luck. He didn't want to be a vampire, he doesn't have a Family to support him, and he's stuck working the night shift at Speedy Mart. I really loved Jake and wanted to find out more about him, and moreover I wanted him to succeed. So here's what happened after he hung up on the phone call with Kitty.

"Long Time Waiting" (Pink Floyd, "Wish You Were Here")

You didn't think Cormac was just sitting around twiddling his thumbs all that time he was off stage, did you?

The challenge of this one was climbing into Cormac's brain for an extended period. He's very different from most of my other viewpoint characters, who tend to be cheerful do-gooders, or at least come from familiar, recognizable backgrounds. Cormac, not so much on either count. Kitty may be the werewolf, but Cormac is the real outsider among the characters. In this one, he finally moves to center stage.

When I was coming up with Cormac's background, even for the early Kitty stories, I wanted to make him more grounded in reality than the typical badasses I encountered in genre fiction. He wouldn't be a former SEAL, a bitter ex-cop with a heart of gold, or a member of an elite paramilitary squad. No, I went local, to rural Colorado. Where did Cormac learn his skills and his outsider attitude? The militia movement, enclaves of which you'll find throughout the Midwest and Rocky Mountains. I found that to be much scarier because it exists in my own backyard, unlike most types of fictional badasses.

I sent Cormac to prison as part of my project of injecting the real world as much as I could into the novels. Lots of urban fantasy novels have kick-ass, badass, gun-nut, hard-core bounty hunter type characters, and they never seem to suffer consequences. In the real world, people who kill people go to jail more often than not. So, my hard-core bounty hunter was going to get caught, and was going to go to jail.

I have gotten more e-mails and feedback over that decision than just about anything else in the series.

A lot of people worried about Cormac being in prison and gave me lots of advice about how to get him out as soon as possible, but it was never my intention to lock him away forever. I planned on bringing him back. That was why I worked so hard to come up with a situation where he'd be convicted of manslaughter (rather than the first-degree murder he's probably actually guilty of . . .). He'd be out on parole in a couple of years. Meanwhile . . .

Where did Amelia come from? I'm a fan of Victorian adventure literature, and Amelia embodies Victorian attitudes about the occult found in a lot of those stories. I'd been wanting to write about a character like her for a long time.

Something I've learned: You get the most interesting results by combining the most disparate ideas in the same story. I decided the Kitty universe needed more magic and wizards, and I could accomplish that by throwing Cormac and Amelia together. That also meant that Cormac in prison would have the most *fascinating* adventures. As you can see from the books, by the time I wrote *Kitty Raises Hell*, I knew exactly what happened to Cormac, and I started writing this novella so I could get it straight in my own mind.